HIJACK THE SEAS

Karen Chance

Karen Chance

Printed in the United States of America First Printing 2024
First Edition 2024

10 9 8 7 6 5 4 3 2 1

CHAPTER ONE

An arrow flew by my ear and would have taken it off, except that I shifted out of the way just in time. I stared around in confusion when I landed on the opposite side of a small clearing because I wasn't Supergirl. I hadn't heard the arrow.

I'd shifted because of a tangled mass of roots on the forest floor ahead which I suspected of being the grabby variety, because Faerie's trees liked human blood. I also liked it—in my veins—so I'd learned the hard way: stay clear of the damned trees. But that was hard to do in a forest, and anyway, it wouldn't help with the arrows.

Why was somebody trying to kill me? I didn't know; I couldn't see much here, with the canopy overhead turning a sunny day into twilight. But it wouldn't be the first time something like this had happened.

In fact, it's pretty much a weekly occurrence. My name is Cassie Palmer, and I'm Pythia, the Chief Seer of the Supernatural World. Nifty title; crap job, and one that frequently resulted in—

Shit!

I had to shift again before I could even finish my monologue because whoever was out there was good. And had eyes that worked better in deep shade than mine. Damn it!

But I could cross territory faster than them since I didn't cross it at all. I spatially shifted from one spot to another. It was one of the Pythian gifts, along with time travel and a bunch of time-related powers, only about half of which I'd had a chance to learn because somebody was always doing *that*, I thought furiously, as an arrow parted my hair.

Okay, now I was getting pissed.

There was a time, not so long ago, when the idea of being pursued by a bunch of murderous fey through a forest would have freaked me the heck out. Especially when I was sans weapons, sans allies, and sans the map I'd lost a while ago. But I'd learned a few things since then and managed to keep my cool despite arrows smacking into stuff all around me.

I'd barely finished that thought when I had to shift away from an incoming barrage, which was tearing up the leaves in my direction and which slammed into a tree in the shape of my body a second later. There must have been twenty arrows quivering out of the bark, mostly grouped in the head and torso region. So, plenty of enemies, and nobody was shooting to wound.

Not that I'd thought they were, but now I had confirmation. And had to decide what to do with that. Or with *that*, I thought, my head jerking up as something started shrieking.

It didn't sound human. Not that I'd expected it to, considering where I was, but the terrible soul-rattling shrieks didn't sound fey, either. Or not any fey that I'd ever encountered or wanted to.

Damn it! Why was everything here so hard? And why were the shrieks not stopping, since whatever it was should have asphyxiated or paused for breath by now!

I crouched in the shade of a clump of bushes I'd shifted into the middle of, holding my hands over my ears and thinking about leaving. Thinking hard, because the shrieking had been joined by yells and curses and a bunch of other stuff indicating that a diversion was going on, if not one that I'd had anything to do with. I could use it, though, to get the hell out of here, to figure out where I was, and maybe to get back on track.

But then the shrieks leveled up in anguish, and I sighed.

Being Pythia came with a boatload of duties, mainly concerning patrolling the timeline, fighting gods, and helping the little guy. And a little guy was yelling his head off. Which did not change the fact that I had shit to do and did not have time for this!

But the wails were pitiful, and I was stupid and—*damn it.* I spotted a perch in a tree in the direction of the screams and shifted there before I had time to talk myself out of it. The perch was in a pine tree, or since this was Faerie possibly not, and there wasn't much cover.

Not that it mattered, as nobody was looking at me anyway.

A bunch of dark-haired fey—think humanoid, if humans were regularly seven feet tall, long-haired, and supercilious looking—had gathered in a clearing where the sunlight had managed to find a hole in the trees. The fey faded into the background thanks to their dark green and brown leather ensembles, which mimicked the shadows even without magic being needed, although they had no shortage of that. But something else didn't.

Something else stuck out like a sore thumb because it was in the middle of the spotlight the sun was providing. Or because it was the focus of all eyes, some of them horrified. Or because it was a monster.

I blinked at it, and it wasn't like I didn't have a good view. I had an awesome view, a center balcony view, a could-only-be-better-with-binoculars view, and I still had no idea what I was looking at. And didn't want one because that . . . was just nasty.

It was large, gelatinous, tentacle-strewn, and formless. If not for the tentacles, it would have looked like a giant had horked something up of the phlegm variety, only not so attractive. It was vile and oozing is what I'm trying to convey, and was grossing the fey out just as much as it was me.

And then I realized there were two of them.

They slorped away from each other like an overgrown cell undergoing mitosis, or maybe one had just been on top of the other. Couldn't tell; didn't care. I just wanted to leave now, and that was before the smell hit me.

What the . . .?

My hair, which was blond and scraggly after the last few days shifting around the wilderness, wilted even more in the funk coming off the oozing pile. And I was pretty damned high in the tree, meaning that it had to count as some kind of germ warfare down there. I gagged and tried to do it quietly while a fey lost his lunch in the bushes.

The rest didn't give him hell for it, maybe because they looked like they were considering joining him. But then one decided to be brave, grabbed a stick, and gingerly poked the nearest bit of horror. The monsters did not appear to mind this or even notice because they were busy.

Screaming at a cow.

I had been too preoccupied with the horror show to notice before now, but that was definitely a cow. And it looked to be of the Earth variety. That wasn't too strange, as the fey had co-opted stuff they liked from Earth over the centuries, including pigs, chickens, and cows, which they found to be as useful as we did.

Some of those had ended up being crossed with fey animals, resulting in some pretty strange hybrids, but this did not appear to be one of them. This was just a cow. A mostly white with brown spots cow standing on the edge of the glade eating grass.

Or rather, it had been doing so, as a tuft was still sticking out of its mouth. Now it was just standing because its tiny cow mind did not know what to make of the current state of affairs. Right there with you, buddy, I thought fervently.

I also thought about leaving again. Because there was a whole host of things I didn't understand here and didn't need to and nobody was bleeding. Until one of the monsters started scrambling away from the horrible spotted monstrosity, that is.

He was looking at the cow with the same expression that everybody else was using to look at him and backing off as fast as his tentacles could manage, which was pretty fast. And not looking where he was going, either because he was panicked or because he only had one eye and it was on a stick. Anyway, he crashed into a fey, who freaked the hell out and promptly stabbed him, and that he *did* notice.

And then he ate the fey.

It happened so fast that I barely had time to realize what was happening before the blob opened half his body, stuffed the fey inside, and closed again. Leaving the shocked-looking warrior peering out of the mostly translucent flesh of his captor while his buddies stared back in disbelief. Giving said creature a chance to take off with his lunch, lurching up and scrabbling through the forest like all the demons of hell were after him.

Or a bunch of really, really freaked-out fey.

The pointy-eared group tore through the undergrowth in pursuit, leaving me, the other monster, and the cow behind. Things were pretty loud for a minute, with the fleeing creature wailing, the fey yelling, and various bits of flora biting the dust as the ball of weird mowed them down. And possibly ran over a few fey in the process; I couldn't really tell.

But then everything calmed back down, as the cavalcade of crazy got too far away to hear, and the forest resumed being quiet and strangely beautiful, which was how Faerie often looked in between cycles of violence.

The cow went back to chewing its grass. The remaining monster sat on the ground, its tentacles spread around it, and began to cuss. And I finally caught a clue and shifted down beside it.

Or rather, I shifted down beside *him* because the monster wasn't a monster, at least not of the oozy variety. As evidenced when its translucent blobbiness opened up to disgorge a rather beat-up-looking man. A very pissed off, very familiar, beat-up-looking man covered in transparent slime.

"Pritkin!"

A dripping blond head jerked up, a pair of green eyes skewered me for a second in utter disbelief, and then the cussing ramped up to epic levels.

"Shhh!" I grabbed his shoulder and then pulled back with a handful of ooze. Which I ignored because I had bigger problems right now. "They'll hear you!"

This was undeniably true. The warriors' ears might look a little strange, but they worked just fine and even better than the human variety. Of course, they were currently busy chasing down a ping-ponging, shrieking nightmare, but still.

There might be others.

Pritkin seemed to agree with my thoughts because he lowered the tone of his voice, if not the viciousness. "What the hell are you doing here?" he demanded, getting back to his feet, probably to shake me.

Or maybe to hug, I amended, leaning into it because I hadn't seen him in a while, and so much had happened since then. The hug was moist and slimy and smelled like the creature he had just been thrown up by, but it was so good to be back in those arms that I almost sobbed anyway. But I bit it back, which was just as well because *then* the shaking commenced.

Of course.

I would have protested, but the blobby thing had reconstituted itself, plumped back up, and was watching us with an interested eye. I regarded it warily until the shaking increased, and I had to smack Pritkin's hands away. "I came to find you, and what is *that*?"

"You should know," he said savagely, turning on the blob. "Get away from there!"

It had been sidling up to the cow while it watched us and had almost been close enough for a touch from a strangely hesitant tentacle, but at Pritkin's comment, it jerked back. And said something in a screechy whine that had my ears wanting to close up and never open again. "Auggghhhh!" I whimpered.

"Stop it!" Pritkin snapped, and we both did. And then the monster and I looked at each other because neither of us knew who he'd meant.

"Um. I'm Cassie," I said since there seemed to be some

intelligence there.

"It knows who you are! You sent the damned thing!" Pritkin informed me while trying to scrape some of the smelly sludge off his clothes.

It didn't work, just sort of smeared it around. He finally gave up and settled for glowering at me instead. I didn't return the favor, being too happy to see him and also too confused.

"*I* did?"

"Yes!"

I regarded the blob some more. I had seen a lot of strange things since becoming Pythia, like a lot a lot, but I thought I'd remember that. "Doesn't ring a bell."

"Oh, for—you sent them to guard Mircea!"

I looked from Pritkin to the blob and back again and wondered which of us was having a senior moment. Considering that the war mage currently dripping in goo looked thirty-ish but was hundreds of years older than that, I knew who I'd put my money on. And I guessed my face showed it because he cursed some more.

"Did you or did you not ask Adramelech for help guarding Mircea?"

Mircea was the third member of the triumvirate of power we shared, a spell that connected the three of us down to the magical level and greatly expanded all our abilities. He was also my ex-lover, which was sometimes awkward as Pritkin was my current one. Or so I hoped, although he was not looking too happy with me at the moment.

"Adra? I only asked him to—"

"Stop calling him that!" Pritkin sat on a root that had conveniently grown into a nice perch, probably so that weary travelers might decide to plop down and be more easily attacked. This whole world was one huge Venus Flytrap, only it didn't eat flies!

But Pritkin saw the smaller root that was inching toward him through the dirt like a snake, with the pointy end serving as its one fang, and shot it a look. "Try it," he invited.

The root paused, then shivered a little before sinking back into the earth with a pissy little wiggle.

The cow chewed on.

I plopped down on the dirt because I was tired and hoped it wouldn't eat me. "It's his name," I pointed out.

"You do not give the head of the Demon High Council a nickname—or a diminutive!" he added before I could protest. "And did you or did you not ask him to assign two of his best demon guards to Mircea?"

"Sure, back when I thought the consul was planning to have him killed." AKA the good old days, when all I had to worry about was a jealous, two-thousand-year-old vampire queen instead of . . . everything. Just everything. I decided not to think about it. "But what does that have to do with—"

I stopped, a horrible thought intruding.

Pritkin just looked at me with a little smile on his face.

My eyes slid over to the blob, which was sidling toward the cow again and trying not to look like it. "Don't eat that," I said before I thought.

He understood me or chose that exact moment to stop and turn that one eyestalk in my direction.

"It's not your cow."

He did not seem to think much of this argument.

"Eat it, and I'll kill you," Pritkin added, at which time it plopped down again, and the eyestalk drooped despondently.

He was hideous and smelly and slimy, with a sheen of mucous-like substance that was already wetting the ground around him. But the eye had ridiculously long lashes, and the tentacles were waving about sadly and plucking up random things—a leaf, a stick, a rock—and examining them before tossing them away. I felt a surge of pity.

And that was especially true if he was one of the previously invisible demons Adra had placed as bodyguards on Mircea. They had been spirits, allowing them to watch over him more easily without anybody being the wiser. Including him because I hadn't known how he would take my possible paranoia.

Sometimes, it was easier just not to ask.

But then he ended up in Faerie, and I guessed his bodyguards got pulled in with him? I wasn't sure how that worked, but it would explain why this one looked so confused. Spirits manifested bodies in Faerie, something that had probably surprised Adra's guys, who might never have had corporeal form before.

It didn't look like this one was enjoying it.

"Is he hungry?" I asked, a little worried. "Should we find something to feed him or—"

"You are not. Going to sympathize. With that bloody thing!" Pritkin yelled.

I frowned at him. "There's no need to yell."

"What are you doing here?"

"Looking for you. Only the fey started shooting arrows at me and—how did you end up with the demons?" I asked because I still wasn't clear on that point.

Pritkin took off a boot, and a gob of slime slugged its way out. "They became lost after following Mircea into Faerie, and before they could adjust—to that and to suddenly having bodies—they encountered some fey. Who immediately became hostile—"

As if they were ever anything else, I thought, being slightly pleased that something I'd done had managed to traumatize the fey for a change.

"—causing the idiot twins to run off, thus making them more lost. They finally calmed down, realized what had happened, and became determined to find Mircea again and, thus, a way home. I believe they planned to stuff him through the nearest portal—"

I very deliberately didn't say anything.

"—but they followed the wrong man. They aren't used to having human-like senses, and I smell more familiar, being half demon. . ." he shrugged.

"And the fey were shooting at me because?"

"They weren't shooting at you; they were shooting at me,"

he said tersely. "You got in the way and are damned lucky you didn't take an arrow through the head. You need to leave."

I frowned as he pulled his slightly less slimy boots back on. "Wait. Why were they shooting at you? They looked like Alorestri. Aren't the Green Fey supposed to be your people?"

Or partly, anyway. Genetically speaking, Pritkin was a bit of a patchwork quilt, but his great-grandmother had been Nimue, Queen of the Green Fey. Which explained what he was doing here because the queen had recently passed away. That had come as a shock to everyone because fey didn't die all that often, other than in battle, and that went double for one who was a daughter of Poseidon and thus a demigod.

But dead she very definitely was, and thus a successor was needed. So, all the claimants, those closely enough related to the queen to qualify and crazy enough to try it, had been invited to participate in a contest to vie for the throne. Or to die trying, which appeared more likely.

But as far as I knew, the contest hadn't started yet, so what the hell? The Green Fey might not like Pritkin much, considering him demon spawn due to his father's blood, but they didn't usually try to kill him. He *was* one of their princes, after all.

That won me a short bark of a laugh when I pointed it out, although Pritkin didn't sound happy. "Tell them that."

I would if they'd stop being homicidal weirdos for five seconds, I didn't say, because I wanted to stay on track. "Don't they know you might be their next king?"

Pritkin had more colorful phrases in reply, perhaps because it was the last thing he wanted on Earth—or Faerie. He'd once longed to be accepted by his mother's people but had finally realized that a part human/part demon/part fey child would never be good enough, even if his fey blood was from the royal house. He had, therefore, concentrated on the human part of his lineage and left his dreams of being a fey prince behind.

But we were currently in an all-out war for survival against another king of the light fey, Aeslinn of the Svarestri, and his godly allies, and needed all the help we could get. Nimue's army was strong and battle-tested, and they knew Faerie as we did not. And as king, Pritkin could command it.

But he had to win it first, which was why I was here. I had no problem at all cheating my ass off if it helped him and damned if I cared what the fey thought about it. There was just one thing I didn't understand.

"Is trying to kill you part of the contest?" I asked, just as Pritkin's head jerked up.

He was staring at something in the trees I couldn't see, but I threw up a time shield anyway because Faerie.

And had no sooner done so than a dozen spells lashed it in a storm of magic that made the whole world crackle around us.

CHAPTER TWO

Sons of bitches!" Pritkin yelled and jumped up, only to have me tackle him before he ran through my time spell. "What the—"

"I'm aging out their weapons. Don't touch it!"

He stared at an arrow a few feet away that some bright spark had shot into the midst of all the magic being flung around. Maybe it was reflexive, or maybe the fey archer had thought it might get through the spell as their curses had not. But he was learning otherwise.

Pritkin stared at it as the wooden shaft cracked and splintered and dusted away, as the white fletching curled up, turned brown, and then was gone, too, and as the metal tip corroded, rusted, and flaked off. The last little nub of what had been an arrowhead fell to the ground, and a fey voice could be heard yelling at the top of his lungs.

"Pythia!"

Caught that one, I thought wryly, even before my translation spell crackled in my ear.

And then the fey were gone as well, melting into the forest like leaves on autumn's wind, which was good because a moment later—

"Are you alright?" Pritkin said, clutching my arm as my spell faltered and fell apart, dissipating like smoke.

"Yeah." I swallowed. "Harder here."

He nodded curtly. And then unleashed his magic, which I assumed was of the demon variety since the blob perked up. Talons of fire went screeching after the fey, with fiery bodies glimpsed briefly in the air like demented birds.

I couldn't see them well; they were only flickers in the vague shape of winged creatures and were quickly lost among the trees. But the fey didn't seem to like them much. I heard screams, warning cries, and then more screams, and the vicious little half-smile on Pritkin's face told me that at least some of his bolts had hit home.

"Okay, that went well—" I began right before he grabbed me again.

"*Go home.*"

"My ass."

"Your arse is very nice," he said, grabbing it and giving a squeeze. "And I like it in one piece. So, get it out of here!"

"I came to help you!"

"I don't need any help."

"Yeah, it looks like it!"

But then he was gone because he was an *asshole*, and between the dark and the trees and the no-doubt cloaking spell he was using, I had no clue what—

I suddenly had an idea.

"Hey! Hey, you!" The blob looked around and then slowly up at me, the stalk-eye appearing somewhat startled. "Follow him!"

The blob did not have hands, but a tentacle stopped messing with a leaf and touched what could, very charitably, have been termed its chest. "Yes, you! Hurry! He's getting away!"

And, okay, part of what followed was my fault. I knew that the blob, AKA one of Adra's top operatives, was having a bit of a moment. It was in a world not its own, in a form that was its own but probably didn't feel like it, and likely only understood English in a rudimentary way.

I should have been more specific. But I was fast losing Pritkin in a forest full of murderous fey, I had not been having fun trying to find him before this, and I didn't know how much longer it would take to do so again—or what I'd see if I did. So, I wasn't thinking about the blob.

Until it ate me, opening up and stuffing me inside and leaving me looking out at the world through a mass of translucent flesh, just like the unfortunate fey.

"Auggh—urp." I opened my mouth to scream because that is what you do when a demon has just eaten you, but that was not a good move. The hollow I found myself in was large enough to accommodate me and had at least a little air. But it also had a lot of phlegm or whatever the goopy clear stuff was, and it was everywhere, including in my mouth!

I spat it out and tried not to hurl, but it smelled. Oh, God, it did! And I didn't know how to—

We were moving.

No, we were *moving*.

I stopped worrying about losing my lunch because of the stench and started worrying about losing my life because of the *speed*. Which was absurd! We were in a *forest*; big trees were everywhere, and some were sapient!

Experience had proven what would happen if we hit one—

Annnnnnd we did, we hit a lot of them, but the blob didn't seem to mind ping-ponging off the rough old bark at sixty miles an hour. Or getting lashed at by angry roots and overhanging limbs and then stung by a bunch of wasp-like insects that had had a nest in one of the branches until it smashed into us. I *did* mind, but not physically, since whatever receptacle encased me did not appear connected to the demon's outer body.

It was like racing around like a gyroscope made from very stinky flesh as we tore through the trees after Pritkin. Or, at least, I guessed we did, although despite remaining relatively upright and stable, I couldn't see much. Everything was thrashing leaves, stabbing roots, and buzzing wasps, and anything I could see past all of that was distorted by the rippling wall of flesh.

Then we hit water—a lake, a river, hell, maybe an ocean for all I knew—but it was deep, and we were diving fast.

I tried to tell the translucent submarine I was in that it

wasn't going the right way. I wanted to find Pritkin, not a watery grave, and it needed to turn around! It needed to turn around right now!

But I couldn't scream without ingesting more terrible goo, and beating on the sides of the thing didn't work, and trying to communicate mentally didn't work, not that it usually did with me, but I thought that maybe a demon might be able to pick something up. But if it could, it was ignoring me. And diving ever deeper, with my frantic stares upward now showing me only a vague glimmer of sunlight on the water . . .

Before it was gone, too.

Leaving me in an eerie, dark world where everything was quiet except for my harsh breathing, and everything was disorienting as the whole world was suddenly one shade of murky blue-black.

Screw *this*, I was shifting, I decided. And I tried. But my power was acting up again as it did everywhere in Faerie, where I had to draw it through whatever portal I could find to Earth.

The Pythian power had been tethered there by the gods millennia ago when Apollo first gifted it to his seers at Delphi, and it couldn't leave. Only I had discovered that that wasn't entirely true. As long as I was near enough to a portal, I could pull some power to my location.

But it was never as strong as on Earth, and the further I got into this crazy world, the more unreliable it became, to the point of just putzing out entirely. It was like trying to find cell phone service in the mountains and never knowing when or if you'd come across a good spot. Or when you'd get cut off since some of Faerie's portals were omnidirectional.

Running a portal was expensive, magically speaking, so having one that cycled from place to place on a set schedule was efficient. It allowed one portal to serve many destinations and saved power. But it also meant that my power could get cut off randomly as the portal I was tapping into cycled away from Earth.

Like that, I thought, as the strands I had been trying to grasp suddenly disappeared, fading into nothingness in my hands. And leaving me at the mercy of the crazed little taxi I was now stuck inside, without knowing how much air I had left or where I was going. Or what the heck that was, I thought, peering through the rippling surface at something in the distance.

It didn't stay distant for long. That was concerning not only because it was huge, a dark, oblong shape that I couldn't see very well in the gloom but also because it appeared to be able to give a whale a decent run for his money. Only whales didn't have teeth that big, did they?

I didn't think they had teeth at all, just a screen for filtering krill and why was I thinking about that when we were about to get *eaten*? Because we were, we very definitely were, and the blob finally appeared to wake up to that fact. And started churning up the water with its tentacles.

But they were short and stubby, and the Not Whale was still coming, and the little burst of speed we'd put on was only doing us the dubious favor of allowing me to see our pursuer better.

That didn't help because I still didn't know what it was. I didn't want to know what it was. It looked like a cross between a whale and a shark, with a tremendous body and a gaping maw, and why did every freaking thing in Faerie have a gaping maw?

With teeth larger than me, by the look of them.

I had a second to stare at the biggest set of chompers I'd ever seen when suddenly, I was no longer trapped. Because my little friend had decided that it was every demon for himself and shat me out before hauling ass, zipping off into the darkness like a fleeing jellyfish. And leaving me as the sole hors d'oeuvre on the tray.

How did I get here, I thought, staring at looming death. And wondering if the set of armor that my dress was quickly transforming into would save me from those teeth. It was dragon scale, but I supposed that even that had limits and—

And *shut up, shut up, shut up*, you're about to *die*!

That was undoubtedly true, as the giant creature was now on top of me, the maw was gaping even wider, and I was about to find out how Jonah had felt—

When what looked like a human fist, if it was fifty times the size and made of golden light, popped out of nowhere. And crashed into the creature's jawline, hard enough to send several of those teeth flying. One of them shot past me, disturbing the water, but not half as much as when the whole great body flipped around, tail thrashing, and sent me tumbling head over heels, lost in a wash of bubbles and a current that left me feeling like I was being torn apart.

But the armor held me together, although it did nothing for my burning lungs because I had no air. And what little I'd had that encounter had forced out of me. Leaving my vision darkening, my body flailing, and my brain telling me that I should have listened to Pritkin and gone home.

Because Faerie was just one big way to die.

And it would have been, but the portal took that moment to cycle back to Earth, and my power immediately reached out to me. It found me just before I lost consciousness, enveloping me in warmth and shooting magic down to my fingertips. And a second later, I had a new enclosure, which smelled much better than the old one.

This one smelled like loamy earth and wildflowers and the rich greenness that permeated this part of Faerie, but not because I'd shifted up there. But because I'd reached out and shifted it down to me. Or a portion of it, anyway, with crumbly soil under my feet, a bunch of little river rocks that threatened to trip me up, and a branch full of leaves that promptly fell into my face.

Not that I cared because *air*.

I gulped it down, my lungs greedy and seemingly impossible to satisfy for a moment, maybe because the damned branch kept getting in the way! I spat out a mouthful of leaves, heaved in a deep, satisfying breath, and coughed much of it back out because I already had a lung full of water. Then, I breathed in more clear, sparkling breaths that a few seconds ago had seemed like a mirage in the desert and something I would never experience again.

Before looking around and realizing the fight wasn't over.

The fight was just gearing up, in fact, and the Not-Whale was *pissed*.

The fist had just made it mad, so I decided to make it madder before my power cut out again, and it succeeded in eating Pritkin. Because that had been his fist, a massive extension of his tiny-looking body, which was still going to town on whatever part of the bastard it could find. But it didn't seem to be making much of a difference.

There was too much blubber in the way, which cushioned the blows, and when Pritkin decided to go for the mouth again, his impressive fist got introduced to the chompers from hell.

And they didn't give a damn about his magic.

Try mine, bitch, I thought, and sent a spell speeding through the ward encasing my air pocket and out into the open water.

It didn't change the water as water doesn't age. But the same could not be said for the Not Whale. I once thought that Faerie's creations were eternal, but apparently not.

Because a large section of its scarred old hide suddenly burst outward, as if from decaying gasses, blowing a hole big enough for me to see what was happening inside. It wasn't pretty. Entrails were churning and dissolving into soup, ribs were cracking and blackening and falling to pieces, and the great spine was liquifying as the spell, shot at an angle, boiled through to the other side and punched a hole there as well, bisecting the creature that was no longer looking quite so angry anymore.

In fact, it wasn't looking so much like a creature anymore and more like something called lunch. Because out of nowhere, the formerly empty water was churning with life, as a myriad of weird aquatic . . . things . . . came zooming in, determined to get a piece of the pie. Or of the whale. Or of something I didn't care about because my power had just cut out again.

Son of a bitch!

The ward I'd been sustaining popped, letting the water rush in and slap me in the face. The tree branch decided it had had enough and floated off, but not up because things were too churned up thanks to the feeding frenzy to obey gravity. And while I had a lungful of air this time, as there was no longer anything to force it out of me, it wouldn't last.

How many minutes had it been between cycles of that portal? I thought frantically. And didn't know, having been busy almost dying that whole time. And was about to do it again, and that wasn't fair.

We'd won, damn it!

But then a hand, normal-sized and not glowing, caught mine. I jerked in surprise and looked up to see Pritkin, visible in the spectral light that some of the water creatures were giving off. He had a bubble over his head and was yelling something at me, which I thought was a bit much right now.

But suddenly, I had one, too. A bubble, that is, filled with air that I gasped in gratefully. So much so that the fact that I could now hear him bitching at me almost didn't matter.

We took off, with me latching onto his back and him plowing through the water faster than he could run on land, and he could run pretty fast. But he could swim even faster, which was lucky as I was so disoriented that I had no idea where we freaking were. Or even which direction we were headed, although it appeared to be mostly down.

Down, down, down, to the point that I didn't know how he could see anymore. The bioluminescent creatures had been left behind, and the murky water had swallowed up what little light they'd shed. My eyes met only blackness, and only the sensation of my fingers digging into the muscles of Pritkin's back and shoulders kept me somewhat grounded.

Then we abruptly hit bottom, on a sandy bed that I could

feel against my skin as it was stirred up by Pritkin scrabbling around as if searching for something.

Something that I guessed he didn't find since he started cursing. And while Pritkin had many different styles of profanity, which he cheerfully used for everything from his coffee not being strong enough to sending his enemies into oblivion, this one was serious. This one meant business.

But then it stopped, he grunted with surprise, and manically started digging again. The next moment, we were on the move, plowing through the clouds of sand he'd stirred up into utter darkness. Before entering a vast cave, with torchlight glimmering on black rocks as we sloshed and then crawled out of the depths and onto a shoreline with people all around, none of whom I cared about because I was too busy collapsing into a soggy pile.

The bubble around my face burst, but there was air in the cave, so it didn't matter. Someone was talking in a sonorous voice that echoed, but which I could barely hear over my heavy gasps. My lungs were not convinced that this air would stick around and were drawing in as much as possible while they could. But my ears finally popped, and a bunch of water ran out, allowing me to hear what was being said.

"—the statue is genuine. The winner of the first Challenge is, therefore, Prince Emrys of the Earthly Realm—"

"I protest!"

"*Prince!* He's no prince of mine!

"Earthly Realm! Say rather the hell regions. He's a demon!"

"He cheated! That damned woman is with him!"

There were a lot of similar comments, shouted at us from all sides, but 'that damned woman' was too tired to pay them much attention. I rolled my head over to look at Pritkin, who was also lying on his back, breathing hard and looking back at me. And picking up my sandy hand and pressing a kiss to the back of it, because he was clearly over them all, too.

"You've landed in it this time," he murmured.

CHAPTER THREE

Okay, so what are we working with here?" I asked, trying not to get distracted by the room we were in.

That was hard, as it was part of the suite that Pritkin had been allotted in the royal palace. According to him, it was garbage-tier compared to what the other heirs had received. But if this was garbage...

I thought back to my court in Vegas, situated in a casino designed to look like hell, and winced. I hoped I didn't get a light fey delegation anytime soon. Because this place was stunning.

For one thing, it was underwater, or at least this part was. Which was why fish were swimming past the windows, and light shadows from the sun somewhere above were streaming in to dance on the floor, walls, and ceiling. An occasional jellyfish-like blob hit the ward keeping all that water out and stayed there, blorping gently for a while before floating off.

They were easy to see as the huge windows were floor-to-ceiling, although they didn't look like windows. The room had an oblong shape with rounded walls, like a half-squashed balloon, and was made up of the same dark stone as the cavern where we'd come in. Now that I could see it better, I realized that the rock was striated with veins of what looked like pointy black glitter, which Pritkin said were crystalline formations within the stone.

Wards covered the fissures in the walls, leaving them looking less like windows and more like what they were: gaps in an undersea cave. The floor had a slightly uneven feel that lent credence to that view, like one giant, black river rock that a stream over untold eons had smoothed out. It glittered, too, but with pieces that looked more like the flecks within terrazzo than the pointy inside of a geode.

And that was just the bones!

It didn't consider the furnishings, which were opulent to the extreme, including braided ropes of tiny pearls used to keep back the filmy white curtains on the platform serving as a bed. Or the massive pieces of coral that made up scattered tables and sconces, the latter holding balls of spell light instead of candles because Nimue's court had magic literally to burn. Or the carpets scattered carelessly about in dark jewel tones that matched the rest of the room—reds for the coral, black for the rock, white for the pearls, and blue for the water—and with a nap that looked like silk but was something even finer.

Pritkin had said that the fey wove it from the secretions of certain ocean mollusks that used it to adhere themselves to rocks. Mussel spit, in other words, but it didn't feel that way when the weavers finished with it. It caressed my abused toes in almost obscene luxury, making me feel more inadequate than I already did in my drenched rat state, with a half-burnt gown from my last adventure because dragonscale doesn't hold up so well to real dragons.

I was also vaguely dizzy as the whole, dimly lit room subtly glittered. Between that and the constantly moving light shadows from outside, it felt like the waves were in here, too. Or, when I briefly lay on the bed, heaped with fluffy mattresses and silky furs and enough velvety pillows for ten people, that I was drifting on a raft under a star-strewn sky, to the point that I started to disassociate.

Looking at it through half-lowered lashes was not recommended.

I got up in self-defense and started pacing around the room, trying to find something to ground me. Pritkin stayed on the bed, exhausted from an ordeal that had lasted far longer than my brief participation. It had been the first in a series of challenges that had been the Alorestri's way of choosing their next monarch until Nimue had shown up and rendered it all moot.

But she was gone now, and the locals had dug out the old scrolls recording how chieftains were selected in ancient times, and it was as bloody as you'd expect from Faerie. That would have been true even if the contest was fair, but it definitely wasn't. Pritkin was part demon, and it seemed that everyone was ganging up on him to make sure that whoever won, at least they wouldn't be ruled by hellspawn.

And the easiest way to do that was to kill him.

He'd been ambushed three times during the Challenge today, and the only thing that had saved him was oozing over by the walls.

Or I should say things, as they were both there, our demonic guardians, looking as abashed as something like that could. I shot the one with a slightly pink tint an evil eye, as it had been my ride before abandoning me to save its smelly hide, and watched it sink even more into itself. Any further, and I was going to see what it looked like on the inside—

Oh, wait.

It made an unhappy sound and tried to hide behind its . . . brother? Friend? Partner in crime?

I still wasn't sure, but I was giving it a pass since it had helped Pritkin when a couple hundred fey ambushed him during the Challenge. Its amorphous skin didn't mind arrows getting shot into it, as it just glorped them back out again, allowing it to pick up Pritkin and run off with him heedless of how many times they were hit. And they'd been hit a lot.

"Did you hear me?" I verbally poked Pritkin a little because he was ignoring me.

"Yes, and let it rest for a moment," he said, with an arm flung over his eyes. Only his tone made it into "Let me rest."

I walked back over to the huge bed and sat down. It was atop a three-step dais like the one I had back at my court in Vegas. Giving me a sudden pang of longing for my tacky penthouse, my pretty blue and sand-colored bedroom, and people who didn't look at me with suspicion and hate. But the job was here, and the job wouldn't wait.

I compromised with duty and lay down beside the exhausted man. The stench had mostly been washed off us by the plunge and what was left ... well, I was getting used to it. Pritkin huffed out a laugh as if he knew what I'd been thinking and turned to face me.

His hand lifted to play with a limp curl by my cheek, making it hard to concentrate as a warm knuckle kept just brushing the skin. It was unpredictable—brush, brush ... brush—and the anticipation in between moments of contact had me holding my breath. And then letting it out again in a soft "ahh" whenever that tiny touch came once more.

It was one of the things about dating a prince of the incubi that nobody else would understand. Pritkin usually put on this fierce, war mage persona—gruff, hard-edged, and fairly profane. Okay, make that really profane, especially when something set off that famous temper. And that was one side of him.

But then there was this.

Brush ...

Brush ...

Wait for it ...

Annnnnd freaking nothing, except for green eyes sparkling at me through pale lashes, because yeah. He knew exactly what he was doing. And it was working.

My body was tingling, my insides were liquifying, and goosebumps were flooding over my skin, and yet—

Nothing.

Nothing.

Nothing.

Auggghhhh!

More nothing, except for the feel of his breath on my face because he was close, close, so very close, and yet nowhere were our bodies actually touching. But close enough for me to feel his heat radiating on my skin and banishing the room's chill. Banishing Faerie, for a moment, because this was home, this was what I longed for, this was why I dreamed of Vegas.

Because he was usually in it.

Brush.

I jumped him, heard him laugh, felt him roll me in the soft silks of an alien world, and looked up into a face full of evil intent if I'd ever seen one. Yeah, I thought enthusiastically. Be mean to me, Daddy—

Just as somebody started pounding on the door.

Pritkin's head dropped to my chest in defeat. "I *hate* this place," he whispered, and I laughed.

Then they were coming in, a bunch of people I didn't know, to invite us somewhere I didn't want to go. And didn't have the clothes for, as my once pretty tissue of silver dress, which had reemerged from the armor once the danger was past, was looking a bit ratty. And smelling worse.

I took a discreet sniff while Pritkin dealt with the flunky brigade, all of whom were staring: at him, at me, at the two horrors squelching by the wall, and speaking of which—

"We need some food," I said abruptly, with the tinny translation spell echoing my words in whatever tongue this particular brand of fey spoke.

Or maybe not, because the chief flunky paused the flowery speech he had launched into to blink at me in confusion.

He was a typical fey, with high cheekbones, a tall, deceptively thin body considering that he could probably heft a tank, and—thankfully—dark brown hair. It was the silver-haired bastards that made my butt clench, although, after today, I was starting to wonder if these were any better. Frankly, it was doubtful.

But this one, dressed in some mighty fancy robes for a flunky, was at least listening, although I appeared to have confused him. "But your . . . Pythianess," he said, frowning and stumbling a bit over the word he'd just made up. "Did you not hear? The victory banquet is in less than an hour—"

"To catch us off guard and exhausted," Pritkin explained in

English, which the flunky didn't appear to understand because he continued blithely in his language.

"—and I can assure you, any delicacy that you could possibly—"

"Are they invited?" I asked, not bothering to be polite, considering that his people had just tried to kill me.

Luckily, my translation spell didn't manage sarcasm well, and he failed to notice.

"They?" his eyes went around the room, carefully avoiding the repugnance along the wall. "You brought others with you?"

Pritkin was trying, not very successfully, to hide a smile.

"They," I said impatiently. "Them. Those." I pointed at Horror #1 and #2 and realized I hadn't thought to ask their names.

"You think they deserve to eat?" Pritkin asked. "After the stunt they pulled?"

"Only one of them noped out," I reminded him. "And both of them did help. I take it that getting help is not illegal?" I assumed not, as he'd have been disqualified otherwise.

"No, I'm allowed a team," Pritkin said, grinning openly now.

"I don't know what's so damned funny," I said. "We won, didn't we?"

That won me an actual laugh.

Pritkin's amusement seemed to take a couple of the fey back almost as much as it did me, as it was not a regular occurrence from a man known to scowl for centuries. But nothing about this day was normal! And if Gross and Nasty over there were our team, we needed them strong.

But the flunky, who had appeared as unruffled as they came on arrival, was starting to have a problem keeping up that façade. His eyes didn't seem to want to light on the horror twins, yet his duty required them to, so it was a lot of blink, slide, blink, slide as he continually readjusted his view. And then Pritkin decided to help him out.

"Or we could just take them with us."

"Take them . . . with you?" the head flunky whispered as if he didn't understand.

"To the banquet," Pritkin said helpfully, which caused one of the flunkies-in-training to gasp and the other literally to clutch his pearls.

He had a lot of them. They all had a lot of them, from the seed variety sewn onto their filmy robes to create patterns in the weave, to normal-sized ones that they wore in long ropes around their necks and threaded through their elaborate hairstyles, to one the size of a robin's egg on the hand that the chief flunky had brought up to his throat. It was black and matched his expression, which had just about worn through the thin veneer of proper manners he had left.

He clearly didn't think that we deserved proper manners. He thought that we smelled. And what he thought about our companions was probably best left unsaid.

So Pritkin helped him out again. "Or you could have some raw meat sent in. Venison will do."

"Venison," the flunky repeated as if he had never heard the term. And then he seemed to snap out of it. "Yes. Yes, we can— venison. Venison. Of course."

"A lot of it," Pritkin clarified, and the three of them nodded together as if their heads were on a string.

Then they fled. Probably to get a bath and change clothes, lest any of our funk persisted. I grinned for some reason.

And looked down to see that I had made a friend.

"You have a name?" I asked Horror #1, who had sidled up beside me.

It opened up a hole in the rippled skin that I guessed was supposed to be a mouth and screeched something. I winced. "I don't think I can pronounce that."

"Perhaps you should just give them names since we're all in this together," Pritkin said dryly from over by the door. He'd followed the flunkies, closed the door after them, and was doing something to it. Probably making sure that they hadn't added a listening spell because he continued to move about afterward, checking other parts of the suite.

"And the rest of the team?" I asked, terribly afraid that I already knew the answer.

"Nobody wished to throw their hats in the bull ring with the certain loser," I was told.

"But you didn't lose."

"No." He frowned, his good humor evaporating as quickly as it had come. "Which just makes this more dangerous. My attackers were clumsy today, assuming that numbers would be enough to overwhelm me. They'll be more strategic next time."

"Next time?" I repeated. "How many of these damned events are there?"

"Five all together. And they get progressively harder." He looked at me seriously, and his head tilted. "Feel like doing that sort of thing four more times?"

"No." I lay back on the bed, and the horror I had decided to name Pinkie curled up next to me. I absently petted it. It wasn't like I could smell any worse.

"Then I take it you'll be leaving?" Pritkin asked, appearing hopeful.

I frowned at him, a fact that did not go over well.

"Don't be stupid, Cassie! You have to see what's going on here!"

"Yes, I do, and don't call me names."

He blinked slightly at that. "I wasn't. I was pointing out that you are, in fact, acting remarkably—"

"I am acting like a Pythia who wants this war over and all of us back home!" I said and shifted to get in his face since I could currently do that. But he recovered quickly; no one had ever said he wasn't resilient.

Which was why I found my wrist captured in an iron grip and a suddenly dangerous-looking man in my face. He had just been chased through a forest by no fewer than three different hunting parties, had gotten into a fistfight with a prehistoric nightmare, and had almost drowned while sharing his limited oxygen supply with me. He should have looked like a twin to my drowned rat.

He didn't.

The tan he'd been working on in Vegas had deepened, probably due to roaming all over the fey countryside, trying to get here. I imagined that that hadn't been easy, as assassinating him before he arrived would have been simpler than this. But they'd missed him, and now they'd missed him again, yet all he could think about was my safety.

I wanted to kiss him, so I did. And it was nice—for half a second. Which was all I had to enjoy the hard lips, the faint scrape of stubble, and the body that felt like it had dropped some weight and put on some muscle since I'd seen him last, not that he'd needed it. But it had left him looking even more stripped down and deadly than usual, with the cheekbones more clearly defined and the jawline sharp enough to cut myself on.

Pair that with blond hair that was no longer dripping but molded to his skull as it never did usually, hard green eyes, and a grip like iron, and I was . . .

I was trying to kiss him again.

But he pulled back, clearly not in the mood, which was not normal for an incubus. But Pritkin was a war mage first and Rosier's son second—or maybe third or fourth as he and the old man were less antagonistic these days but hardly friends. And business took precedence.

"What?" I asked.

And then wished I hadn't as a silence spell clicked shut over our heads.

Damn it.

"Let me spell this out for you," he said grimly. "You asked what we're working with? Them," he hiked a thumb at the horror twins. "That's it. And your power is wonky and dependent on portals that can be shut down, should anyone figure out that that is the way to stop you. And whilst I absorbed a good deal of power from recent events," I stiffened, but he didn't go into detail, thank God, "it is limited, and I expended a good deal of it getting this far. And for some reason, I can no longer feel my connection to Mircea."

I bit my lip. "Yeah. About that."

"Cassie . . ." Pritkin could make a single word into a whole paragraph, maybe an entire page, I thought.

"I was going to tell you later—"

"Tell me now." It wasn't a request.

Which was fair, as Mircea formed the third part of our triumvirate, and without him, the spell binding us together didn't work. Not that that mattered since Pritkin had taken it off when he and Mircea went on different errands in Faerie, not wanting to risk me. But it was easy enough to reengage in emergencies, which was what had happened because Mircea had had a crisis involving a pissed-off Athena.

Yes, *that* Athena. Luckily, he'd had a witch with him, who I guessed had cast Lover's Knot at his request. Because seconds before his daughter Dorina, who had been fighting an ancient goddess on her own, was about to meet a predictable end, Mircea had absorbed some of the goddesses' power through a smear of her blood.

And used our bond to borrow one of Pritkin's abilities.

The next thing I knew, a giant-sized Mircea was meeting the towering Athena on her level. Because one of Pritkin's abilities as the son of the Prince of the Incubi was to steal talents from the souls he ingested. Not that he went around ingesting souls, as he hated his demon half, but Mircea had no such qualms.

Like most vamps, Mircea loved power, especially a new one that appeared when he most needed it. Which was why Athena's intended butchering of Dorina did not go as planned. A furious father, every bit as big and strong as she was, had jumped her, huge vamp fangs glistening under the cold skies of an alien world, and shortly after that, RIP Athena.

That would have been great if, shortly afterward, he hadn't ended up stranded in said world when the portal linking it to

Faerie was blown up by a vengeful pixie.

It's a long story.

But the point was that the Lover's Knot spell binding the three of us was now well and truly dead, with one of its parts not only out of town but out of this universe. Because Jotunheim wasn't like Faerie, which was within a stone's throw from Earth, metaphysically speaking. No, Jontunheim was well into the universe that Faerie had initially come from, and that was a problem.

That was a big problem, as the spell was acting like Mircea had died. I didn't think that was the case, as his vampire family hadn't run amuck, and Pritkin and I hadn't keeled over, which a dead triumvir would have definitely caused. But as far as our link went, it didn't matter.

Lover's Knot was kaput since a partial spell was an inoperative spell. I didn't need to tell Pritkin that, who had forgotten more magic than I was ever likely to know. I just needed to tell him why.

And there was no way to make it any easier.

"He went through a portal into Jotunheim," I said, fessing up. "Which was destroyed soon after—"

"What?"

"—so he's stranded there for the moment. His daughter is planning to go through a similar gateway in my court's library —"

"Gateway? What gateway?"

"—which has been inactive since the gods left but which her family lineage may allow her to open. But even if she gets through—"

"Wait. Go back."

"—and somehow links up with him and manages to rescue him, it won't be for weeks, as she was pretty banged up the last time I saw her—"

But Pritkin wasn't listening. Pritkin was talking. "What the *hell?* The portals to other worlds are barred, save for Earth and Faerie! That's what this whole damned war is about, to keep them that way and the gods out!"

He had flung out a hand as he spoke, I guessed at the collective crap fest the universe insisted on handing us, so I knew he was seriously pissed. Pritkin was usually tightly controlled, especially regarding physical actions, since war mages were essentially magical nukes. They could take out a building by a stray spell, especially those who had learned silent casting.

I'd often wondered if that was where all the swearing came from; it was literally his only safe outlet. But it hadn't been enough this time, and he didn't even know the half of it yet. This was going to be fun.

"Yeah, I know," I said, wondering where to even start. "But Dory has a pass through the barrier from her family background, which is even more messed up than, uh. . ." The green eyes flashed, and I wondered if there was any way to postpone this to a time when I wasn't tired and hungry and could think straight.

But I guessed not. Because, before I could come up with a good excuse, he came out with it: the question I'd been dreading. "And how the hell do you know all this?"

There was no point beating around the bush, as Pritkin was like a bloodhound on a scent. He'd have it out of me sooner or later. I sighed and womaned up.

"Because I was there when it happened."

CHAPTER FOUR

Fifteen minutes later, things had not improved, even though I'd finished filling Pritkin in on recent events.

Or maybe because of that.

"I sent you back to Earth to keep you safe!" he snarled. "Not to have you fighting gods!"

Yeah, that was what he'd thought was happening since I'd had information that I hadn't shared with him. It hadn't been a lie, unless by omission, but it hadn't been the entire truth, either. Because he'd been coming here and needed to concentrate on what he was doing, not be constantly worried about me.

But I'd made that decision for him, and he was pissed about it. It had been one of those times when duty had to supersede our relationship, but I didn't think now was the time to bring that up. Or to remind him exactly why we were here.

Once upon a time, having the spirit of Faerie, essentially the soul of a planet, giving me orders would have sounded weird, but that time was long past. I had accepted that she was real, was tired of seeing her creations destroyed by a bunch of vagabond gods from another universe, and wanted said gods dead. And since she'd noticed that we felt the same, we'd gotten an ally.

But she didn't communicate through speech, so her instructions had been murky. I'd understood enough through the visions she'd been shooting into my head, however, to know that there were some pressing issues that she needed help with. The one I hadn't told Pritkin about had involved Zeus, AKA Jupiter, AKA Odin—the father of the gods and the biggest asshole I had ever met—getting up to some very bad stuff in old Romania.

I'd tackled that one, as it required a time traveler. It had been the most brutal battle of my life, something that I guessed I should have expected, and I'd spent more than half of it dead. Having a dad who was a necromancer comes in handy when you have to animate your own corpse.

Mircea, meanwhile, had been sent on the second task, namely to find his long-lost wife, who had been fighting the gods in another world. Only we hadn't known about that last part until I caught up with him again, and we showed up just in time for the big battle. And turned the tide; well, mostly Mircea and his daughter had, by him borrowing some of Pritkin's abilities through our bond and meeting a goddess as a peer.

And annihilating her.

Pritkin had been stuck with the third task, which we assumed was about getting one of the strongest fey armies on our side before they joined the other guys. But considering how the last few errands had gone, I didn't know for sure what we were facing here. And the fact that I hadn't gotten any more visions lately probably meant that Faerie didn't, either.

She theoretically saw whatever her creatures did, and that included the fey. But the gods could cloud her sight or play tricks on it, leaving her knowing where the hot spots were but not necessarily what they were. Or else she did know and didn't want to tell me, thinking we'd run for the hills if we knew the truth, and we just might!

"I only fought Zeus," I pointed out, trying to drag my thoughts somewhere else. "Athena was more of an assist. . ."

And, okay, not helping. Pritkin had been sitting on the edge of his bed with his head in his hands, but at that, he looked up. And there was savagery there that I had rarely seen, at least directed at me.

It radiated out of hard green eyes, flushed stubbled cheeks, and exposed teeth as flat and normal as mine but which suddenly reminded me of fangs. That look alone would have given most people palpitations, like being stuck in a cage with an angry tiger. It didn't me.

This man had suffered, risked, and almost died a hundred times to save me. He had battled through trauma that he'd repressed for centuries, had bared a soul that few had ever seen, and which had probably been more challenging for him —so private, so guarded, so careful—than any physical fight would have been. So, no, I wasn't frightened.

But I didn't like seeing him in pain and with an added layer of confusion in his eyes because he wasn't sure that he could protect me anymore, not against the kinds of things that we were facing these days.

That made me sad, which in turn made me angry because we'd had enough of that, of stupid angst that didn't get us anywhere, of pain that neither of us deserved, of greedy assholes who thought they could come barging into our world and upend everyone's lives, or end them. Yes, we'd had enough, and I was tired. Like I was tired of this conversation because he didn't get it despite being way smarter than me.

But not about this.

I walked over and knelt between his legs, my head on his chest, my heartbeat and his mingling in my ears. His was rapid, hard, and angry as if he was gearing up for a fight, but I didn't give him one. I didn't do anything except hold him, and slowly, the furious beating under my ear started to ease, to slow, to melt back into a normal rhythm until I could barely hear it anymore.

And the tiger began to purr.

Or at least to sigh and run a hand up and down my back. One that was lethal to his enemies, as evidenced by the gun calluses I could feel through the thin layers of chiffon. And the potion stains that I couldn't see but knew were there because they never went away.

Over time, I'd learned to use them as a kind of mood ring. Brown or yellow meant that he was mellow and happy because he'd been experimenting with weird stuff from three different realms that the Silver Circle, the leading magical authority on Earth, didn't need to know about. Purple, blue, or green meant that he was worried and busy crafting protection spells and wards, or nasty little traps to litter around the outside of my court to terrorize anyone trying to break in. And then there was red...

Red, mauve, and the pinkish, washed-out salmon color that resulted from him scrubbing his skin so that I wouldn't know what he'd been up to, indicated that he had been working on lethal potion bombs, vials of poisonous gases, and bullets that did a lot more than go boom. We'd argued over red because the Silver Circle had plenty of weapons he could access, as protecting the Pythia was one of their many jobs, and Pritkin had been a war mage in their employ before quitting to guard me. I wanted him to use their stuff, not to experiment with crazy shit that could make flesh drip like water and eat through bone—and two layers of wards!

But he didn't trust anything he hadn't made himself and insisted that the Circle was always behind the times. Our enemies constantly developed new weapons, so we had to follow suit. And as someone no longer employed by the Corps, he didn't get the experimental, cutting-edge stuff anymore.

So, I knew, I *knew*, without turning my head, that his hands were speckled with red. Because he'd used up the weapons he'd had when he came here and had had to craft more on the run. It told me something of the battle to get this far, how savage it must have been, and the toll it must have taken on him.

It also told me that he hadn't expected to see me, hadn't thought I'd come after him, had believed that he would be all alone.

And he probably wanted to be because he'd come here expecting to lose, knowing the competition. And that he would be fighting in an arena of their choosing, in their world, because they were too cowardly to come into ours. Meet me on my turf, I thought viciously, and this will be a very different contest.

And a damned short one!

I felt my breathing quicken and my heartbeat speed up, but the rhythmic stroking never faltered, although I knew he'd noticed. Pritkin noticed everything about me. I sometimes thought he knew me better than I knew myself.

The long, slow strokes continued as if he understood how much I needed them, and he was right. I'd had a grip on my emotions for so long that it had become a stranglehold. I hadn't been able to let them out or relax enough to grieve everything that had happened recently; I couldn't when I had to be strong for my court, my job, my*self*.

So, I'd sucked it up and did so again, only it was easier this time with the power that seemed to be leeching into me from that soothing touch. I didn't know if it was a spell, but I didn't think so. We didn't need a spell.

Just this, just him, just those arms holding me and those hands on my bare skin through the rips that battle had left in my protection. I wasn't sure which battle anymore, but it didn't matter. None of it did.

Just that we'd survived them all and were back together, something I hadn't been sure would ever happen. And I guessed Pritkin hadn't, either. Because his hands suddenly tightened, as if he was afraid that I would disappear if he let go, like a mirage in the desert.

"You fought so hard," I finally whispered. "When I had the Pythian power dropped onto me like a boulder out of nowhere, you fought for me, to help me, to train me, to defend me when I couldn't defend myself. So that I could someday become a Pythia who didn't need it anymore. And I did."

I looked up at him. "Or as close as anyone can be in war. I can hold my own."

"I know that." It was a rasp I didn't understand.

"Then what . . .?"

He looked at me, and his eyes were haunted. "Then what the hell can I offer you? What am I good for anymore except to put you in danger? You shouldn't be here, Cassie! This is my fight!"

I stared at him, caught off guard. And then repeated the most absurd claim in a string of them. "What are you good for?"

Green eyes blazed into mine, and there was anger again, but it wasn't for me. "I let you be assaulted, tortured, beaten to a bloody pulp," he rasped. "And almost—"

"You didn't let anything happen," I said low and vicious, before he uttered the word that rang in both our heads.

"I didn't prevent it, either," he said, his jaw tight.

I glared at him, suddenly furious, because we'd discussed this once before, and I didn't want to do it again. I didn't want to remember the prelude to my fight with Zeus, which had been a much smaller but no less horrifying battle to escape from a camp run by his creature, Aeslinn. He was the fey king with whom we were currently at war, who had allied with the gods against his own world.

His silver-haired servants had taken me prisoner, and it was from them that I'd learned the true meaning of fear. And of the sensation of bones snapping under my skin, of limbs turning unresponsive, of breathing becoming labored when I could manage it at all, and of eyesight fading after I escaped my tormentors and dragged myself toward a portal that I couldn't even see properly. Luckily, its brilliance had blinded the fey, too, ensuring that at least some of their boots, fists, and clubs had missed.

But not all.

Not even most.

Yet the portal had caught me right before my strength gave out, with the strangest feeling of weightlessness as my almost dead body fell away. It had been the one Faerie had made for me when I'd visited her realm in spirit form, or else what would have tumbled out the other side probably wouldn't have lasted long. Instead, the next thing I knew, I was waking up in my mentor's cozy court, with my whole, unbroken flesh embracing me.

I should have felt relieved and grateful. Instead, I'd been terrified, hearing those jeering, angry voices over and over in my head, feeling phantom pain that didn't have a source anymore but was so real nonetheless, and being afraid to close my eyes in case I got caught in that nightmare all over again. It had felt obscene, like there should be a price for cheating death.

And, of course, there had been. Because the nightmares *had* come when I was too weary to stay awake another moment, sending me plunging back into a vortex of leering faces and grasping hands. And abject panic, as if I was right back there again, helpless, alone, and terrified, and unsure whether I'd ever see anyone I loved again.

The fight with Zeus had come later, and strangely, another trauma seemed to have partially healed the first. Maybe because, while I might not have won that contest, I hadn't lost it, either. I had come face to face with the biggest threat of them all and lived to tell about it.

And I wasn't sure which of us had been more beat up at the end.

The momentary victory had done wonders for my belief in myself, my training, and my competence. For so long, I had been flailing around like a drowning victim, just trying to keep my head above water and wondering if I would ever be worthy of the position I held. I didn't worry anymore.

I was Pythia, I was a damned good one, and if I had beaten Zeus once, I could do it again. Of course, I could also die trying, but that was old news. But this, this *chance*, this possibility that maybe we could survive, even win . . .

That was new.

But Pritkin hadn't been there. He hadn't seen that fight, and the look on his face reminded me a lot of the one I'd seen in my mirror before I left to face my biggest challenge ever. He didn't know that we could do this, and the last thing he'd seen had not been positive.

He and Mircea had been linked with me when the terror

and torture and savage beating happened at that horrible camp. They had helped me to escape through Pritkin's abilities and Mircea's mental powers, all of which we'd shared through our bond. But not before experiencing it right along with me.

I'd been so busy ever since that I hadn't had much time to think, especially about things I'd rather forget. But I realized now: Pritkin had had nothing *but* time, fighting his way across a land rent by war and full of enemies. I could see him sitting by a fire in some godforsaken wood, trying to craft weapons out of the locally available flora that might keep him alive a little longer, with nothing but his thoughts for company.

Waiting on another attack and thinking—entirely too much.

"I saw what condition you were in at the end of it," he growled. "If you hadn't been traveling in spirit, clothed in a body that Faerie gave you, you wouldn't have made it. You'd have come back a corpse!"

I didn't say anything because I couldn't argue with that.

I'd thought a few times since that being injured in battle came with one advantage: the long recovery time. I'd had a bit of that after the fight with Zeus, which had mostly involved lying in bed for a week with my head spinning. But it had given me a chance to come to some kind of grip with what had happened and how my world had changed.

But his hadn't yet.

Mircea's may have because the last time I saw him, he was soaked in the blood of a goddess whose head he'd just cut off, which you had to assume changed a person. But Pritkin had yet to cross his Rubicon, to evolve in the way that this war was causing all of us to, and while I'd come to help him, there was only so much I could do. Physically, because my power didn't half work here, or emotionally because I didn't understand what he was feeling.

But maybe there was one thing I could give him.

"Every time the nightmares came," I said softly. "Every time I felt helpless, like I couldn't handle another day, like the war would never end and all the hopes we'd had were just that. Just hope, just straws we clutched because what else was there? To lay down and die? I won't do that."

"Cassie—"

"No, let me finish." I looked up at him and let my anger show for once instead of hiding it as I did with most people. I didn't need to pretend here.

I never had with him.

"Every time, *every time*, I banished the pain by thinking of you. You and Mircea and Rhea and Tami and Gertie and so many others. But mostly you. Your face got me through that night, just as your power gave me light in the darkness. I followed your footsteps to that portal, and it was the thought that they *were* yours that kept me going. I don't know that I would have had the courage to do it otherwise."

"You would. You always do—"

"Shut up!" This time, it was my eyes blazing. "I'm trying to tell you that I do need you! I needed you that night like I need you now, by my side to the end. We can do this—I know we can. And the damned fey can go hang!"

"You came to rescue me, then?" Pritkin asked, his voice raw but his eyes lightening with something he didn't want to let himself feel.

"I came to fight beside you. Because I need you, in so many ways I've lost count. And because I love you." I stared up at him. "Are you really going to turn me away?"

I didn't get an answer in words that time, but I didn't need them. Incubi spoke with other things, with lips and tongues and fingers pressing harder now, as if to reassure himself that I was really there and hadn't dusted away in some magical battle he hadn't even known was happening. Maybe that was what was eating at him, as it had me, not knowing what the other was doing and whether all this fighting was for a brighter future we wouldn't share because the most important person in our lives might not survive to see it.

But we were together now, I thought, kissing him back.

And this was what I'd wanted, what I'd needed, what I didn't think I could live without. What I'd dreamed about when he was gone, and the world had felt so big and empty without him.

He was still angry; I could feel it in the rigid set of his shoulders, see it in the frown on his forehead, taste it in his kiss. But he was more relieved, vastly, vastly relieved, that we were together. And together, I thought, drawing him closer, we could handle anything.

CHAPTER FIVE

O ur lips met, and he immediately deepened the kiss. I made a little sound and started trying to figure out how to get the damp shirt off of those broad shoulders. It was the last one I'd bought him, the one that said "I may look calm, but in my head I've killed you five times" and I didn't want to tear it.

But before I could get it over his head, he picked me up, I assumed to lay me on the bed, but he appeared to have a different destination in mind.

"Is the smell really that bad?" I asked as we crossed the room and entered what I guessed was a bathroom.

"No. But I thought you might prefer not to have an audience."

I didn't know who he was talking about until one of the Horror Twins gave out a screech of what might have been approval. Or absolutely anything else since their language made nails on a chalkboard sound soothing. I couldn't believe I'd forgotten about them already.

But they didn't follow us inside, although there would have been plenty of space. The bathroom was big, black, and weird, with half the size of the expansive outer room but without the windows that lightened things up. Instead, there was a plunge pool almost big enough for somebody's backyard, surrounded by plants and mist that didn't seem to be coming from anywhere but was wafting among the leaves. There were also small lights in all that, like fairy lights on a string only without the string, and possibly made out of real fairies.

I wanted to poke one, just in case, but couldn't reach it.

There was another archway to the left, which I guessed led to the facilities or a closet, and a large, black stone area on the far, right-hand side down a short hall that looked like it might be a shower, although there were no nozzles for the water. Just a jutting piece of black rock that looked naturally occurring but probably wasn't, that formed a sort of bench. On which Pritkin sat down after carrying me over there since it was the only option.

I was disappointed, as the bed would have been more comfortable. But I could make do, I decided, and finally got the damned shirt off. And then everything else before straddling him, still dressed myself because I was in too much of a hurry to worry about me.

"Take it easy," he said, as I accidentally bit his lip.

"This from an incubus?"

"Half incubus, and one who doesn't want to get stabbed by—what is this?" he demanded, and I looked down to find out that my dress was morphing back and forth from pretty evening wear to a set of full-on, medieval-and-then-some, silver scale armor. It seemed confused, and then so was I as I looked about.

Because this shower wasn't like any I'd ever seen.

"What's happening?" I whispered, wondering if we'd triggered a ward.

Pritkin chuckled, his bad mood momentarily forgotten, maybe because he'd just figured out how to collapse the top half of my suit into the base, leaving me topless. And trying to think past the hands, lips, and tongue that immediately took advantage of that fact wasn't easy. But my eyes nonetheless kept following the floating water globules that were suddenly everywhere.

I didn't know why or how they were floating about as weightlessly as if they were on the space station. But there they were, with an iridescence that showed me back my clueless face as I stared at them in surprise. Some of them were larger than my head.

They kept coming from all directions, even the floor, starting small but then fusing together to make floating puddles or shattering apart into fragments by collisions. There were a lot of the latter because they were coming fast and furious, until it was less like being caught in a rainstorm and more like swimming with occasional air pockets. It left me trying to breathe between getting punched in the face by the latest water-balloon-sized burst.

Until I miscalculated and breathed in when I should have exhaled and choked.

Pritkin paused what he was doing to make a slash at the air with his hand, and suddenly, the watery smacks became more like caresses as the globules slowed way, way down. I found myself in a wonderland of vaguely green and pink-tinted bubbles that had an iridescence on them I hadn't noticed before. Some kind of soap . . .

I turned toward Pritkin, a vaguely pink puddle balanced on one hand, grinning delightedly, and caught him looking at me with a strange expression. It was a cross between wonder and terror, which quickly morphed into a frown when he noticed me noticing. I sighed.

And kissed his neck because I wanted to kiss his neck. It tasted like salt, sweat, and soap because he had been getting smacked, too. But mostly, it tasted like him.

It tasted wonderful.

"You act like we've decided something. We haven't decided anything," he informed me sternly. I mouthed his Adam's apple, one of my favorite bits on a smorgasbord of delicacies, and felt him shiver. "I know what you're trying to do," he added as if there was any doubt.

"Hope so. Didn't think I was being subtle," I murmured and bit down.

"Damn it, Cassie!"

I managed to get my armor to collapse a bit further, to the point that it looked like I was wearing dragon scale thigh highs, which . . .

Badass, I decided, and from Pritkin's expression, he seemed to feel the same. He swallowed and then did it again when I grabbed him, getting an almost comically confused expression on his face. I guessed because it was hard to be stern with a blond trying to sit on your dick.

And succeeding, I thought, groaning loudly enough to drown out whatever stupidity he was spouting because yes, this, this right . . . freaking . . . here, I thought, panting a little as I took all of him, because he was a big boy and I couldn't always do that immediately.

But I was hungry tonight; no, I was *starving*, and I guessed he was, too. A moment later, when I was still trying to find a good seat, he helped me out, making me groan as he grabbed my bare backside and shifted my position. And then kissed me, and it told me everything I needed to know.

That he was as starved as I was, that he had missed me, too, so much, that whatever his mouth was saying, his body was glad I was here—

Make that very glad, I thought, screaming a little as he started to thrust. And how the hell he managed to get into a rhythm while being straddled on a narrow rock shelf, which was probably meant for toiletries, and slapped in the face by soap-laden water bubbles, I didn't know. But damned if he didn't make it work.

And, of course, I couldn't let that pass, so I stepped up my game. And would have done even more, but I was too emotional to think straight. I had visualized this moment so many times over the last month while healing from my latest brush with death, and then all the time I was at the dark fey court, which had been a mind trip all on its own, and then during the mad rush to get here, but it had never been like this.

I didn't care. A prince of the incubi makes damned sure you don't care, that you can't think, that your eyes keep wanting to cross and simultaneously roll up into your head and sometimes do. And that your throat is so busy groaning and yelling and shrieking and then laughing as you bounce on his lap and come again and again, as the world slings around you, and as pretty pink water balloons burst in your face so that you can't even speak.

But my body could. And incubi know that language better than any other. It grabbed him, even while I was still giggling my way through orgasm number three, hard enough to make him gasp for a change. And then groan and laugh as I found a rhythm of my own.

I wrung his pleasure right out of him with wriggles and writhing circles and inner squeezes that I was proud to see had *his* eyes rolling back into his head. Twice; they did it twice. I was about to go for three, an all-time best, when he had enough of my antics, grabbed my ass, and squeezed while I laughed and squealed and giggled into the skin of his neck.

And even the ripping, tearing noises from outside, where I guessed the requested venison had finally been delivered by a couple of probably scandalized fey, didn't faze me.

"Think they're eating the deer or the waiters?" I gasped at Pritkin, who only laughed and kissed me. And kept on doing so while finishing up, to the point that I was breathless and energized and tingly and satiated before my butt hit the plunge pool.

I supposed it said something about the whole experience that I hadn't even noticed we were moving.

I floated in a post-coital haze in a fey jacuzzi while my new demon pets tore something to pieces next door. Wasn't how I really thought my life was gonna go, but I'd take it, I thought. And glanced over at Pritkin, who was looking more serene than I could remember in a long time.

I'd take it all day.

But we didn't have all day, so I was happy that the pool seemed designed to clean off all that soap. It felt like little fingers were running over my skin, stripping away the remains of the last few days' worth of sweat and grime and finally getting me clean. It was amazing.

"I could get used to this place," I murmured, sinking lower

so the bubbles could do their thing on my scalp.

Oh, yeah. Yeah, I could absolutely stay here for a while, enjoying the fey version of a spa. Only Pritkin didn't seem to agree.

"You won't find everything so enjoyable," he said grimly. "I know how stubborn you are, but you need to consider—"

"Leaving you here to fight alone?" I considered it. "Nope."

"Don't be so flippant! You don't know what's ahead!"

"Like we ever do?" I cracked an eye because he was harshing my buzz, and it was a good one.

"I'm serious. You don't understand what—"

I gave up, sat up, and put a finger to his lips. Which he instant grabbed in a fist because he was determined not to be distracted this time. Unfortunately for him, so was I.

"Among the many lessons of the past eight months or so," I told him, seriously because he'd asked for it, "one stands above the rest: enjoy the downtimes. They don't come along often, and if you spend them uselessly arguing, you'll regret it when the pressure builds up and you explode."

He kissed the finger before releasing it. "I'm more concerned about you exploding."

I sighed and sank back into the evil, evil bubbles. The fey might have finally found a way to trap me. Right now, I didn't care if I ever got out.

"Okay, you send me away," I said. "And you lose because there are tons of them and only one of you, and they don't care if they cheat. And then *we* lose, all of us, 'cause Faerie wouldn't have sent us here if she thought we could win this without the Green Fey. Then the gods come back and kill us all, including me.

"So, I get to spend the last few weeks or months of my life wracked with guilt and fear and mourning your loss.

"Thanks for that."

Pritkin didn't reply for a moment, and his voice sounded different when he did. "You've changed."

I sucked in some bubbles, then spluttered and coughed

them out again while flapping a hand at him to let him know I was okay. "You think?" I gasped.

I blinked water out of my eyes to see him regarding me soberly. "I wouldn't have—I didn't want this for you," he finally said.

"This?"

"This fear. This pressure. The constant weight of the world on your shoulders, any number of worlds. That ridiculous happy-face T-shirt you wore the first time I saw you—that's what I wanted for you."

His hand cupped my cheek, and I smiled at him wearily. "Pythias don't wear happy-faced Tee's."

"They don't smile much, either. Lady Phemonoe rarely did, and her predecessor wasn't much better from what I could tell."

"Gertie smiled," I said, remembering my old mentor fondly.

"Name once."

I could name several, but one stuck out. "After a training mission on the Devon coast. She'd set Agnes and me the same job: find the item she'd buried with a time signature that showed it wasn't from our era."

"Not from your era?" Pritkin's brow wrinkled, maybe because he didn't know Gertie, who had been the Victorian/early Edwardian Pythia. I'd had to go back that far to find someone willing to train me.

I nodded. "Doesn't happen very often, but sometimes a naughty witch or wizard trying a time spell actually survives and has to be hunted down. But of course, they know we'll be after them and cast spells to make themselves hard to find. One way to get around that is to zero in on an object they dropped."

"What kind of object?"

"Doesn't matter. You start with the easy things to spot, the kind of stuff that anybody might lose—a handkerchief, a piece of jewelry, even a hairpin—and eventually progress to harder items like a leaf caught on their shoe.

"They all feel . . . different, wrong, out of place, like a puzzle piece that doesn't fit. The Pythian power knows that whatever it is doesn't belong in that time and sends up an alert—"

"And you do a locator charm to take you right to them," Pritkin finished. Because while he might not know Pythian magic, he knew just about everything else.

"That's the idea. Only no time traveler had dropped this particular object. Gertie put it there to give Agnes a test and sent me along to add an extra layer of difficulty because she was running out of things to challenge her with. Agnes was a bitch, but she was a talented bitch."

"Another layer of difficulty?"

I smiled slightly. "There was only one object and two of us."

"Ah."

"I ended up covered in rotten seaweed, thanks to Agnes shifting me into a pile on the beach. But roughly the same time, my spell caught her and flung her half a mile into a mountain of fish remains beside a pier where the fisherman cleaned their catch."

Pritkin didn't say anything but blinked slightly as if he'd thought Pythian training was full of tea parties and tarot readings. Not that there hadn't been some of those, but there'd been a lot more stuff like Devon. Because our enemies were like the fey, they didn't play fair, so we had to be prepared for anything.

Including knickers full of seaweed.

Or a really, really pissed-off heir.

"Agnes dropped the object—a lady's hand mirror—which she'd stolen from me when my spell hit her," I continued. "I thrashed my way out of the seaweed, grabbed it, and shifted the hell out of there before she could recover. It was a Pyrrhic victory, considering the state of my dress and the fact that I was likely to smell like a corpse for a week, not to mention that I kept making myself gag. But it was a victory nonetheless."

"Of course it was," Pritkin said. "You're a demigoddess."

I huffed out a laugh. "Yeah, and she was Agnes. I limped

back to court, dripping and towing a couple of strands of blackish-green rot, like toilet paper that had gotten attached to my shoe. But before I'd even gotten across the front hall, there she was, snorting like a dray horse and covered in fish guts. And still clutching one of the seagulls, which I guessed had attacked her when she landed in the middle of its dinner."

Pritkin blinked again like he was having difficulty imagining the elegant lady he'd known that way.

He had no idea.

"It got loose," I said, "or maybe she threw it at me; I was never really sure. But it flew squawking around the front hall, setting the chandelier swaying and the initiates screaming and me ducking, just before that bitch grabbed me."

"What happened?" He actually looked interested.

"She was a savage, is what happened. Almost pulled me bald and practically beat me to death trying to get that mirror away from me."

"Did she succeed?"

I shot him a look. "What do you think?"

Pritkin looked confused. "And Lady Herophile didn't intervene?" he asked, using Gertie's reign title.

"Do you remember how we started this subject?" I demanded. "She was laughing so hard she could barely stay upright. Had to clutch the balcony railing so as not to fall off!"

Agnes hadn't been the only bitch in town.

"But my point in telling you all this was that I spoke the truth earlier. I can hold my own."

The grin that had been spreading over his face faded. "You shouldn't have to."

"None of us should. But that isn't how life works, is it?"

He grasped the back of my head with one strong hand. "If you stay, you're going to be careful."

"I'm always—"

"*Really* careful." Stern green eyes looked into mine, and my stomach, so satisfied a moment ago, started fluttering again. "If it comes down to it, and it's me or you, you let me take the hit—"

As if!

"—or you go home now. I will have your word, Cassie."

He looked like he meant it. Which did not make him right! "You always act like I'm the

most important one in this fight," I said. "While you and Mircea—"

"Right now."

"—and a lot of other people have played major roles in this war! If you die, how do you

know it won't be just as devastating to—"

But Pritkin wasn't listening. "Or you can leave immediately."

"And if I don't?"

"I'll remove myself from this contest, and both you and Faerie can find another champion."

I glared at him, but he meant it. His eyes never wavered. "You know, you're being a complete and utter—"

"Your. Word."

He let me go and stuck out a hand like we were in a boardroom instead of naked and wet and bubbling. But something about the man made me take him seriously anyway, and he looked like he was taking me the same way. There was a time when I would have given a lot for that, for him to trust me, even respect me.

Now wasn't one of those times.

But I took his hand because I wasn't leaving. And because Gertie had taught me something else that I hadn't mentioned. "A Pythia's word is a complex thing," she'd mused one night over tea. "Others don't know what we know or experience what we experience. When they ask for my word, I want to ask them, in what world? At what time? Under what circumstances?

"Those that you would understand, in this one, flat plane of existence that you inhabit, or in the realms that I do? For me, a yes may mean no, and a no yes, for time distorts everything and plays havoc with what we think we know. And frequently leaves all our good intentions in the dust.

"But I don't tell them that, for they wouldn't understand. But you. . . Forget about words, Cassie, demanded from you or otherwise. Follow your heart; you have a good one. And do what it tells you.

"It's the closest thing to truth you're going to get in this life."

So, yeah, I took Pritkin's hand. And shook it. And when he said, "Deal?"

My voice was steady, and my eyes were clear when I answered.

"Deal."

CHAPTER SIX

I went to dinner in my armor. Only it was different armor since it had morphed again, as it had a habit of doing. Because, as the designer who'd created it had put it, "I never know what the hell you'll be up to!"

So, instead of a halter-necked chiffon gown, softly cascading, or a dragonscale battledress silver bright and gleaming, I was currently sporting a swanky silver bodysuit with a high neck, long sleeves, and a fit that left little to the imagination.

And I do mean little.

It hugged every curve in a way that would have made me uncomfortable if it hadn't also been covered in tiny, liquid-looking scales. They shone like polished metal but were harder than diamonds, which was fair since that was roughly what they cost. Leaving me clad neck to toe in squeaky clean, silver badassery.

To accompany it, I slicked my still-wet hair down with something that smelled divine from the spa and that Pritkin had said was a popular hair gel. Trust the fey; the world could be imploding around them but damned if their hair wasn't going to look good. But I wasn't complaining because mine did, too, all sleek and shiny, just like my armor.

I looked like trouble, and since I was, in fact, a freaking lot of trouble for the fey, I felt good about it.

The days of hiding behind a harmless exterior were over. They knew who I was and what I could do. So, the idea was to lean into it and maybe make at least a few of them rethink their plans.

Of course, they might rethink them to make them worse, but I didn't think going to dinner looking like I'd just crawled out from under a bridge would help, either. This court was clearly about making an impression. If I'd had any doubts about that, they would have been quelled by one glance at Pritkin's ensemble.

I'd been dealing with my hair in the bathroom, so hadn't seen the transformation. And it was so extreme that, at first, I didn't know who I was looking at. For a second, I thought a fey had shown up to drag off the deer bones.

But then my brain registered the truth and almost shut down. He must have used the same gel as me because his hair was flat and shining and lying in place for once. He'd smoothed it back from his face and kept it there with a golden circlet around his brow, leaving the newly paired down features on full display.

And they were so *handsome*.

I don't know why that fact always surprised me. Rosier was stunning when he wanted to be, and Pritkin was basically his clone. But he'd spent so much time denying his incubus heritage, of schlepping around in scuffed boots, a scarred old leather coat, a three-day beard, and hair that looked like it was taunting God, that I sometimes forgot.

But the beard was gone now, and the planes of his face were on full display, along with his fey heritage. I wondered if that was why he'd done it, to remind everyone of his royal Alorestri blood. Or, knowing Pritkin, to piss them off because they hated the fact that a part demon, part human, mongrel mutt was even here, staining their pristine halls with his presence, much less competing for the throne.

I grinned. "You're rubbing their faces in it, aren't you?"

"I don't know what you mean." The green eyes were innocent, which they never were. So, yeah. He was trolling.

Fine with me.

But the troll went a lot farther than a shave and a hairstyle.

"Nice threads," I said, because he'd somehow managed to

get his hands on an outfit that looked like it should be in a Hollywood superhero movie, only they'd have probably struck it for being too sexy.

Skin-tight trousers hugged muscular calves and thighs as if he was wearing a scuba suit. They were black, with a faint green iridescence when the light hit them just right, and a subtle pattern of fish scales. Nothing hugged the equally impressive muscles of his chest as it was bare under a floor-length, sleeveless, open-front tunic in the same material. Golden armbands circled bulging biceps, probably because the fey tended to be more slightly built than humans, so that was more salt in the wound.

And there was a cape because, of course, there was.

It was made of the same almost black material and lined with matching fur that looked like sable but was probably from an aquatic creature like a beaver. These folks had a theme, and they were going with it. It also swept the floor when he carelessly threw it on and attached it in the front with golden chains.

There were no boots to finish it off. Just that blinged-out *Aquaman* suit and bare feet, like he was headed to some billionaires' beach wedding. And while it should have looked ridiculous, somehow, it didn't. It left him a pared-down, gold and black figure that resembled a cross between a merman and an ancient king.

An ancient king with a hairy chest, something else the fey didn't usually have, but which added to the slightly barbaric air. And with the fur caressing his shoulders and the way those trousers fit, all together it was . . . it was. . . Yeah.

I needed another shower.

Pritkin noticed, and his lips quirked. "We don't have time for that. You still need to get dressed."

I blinked at him because I was dressed, only to notice some filmy thing lying on the bed.

I walked over to have a look, and no. Just no. In fact, hell no, I thought, holding it up.

Its weave was so fine that it was practically transparent despite having about ten layers of material. It was pretty, in a soft blue to match my eyes, and floaty enough to make my armor's alter ego look like heavy wool. But it was still a no.

I dropped it back on the bed.

"Why did I think that would be your reaction?" he murmured against my neck.

I turned my head and there he was, eyes sparkling with mischief because he was enjoying this. "I'm not doing girlie-girl today," I told him.

"What are you doing?"

"Wartime Pythia. It's a look."

"It is indeed."

Lips found my neck, quickly followed by teeth. They didn't bite down, at least not hard, but it was right over the mark that Mircea had left when he claimed me. Pritkin deliberately traced it with his tongue, taking his time, learning every slight ridge and dip in the skin.

And causing a shudder to shoot through me like lightning.

It reminded me of the one and only time that all three of us had been together . . . like that. It had been a desperate attempt to fully utilize our power, which was linked by incubus energy, and fight off a god, and it had worked. But I'd been so busy not dying that I didn't remember much of it.

Probably just as well, I thought, as liquid heat spread through my body, rushing down my spine, arms, and legs until everything tingled with it.

Everything.

Then he bit down, still not hard, but enough that I felt it. Enough that my body jerked several times and then kept on trembling as sensation after sensation crashed through me. Okay, I did remember a little bit, I thought, my mouth going dry, so much so that I had difficulty getting words out.

"I thought . . . you said . . . we didn't have time," I gasped as strong arms came around me.

"We don't."

"So, what—"

"So, let them wait."

*   *   *

We were late. We were, like, seriously late. Maybe an hour or more, I didn't even know. I was still trying to slick my hair back down and hoping that the trip through a bunch of broad, cool corridors had faded some of the blush from my cheeks.

I didn't even know why I was blushing. I didn't have anything to blush about! Pritkin and I had been together before, and it had always been, uh, memorable.

But today had been even more so. To the point that I'd started to wonder if there was something in the water around here when we suddenly arrived. And I do mean suddenly.

One minute, we were in the hallway, beautifully decorated with flowing, water-themed mosaics on both sides, studded here and there with what looked like genuine pearls for bubbles, gemstone scales on some of the fish, and a gigantic jade tortoise in 3-D that looked like it was coming out of the wall at you because part of it was.

And the next, we were through an archway and onto a landing with a balcony looking over an expansive room. Two impressive stairs were going down, one on either side of the landing. The stairs were terrazzo, with little shells and shiny bits of mother of pearl in the mix, and the handrails were massive pieces of driftwood, bleached in the sun to appear white and polished to bring out their full beauty, yet I barely noticed because the rest of the room was . . . was . . .

Yeah.

It was definitely yeah. And some uh huh and a bunch of oh, wow, and maybe a little damn. And then I lost words entirely because it hit like a blinged-out fist to the face, with all the mind-blowing colors and textures and *people*—

I decided to start with them because the rest of the place was making my head swim. So, I ignored the masses of hovering balls of light roaming around the high arched ceiling, suspended on nothing and constantly changing their patterns and orientation because static chandeliers were for peasants; and the lack of walls because the whole place was surrounded by a seascape, like the "windows" in our room, only these weren't windows, they were huge expanses with nothing but powerful wards keeping back all that water; and the black stone floor that made the white draped, circular tables seem to float like rafts on the sea, surrounded by hundreds of laughing, talking, entirely crazy-looking people. And I belatedly realized that the overdressed flunkies hadn't been overdressed after all.

And that neither was Pritkin. He was practically spartan by comparison because conspicuous consumption was very definitely the order of the day. My God, it was!

A guy at a nearby table had a headpiece made out of a complete set of antlers, only these must have been from some mutant kind of deer. Because they were so big that his neck should have buckled under the sheer weight. Particularly as the headdress was also decked out like a crazy Christmas tree, with dangling shells, jewels, ropes of pearls—of course—and bunches of fresh flowers on each antler.

His chest was bare, too—there was a lot of that going around—although a filmy piece of the nothingness the fey called cloth was draped about his shoulders like a frame. Probably so that his nipple piercing—dripping with a huge, teardrop-shaped pearl—would have something to set it off. He also had a full face of makeup, with seed pearls so thickly encrusted around his oversized eyes that he looked like he was wearing wild, Elton John-type glasses with wave-like flourishes that reached into his hairline, and skin that looked like it had iridescent scale-like tattoos on it when the light hit it just right.

And he was not remotely out of place. If anything, the men outdid the women, the latter of whom were content to show off their perfect, lithe bodies in dozens of layers of diaphanous nothing while seeing how many jeweled belts and pearl necklaces they could pile on top. Fortunately, it was enough to save their modesty most of the time.

And since nobody had on shoes, except for a few wearing backless, jeweled sandals, the whole thing gave off party-at-the-poolside vibes from some deranged club. But I wasn't feeling it. The glare of all those jewels, silks, precious metals, and gleaming furs made me dizzy.

Pritkin wasn't fazed, maybe because he'd seen it before or because he'd seen stranger things in the hells. But I had to work hard to keep from tripping over my own two feet as we slowly descended the stairs. I kept glancing away at the serene coolness of the water, deep and dark and restful to the eyes.

That was how I noticed: not everyone was so ridiculously overdressed. Some of what I guessed were waiters were lined up by the wards and barely dressed at all in short, plain tunics in dark shades that almost matched the water. I might not have noticed them, except that they had their own sort of bling, only I was pretty sure that theirs was all natural.

"Servants," Pritkin confirmed, noticing my interest. "Part human and part fey—of all kinds. That's where the variety comes from. You remember Wales?"

As if I'd forget. He'd had a problem for a while with the Demon High Council, who had cursed his soul backward through time, skipping across past iterations of himself like a stone on a pond. The idea had been to have him snuffed out of existence when he arrived at his birth and to kill him by basically erasing him from ever having lived in the first place. And while that would have solved their problem, it would have exponentially increased mine.

Not only would it have screwed up the timeline, as Pritkin had played a not-insignificant part in it, but it would have resulted in my death. Without him, I would never have made it past the first month of this job. But the demons didn't like the gods, either, so offing the daughter of Artemis, even if she was on their side in the war, didn't appear to worry them too much.

Or maybe they figured I'd survive alone if I had no choice.

I severely doubted that, but nobody had asked me. So, I hadn't asked them when I went pelting back through time after him.

I'd made it—barely—catching up to the fleeing soul when he was a young man in Wales, where he'd been born in the 6th century and known by a different name. There, I'd met many other mixed-species kids since Wales was the sight of one of the Green Fey's portals to Earth. They'd used it to kidnap human women to breed with their fey and create hybrids to act as cannon fodder in their constant wars.

They'd also used it as a dumping ground for the kids who didn't have enough magic to be useful or had been born with other defects that made them unsuitable to fight or to raise the next generation to do so. Those were returned to Earth to fend for themselves as best they could or to die trying. I didn't get the impression that the fey cared much either way.

Yet women continued to go through that portal, some by force, others willingly, to escape the war and deprivation back home. The Green Fey, therefore, had more part humans wandering around their lands than any of the other great houses. And I guessed that not everybody had been dumped who wouldn't make good soldiers because there were a *lot* of mixed-race servants.

"Why are they so . . . colorful?" I asked Pritkin, gazing at the lineup.

"Same reason that some of those in Wales were. A sizeable group has built up here through the years, but marriage is forbidden with the Alorestri—"

"But I thought that was the point."

Pritkin cocked an eyebrow at me. "Breeding, yes; marriage, no."

I scowled.

"They don't want to 'pollute the bloodline,' which is how they view those of us who aren't pure enough for their standards," he added. "The half-castes have to intermarry with each other or the dark fey, who aren't so particular. The result is what you see."

What I saw were skin tones in vibrant yellow, true green, pale lavender, or puce. And a few plain old human shades, but with hair the color of newly mown grass, vivid purple, or Crayola orange. I assumed that some of those shades might have come out of a bottle, but not all, maybe not even most, as they didn't have any other sign of having spent money on their looks.

"They're called Abrovs, named after the first village the fey established for them," Pritkin said. "Well, that's one name. Derebesh is another, meaning contaminated, and others are even less nice."

"Why hate them? They made them," I pointed out. "Those witches I saw in Wales didn't look like they were going willingly!"

He shook his head. "They weren't. The fey prefer magic users for their slaves, as human magic sometimes boosts their own, resulting in stronger soldiers. But coven witches could protect themselves from the era's wars and did not wish to serve the fey."

"But they were taken anyway," I said, remembering my rage at the sight and at the knowledge that I couldn't help them without massively screwing up the timeline. Those women had lived their lives in Faerie, influencing the history of this place, or else had escaped back to Earth and influenced ours. Either way, I'd had to leave them, something that still caused a bitter taste in my mouth.

"Yes," Pritkin agreed. "Something that turned out to be a two-edged sword. All those fey volunteering to father sons on the human women—"

"So noble of them," I murmured furiously.

"—have transmitted some of the strongest magical blood into the mix, and more than occasionally, it has proved dominant."

"You mean—"

He nodded. "You won't see that kind here. They're kept guarding the borders for the most part so that they can die on cue. But if you did, you'd be hard-pressed to pick out the "polluted" from the true-born. It's one reason they are so obsessed by bloodlines here."

"And why you're seen as such a threat."

"Oh, I'm more than that. Being part human makes me polluted; being half demon makes me a monster. There are plenty here who would prefer to kill me on sight rather than let me compete."

"Then why don't they?" I glanced at the nearest tables of people, a few of whom were shooting us poisoned glances as we passed. "They tried hard enough on the way here!"

"Challenge rules. I was protected once I announced my intention to compete for the throne."

Yeah, it really looked like it.

"Except in the Challenge," he added. "There, anything goes. But here . . . if they want to murder me, they'll have to be more subtle about it. Until then, they demean me whenever they can."

"Like giving you subpar rooms?"

He nodded. "And then there's this."

For a moment, I didn't know what he was talking about. Until I realized that we had stopped by a tiny table that might have sat four in a pinch. It was missing the gorgeous, over-the-top centerpieces that the other tables could boast, along with a tablecloth and cutlery. There were only a couple of plates and a few dull-looking goblets—in pewter when the rest of the tables had gold.

It was the fey equivalent of sitting by the bathroom, or where the door from the kitchen could hit your chair every time a waiter went in or out. We easily had the worst table in the room, which was barely in the room at all, being in a dark spot a good football field away from the brightly lit, elevated area at the far end across from the now distant staircase, where I guessed the beautiful people sat. Or at least, the "pure."

I looked at the pathetic place they'd planned to stash Pritkin and felt a wash of fury flood over me. He was worth a hundred of them—a thousand! And he had the slashes on his shoulder to prove it!

A demon lord had gotten his claws into him once for saving a couple of slave girls who had ended up in the hells. The demon had kidnapped them, and for a worse fate than the fey intended, planning to drain the life out of them to increase his power. Pritkin had heard about it, and the ensuing battle had been as close as they came, with him receiving the scars he wore to this day.

But he'd survived, rescued the girls, and won the enmity of the Demon High Council in the process, although not for the damage he'd inflicted on one of their own, who they didn't like anyway. But because he'd broken the cardinal rule—he'd made them afraid—and they'd never forgotten it. It had been one factor in the aforementioned trip to Wales and plenty of other nastiness through the years.

Yet he'd done it anyway; he'd bled to help slaves instead of raping and breeding them! He deserved better than the bastards here, not worse. And frankly, so did I.

So, I moved us—and the table—to an open spot on the brilliantly lit dais and almost scared a poor servant girl to death in the process.

We popped out of nowhere in front of her, and she gave a little shriek, barely holding onto the golden jug she was carrying. And the shriek carried. Because suddenly, the entire huge room was deathly silent.

I ignored them since they deserved no better, picked up one of the pewter goblets, gave it the look it deserved, and held it out to her. "Thanks," I said as she stared at me wide-eyed.

And then hurriedly filled my cup and Pritkin's, too, before scurrying off somewhere.

I took my seat. "We'll pay for that," Pritkin said, joining me. But his lips were quirking.

"If we're ever sat there again, so will they," I said and didn't bother lowering my voice.

Then I drank my wine, and damn if it didn't taste divine.

CHAPTER SEVEN

Besides us, there were two big tables on the raised expanse and three smaller ones. Of course, "smaller" meant maybe fifty people each, whereas the biggest had to hold several hundred or more. All of whom were glaring at me as if they'd understood my threat.

And maybe they had. I hadn't been addressing a fey, so my translator hadn't kicked in. But if anybody in Faerie could speak English, it would be the Alorestri.

One of them, I was sure could, a surprisingly golden-haired guy in the middle of the most extensive table, in a mass of silver robes embroidered with tiny blue carp. He had on silver blue eyeshadow because the Alorestri noblemen seemed to wear as much make-up as their women, but he didn't look effeminate. In fact, he looked like he might be part human, with a more muscular build than most of the fey could boast and a strong jawline.

He looked like he'd be more at home in Malibu on a surfboard than here, but maybe the Alorestri had those. I mean, why wouldn't they? Too bad he was drinking wine and pretending he couldn't see us.

But his hand, sporting the largest sapphire I'd ever seen, had just clenched on the bowl of his goblet, so I was pretty sure he'd heard me. He wasn't ordering us off the platform, though, so I supposed that was something. I glanced at Pritkin.

"Feltin, Nimue's old lover," he told me in a low voice. "He's part human, too, although he denies it. She plucked him out of obscurity centuries ago and elevated him to royal favorite. He enjoyed a good deal of power when she was alive and isn't happy about losing it."

"Is he challenging?"

"No, he can't. He has no standing without a blood tie. But whoever he backs will have a definite advantage."

Probably shouldn't be antagonizing him then, I thought, and looked away.

I didn't have a chance to ask anything else, as the momentary silence was interrupted by the arrival of Lord Bling. At least, I assumed that was his name; if not, it should have been. And like all true showmen, he made an *entrance*.

There was a blast from some guys with huge, sea-shell trumpets, who I'd noticed framing the main doors when we came in but who hadn't made a peep for us, and there he was, pausing on the landing at the top of the stairs so that we could all feast our eyes. Or gouge them out because the light coming off him was blinding. And not just because he was covered in about an acre of emeralds, aquamarines, and sapphires.

But because all the chandeliers had suddenly turned to spotlight him.

Guess he knew the magic worker controlling them, I thought wryly.

The light show left the rest of us in shadow, even on the dais, and him in dazzling solitude. Frankly, he deserved it, considering that his Liberace outfit made even Antlers down there look shabby. For a moment, I just took it in.

As usual around here, he had opted for a caftan open to the waist to show off his nice chest muscles. But his weren't pierced, tattooed, or draped in jewels like half of the guys' here. They were bare and were literally the only part of him that was.

Other than for that vee of perfect skin, he might have been some jeweled creature come to life because he *glittered*. Besides the fantastic caftan, which was so heavily encrusted that I couldn't even tell what material was under there, he had on see-through gloves spotted with precious stones, a sash around his waist with huge, clear cabochons of some crystal that clustered together gave the appearance of seafoam, and then there was the cape. Or no, that wasn't right.

It was a *cape*. It was at least fifteen feet long, and unlike the rest of the outfit, which was designed to mimic the colors of the ocean and the breaking surf, the cape was fiery red since it was covered in golden crabs with ruby-encrusted shells. It was held up by six-page boys, three on each side dressed as mini-me's in short but equally jeweled tunics, probably because it weighed a ton.

Several looked to be having trouble just heaving the thing in the door.

Their boss posed like a supermodel for a long moment, giving everyone time to take in the magnificence before slowly beginning to descend the stairs. He took it easy to allow the spotlight to follow him, but not easy enough. The crabs were spelled to move about, I guessed to make their stones glitter even more since that was definitely what that outfit needed, but they got a little too feisty.

They kept crawling onto the pages, several of whom started batting them back down, which ruined the elegant effect somewhat. And not just for me. I heard tittering in the audience, who had forgotten about us in favor of making fun of whoever the hell.

"What is that?" I asked, as the vision was tripped up by some of his crabby accessories but recovered just in time. The titters grew. Pritkin drank wine.

"Lord Algaut. Wealthier than Croesus and about as lucky. Not a problem."

I'd already figured that out by the fact that he'd tripped up two more times just getting to ground level or sea level or wherever we were and was now snapping at his train of boys about something. Probably the fact that the small, jeweled crabs had broken loose from whatever enchantment had bound them and were now crawling everywhere. Including over the lord himself, where they were pinching his aristocratic skin.

"Then what was that entrance for?" I asked as the servant girl came hurrying back with cutlery, better plates, and fine golden goblets that she exchanged for our sad pewter things.

"Politics." Pritkin shot her a smile and she blushed to the roots of her fire-engine red hair. And curtsied before being summoned by an unhappy voice from a nearby table.

"Politics?"

He nodded and leaned closer so that I could hear him. That was harder than you'd think because the crabs had spread to nearby tables, causing a ruckus. Some lady with pale, silver-green hair, which made me wonder what she was doing with the upper crust, started screaming; the pages were running around, trying to scoop the bitey miscreants back into their own smaller capes; and a few men were attempting to crush the escapees underfoot, which wasn't easy shoeless and was making Lord Algaut even less happy as he'd probably paid a lot for those.

"This isn't just a contest," Pritkin told me. "It's an election. The contest gives people an idea of who they want to vote for. Consider it a very bloody stump speech."

"I don't understand," I said because I really didn't.

"Take Algaut over there," Pritkin said, nodding at the angry fey lord, who had lost all dignity and was scrabbling around on himself, trying to throw the crabs off. Only they'd gotten under his magnificent caftan and appeared to be trying to eat him. He screamed, but nobody went to help him save for his beleaguered pages.

"Somebody tinkered with the spell to have that happen. To embarrass him and make him look a fool in front of the rest of the nobility."

They got value for their time, I thought, as Algaut gave up, ripped off his priceless attire, and went running back up the stairs in the fey version of tighty-whities, namely a very unblinged-out loincloth.

"Why bother?" I asked as he disappeared back through the door to raucous laughter. "You just said he wasn't a problem."

"In the Challenge, no. But anyone that rich is always a threat. He might have bribed his way to the throne had things gone differently, but now that he looks a fool, without even enough magic to counter some enchanted crabs—"

"Anyone who votes for him might as well be waving a banner saying 'I was bought.'"

"Exactly. Someone just removed a threat for the price of a few minutes of spell-binding."

I narrowed my eyes at him because the tone of that last comment had been verging on smug. "Or paid someone else to do it," I said.

"Of course. They could have done that."

Unless they were a war mage and an expert magic worker and didn't have to, I thought, wondering if I'd underestimated my partner. Pritkin didn't help me decide, being too busy smiling at the servant girl again, who had returned with a whopping platter of fish in some brown sauce. She smiled back, and she smiled big.

My eyes narrowed a bit more.

And then widened to roughly saucer-shape when I saw who was behind her and had just paused by the third chair at our table. "What the—"

"Hey, sweetheart. Mind if I join you?"

I just stared, my mouth hanging open in a way that probably didn't help with the badass, but I didn't care right then. *"Alphonse?"*

"The one and only." He started to sit, but Pritkin put out a hand.

"No offense," he said because Alphonse was a vampire, the approximate size of a small mountain, and mean with it. He was also ugly enough to have some of the fey currently staring at us start doing the look-slide thing that the flunkies had tried on the Horror Twins because he offended their delicate sensibilities. Several even looked like they might lose their expensive dinner.

It made me warm up to Alphonse, which was not an easy

task.

"Offense taken," Alphonse growled. "You got a problem with me, war mage?"

"No. But sitting here might be dangerous. You know what it means?"

"What does it mean?" I asked before Alphonse could.

"It means," Alphonse said, removing Pritkin's hand from his arm with the very deliberate motions of a man who could have just as easily ripped it off. "That I'm signing on. Which I am."

His butt hit the seat, and he smiled at me, which did not help matters much. Alphonse was the guy normies envision when somebody says "vampire," only not as suave. Or as sexy. Or as wealthy or influential or—

You get the idea. But the tall, dark, and brutal thing? He had that in spades and at least eighty pounds of added muscle that vamps didn't need.

"Signing on to what?" I asked, thinking that maybe Pritkin and I should have done more than "take a shower" while we'd had the time.

"To team Cassie. And this guy," he added, hiking a thumb at Pritkin when I opened my mouth to protest. "But mainly you."

"Me?" My eyes tried narrowing again, but they were still too shocked. "Why me? And what are you doing here? You realize we're in *Faerie*?"

"Yeah. All the pointy ears kinda gave it away." He tucked a giant napkin into the front of his very Earthly tuxedo. With his oily, slicked-back, dark hair, his pockmarked face, and his cauliflower nose, he looked like a mafia don who had somehow wandered into the land of the fey, which wasn't far off.

He had been second-in-command to the mafia don.

And, suddenly, something started to make sense.

"Hold it," Alphonse's huge hand covered mine and pressed down hard enough to keep me in place. But not to keep me from looking around wildly, trying to spot—

"Where is he?" I demanded.

"You need to calm down, okay?"

"You calm down!" I turned back to him, my eyes furious. *"Where is he?"*

"I don't know, and that's the truth. That's why I'm here. I tracked him to Faerie and—"

A trumpet sounded somewhere behind us, or maybe a couple of them. It was deafening, probably announcing another contender who had waited to make a grand entrance. I didn't know, didn't care.

"You tracked him?" I said furiously, leaning over the table. "All the way here? You expect me to believe—"

"I frankly don't care what you believe. All I know is that that fat fuck is here somewhere, and now so are you. And he has a major hate on for you. So, I figure he'll turn up sooner or later, and as long as I stick to you—" he made a meaty fist and crashed it into the palm of his other hand, thus releasing me.

I didn't go anywhere. Because the image of that huge fist pounding the face of the vampire I'd once called master was so seductive that, for a minute, I could almost see it. And I *wanted* to see it.

Antonio Gallina, better known as Tony and even better known by a series of expletives as long as my arm, was a massive piece of shit. The kind that sees a little girl who just might grow up to be a valuable seer someday and grabs her, and the fact that he had to kill said girl's parents to make that happen. . . Well, for Tony, that was just Tuesday.

He'd also killed my governess, Eugenie, one of the only people I'd had growing up who gave a damn about me because he thought she knew where I went when I fled from him. She didn't know anything, but again, did he care? Ripping her apart was a good way to alleviate the fury he couldn't take out on me.

These days, I had my own fury and the power to do something about it. But Tony had done a disappearing routine before I could get my hands on him to join the other side in the war, or so I'd heard. Faerie was vast and treacherous, and searching for him could take months, even years, which I didn't have right now. And that was assuming that it hadn't done what it usually did with outsiders and eaten him alive.

Possibly literally.

But no, he'd survive. Snakes like that always did. If the good died young, Tony would live forever, or at least for as long as it took me to find him.

Alphonse had been watching me, those sharp dark eyes shrewd behind surprising long lashes, a strangely beautiful touch on a face that even a mother couldn't love. But someone had once. Or had made him believe that she did.

Before Tony killed her, too, or at least helped with the process.

"Yeah, I know what it feels like," he told me softly as we thought about Sal, Alphonse's old flame. She'd technically been killed by one of Mircea's vamps who was trying to protect me, but she'd only been after me on Tony's orders. And for someone as weak as Sal, her master's commands were little less than mind control.

She hadn't had a choice, and so she'd died, a tragedy that I still regretted and that Alphonse. . .

Well, regret wasn't what he knew how to do. Or grieve or process this in any other normal human way. Alphonse hadn't been a human in centuries, and I frankly doubted he'd been normal even then.

Alphonse knew how to kill, how to hunt, and how to brutalize.

I felt a small smile curve my lips.

"Yeah," he said, seeing it. "I want him every bit as much as you do. Maybe we can help each other out."

"Or maybe you can die trying," Pritkin said flatly. "This isn't Earth—"

"I know what it is, war mage, and I die only if you lose."

"What?" I said, jolted out of the trip down memory lane. And then said it a few more times because *what?*

"Oh, didn't he tell you?" Alphonse shot Pritkin a sly glance. "That's what traditionally happens to challengers and their retinues who fail. At least those that are still in the contest by the last round. It's a way of making sure that the next monarch don't have a bunch of butt-hurt wannabees around to plot against him or her."

He ate some of the fish off my plate.

"Mhmm, nice. Too bad it's poisoned," he said, tapping the china with the tines of one of the weird, two-pronged forks they'd given us. "I'd decline if I were you."

"What?"

"Poisoned?" Pritkin stood up and started toward the tables behind us, but Alphonse pulled him back.

"Save it for the Challenge. Attacking the challengers outside the arena is a quick way to get disqualified, remember?"

"How the hell do you know that?"

Alphonse looked at him calmly. "I know a lot about this stupid fight. It's all anyone talks about around here, and my ears work good. Specially with that nice translation spell I paid a mage way more than it was worth to conjure up for me."

"You don't conjure—" Pritkin began automatically, but Alphonse waved him off.

"My point is, I know what I'm getting into." He switched his gaze to me. "Do you?"

"She's Pythia, dark fey friend and ally of Caedmon, the Blarestri king," Pritkin snapped. "They wouldn't dare touch her."

"Is that what you've been telling yourself?" Alphonse asked, a dark eyebrow going up. "They just served her poison, but okay."

"That was meant for me!"

"And that's better? 'Cause I gotta say, your chances aren't looking too good. There's," he paused and ostentatiously counted, "two of you—"

"We have two more in our room," I said, glaring at Pritkin. Who had forgotten to mention that this was a duel to the death.

"So I heard." Alphonse chuckled. "And you guys think that's gonna help you? Bringing two demons to court? Well, two and a half," he shot another look at Pritkin. "You know you can win every challenge and still lose if everybody votes against you, right?"

"What?" I said, upping the glare. Because it seemed there was a damned lot I didn't know!

But Pritkin didn't look too disturbed as he sat back down. "In theory, yes."

"In *theory?*"

"Look."

He didn't tell me where to look, but I discovered it didn't matter. There was another preening popinjay on the landing, which I guessed was who the trumpets had been for. He was in a silver-white get-up that glittered in diamonds and looked like he was cosplaying Poseidon.

With a million-dollar budget.

A cape of silver and white, with the loose weave evoking fishing nets, hung from his shoulders, with tiny diamond fishes dangling from the webbing. He wore silver-colored armor underneath that was every bit as nice as mine and maybe nicer since it was set with more sparkly stuff, as were the silver tattoos or maybe makeup on his face. He was nonetheless frowning, possibly because nobody in his entourage had told him that boots were déclassé at court, which was why no one else was wearing them.

Or maybe because of us.

Yeah, it was us, I thought, catching that lordly gaze.

But I barely noticed because I was too busy adjusting my worldview and, therefore, also wearing a scowl myself. Each table behind us and the many spread out below, including the ones sitting hundreds, was now a competitor. I felt my stomach knot itself into a tiny, hard lump.

At least I couldn't eat the poison that way.

"After every round, they have a banquet like this one," Pritkin said. "Supposedly to celebrate, but in reality, it's a vote.

People decide who they think will be the likely winner and join his or her table. As the contest continues, the smaller tables shrink to nothing as their members join the larger groups. By the end, there's only a handful left standing, and the final night is the final vote."

"And there are three of us!" I said, suddenly seeing Alphonse's point.

"Yes, but tides change quickly, and no one wants to be on the losing side."

"How can you say that when *we're* the losing side?"

"Look again," he told me, and I did because I didn't know what else to do.

But this time, I saw what he meant. No one else was paying attention to us anymore because they were too busy scowling at the newcomer—and everyone else. The factions in this court hated each other, probably as much or more than they hated us.

We were the nasty, tainted outworlders, but looking at the vengeful, prideful, superior faces, it looked like there were old grievances and long-standing feuds that cut far deeper. I understood that as much as anyone, although my personal vendetta hadn't had the centuries to fester that many of these probably had. But it was nonetheless hot enough.

Which was why I was on my feet again a second later at the sight of the fat face poking out from behind the latest blinged-out backside.

Tony.

Son of a *bitch*.

CHAPTER EIGHT

I shifted to the landing when I could have just shifted him to me and my backup. But I wasn't thinking, and anyway, I didn't need backup for Tony. I didn't need anything except to catch him!

But that was harder than it sounds, as an entire retinue was behind the silver, god-like creature that I appeared beside. And this one was a little different. The latest heir had been posing on the balcony and sharing his sneer with the room a second before, looking like this was all beneath him.

But an instant after I arrived, that changed. A silver sword almost magically materialized in his hand because the fey had lightning reflexes when they chose. But my reflexes were fast, too, thanks to Gertie's relentless training, and with the aid of the Pythian power, I disappeared before he could slash at me.

And reappeared down the corridor at the end of a glittering train of people, also all in white and diamonds and with the same sneers on their faces, as if they smelled something and suspected it was me. They all turned my way, including their leader down the hall, who I belatedly noticed had long, silver-blond hair. Crap.

I dodged the sword the bastard threw a second later by catching it mid-air with my power and shifting it to the middle of the sea outside. And then stared around at the now shocked faces of his crew, searching for Tony. I didn't see him, but I did see a hundred swords suddenly appear and lunge at me.

Crap!

I shifted back to the dining room because I must have missed him somehow. Although I didn't see how, as he'd been in black, something that should have stood out against all that dazzling white. But all I found was a silver blur leaping for me, who I caught halfway through the motion and shifted him to the same place as his sword.

His crew gasped with surprise as their champion reappeared on the water side of the ward, facing the other way. He spun to boggle us for a second with all that otherworldly hair floating around his head. And then I was almost trampled by his retinue bolting down the stairs, with several already trying to take down the ward on the run.

Since that would flood the dining hall, they were immediately countered by some of what I guessed were the old royal guards. Nimue hadn't been about to let her people be outshone by overdressed guests, which was why they were wearing peacock-colored armor that started as dark blue in the midsection and radiated outward in every color of blue, green, gold, and, on the very outer bits, flashes of red. It looked less like dragon scale and more like the fish variety, with tiny, overlapping platelets that hugged their bodies like a second skin, but I guessed it did the trick.

Because they stopped the throng, being determined that the ward wasn't going down. Unfortunately, the other side was just as determined that it was and pulled weapons. The two forces met with a clash of metal on metal that clanged horribly in the room's excellent acoustics.

I was with the guards on this one. If Silver Hair was coming to compete, presumably, he knew how to swim. I was more concerned about Tony but still didn't see him.

"Cassie!" Pritkin was fighting to get to me, but the room was suddenly full of standing, jostling, unhappy people.

Some of the latter were a bunch of newly arrived guards, flooding through the door behind me and looking around in confusion. Others were the diners, many of whom were staring at the ward in what looked like terror, why I didn't know. They were members of Nimue's court; even if the worst happened, they could handle it, right?

Only they didn't seem to think so. One woman pointed at something and started screaming something that my translator didn't know, and then everybody broke and ran. And I do mean everybody.

It was like the starting gun at a race track had just been fired. They were all coming and coming fast, leaping over tables, clawing at each other to get to the exits, and clogging the stairs. And one—

Was Tony.

"There!" I screamed at Alphonse, who was almost on top of the bastard.

I tried to shift him to me this time, as there were so many fleeing people that I couldn't get a good landing spot beside him. But grabbing him in the chaos proved difficult, and my spell caught several other richly dressed diners instead, who went utterly ape-shit when they suddenly appeared beside me on the stairs. And now I couldn't hear anything, with them screaming bloody murder.

Including whatever Alphonse was saying because he'd heard me but hadn't seen the fat man. And neither did I anymore, as Tony was a good foot and a half shorter than the average for the room and was as dark-haired as most of the court. I lost him in the throng, and shifting bunches of people to the peripheries and out of the way didn't help.

In fact, it did the opposite, as suddenly I was the problem instead of the murderous bastard they'd been hiding at their court. The guards must have gotten a message from someone because they stopped looking around cluelessly and started fighting their way toward me. That didn't work so well, as the doorway was now clogged with partygoers, all desperate to escape the ongoing fight through the same doors the guards had used.

I figured I had a few seconds.

So, I shifted more people off the dais, clearing a path around Alphonse and hunting for the bastard that had to be there somewhere. Until my power abruptly cut out thanks to that infernal portal, and I still didn't see him. It was like he'd vanished into thin air!

And I guessed that Alphonse couldn't track his scent, which he damned well should have been able to as a vamp who had known Tony for a couple of centuries. But instead, he was shouting and pointing, only not at him. At the guards, I realized, who were almost on top of me, and now I couldn't shift!

But Pritkin saw the problem from halfway across the ballroom and came up with a solution that hadn't occurred to me. The next moment, he flung a hand at the straining ward, where a soaked and furious fey was about halfway through the spurting hole some of his people had managed to make while others held off the guards. His finery was a lot less fine now, and there was murder on his face.

Which was quickly replaced by shock when he was suddenly all the way through, along with thousands of gallons of water, as that entire section of the ward abruptly gave way.

A wall of ocean fell in, swamping that half of the hall and quickly washing across the great space. That would have been more of a problem anywhere else, but here. . . Well, look at that, I thought in amazement, as mermaid tails suddenly flashed everywhere.

It looked like maybe one in ten of the guests were shifters, with their scales gleaming brightly under the lights still spinning above us. That included antler-head, who morphed and slipped out of his clothes through the expansive neck hole. I was starting to understand the fashions here, I thought, as he flaunted a heavily muscled tail before surging off into the deep.

The guests with brighter hair colors were all doing the same, their lower bodies flooding with blue, turquoise, or silver-green scales and a few pale lavenders. The tails usually matched their hair, the latter of which should have clued me into the fact that Nimue's court wasn't as homogenous as it seemed, even among the elite. And now it looked like the world's craziest disco, as water frothed and bubbled around the fleeing merfolk, as their legged counterparts thrashed and flailed, and as the sea continued to rise and rise fast.

And as Tony got away, because there was no way I could find him in all that.

Damn it!

If you'd stayed calm, you could have had him, I thought, furious at myself. I was supposed to be better than this; I'd been taught to be better! Gertie would be chewing my ass out right now, and she'd be right.

And then someone grabbed me from behind because the guards had kept their eyes on the prize while I'd been daydreaming.

Two mistakes, I thought grimly and shoved my elbow back into somebody I couldn't see because he'd latched onto me too tight. But he let go at that, and not because I'd hit his solar plexus, where I'd been aiming. I'd forgotten: the fey were typically at least a foot taller than most humans, meaning that his stomach wasn't where my blow had landed.

He gasped and let me go; I spun and ducked under another guard's reaching arms and was then confronted by four more beyond him. The only good thing was that they didn't have swords out. The bad was that, with fey strength and agility, they didn't need them.

But they weren't the only menace in town, as demonstrated when I was snatched backward off the balcony by what looked like a giant, purple octopus' leg.

Maybe because it was a giant, purple octopus' leg, I realized in shock, as the creature it was attached to waved me around in the air, giving me a skewed view of the dining hall. And of a bunch of equally surprised fey staring up at us. And of the guards diving off the stairs after me.

I didn't see anything else as the creature shoved me under the waves and tried to drown me.

It did a pretty good job, even when I grabbed a knife off a now-submerged table and shoved it into its leg. I'd hoped the pain would cause it to let me go, but instead, it just made it mad. And so did the guards' actions, who, weirdly enough, seemed to be on my side.

I saw them when I ended up back in the air briefly, sucking in oxygen and noticing that they'd pulled swords, a couple of spears, and an honest-to-God trident from somewhere and were trying to skewer my attacker. Or maybe they were trying to skewer me, but I didn't think so. Because one of them threw the trident straight into one of the creature's giant eyeballs, only for the beast to start flailing furiously in a storm of massive suckered legs, one of which sent the guard sailing across the hall.

It then turned and headed out to sea with its prize, I guessed to eat me in private.

I finally got a good look at it and didn't enjoy it any more than I had the whale. It was less like an octopus and more like Cthulhu, being almost as tall as the dining hall's expansive ceiling and having way more than the standard eight legs. There must have been fifty under there, along with a ruff of smaller ones around its neck, which could telescope out to many times their length.

I saw one of the "little" kind stretch to sock a fey who was readying a spell a third of the way across the ballroom while another took a trident from an attacker and tried to skewer him with it. But it couldn't penetrate his armor, resulting in the beast settling for smacking him over the head. All while fighting a dozen other battles, because yeah. Each of those arms probably had its own brain.

At least, that was how Earth octopi worked, and it looked like Big Daddy was no different. The larger legs had heft, and the smaller had range, and each likely had its own crazed little brain bent on destruction. Meaning that we weren't fighting a single adversary but a whole platoon.

Not surprisingly, the beast was winning.

Nimue's guards and Silver Hair's posse found themselves on the same side, battling for their lives, which wasn't going well based on how many were being tossed around. And I wasn't doing any better. The mini-mind concentrating on me was flushing dark aubergine in annoyance at the fact that I stubbornly kept breathing.

But dragonscale doesn't crush easily, no matter how much the beast tried. So the creature jerked, making the arm holding me whip around hard enough almost to snap my neck. But allowing me to see—

"*Alphonse?*" I yelled, catching sight of the dark figure who had just grabbed one of the massive arms despite looking ridiculously small next to his enormous adversary.

But master-level vamps don't care what size you are. Master-level vamps just put a hurting on whatever was pissing them off. And Alphonse was no exception.

Guess he really did join our side, I thought, as he and the behemoth fought it out.

It was a little hard to tell what was going on because of all the water and people being flung about and because the guards trying to heal the ward had only managed to get part of it back up. The ocean was still pouring in through a sizeable gap, and the screaming, shouting, and cursing hadn't diminished. The fey didn't seem any less horrified at the party crasher than I was, and they sure weren't volunteering to help battle it, being too busy trampling each other while fighting their way to the exits.

That kind of thing sped up even more when Pritkin joined the fight. I couldn't see him from this angle, but I knew the feel of his magic as well as my own and felt a smile break over my face. Alphonse could seemingly keep the beast from escaping but couldn't do much else.

Pritkin could.

As demonstrated when a line of spell fire sliced through the huge arm holding me and sent me plunging into the sea.

I wasn't free, as the tentacle refused to let me go despite not being attached to its host anymore. But I heaved and struggled and managed to pull myself partway out of its grip, enough to break the churned-up surface of the water, gasping and trying to see what was going on. Only to find that I wasn't sure I wanted to.

Bright red rings had appeared all over the great creature's skin, the color of freshly spilled blood. I didn't know what that meant, but it didn't look good. And then I knew it wasn't when the beast spurted an oily, black substance everywhere, clouding the water and fountaining through the air like a fire hose.

People screamed and dove, and a line of black ooze hit Silver-Hair, melting his pretty get-up instantly and stopping only when it hit dragonscale. But while his entourage were cursing and backing the hell up as fast as their heavy armor would let them, he stood his ground. And unlike the other overdressed popinjays I'd seen tonight, he seemed to have a spine because he snarled, pulled a spear off his back, and lunged for the beast.

He'd been trying to gut me a moment ago, but I was glad to have him on board. Because Alphonse had just gone sailing, having been whip-cracked halfway across the room by the tentacle he'd been fighting. And the guards had backed off, probably realizing that they were just getting in the way.

Or maybe they were waiting for reinforcements. Because maybe ten of them were still in action, and they didn't seem to think that was enough. Which it wasn't for tackling Behemoth up there, but they could have freed me!

Only nobody seemed interested in freeing me.

Quite the contrary, I realized as a spear sliced through the air and missed my head by inches. I stared around, wondering how bad someone's aim had to be to miss the writhing mountain of flesh up there with legs bigger than ancient oaks and suckers the size of the guards' shields. And then two other spears and a spell came whizzing past, the latter bouncing off my armor, and I caught a clue.

But I still didn't see the culprits, and who could in all this? Water was being thrown around everywhere, grand sprays of it, like the ocean hitting a seawall in a hurricane. The ink was hitting the water and sizzling like fire, only this kind didn't go out. It did leave puddles of acid-like fury, however, floating around and eating anything or anyone unlucky enough to get in their path.

Which could be anyone since those thousand damned tentacles were churning things up like the swells in a mighty gale. I was bobbing up and down helplessly and couldn't half see. Like who was trying to kill me in the middle of all this!

It could have been anybody, or everybody, because they all had reason, didn't they? This whole poisonous court was at each other's throats, which went doubly for me. I'd probably have more of them targeting me if they could see worth a damn.

Wouldn't it be nice if I died in this, and they could blame it on the monster?

Or if Pritkin did, I realized.

And fuck that!

I started hacking with renewed interest at the severed limb, trying to cut a wedge with my knife that might free up the rest of my body or at least give me some wiggle room. Pritkin threw another fiery spear and dove underwater to avoid an attack by half a dozen of those great arms. And Silver-Hair got in a few spear thrusts that the creature didn't even feel.

Or maybe it did, as one of the wildly whipping arms snatched up a member of his entourage, and this one wasn't wearing dragonscale. The man's scream cut off with a wet-sounding crunch, and blood splattered down like rain, hot and sticky against my face. I spat it out, Silver-Hair's entourage broke and swam, and Alphonse reappeared and grabbed the tentacle still holding me.

Finally!

He seized it by the wound I'd made and ripped out a large enough chunk that I could slither out of its grip. It was still thrashing around, trying to find me, but it had no vision anymore, being just a severed arm. We left it curling and frothing up the water behind us as we swam away.

"You okay?" Alphonse screamed, which still wasn't enough for me to hear him. But I read his lips and nodded, the concern on his face unexpectedly endearing.

And then Pritkin surfaced, gasping and looking around for me.

Just in time to get hit in the face by a massive spray of black.

CHAPTER NINE

I screamed, fear clawing at my chest, and desperately searched the churning waves for Pritkin but couldn't see him. Just an oil slick of that hideous black stuff, puddling and steaming in the water. But then he surfaced again, and I noticed that the stain stopped a foot away from his face and started dripping down something I couldn't see.

Because he was shielded; of course, he was!

I felt my heart start up again as he sent a spear of fire at the great head, aiming for the remaining good eye. But the creature moved with liquid speed and the bolt missed, flung aside by one of the larger tentacles and hitting the ceiling instead. It took out some of the roaming lights, causing an uptick in the panicked screaming from the crowd, but other than for a burn on the arm that had hit it, the creature suffered no damage.

So, on top of everything else, it was spell-resistant.

Great.

And Pritkin couldn't risk firing again until he cleared his vision because too many people were around. Including more guards, a few dozen of whom ran onto the landing above us. And stopped dead right before a line of acid ink was flung at them.

They got shields up but did not advance, maybe because they were used to having a demigoddess fight their battles for them. Which might be why they were looking at me. And Alphonse seemed to agree with them.

"If you're gonna do anything, now would be the time," he rasped, staring around with an expression that that unfortunate face wasn't used to.

Alphonse was a lot of things, but a coward wasn't among them, as he'd already proven. But he didn't know what to do about this. Which, two of us, Alphonse!

But I knew one thing. "That's not going to be enough!" I yelled up at the guards, who were holding the standard issue spears, swords, and a couple of tridents. "Get some decent weapons! Now!" And when they just stood there, I flung out a hand, which was a total bluff as I couldn't do a damned thing at the moment. *"Go!"*

To my surprise, they went. Of course, whether they intended to return was anybody's guess, but we couldn't depend on it. Which Alphonse seemed to agree with.

"God . . . damn it!" he yelled, being interrupted by a wave splatting him in the face. "You're . . . a goddess!"

Which was not strictly true and completely unhelpful. But that was, I thought, as my power returned, like a glittering hand reaching out to engulf me. And for once, it was right on time.

Okay, I thought, let's see what all that training was worth.

I sent a bolt flowing at the hulking bastard towering above us, and I didn't miss. The remaining great milky eye had been staring around, searching the bobbing crowd, and had finally spotted me. But I spotted it, too, and the next second, one of the biggest tentacles aged out of existence, poofing away in a storm of ashes.

And I do mean a storm. That thing must have weighed a thousand pounds because it ate a spell strong enough to take down ten men. Unfortunately, I'd been aiming for the head but couldn't get near it since those thousand thrashing arms served as their own kind of shield.

I sent a few more rapid-fire spells, but the same thing happened. The creature was smart enough to have learned from the initial attack, which it had ignored until a guard took out its eye. It wasn't going to risk that again, meaning that I couldn't get to the head until I took down those damned arms, which were moving so fast I could barely see them!

But it could see us and came rushing through the ash cloud with telescoping tentacles punching all around us and a great leg slapping the waves where we'd just been.

But Alphonse had already grabbed me and plunged us underwater, with debris hitting down everywhere from the creature's attack. We surfaced in time to watch the latest group of guards who'd just come in turn around and flee. Along with half of the ballroom, who looked like they'd lost faith in this particular goddess, and they knew the monster better than I did.

"Shit!" Alphonse said, grabbing an abandoned trident off a small, floating table. "Stop time!" he yelled.

And, yeah, I could do that, but that was one of the hardest Pythian spells. It would sap my energy for the rest of the day, no portal needed. So, if I pulled that trick out of the bag and it wasn't enough. . .

"Damn it, do *something!*" Alphonse yelled because the colossal creature had just spotted us again.

"Chimera!" I said, defaulting to a slightly less taxing spell, and felt the intensely creepy sensation of my body splitting into two identical Cassies. We could only channel half of the power each this way, but half was better than dead.

My doppelganger broke away from me, and we went in opposite directions, with Alphonse grabbing me and swimming below a mass of small, floating tables that obscured the world above us like water lilies on a pond. But it must have also obscured the view from up top since Cthulhu turned the other way. And started even more waves crashing about as it searched for my double.

We surfaced to see the other Cassie fire off a spell and miss and then show off some of the next-level shit Gertie had beaten into me, sometimes literally. So many times, I had gone to bed aching in every muscle, feeling drained and inadequate, and sometimes having to get up again to puke my guts out, but I *had* learned. As demonstrated when I watched myself disappear, but not because I'd shifted.

"What happened?" Alphonse said. "Where'd she go?"

"There," I said as my doppelganger reappeared after speeding up time for her and her only and covering half the length of a football field in an eyeblink. And firing again from behind the behemoth.

And this time, she hit.

One of the biggest limbs was erased in a storm of ash, and with the next blow, she tore a furrow across the huge head because it hadn't quite knocked her spell aside fast enough. She disappeared again before another leg splashed down into the water where she'd been floating, and three more limbs vanished in seconds, with her firing while still in quick time. It was an impressive display, not least because it had taken maybe five seconds from our perspective.

Throughout training, I'd usually been eating Agnes' dust, but as it turned out, I wasn't so bad myself. I grinned. Wonder what two of us can do, I thought, preparing to join the fight— right before a spell flashed across my eyes.

I got a shield up in time—just—because I'd been trained to feel magic coming at me. When you're blindfolded and surrounded by a bunch of gleeful initiates who have been given carte blanche to beat the hell out of you, you learn fast. I'd had welts on my body for days from that particular piece of fun, but it had sharpened my instincts considerably, as had the many subsequent repeats.

So, yeah, I got a shield up, but there wasn't one spell coming at me; there were a dozen or more, all spattering the shield's surface with a multitude of colors in the red-to-orange spectrum, cutting off my view. Somebody meant business, and apparently, I wasn't dying fast enough to suit them. And then I was diving again and taking Alphonse with me because I had shielded him, too.

"Fuck!" he stared at me as we shot away underwater, using the debris field as cover once again. "Where the hell did that come from?"

"You have vampire eyes," I snarled, already feeling the heat of the rapidly depleting air inside the shield, because I hadn't made it big enough, damn it! "What direction?"

"Don't know. Multiple. I didn't know what was happening 'till your shield closed over us, and the next second, the bastards were hitting us. But somebody's got good aim."

And they still did. We'd been close to the staircase, and the crowd clogging it, meaning the blows had probably come from there. We'd put some distance between us now, but the spell light followed us, blooming on the water's surface like distant suns.

Or not so distant, as I felt the impact of several more blows and the subsequent drain on my power to support the shield. And considering that spells are like bullets in a way, namely that water usually stops them after a short distance, somebody was putting some power behind those bolts. Or using water magic for all I knew, which was nothing as I hadn't studied elemental!

I'd barely had time to learn my brand of magic, but I *did* know it. Which was why I let the next spell penetrate the shield, just far enough for my magic to loop around it and catch hold. And then I did a return to sender that would have made Gertie proud.

I didn't hear anybody scream because everyone was, but the attack abruptly cut out, allowing Alphonse and me to surface. I watched water bead on my shield and stared around, looking for another problem. Only we didn't find one—except for the massive monster that was trashing the room and, a moment later, took out the surviving lights overhead.

Someone had gotten smart and spelled them to shine directly into its one eye, or maybe they were designed that way, to highlight whatever the big deal was at the moment. Either way, our current big deal didn't like that and had swiped them off the ceiling with one gigantic arm, plunging them into the depths and us into darkness. For about ten seconds, I blinked with only multicolored after-effects strobing my vision.

And then we got a new and much more deadly form of light.

Pritkin took advantage of the cover of darkness and started throwing firebolts like they were going out of style while constantly moving, having the creature attack where he'd just been and where the residual spell light was still lighting up the night. But the creature's spell resistance threw off the effects of some of the blasts, and it dodged the rest. Until he hurled something substantially bigger, something that had all the staring faces around the hall illuminated in bright red, including that of the creature.

Which flung up an arm at the last second to save itself, and spell-resistance or no, the massive limb promptly burst into flames.

"Looks like it's got a new enemy number one," Alphonse said, as it started after Pritkin, not by finding him but by using the telescoping tentacles to attack on all sides, all at once.

So, I sent a bolt of the Pythian power in an attempt to regain my title, but barely clipped it because those arms were moving like lightning. And it seemed to be able to sense magic, too, anticipating my bolt. But a time spell from the other direction finished the giant arm off, with my doppelganger coming in clutch and then yelping when the creature turned on her in a fury.

I heard my voice abruptly cut off, and a second later, the other half of my soul slammed back into me like a freight train, indicating my spell's demise. My double must have dropped her shield to up her firepower, and it had been a mistake. One that caused me to stagger as my two halves knitted themselves back together, something almost as uncomfortable as the ripping apart had been.

And then I heard Pritkin scream.

My head jerked up because that was not normal. Pritkin could be loud, and I'd heard enough yelling, bitching and weird profanity from him to fill a good-sized library. But he didn't scream, and certainly not like that.

For a moment, I feared the worst. But then a fury of spells, more than I could hope to count, exploded around the creature all at once, lighting it up in a red, orange, and yellow halo. It looked like a fireworks display where someone had misjudged the timing and let everything off at once, so bright and breakneck that I could barely even see.

And when I could, it was to notice what had to be a hundred levitating weapons silhouetted against the brilliance, which I guessed Pritkin must have spelled on the fly because he hadn't had them in that skin-tight suit. But they were there now, and the creature couldn't anticipate them as easily.

The little magic they used was lost in the flood around the room from people's protection spells, the guys working on getting the patchy ward to solidify, and others banishing water from the room before we all drowned.

So, no, it couldn't spot them all, and as a result, it was getting skewered, as well as fried from the spell light suddenly crawling all over its body. It looked as if an entire war mage battalion had descended onto the place, but they hadn't. It was just one man.

A man who believed I was dead, I realized with a lurch; he thought my doppelganger had been me.

"He's going HAM," Alphonse said, sounding impressed. "And he better hope it works, or that thing's gonna kill him as soon as his magic runs out."

And it would because no one could sustain something like that for long, even Pritkin.

"Like hell," I gasped, the light, heat, and burning stench from the battle making me dizzy. But dizzy or not, we weren't going out like this. Not as freaking after-dinner entertainment for this bunch of bastards!

"Over here!" I screamed, magically enhancing my voice, to the point that it echoed deafeningly round the space. "Hey, big boy! You're looking in the wrong place!"

I didn't know whether it could understand English or if the sheer volume was enough. But it got the idea. And whirled with an almost comical look of shock as if to say: "Didn't I kill you already?"

"Try again," I told it grimly as Alphonse cursed. Because immediately, a burning, furious, possibly elder god was storming our way in a cyclone of murderous limbs and spurting black acid.

And, okay, yeah.

That had worked.

"I hate you," Alphonse said and plunged us underwater again.

The screaming cut out, more or less, except for the sound of the merpeople screeching in their strange language. It didn't sound happy, and neither was I, as tentacles of all sizes started stabbing down all around us, sloshing tables everywhere as they followed us through the water, vampire speed notwithstanding. I should have worn something less shiny, I thought, right before my outfit abruptly went dark.

Thank you, Augustine, I thought fervently, thinking of the part-fey designer who had made my current ensemble. He charged a fortune but was worth every penny and was partly how I managed to evade getting ground against the floor. The other part was Alphonse, who shoved me away and went thrashing in the other direction, and considering how smoothly he'd been swimming before, I had to assume that was deliberate.

I broke through the water, gasping and exhausted. Swimming in armor, even the ultralightweight dragon scale variety, is not fun. And neither was that, I thought, turning to see Pritkin, Alphonse, and the silver-haired fey each wrapped in a giant arm and getting smashed into anything and everything the creature could find.

Pritkin still had his shield up and was firing between blows, but it looked like the pounding was throwing off his aim. Alphonse, who was immobilized except for his head, appeared to be trying to gnaw the creature's arm off but had a long way to go. And the silver-haired fey still had one arm loose and was stabbing whatever he could find with his sword in between getting slammed against floating debris, the stairs, the ceiling, and the nearby wall.

The only good news was that the guards had started to remember that they were actually supposed to guard things instead of standing around looking pretty. And at least some of those who had run off had come back with a chest of potion bombs that appeared to be causing the behemoth some distress. I couldn't be sure, as it remained eerily silent, with the only sound coming from the remaining crowd because the flying debris the creature was flinging at the guards was also hitting them.

But behemoth was looking the worse for the wear himself, with noticeable gaps in the forest of arms, a missing eye, and burn marks all over its huge head. Which had turned to look at the ward as if it was thinking of getting the hell out of Dodge. Only it couldn't, as the room's protection was back up, Nimue's magic workers having earned their money twice over tonight, so it had nowhere to go.

Neither did I, and I was woozy and exhausted. Even worse, I was learning to tell when the portal was about to cycle away as my power started to thin. I had time for one more blast of dubious quality, but I had to take it now.

So, I did, throwing everything I could muster at the only target that made sense: the reinvigorated ward.

That gave the creature an escape route in case it was as tired of this fight as I was and just wanted out. I couldn't tell if it did because a new wall of water hit me a moment later, slamming me back against a mass of floating tables and chairs that had washed up together like a beaver dam. And by the time I dragged my battered body out of all that wood, I still couldn't see much as the lights remained out.

The only illumination was cascading through the flung wide main doors at the top of the staircases, which the crowd had mostly blocked before but which was clear now that they'd fled.

What happened, I thought dizzily, staring around, right before Pritkin grabbed me. And shook me like a maraca while screeching something I couldn't make out because my ears were full of water. But the shaking took care of that in a minute, and they popped, only to immediately get assaulted in a new way.

"Answer me, goddamnit!"

I didn't know the question, but I nodded because there was a terrible expression on his face that I'd never seen before. And because I was still trying to cough up enough water to be able to speak. And I guess that was good enough.

"Alphonse!" he yelled.

"Yo," the voice came from somewhere near the stairs.

I stared at the big guy, half in disbelief, because he was okay. He looked okay! And then back at Pritkin and me, who were still somehow in one piece.

Battered and bloody, but in one piece!

"We made it," I said, wonder in my breathless voice. "We all . . . made it."

"We did," Pritkin's tone was as grim as I'd ever heard. "But the Svarestri heir was just carried out to sea."

CHAPTER TEN

Want some?" Alphonse asked, pushing a small brown paper spill at me sometime later.

I looked up from examining my tarot deck, which I'd been carrying as a good luck charm but which looked like it could use some luck itself right now. And peered inside the spill. I made a face.

"You think you're funny," I told him. "But you're not."

"No, seriously. You didn't have dinner, and you gotta eat. You're puny as it is."

I looked at the contents of the spill again, which was stuffed with small, charred, suckered legs, and felt my stomach churn. "You couldn't have gotten something else?"

"I got all kinds of stuff." He pulled open his coat to display more little spills, shoved haphazardly into pockets.

Most of the time, said pockets held guns, knives, brass knuckles, and assorted mayhem equipment, as Alphonse liked to be prepared. But right now, they were full of food—wonderful-smelling food. I heard my stomach grumble.

"Where did you get this?" I asked because if it was the ballroom, hungry or not, I was taking a pass.

"Relax," he told me. "They got a market down at Fountain Court—the main one with the big ass waterfall?" I looked at him blankly. Like I'd had time to sightsee. "Anyway, I stopped by before coming here as it's got all these vendors. You can even eat the container; it's made out of pressed algae." He crunched off a bit to demonstrate, then made a face. "*Can* eat. Not should."

He handed me a different spill of what appeared to be fried

fish nuggets, and I tentatively took a bite. They were good and even a little warm still. Before I knew it, I'd finished the whole thing.

I moved on to wonderfully flavorful mussels cooked with herbs and citrus, some bland-tasting fish cakes, a ceviche of mostly lobster, and a half-dozen grilled scallops. But my stomach only grumbled ungratefully, as if the food had just woken it up, and demanded more. I pawed through Alphonse's coat to see what else he had.

Meanwhile, Pritkin yelled next door.

We weren't back in our room, and I wasn't sure when we would be. Feltin, Nimue's old flame and the resident power broker around here, at least until the end of the Challenge, had had his guards scoop us up following the fight and usher Pritkin and me here. Alphonse had come sauntering in a little later after a stop for takeout, as even the fey didn't mess with a hungry master vamp.

Now, Pritkin was in what I guessed was Feltin's office, along with the other heirs. I could hear them dimly through the door but couldn't make out what they were saying, as my translator spell got confused when so many people were shouting at once. It had started giving me random words and sentences in a confused gobble-gobble that reminded me of a bunch of turkeys.

Luckily, Alphone's ears were better, and since translator spells relied on them, his was better, too. He'd kept me up on things, not that I'd enjoyed it. The other heirs seemed to want Pritkin disqualified over what had happened to Aeslinn's son, and Feltin seemed to be seriously considering it.

Not that it had had anything to do with us; one of the creature's arms had refused to let the prince go when it escaped. It was something Feltin knew perfectly well, as he'd been there the whole time directing some of the guards. Or so he claimed.

But he was worried about possible Svarestri retaliation if the prince died under suspicious circumstances while at his court. And yeah, trying to explain to a murderous bastard that a giant octopus ate his son might be a hard talk. But I didn't think that Feltin had anything to worry about.

Aeslinn had enough on his plate right now, and anyway, his son appeared to agree with his mother that dear old dad had really ruled long enough and needed to step aside for the next generation.

Or, you know, die.

I thought death was something they'd happily take instead.

In fact, from what I'd heard in council sessions, Efridis, Aeslinn's queen, had tried to murder the old man, having had enough of his abuse over the years. And when that failed, she'd fled the court and attacked Nimue to open up another throne for her baby to take. I assumed that was why Æsubrand, her silver-haired son, was here.

Or had been here, I thought slightly guiltily.

"Don't start that," Alphonse said, handing me another spill, this one full of little squid rings.

"Start what?"

"The agonizing. The guilt. The goddamned angst. 'Cause, seriously, I can't do that with you right now. I really can't."

"How did you know what I was thinking?" I demanded. "And is there any sauce?"

"What kind of sauce?"

"Marinara. Or ranch. Or anything that goes with calamari."

"You eat calamari with *ranch*?"

He looked genuinely appalled.

"I eat everything with ranch. And don't get all Italian on me," I said because he was going to. I'd had this lecture before.

He stopped, but it was clearly a struggle. "I don't think the fey know about marinara," he said as I searched the half-acre of coat.

"Well, that's it then. That's how we win. Let the others battle it out; we'll bring the marinara and get crowned."

"It's a concept." He eyed me. "So, I come up with a sauce,

and we drop the angsting?"

I thought about it. I was tired tonight anyway. "What sort of sauce?"

"Well, you got your choice," he said, going to the other side of the coat and pulling out some even smaller spills, these with their tops cleverly made to fit together to seal them up.

He started describing the contents, none of which sounded very appetizing, with frequent uses of the words fermented and krill. I took the opportunity to examine my cards and decided that I should have left them at home. They'd gotten wet before and come through mostly okay, but this time. . .

They weren't even yelling at me, which was a bad sign. They'd been spelled to describe the meaning of each tarot card, often at length, and while it was an old enchantment, it had never failed me before. But I didn't get so much as some confused muttering this time, not even when I shook them, and one looked to be—

"Oh, no," I said, peeling off the two halves of the World card from the end of the pack, where it was clinging to the next card in line after having been torn in two.

I didn't understand that, as the deck had been inside my armor in one of the pockets that moved around as it morphed. This one had ended up on my belt and must have gotten the brunt of some blow or other, probably when that damned tentacle was trying to squeeze me to death. And now—

"What's wrong?" Alphonse said, seeing my face.

"Eugenie's cards," I told him, feeling teary-eyed. Which was stupid, but the deck was the only thing I had from my old governess. She'd had them enchanted for me when I was a kid, and I'd kept them ever since.

Now, they were ruined.

"Hey," Alphonse said because he'd known her, too. "Don't do that."

"What?" I said, not looking at him because big, bad Pythias didn't cry. Especially not over a ratty old pack of tarot cards!

"Cards can be fixed. See, there's your problem," he said,

pointing at the ruined World card. "It's messing up the enchantment. It got torn somehow."

"I know that!"

"So you also know that, if you mend it, the enchantment will work again."

I looked up at him. "Really?"

He nodded. "Not all of us have a ton of decent mages around. That Pritkin guy, he don't have to fix anything. He just casts a new spell. But when you're one of us untalented slobs and shell out for a thing, well, you gotta have that thing. So, you get it fixed, right?"

"I guess." I didn't know if something as delicate as a ruined card could be fixed.

But Alphonse seemed to feel differently. "Yeah, this won't be too hard. Your Dad repaired something similar for me once."

"My Dad did?" I blinked. I hadn't known that he and Alphonse had interacted much, mainly because Tony hadn't allowed anybody to talk to me about my parents. But nobody cared what Tony thought now.

"Yeah." Alphonse looked uncomfortable suddenly, as if he was sorry he'd brought it up. "It was nothing."

"What kind of nothing?"

He scowled. "The poem kind, okay?"

I blinked some more, absorbing this new information. "You write *poetry*?"

"Hey, I got an artistic side."

Yeah, but I didn't think that photographing corpses counted. "What kind of poem was it?"

"Like I said, nothing. I just took a pic of Sal one day when we were running some errands for Tony. It was when the casino was being built, and he was going back and forth between Philly and Vegas to keep an eye on the place. He'd have preferred to put it in Atlantic City, but Mircea was insistent on Vegas, so. . .

"Anyway, some of the contractors screwed up, and he fired 'em, but they'd just taken a draw and didn't seem interested in doing a refund. Sal and I were sent to expedite the process. And it was pretty easy.

"They folded like a house of cards when she brought out the nutcrackers."

"I bet."

"So we figured, why not take the rest of the day off and go to the lake? She looked real pretty, hanging over the pier to throw popcorn to the ducks. Or she was trying to. They had birds that hung around that pier to get tourists to feed them popcorn from this stand, you know?"

"Ducks eat popcorn?"

"Ducks eat everything, but there's not much *to* eat there. You seen Lake Meade, there's not a lot of vegetation going on, so I don't know what they usually snack on. But they like popcorn.

"Only so do the fish, these big goldfish types. Somebody must have released 'em into the water, and they got busy. Now there's a ton of 'em, and they're like a foot long or bigger, and they and the ducks were going at it.

"The ducks would peck at the fish whenever they went for some popcorn, and the fish would whack 'em with their tails in response, like really smack 'em around. It was all-out war, with quacking and splashing and *whack whack whack*, better than some fights I seen in Vegas. Sal fed 'em like ten containers of popcorn she was laughing so hard. The stand made out good that day. . ."

He trailed off, staring into the distance as if he could see it all again.

"I'm sorry," I told him after a minute. "About Sal, I mean. It wasn't fair what happened to her."

"No, it wasn't," Alphonse said, his face expressionless. "And somebody's got to answer for that." After a minute, he glanced at me, and life flooded back into those features. Taking his face from serial killer to slightly more animated serial killer. "Anyway, I took a picture of her, laughing her ass off, and later, after I saw how well it came out, I had one of the mages Tony kept around enchant it for me, so it moved.

"It was nice. You could hear her laugh and almost smell the popcorn. Then I wrote her a poem on the back."

"What did it say?"

"You know, I don't remember?" Since he was blushing slightly, I doubted that but didn't press it. "I was gonna give it to her for our anniversary, but that dumbass Hanson spilled coffee all over it, and then tried to fix it and ended up tearing the thing! I took it back to the mage, but he said he couldn't do anything, something about rupturing the structural integrity of the piece.

"We were all set to go out. Sal was finishing her makeup, and I was panicking. Until your Dad happened by and fixed it."

I tried to imagine Alphonse panicking and failed utterly. "I thought you said it couldn't be fixed," I said.

"No, that's what that punk-ass mage claimed. Your Dad wasn't a punk ass. He did a spell to knit it back together and clean it up. He said he did things like that all the time when he was a garbage man—"

"He disenchanted unstable magical objects," I corrected. "He wasn't a garbage man."

"Okay," Alphonse said. "But the point was, he would sometimes find usable stuff when pawing through the trash— excuse me, the unstable magical objects—and some could be repaired and resold. It was a nice little sideline, even while he was with Tony. I don't know why I didn't go to him first.

"Anyway, he was going to reapply the spell, but he didn't have to. Once it was whole again, the original enchantment worked just fine. So, all you probably need is a hairdryer and some tape."

"Neither of which I have," I said, but I cheered up slightly. Maybe I could save them after all once I got back home.

If I got back.

"I'm surprised it tore," he added. "Being in a deck and all. Are the rest okay?"

I checked them out. They were currently welded into a

block, like paper mache. But they didn't look damaged and the plastic coating should help me pry them apart once they dried.

"I think this is the only one."

"Maybe it's a sign," Alphonse said, sitting back and raising a black brow. "Isn't that what those cards do? Predict the future?"

"Kind of. The witch who enchanted them for Eugeniue said that they could predict the overall climate of a situation, but yeah."

"So, is it a good card?"

"It can be. Tarot cards aren't exactly good or bad. It depends on where they fall in a reading."

"Then what does it mean on its own?"

I knew Alphonse was only keeping me talking to cheer me up, but I answered him anyway. I could almost hear the card's usual happy burble informing me of the various possibilities. I'd listened to them so often growing up that I could recite them from memory.

"The World shows a woman dressed in purple cloth stepping through a large laurel wreath," I said. "Her head is turned behind her, toward the past, while her body moves forward into the future. She holds two wands in her hands, like the one seen on the Magician card, symbolizing that what began with the Magician has now come to fruition in the World—"

"What began with the magician?"

I shrugged. "Again, it can be a lot of things. Unlimited potential is the usual meaning, but it depends. Or, in this case, potential realized."

"Okay."

"Likewise, the wreath is circular, like a portal to another world. It also recalls the Wheel of Fortune, symbolizing life's cyclical nature, where one cycle closes to allow another to begin. The four figures at the card's corners are a lion, a bull, a cherub, and an eagle. They represent the four elements, the four fixed signs of the zodiac, the four compass points, and the four suits of the tarot. They are here to act as guides in the new cycle, bringing aid on the journey.

"One World is ending and telling you it's time to move on to the next. Is this always positive? No. But is it necessary? Yes. It's a sign of a significant and inevitable change, one of tectonic magnitude. It's also a warning not to let your fears hold you back and instead embrace the knowledge that your journey has brought you, using it as a catalyst for growth.

"Reversed it means refusing to let go of the past to experience the fresh start you're longing for. You can become your own worst enemy if you don't listen to the advice of the World."

"Impressive," Alphonse said. "How many times have you heard that?"

"A couple thousand," I admitted. "Maybe more."

"So, upright, new phase, embrace it. Reversed, new phase, embrace it or else."

"Kinda."

"And what does it mean if it's torn in two?"

But for that, I didn't have an answer.

And we didn't have time anyway, as the outer door to the little antechamber we had parked our dripping butts in suddenly slammed open. And there he stood, in all his mangled glory: Æsubrand, heir to the Svarestri throne, dragging a familiar purple tentacle and breathing like an ox on steroids. Until he saw me, that was, and the pewter-colored eyes narrowed to slits.

Well, crap, I thought and dropped my calamari. And managed to catch him with the Pythian power halfway through a lunge so fast that I hadn't even seen it, I'd just known that it was coming. Which was why, when the shit show next door suddenly came running, the Svarestri hope was suspended off of the floor, cussing up a storm and with his hands grasping for my neck.

It got messy after that, with lots of shouting and people, because the prince's entourage had muscled in, too, and they didn't like me any more than their master did. And lots of jostling for room, which didn't make Alphonse happy, who started snapping and snarling at anybody who got too close because he knew how quickly a shiv could go into vulnerable flesh. He'd done it often enough himself.

Pritkin finally fought his way over and grabbed me. "Can you?" he asked grimly.

I assumed he meant drop Æsubrand on his face, so I did, but that caused another stir, so I decided to assume that he also meant "get us out of here." So, I did that, too, while the juice was still flowing, and I could. Leaving the whole squirming, furious mess behind.

CHAPTER ELEVEN

We ended up back in our room in a pile, almost landing on the Horror Twins and setting them to screeching. I just lay there momentarily while everybody sorted themselves out, staring at the glittering ceiling and wondering how I got into these things. I had assumed that, eventually, I would start to morph into one of those serene, elegant, powerful women that the Pythian name evoked, and maybe I would.

But it was taking its own sweet time.

"Holy shit!" Alphonse said. "You gotta warn a guy when you're going to do—*what the fuck is that?*"

It looked like his freak-out about shifting was about to be overtaken by a freak-out about the twins. And when a master vamp freaks out, it is a very scary thing. I looked up to see extra-long fangs fully extended, a knife he didn't need in one hand, and the big body in a superhero pose ready to launch itself at—

"Don't overreact," Pritkin told him, which didn't help. And neither did the knife, which Pinkie didn't seem to like around me. Which was how the big bad vamp met the big bad demon, or at least a smallish pissed-off demon, who stuck out a tentacle and . . .

Bopped him on the nose.

It was less of an attack than a sit-down-and-behave move, such as a large dog might give the young, yappy member of the pack, but it was not well-received.

"Grab him!" I said to Pritkin, as my power had just gone AWOL again, and damn, that was getting old!

Pritkin did not grab him, maybe because there wasn't time. Master vamps can move like the wind, which was why Alphonse completed the launch at Pinkie. And, this time, he was bopped all the way to the other side of the room, still screeching.

"Stop yelling!" I told him. I already had a headache.

And then Pinkie started mimicking him, or maybe he just thought that was what the gang was doing now; we were all yelling. Only he did it better than the rest of us. He did it better than everybody.

"*What the fuck?*" Alphonse shrieked, back on his feet and no happier, having just peeled himself off a wall.

"You said you knew we had them with us," I reminded him, wincing.

"You—*that's* your team?" he stared incredulously from the blob twins to me and back again. "The *fuck*?"

It was the only word he seemed to be able to remember right now, which . . . okay. They did require a minor mental rewiring, but still. I'd have been worried about their feelings, except that Pinkie was still shrieking happily.

"I told you not to sit down," Pritkin reminded him dryly.

"But . . . but . . . *demons*," Alphonse said. "They're supposed to be—I don't know—scary and shit!"

"Who just got thrown across the room?"

"I wasn't ready! Cassie shifts us with no warning, and the next second, that . . . that . . . that . . . *the fuck*?"

"They're scary!" I said, feeling vaguely outraged on the twins' behalf. It wasn't their fault that the corporeal form they'd gotten stuck with was less badass demon than . . . phlegm with eyeball stick.

"They're hideous," Alphonse said with feeling.

"They're not so bad—"

"*Hideous!*"

"Stop saying that!"

Pritkin helped me back to my feet. Only judging by his expression, that wasn't a good thing, as he preferred to yell at people standing up. But I noticed something before he could start whatever lecture I was about to get.

"What is that?" I crossed to the bed, where Pinkie was sitting proudly, if you could call that sitting, in front of a variety of . . . things. Lovely slimy things, but I had no idea what the hell. . .

I picked one up, which was dark pink silk with what looked like rubies of various shades encrusting it in pretty flower patterns. There were also tiny emerald leaves, perfectly formed, each exquisite enough to adorn a ring on Earth. And even tinier diamonds scattered here and there like dew drops on the flowers.

Under that was a translucent piece of lavender fluff with what looked like eighty layers. Seed pearls carved intricate patterns across the weave on top, while some much larger ones adorned a belt. The piece under that was a beautiful sea green with drifting fields of kelp along the bottom made of emerald, tourmaline, and peridot, with tiny citrine fish playing amongst the leaves. And under *that* was a blue so heavily encrusted with aquamarine, sapphire, and blue topaz that I could hardly see the material.

They were gowns, I realized, dozens and dozens of beautiful, exquisite gowns in every color of the rainbow. All were gorgeous, to the point of making a human designer weep with envy, and entirely unlike the rather plain outfit I'd been provided previously. I wondered why the dress gods had changed their minds. . .

And then I understood, and my eyes got big.

"Oh, shit. Oh, no."

"I think that deserves more than an 'oh, shit,'" Alphonse said. "What is that stench?"

"They always smell like that," Pritkin snapped, following me over to see what we had to deal with this time—and giving me no chance to hide the terrible truth even if I'd had the power to do so. "What is it?" he demanded.

"Trouble," I said, looking at the mass of purloined finery.

Because I doubted that either of our delinquents had a wallet stashed somewhere, so I assumed they'd taken the opportunity while we were at dinner to raid the surrounding rooms. And they'd raided a lot.

Pritkin must have reached the same conclusion because he looked at the pile of loveliness spread out on the furs and then turned to glare at Pinkie and the Brain. Before going off in some language that my translator didn't know, thank God. I already knew more demon curse words than was healthy.

"This is what we got?" Alphonse said, still staring at the twins. *"This?"*

"They're more competent than they look," I told him. Probably.

"I need a drink," he announced and started pawing through some drawers set into the walls that I hadn't even noticed. "And can we open a window or something 'cause I'm about to hurl."

"The windows would flood the room," I reminded him, and he sighed.

"That stuff could be a bioweapon," he muttered because vamps have super sensitive noses, which was not a plus right now. "And what is all this?" he added, coming up with a bottle I hadn't known we'd had and finally noticing the gossamer stuff on the bed.

"A thank you, I think," I said, smiling weakly at Pinkie. Because it had been thoughtful, in a demonic kind of way.

He waved a few tentacles in return, which reminded me.

"Hey, you guys like octopus?" Because Æsubrand's little trophy had come along for the ride, only it wasn't so little. The severed tentacle would have been longer than a car, except it was all curled up and had to weigh a few hundred pounds. And was still taking up most of the available room.

Pinkie looked quizzical for a moment before his eyestalk bent and peered around me. And then the pupil blew wide, and the screeching restarted, excitedly this time. After which, I was dragged into the bathroom for a confab because Pritkin had finished with the twins and was now ready to rake me over the coals, only he couldn't do it properly because of all the tearing, ripping, and munching noises going on.

"Do they ever get full?" I asked right before I was pushed against a wall.

Yeah, you could really see the fey, I thought, staring up at him. Æsubrand had had an almost identical expression when he'd slammed in that door. Only when it came to murderous fury demons had the advantage.

Too bad that Pritkin was both.

"Okay, what?" I said, crossing my arms.

"What? *What?*" This was followed by some outraged spluttering.

Oh, yeah, this was going to be good. When the guy who could swear in a dozen languages and half of them dead, couldn't even properly articulate the problem. . . We were gonna be here for a while.

And we were. But to my surprise, it wasn't Æsubrand that he was mad about. Or even the attempted disqualification for helping to murder a guy who wasn't even murdered. Or the trashing of Nimue's ballroom, which, in fairness, he'd done himself.

No, the problem was the promise.

"You gave me your *word*," he seethed.

"I know, but—"

"And the first time—*the very first time*—you get a chance to keep that word, you do the exact opposite!"

"Because you lost your damned mind and forgot about tactics," I reminded him. "And stealth, and even basic—"

"Do not attempt to put this on me!"

"—self-preservation. Even Alphonse said it—"

"Hey, leave me out of this," Alphonse said from beside the door. Where he was eating squid on a stick and leaning in the archway, watching the show. And was framed by the twins, who had already scarfed down their dinner and were ready for some entertainment.

I didn't even care.

"—you went HAM on that thing," I said, my blood pressure rising in memory. "And were about to get yourself *eaten*—"

Pritkin's eyes flashed emerald. "You *called it over!* You didn't just—you called for it! And I had just seen it kill you, seen your bloody body floating on the waves—"

"That was a doppelganger; I cast Chimera—"

"And how was I supposed to know that? I thought you were *dead*—"

"So, the idea was to go with me?" I demanded because I wasn't any happier about that fight than he was. We might have won, but it hadn't been pretty. And the worst thing was that it wasn't even part of the Challenge. All that effort, all that risk, and we got precisely bupkis.

Not to mention that that hadn't been an accident. Someone had sicced that thing on me so Pritkin wouldn't leave. So that he'd stay around and get eaten. Or beaten to death against the walls, or drowned, or skewered.

And he'd done exactly that! Yet he was mad at me for not abandoning him or standing back and watching it happen? When he'd done the exact same thing?

Something that did not go down well when I pointed it out.

"It's my *job*," he seethed.

"It *was* your job! I can take care of myself—"

"Yes, it looked like it!"

I felt my eyes narrow. "I wasn't the one they were targeting, Pritkin! I was bait. It was a trap for you—"

"One you could have died in just as easily!"

"—and you gave them exactly what they wanted! I could have shifted out of there in a minute, but you had to go ballistic! You know, I thought we were past this. I thought that suicidal streak had worked its way out of your system, but instead—hey! Hey!"

I broke off because he suddenly wasn't there anymore.

"Out of the way," he growled at Alphonse, who . . . got out of the way.

Alphonse was big and bad and could throw down when he had to, but he looked like he'd had enough for one night. And did not seem interested in taking on a furious half-demon with an attitude, and neither was I. But I didn't have a choice.

"Where are you going?" I demanded, following Pritkin into the bedroom. And then out of the door and into the hall, or at least, I tried. But there was a crowd out there already, although it seemed to be composed mainly of tall, sylph-like women and the flunky brigade from earlier. "Pritkin!"

"I'm going to quit," he threw back over his shoulder.

It was currently naked because he'd lost his fancy vest in the fight, and I saw a fey woman with a cascade of rippling dark hair intertwined with tiny pearls, admiring what was visible. Which was a lot, as the skin-tight trouser/leggings didn't conceal so much as highlight. I shot her a dirty look, got an amused eyebrow lift in return, and chased Pritkin down the hall since I couldn't currently shift.

"What do you mean you're quitting?" I demanded, catching up. "You risked your life to get here—"

"And it seems that I have to risk yours to stay." He didn't break stride or even slow down, making me have to run to keep up, damn him!

"You aren't risking mine! What happened in there wasn't part of the Challenge—"

"Like hell, it wasn't!" And, okay, that got him to stop, if only to back me into a wall again. "Someone tried to poison you unless you've forgotten. And when that didn't work, they used an illusion to separate us—"

I didn't know what he was talking about for a second, and then I did. "That wasn't an illusion! I saw Tony—"

"So did I—for half a second—then he was gone. So, unless he has the power to shift, what you saw wasn't really there—"

"It was! It had to be! I'd know him anywhere—"

"And so would anyone else who'd met him, and plenty around here could have. This court is full of factions, some of which are on the other side. They knew what he looked like, heard us discussing him, realized how badly you wanted him —"

"All that in a couple of minutes?"

"—and did an illusion, which water fey are better at than anyone, to distract you. And it *worked*. You shifted off without a word and were almost gutted by Æsubrand, who is as jumpy as everyone else at present. Which, if I can remind you, would have removed two birds with one stone for the rest of these bastards. Æsubrand kills you, which weakens me and disqualifies him for taking out a rival combatant's group member. And all the others win."

I stared at him. "You think that's what happened?"

"I know that's what happened!" He grabbed me by my shoulders. "Cassie, you may think you know court politics, but you don't, not on this level. This place will eat you alive, and I was a fool to make that deal with you. I am only glad that you showed immediately that it won't work, that you can't be trusted—"

"You can trust me!" I stared up at him, my heart in my throat, and his face softened. He still looked pissed but also conflicted as he stroked my damp hair with both hands, grasped my head, and kissed me on top of it.

"I can trust you to have my back, to risk yourself to save me, to refuse with blind, stubborn faith to leave me, no matter how grim it looks. You've proven that over and over in the past. Which is why I can't stay here. You won't leave unless I do, and if you don't leave, you'll die."

He kissed me very softly, on the lips this time, then took off down the corridor before I realized what was happening.

So, I had to run after him again, which did not improve my temper! Which was why *he* got pushed against the wall this time, and harder than I'd intended. It wasn't enough to knock that ridiculously sloppy fondness off his face, however, and that—

Oooh!

"I've died before," I snarled. "I went toe to toe with Zeus, and yes, I died for it—and then he almost did! Because I'm not the weakling you seem to think—"

"I've never thought that—"

"—and I'm back now and fighting fit—"

"Only because Faerie chose to save you and was in a position to do so," he reminded me. "What if she can't next time? Or won't? I don't trust her—"

"You don't trust anybody, it seems!"

His eyes flashed, and his cheeks flushed, which I liked much better than sappy male superiority.

"Pritkin, we *need* this army."

"And I won't trade you for it." It was implacable.

"You don't need to worry about me. *They* need to worry about me!" I flung out an arm in the direction of the assholes behind us, somewhere down the corridor, and all the others spread throughout this poisonous place.

It didn't help. I could see it on his face; he wasn't listening to me. He was the one person who always did, yet he was deaf this time.

"Faerie helped," I said angrily. "But she didn't fight that battle—*I* did. And it taught me something. I *am* Artemis' daughter and stronger than I ever thought I could be. Maybe I do die in this war, permanently, finally; I don't know. But I can tell you one thing. It won't be anybody at this court who ends me!"

"And if you're wrong?"

And it was all there, suddenly: the worry, the anger, the helplessness, the fear—especially that last one. Pritkin wasn't afraid for himself, but he was terrified for me. He had always leaned to the overprotective side, but that damned camp had really done a number on him, and it was clouding his judgment.

There was more at stake here than me, but he couldn't see it.

All he could see was that bloody corpse in the water.

So, I kissed him because it was all I could do, as there was no reassurance I could give that wouldn't be a lie. "Then you'll go on," I whispered against his lips. "You'll *win this*, and you'll win the war in my memory. As I would do for you."

"I'm not that strong," said the most powerful man I'd ever known, his face contorted.

"Yes, you are," I said, hugging him. "Yes, you are."

CHAPTER TWELVE

O kay, but what about Tony?" Alphonse said as we sat on the floor of our room, with the bottle that Pritkin had stashed away getting passed around and the guys snacking out of Alphonse's coat.

I wasn't eating, although my stomach was still actively complaining about that, maybe because most of the little offerings looked good. But they didn't smell good. Nothing in here did.

And, for once, it wasn't just the twins' fault.

The flunkies must have cast a spell to mask the demonic scent while the ladies were retrieving their stolen items, and they'd cast it hard. It was the kind of passive aggressiveness I could have done without, despite the stuff being everywhere in the royal palace. It was called "ocean breeze," according to Pritkin, and was supposedly the clean smell of wind across the sea, with a tinge of salt and a hint of pine.

And maybe it was. Unfortunately, the twins continued to emit what I hoped was merely passive odor, but frankly doubted it. The monster's leg seemed to have made them gassy, and the spell wasn't having it.

So, every time they erupted, it did, too, in a duel to the death that had the room taking on a smell that I wasn't entirely sure was quantifiable or an improvement over the original.

"What about him?" I asked, trying not to choke.

"Okay," Alphonse said, chewing on some seaweed candy because his nose seemed to have already adjusted, damn it. "I get what you're saying about the illusion, and it's possible. I didn't scent the fat man, although, in a crowd like that, I might not have. I'm not a Hound," he added, talking about the vamps with super sensitive noses that could pick up almost any scent, even one days old.

Lucky we didn't have one of them with us, I thought, shooting the twins a look.

The poor thing would be dead.

"But here's where it gets hinky," Alphonse went on. "Tony might have been a fake out, and the poison could have been meant for any or all of us. But that damned octopus—"

"Kraken," Pritkin said, drinking more blue liquid that tasted like mint and hit like a dozen semi-trucks. He belted it back like a man intending to get drunk, which had me worried.

And then what he'd said registered. "Is that what we fought?"

Pritkin looked at me. "What the hell did you think it was?"

"I . . . didn't really have time to think all that much."

"Obviously."

I frowned at him and took the bottle away.

"—showed up at the perfect time to kill her!" Alphonse continued, pointing at me with the seaweed-covered stick. "The poisoned plate was also put in front of her—"

"Alphonse," I said because I didn't want to go through all that again, not with Pritkin already so touchy.

"—and the illusion could only have been aimed at two people, one of which—"

"Alphonse!"

"—was *her*. And then, when the Ice Prince didn't manage to gut her, they loosed the big boy. Who immediately went after her and nobody else. I don't think you were the target. I think she was and still is."

"I know," Pritkin said, his jaw tight. "But what the hell am I supposed to do about it? She's Pythia. I can't throw her over my shoulder and carry her out!"

His look said that we wouldn't be here now if he could.

"Carry her out?" Alphonse looked confused.

"And neither can you! If they're targeting her—"

"Well, of course, they're targeting her! That's why we didn't come to your aid sooner; we had a fight with a bunch of would-be assassins. Or she had a fight. I mostly treaded water and swore—"

"You didn't tell me that," Pritkin said, looking at me accusingly.

"Didn't I?"

"—and this court used to be run by an iron-fisted demigoddess," Alphonse continued. "They're not happy to see another one show up. But that's not the point. The point is that the attack was *planned* and we know by who—"

"We know no such thing!" Pritkin snapped, his mood darkening by the minute. "I can name a hundred other suspects, and that's just off the top of my head! And half of them have mental abilities that might have allowed them to control that thing. Tony doesn't!"

"And I thought he was an illusion," I added.

"Something he could have arranged as easily as anybody else," Alphonse said. "He's been here a while; he's got friends. Not to mention the ones on the other side in this war. The fact that what you saw was probably fake don't mean he wasn't behind it—"

"You're obsessed with him," Pritkin accused. "Or else you're trying to trick us—"

"Careful," Alphonse growled.

"—into helping you take your revenge. I don't care if you want to target this vampire, but leave us out of it! We have enough—"

"Don't underestimate the fat man," Alphonse snapped. "And I may be obsessed, but it don't mean I'm wrong. Look, he had to know she was coming—"

"How? *I* didn't know—"

"Then you're not as smart as everybody says." He looked back and forth between the two of us. "You know, you guys may think you're subtle, but I got news: you ain't subtle."

"Meaning?"

"Meaning that the whole magical world knows you're bonking—"

"Bonking?" I said worriedly.

"Doing the horizontal mambo," Alphonse clarified. "Riding the bedroom rodeo, bow-chick-a-wow-wow—"

"We know what it means!" Pritkin said.

"The whole world?" I asked. Because who the Pythia was dating was considered a matter of political importance since that person could supposedly influence her. I didn't intend to live my whole life undercover, skulking around like my predecessor did, but I wasn't ready to make a big announcement yet, either.

Alphonse shrugged. "Some people think you dumped Mircea and took up with this guy," he hiked a thumb. "Or else all three of you are getting jiggy with it on the regular because you can't make up your mind—"

"We are not!"

Alphonse hiked an eyebrow.

"Not on the regular. . ."

He hiked two.

"What is your damned point?" Pritkin snarled.

"I have no idea anymore . . . oh, wait. Yeah, my point was that you two are an item, and Cassie is loyal to those she loves. So, yeah, Tony knew you were coming. Probably his masters on the other side told him you might try for the army, even before the court here figured it out. And," he added, before Pritkin could interrupt. "These assholes knew weeks ago. You were spotted heading this way, and there was only one reason why you'd come back, 'specially now. That's why they could lay all those traps for you, to cut you off at the pass."

"And how do you know that?" Pritkin demanded.

Alphonse tapped his ear. "Vampire hearing. They talk; I listen. But Tony . . ." he shook his head. "He's smarter than that. He knew you'd expect it on the road; you know how many scouts they got. So, he laid his plans and waited for you to fall into them like an oversized spider."

"You're giving him a good deal of credit," Pritkin said skeptically.

Alphonse and I exchanged a look. "Everybody always underestimates him," Alphonse said. "He looks like a joke, like a fat Gomez Addams, and like somebody tryin' to be bad who ain't all that bad. But he had his own court for hundreds of years. You know the only people who can usually do that? First and second-level masters, which he ain't.

"He's third, and barely that, to the point that he don't like being out in direct sunlight. Which makes him fodder, even with Mircea backing him up, which he usually don't. You go out on your own, it's expected that you can handle yourself and your court. Your master ain't going to come riding to the rescue all the time, or any time, least not that you can count on. Tony shoulda been meat."

"But he wasn't," Pritkin said, looking like he was listening for the first time.

"No. And it wasn't about power, 'cause it ain't for most of us." Alphonse grabbed the bottle from me and took a swig, and his eyes widened slightly. "What the hell is this?"

"Merlik. The merfolk make it from giant kelp and neon blue algae."

"Why don't that surprise me?" Alphonse looked at it some more, shrugged, and took another drink. "Anyway, like I was saying," he wheezed. "You guys have been hanging out with the big boys—the ones with power to burn who can afford to be stupid sometimes and make mistakes. We don't get that luxury. The losers farther down the scale have to make it by our wits or our fangs, or a little bit of both."

"And Tony did."

"Yeah. I was the fangs; he was the wits. So, he knew she was comin' 'cause you were comin', and she wasn't gonna leave you hanging out to dry. He knows her better than that.

"So, he made plans. And since he ain't the type to trust anybody, he's likely here to oversee those plans. You got a bigger problem than the other heirs."

"Tell her that," Pritkin said, and they both looked at me.

Like that didn't make me even more determined to stay!

Alphonse was right about one thing: people underestimated Tony all the time. It was one reason I hadn't minded the looks I received when I first became Pythia. They had ranged from "Poor thing, wonder how long she'll last" to "You have got to be kidding me." Nobody thought I could do this job, and that included me half the time.

But I hadn't argued with them because I'd learned from the best. Having people underestimate me was a bigger shield than anything magic could create. They didn't target me when they thought I was going to die on my own, just any minute now.

The same attitude had served Tony well for centuries, leaving him to work his nasty little plans in the shadows while everyone else thought he was a lightweight. And now he was on the other side in this war, and his buddies didn't want the Alorestri forces under Pritkin's control. So, Alphonse was likely correct; Tony or people loyal to him were here, which made my leaving utterly useless.

It would just switch the focus from me to the only guy left standing, and that wasn't happening!

I didn't say that, though, since I didn't want another argument, but I didn't need to. Pritkin was more than capable of reading my face, and his jaw had set into that mulish expression I remembered from when we first met. The one that said he *hated* this.

"I haven't said I'm competing," he reminded me. "If you stay, I'll sit on the sidelines. I won't participate—"

"Then I will."

"What?"

I hadn't wanted to do this, but he was leaving me no choice. "If you don't challenge, I will."

He looked at me like I was crazy. "You don't have standing —"

"Of course I do. All the gods were related; they practically made incest a family pastime.

And Nimue was a daughter of Poseidon. The same Poseidon who was a brother to Zeus. The same Zeus who fathered Artemis, or so some legends say—"

"The legends be damned!"

"—and whether it's true or not, no one here can dispute it. So, as Artemis's daughter, I'm Nimue's second cousin. Or something."

"That close enough?" Alphonse asked.

I shrugged. "I don't think it matters, just so long as you have some connection to the throne. Look at him. He's Nimue's *great-grandson*."

Pritkin's eyes narrowed. "You planned this ahead of time," he accused.

"Of course I did." I hadn't had much else to do on the way here.

"And didn't tell me."

I frowned. "I hoped I wouldn't have to! But I know you. I knew what you were likely to say—"

"So, you held this in reserve to blackmail me?"

Alphonse whistled through his teeth, and I felt my cheeks flush. "I'm not blackmailing you! I'm saying we need that army, and if you won't challenge for it, I will. And if you want to leave me here to fight alone, well, I guess that's your—"

Pritkin abruptly got up and went into the bathroom. The Brain's eyestalk moved back and forth between him and me for a moment, and then the vaguely blue-tinted creature slowly glorped after him. Pinkie stayed with me; I didn't know why.

I guessed octopus bought a lot of loyalty.

I sighed, but Alphonse seemed pleased. "Okay, good, he's gone. We can talk."

"He'll be back. He just wants to beat up some rocks first."

Alphonse lifted an eyebrow but didn't comment. He'd gotten good at that at Tony's, where a wrong word could get your tongue cut out. "Then I'll be fast. The point I've been trying to make is that the fat bastard is coming for you. That was him tonight. Some of it, maybe all of it, but it was him—"

"If he's here."

"He's here. You know it as well as I do. You might not know it up here yet," he tapped my head. "But your gut knows. Don't tell me it doesn't."

I didn't say anything. But frankly, I agreed with Alphonse. Tony might have been a middle-of-the-road vamp back home, with a decent-sized court and an income to match, but here. . . He was nothing, just nothing.

I still didn't know how he'd ended up backing the gods, but he'd served his purpose on Earth and had no more to offer them. And they didn't stay loyal to dead weight. So, whatever they'd promised, he was now uncertain about receiving it.

Probably protection; the fat man had always been paranoid. And now there was a less-than-zero chance that his future depended on offering them something big. Something that they hadn't been able to get on their own.

Something like my head.

"Yeah, you know," Alphonse said, watching me. "That's good. It saves time. So, can we stop arguing about whether he's behind this and start talking about how to *use it*?"

"Use it how?" I asked, looking at him suspiciously.

"That's fair," he said, seeing my expression. "'Cause yeah, you're the best chance we got to catch him. I've been here for weeks and haven't had a sniff until you turned up. And suddenly, he's popping out of the woodwork—"

"You want to repeat tonight and use me as bait, only with our plan instead of his."

"*What?*" That was Pritkin again, coming back in with a terrible expression.

Alphonse and I both sighed that time.

"They're coming after her anyways," Alphonse pointed out. "But that's good, 'cause we can use it to—"

That was the last coherent thing he said for a while since talking through a broken jaw is hard, even for vampires.

The two men tumbled into the hall, and I tried some seaweed candy. And made a face because it was terrible, or maybe that was the stench. Pinkie had come over to drag a slimy, odorous appendage up and down my arm in what I guessed was supposed to be a comforting caress, only it had the opposite effect.

And, suddenly, I couldn't take it anymore.

Not the smell, not the view of Pinkie's dinner swirling around and around that transparent flesh, not Pritkin's attitude—none of it! Not this *room*, which I knew would ensure zero sleep. I needed rest to be any good tomorrow, and this wouldn't cut it.

I got up, wiped my arm on the bedspread, and paused, noticing a plain black cloak that somebody had left behind because it blended in too well with the fur. I grabbed it, flung it around me, and went out to find Alphonse and Pritkin. Who were halfway down the hall and still going at it.

"I'm staying with Alphonse," I said. "Come on."

"What?" Pritkin looked up with a bruised jaw that didn't appear broken, but not for lack of trying on someone's part.

"You heard me. I can't breathe in there—"

"Someone tried to kill you three times tonight!"

"—and I need to breathe to sleep. So—"

"That's not a bad idea," Alphonse said from under Pritkin's arm.

"You stay out of this!" Pritkin snarled.

"Just hear me out. Three times *so far*."

He was abruptly released. "And what does that mean?"

Alphonse took his time standing up and shaking out the latest wrinkles in his once-nice tuxedo. "It means they know where she's staying. She might be better off with me. Least until you get this place warded halfway to hell."

"I have wards. And if I'm here, she's safe. I don't have to worry!"

Alphonse didn't say anything, but his look was eloquent.

"What?" Pritkin demanded.

"Nothing. I know better than to get between a man and his woman," he said diplomatically. And then he did it anyway.

"But if I was gonna comment—"

Pritkin said something rude.

"—I'd point out that she throws down pretty good. She ended that fight tonight—"

"By flooding the damned room!"

"Well, that ended it. That thing was lookin' for a way out, and she gave it one. You know there are other ways to win a fight than violence, right?"

Pritkin and I both stared at him.

"And besides, she can shift away if anything happens, can't she?"

"But she won't!" Pritkin snapped. "She'll stay right there, as she's proved a dozen times—"

"You sound like a broken record," I said, grabbing Alphonse again.

"You wouldn't dare," Pritkin said, his green eyes darkening.

"Watch me." My power had just returned, and it was itching to get me out of here.

"Cassie!"

"See you at the Challenge," I said and shifted.

CHAPTER THIRTEEN

H e always like that?" Alphonse asked as we wound our way through dazzling corridor after dazzling corridor.

The fey, especially these fey, loved ostentation, and some of the murals must have taken decades to do. They were huge and 3-D in cases, almost jumping off the wall. I had to move towards the center of the hall to avoid an abalone shell-covered fish leaping from the "water," and a little further on, I had to do it again, this time for the fisherman who held the rod at the end of the line.

I'd never seen anything like it: jade sea turtles watched me from hidden caves, small mother-of-pearl octopi changed hues depending on what direction they were viewed from, and crystal sea serpents slid by overhead, where some light source I couldn't see lit them from the other side like stained glass. It also shed varicolored light on us as we passed by as if we were under the sea. It was beautiful.

It was also intimidating, and I thought that last was on purpose. Nimue's court was rich and powerful enough to afford world-class decor even in minor corridors, and wanted you to know it. But it wasn't working as intended, as I was too busy wondering what was wrong with Pritkin.

"No. He's been acting weird since I got here," I told Alphonse.

"Well, I hope he snaps out of it by tomorrow and gets his game face on. You two die, and Tony might take off."

I shot him a glance. "Thanks."

"Just keeping it real."

And yeah, I was starting to remember that about Alphonse. He had been the exception at a court ruled by deception and backstabbing. Not that he wouldn't shiv you, but it would be face-to-face.

I guessed that was something.

"Pritkin always insisted that I learn how to fight," I said, aggrieved. "Because he knew I'd have to. When everyone else was trying to bury me under a pile of bodyguards or hide me in the closet, he was throwing me off of cliffs."

"And you . . . liked that?"

"No! But if the bad guys were going to do it to me sooner or later, better that he did it first, and I figured out how to deal with it. Pritkin saw that when nobody else did. And if he hadn't made me see the importance of learning to defend myself instead of depending on others, I wouldn't be here now.

"But when I finally get at least somewhat competent, he changes his mind! It doesn't make sense."

"Sure it does," Alphonse said.

"No, it doesn't!"

"It doesn't make sense to the head; the heart has its own logic."

I blinked at him. "I guess you are a poet."

He shrugged. "Poetic or not, it's true. You know, when I first met Sal, what I liked about her was how feisty she was. She grew up in a saloon—her ma was one of the "ladies" there if you know what I mean—and she had to learn to fight early. Cut a guy's ear off when she was eight 'cause he liked 'em young and didn't take no for an answer. She never backed down from anything."

I remembered the hard-edged, one-eyed blonde who had been Alphonse's other half and thought that that sounded about right. Sal had grown up in the Old West with a dagger in her garter belt and a gun in her purse. And nothing had changed over time.

When I knew her, her stiletto heels had transformed into the real thing because vampire or no, Sal never went out unarmed. She saw the world for what it was, always expected a fight, and made sure she had the means to win it. Alphonse was right; she hadn't been scared of anyone—except her master.

"After we started dating, nothing changed," Alphonse added. "I always made sure Sal was on my crew for any little errand the boss had 'cause I didn't have to watch her. She didn't screw up instructions, and she didn't run. We were the dream team.

"Until this one mission, when a first-level master—that Barrio guy from Jersey; you remember him?"

I nodded, even though I did not remember him. And if he was first-level, I should have because they weren't exactly thick on the ground. So, he was probably a screw-up or into some highly illegal stuff—and illegal by our Senate's definition, not that of the local police—or else he'd have been at court instead of trading blows with lowlifes like Tony.

"Anyway, the boss had gotten into a . . . difference of opinion . . . with one of Barrio's boys," Alphonse remembered, "and I was sent to mediate."

"With or without his head on a pike?"

Alphonse shrugged. "Depended on how reasonable he was willing to be. Which was not very reasonable, as it turned out, since his master was visiting him."

"I thought you said masters didn't back up their pawns," I reminded him.

"They don't unless said pawn ain't one, and Barrio's boy, a guy by the name of Fletcher, was working directly for the boss. He was pretending to be out on his own, so if he screwed up, the boss had plausible deniability. But he was under orders the whole time."

"To do what?"

"Barrio had him giving fey wine to normies, getting 'em sloshed, and seeing if any latent magical abilities showed up. If any did, he held 'em for Barrio, who sold 'em on to some dark mages for extraction. It was a nice gig, too—the Circle gets all pissy when magic workers go missing, but if it don't know they were magic workers?"

I scowled. That sort of thing wasn't unknown and was one of the reasons why the many concoctions known on Earth as "fey wine" were banned. They brought out all kinds of latent abilities in the human population that would have never surfaced otherwise.

Most people with a witch as their six-times great-grandmother didn't know it and acted like the regular old, garden-variety humans they believed themselves to be. But they weren't regular humans, and nobody knew how many there were. Many of the old records had been lost through the years in wars and fires and what-have-you, not to mention mages fathering kids in brothels or through one-night stands and not knowing it.

As a result, magic blood was more common in the human population than the Circle liked to admit, mainly because they couldn't keep track of it all. That was usually fine, as it tended to be recessive anyway. Right up until fey wine brought it out, that was, just in time for the newly minted witch or wizard to get grabbed up and sold to some dark mages, who sucked the power, and the life, right out of them.

That was even more the case these days since the Black Circle was on the other side of the war and needed all the weapons they could get. And all the magic it took to make them. And humans went missing all the time. . .

"Nasty business," I said because Alphonse already knew all that.

"It was that night," he agreed. "We showed up about a different matter, only to find a hundred or so freaked out people in cages, a couple dozen of Fletcher's guys armed to the teeth, and Barrio the Bastard himself. He was there to take a new shipment and was not pleased about being interrupted.

"We were boned."

"How did you get out of it?" I asked because obviously he had. Yet I didn't see how.

A first-level master didn't need Fletcher's people to back him up, not when facing a group ranked at fourth or fifth level, with maybe a few strong sixes thrown in. And working with the Black Circle would likely end with Barrio's head in a bag if the Senate ever found out about it. So, he had every reason to ensure that Tony's men didn't live long enough to tell anybody what they'd seen.

"It wasn't fun," Alphonse said dryly. "I lost five guys that night, and I only had six to begin with. Me and Sal were the two survivors, and she was disemboweled. I dragged her out of there, holding her guts in my hands while she was double-fisting a couple of semi-automatics and firing incendiary rounds from both barrels. Luckily, one of 'em caught Barrio himself, and he went up like a Roman candle.

"Must have had a little too much of that "wine" he was giving the normies, and when one of her bullets ripped his gut open, it spilled like gasoline."

I winced, but Alphonse smiled at the memory.

"His boys stopped to save the boss," he added, "and I threw Sal on my back and ran like hell. And even after we got back to the farmhouse, when they told me she'd be okay, when I knew a vamp don't die from shit like that, it didn't matter. It changed things. You know what I'm saying?"

He threw me a glance, but it didn't help.

Because no, I didn't know.

He sighed. "Anyway, I anonymously reported Barrio, even knowing what might happen if he found out it was us. Or me, 'cause Tony didn't want to know. He was too scared to risk taking on a first-level master, even at the loss of five guys, and was holed up in the basement to wait it out."

"What happened?" I asked, pretty sure that I already knew.

I had a feeling there was a reason that Barrio's name didn't ring a bell.

"Barrio had an accident a week later," Alphonse confirmed.

"Nobody knew exactly what happened, but everybody knew it was the Senate 'cause they took his head. It allowed Tony to move in on Fletcher, making him one of his satellite houses. The fat man shut down the human trade soon after as it was too risky, and that was that.

"Only it wasn't. Cause the next time I had a little errand, I left Sal behind. She was healed by then and well and truly pissed about me ditching her, getting all up in my face when I got back. But it wasn't like she thought; I didn't blame her for anything. She was the reason we got away that night, and the roasting she gave that bastard allowed the Senate time to finish him off before he came after us."

"Then what was the problem?"

"What was the problem?" Alphonse, who had been going at a good clip, his legs being considerably longer than mine, stopped to stare at me. "What was the *problem*? I'd held her guts in my hands was the damned problem! Felt her bleeding out all over me! Saw the agony and fear on her face and thought I'd lost her. Like Pritkin saw your dead body tonight, floating on the waves in a pool of blood."

"Ah."

"Yeah, ah. And from what I hear, that ain't the only close call you've had recently. So, whether you get it or not, cut the guy some slack, alright? He's not okay right now."

Maybe not. But Alphonse had no idea of the kind of crap Pritkin and I had seen. This wasn't our first time at the rodeo.

So, what was different now?

Maybe the answer was nothing. Maybe Pritkin was having a perfectly normal reaction to recent events, and I was the weirdo. It wouldn't surprise me.

Alphonse took off down the corridor again, and I hurried to catch up. But not to continue the conversation, as I was too busy with my thoughts. None of which I liked.

Gertie's training had taken place back in time and over months, too many to count as it had involved whizzing around in between the centuries half the time, when she decided that things were too tame in old London to challenge Agnes and me properly. I didn't know how long it had been as a result, as the mind got confused after a while. But the body didn't, and I'd needed three haircuts while there, all of which had been overdue.

And every day, she'd put me through the wringer, knowing that if she didn't, someone else would. And that she wouldn't be there to pull my butt out of the fire when I failed. It had been a harsh apprenticeship, and whenever I returned to my court, only a day or so after leaving from their point of view, it felt strange and left me off balance.

Like coming back to a place that I vaguely remembered, when another court and another time had started to feel like home.

Until the next attack came, as it always did, and then it felt okay. I felt okay because I had a new normal now, one of hypervigilance and constant fighting for my life, and . . . yeah. Maybe it was me who had changed.

Like tonight, when I was tired and hungry and had bruised my elbow somewhere in all that, to the point that it ached like a struck tuning fork. But other than that, I was fine. And I shouldn't be. I should be . . . I didn't know. But not this battle-hardened warrior thing I seemed to have going on. Because I wasn't invulnerable, and I knew it.

Dying tends to bring that home real quick.

And I still made mistakes, although fewer than before, after having Agnes' scornful laughter ringing in my ears. I'd made several tonight. I'd probably make more because that was what humans did, and mother's blood notwithstanding, I had always been very human.

But the fey made mistakes, too. And, for that matter, so did war mages. Yet nobody said they couldn't fight!

I remembered a story Pritkin had told me about a watering hole in Stratford where the Corpsmen went after particularly grim missions. It had a wall in a back room covered in the pins they received when promoted, which identified them as the

Circle's elite and which they never took off when on duty, any more than a police officer would go without their badge. And when one of them fell, their brothers-in-arms brought his pin back to that particular pub and put it on the wall, which had become an unofficial memorial for the fallen.

There were a lot more pins since the war began, some of which Pritkin had placed on that wall himself. Including the one belonging to Mac, his longtime partner, who had died protecting me. Pritkin had honored his sacrifice; he hadn't tried to lock him up to keep him safe as he had me.

Because he didn't know me anymore, I suddenly realized. He had been surprised to hear about one minor training exercise, something Gertie had thrown out on a weekend afternoon because we'd been getting on her nerves. It was nothing to some of the ones she'd planned, several of which I hadn't been sure I'd come back from.

But he hadn't seen those, had he? The months of hard training, the battles against ridiculous odds, the decisions I'd had to make alone. He hadn't been there.

Maybe that was why he'd never questioned Agnes, Gertie's heir and my predecessor. Because he'd met her when she was a majestic older woman with power to burn and a presence that could knock a man down at ten paces. He hadn't seen her shlepping back to court clutching a pissed-off seagull with fish guts in her hair and murder on her mind.

But that had been part of her story, too. Part of the price we paid for the power we wielded. Part of the price I had been paying all these months to earn the right to the position I held.

I wasn't a frightened, confused girl anymore, with more chutzpah than sense, who had somehow failed her way upward. I didn't need another war mage to die protecting me. It was my job to die, if need be, to protect everyone else.

And keeping me back, like a queen on a chessboard that some newbie was too afraid to risk, was the best way I knew to lose. This was the war of all wars, and there was no sitting on the sidelines, no matter how much Pritkin might prefer it. I needed to be here, whether either of us liked it or not, and if I fell...

Well, I had an heir back at court, a brilliant Pythia-in-waiting who was furious with me for leaving her behind. Not so much because she feared for me but because she wanted to fight alongside me. She was as fierce as her mother, and yes, I recognized the irony in the fact that Agnes' daughter would succeed me.

But it was comforting, too. She'd already had to act for me once and handled it with all the ability and grace I would have expected from someone of her bloodline. And if the worst happened, she would mourn me when the power came to her again, this time permanently, and then she'd get up and do the damned job.

Just as I had. And just as I would, whether or not anybody ever saw me as Pythia. Including my supposed partner!

"You okay?" Alphonse said, looking at me strangely.

"Yeah." I cleared my throat. "Is what happened with Sal why you didn't break Pritkin's jaw?"

"Partly. And partly because he got a shield up before my fist hit him." He shook his right hand and scowled. "I hate breaking the little bones. If they don't heal back right, you gotta break 'em again and start over."

He banged his hand on the wall, and I tried not to wince at the crunching sounds.

"But I probably wouldn't have anyway, 'cause he's got enough problems," he added, sliding those dark eyes over at me.

And yeah, I got it. I was the problem, at least in Alphonse's eyes. I didn't know what to do about it because feeding into Pritkin's freak-out wasn't likely to help.

"How did you get past it?" I asked him.

"Get past what?"

"Worrying about Sal?"

"She died," he said grimly and pushed open a door.

CHAPTER FOURTEEN

I had shifted us into the main corridor leading to the dining hall, as I didn't know this place well enough to go anywhere else. Alphonse had taken over at that point and been steering us along winding passageways and up endless staircases as he'd said he had a quick errand to do. And I guessed it involved food since we'd just entered a kitchen.

It was a big one without the subtle elegance of the halls outside. Which had been becoming steadily less refined as we went on, with brilliantly colored mosaics giving way to bare walls, intricate tilework becoming rough slabs of stone underfoot, and expensive spell light dropping away in favor of copper lanterns, the heat of which had stained the plaster behind them in places. I hadn't paid much attention until now, though, when Alphonse pushed through a rough, scarred wooden door, and we stepped into a blast of heat.

That was thanks to a long, whitewashed wall full of bread ovens on this side of the room, tended by an army of women with stained aprons thrown over their tunics. There was a mass of sturdy wooden tables in the middle of the space, being worked on by another hundred or so people, and a row of enormous stone fireplaces along the wall opposite us. Like the bread ovens, they were going all out and blasting the workers in between with a double dose of heat.

That might have been why the spit-turners, sitting on little stools to the right of each fireplace, looked exhausted. They were all men drenched in sweat, to the point that they looked like they'd been in the dining hall with us. Only I didn't think so.

The servants there had been freshly scrubbed and pristine, with their tunics plain but clean and pressed to fall in elegant folds. These guys were in rags, and not many of those, because who would want to ruin decent clothes with that job? And they were decorated with ash from the fireplaces, which had clung to all that sweat and created almost a paste over their skin.

They looked like chimney sweeps after a hard day and were busy cranking haunches of meat and huge, trussed-up fish over the flames, why I didn't know, as dinner had been canceled. Only maybe not. A bunch of teenagers were rushing around, grabbing platters of food, throwing wards over them that immediately became steamed up, and rushing out again.

Ye olde room service was booming tonight.

"They gotta have the kitchens above the water line so that the smoke has somewhere to go," Alphonse explained as we skirted around the edge of the room. "So, the nicer areas are all below the sea, with the workspaces above it."

"Seems like a strange choice since most of the court breathes air," I pointed out.

"Yeah, but so do their enemies. This place was built for defense. The palace is basically a hollow mountain, and the fey got ways of flooding whatever parts of it they want. They know how to survive that kind of thing, having done it for thousands of years. But their enemies—"

"Don't," I finished for him.

He nodded. "Armies come in, but they don't come out. Or at least, they used to. They don't come in so much anymore."

I thought back to the flooded ballroom and the people who had been busy fleeing the attacking monster. But none had seemed overly worried about all that water. And then I thought about the twisty corridors outside and how much fun it would be to meet a trident-carrying bunch of fey while lost in the maze and busy drowning.

No, I didn't suppose armies came in much anymore, either.

But this part of the palace seemed like another world, being bone dry and without the cool breeziness of the rest of the complex. There weren't even any windows to open, giving the tiniest bit of fresh air. Just massive expanses of smoke-blackened chimneys above the roasting stations, their scars getting steadily darker from the heat.

The air shimmered with it to the point that the room seemed to ripple, and within seconds, I was sweating up a storm under my armor. I glanced at Alphonse, who wasn't perspiring because vampires didn't, but he also wasn't looking comfortable. Even in minimal tunics, I didn't know how the servants took it.

"Slaves," Alphonse said when I voiced my thoughts.

"What?"

"Oh, they don't call 'em that, but that's what most of 'em are. I mean, they don't technically have to work for the Green Fey, but there's not a lot of other options around here if you wanna eat."

"Then why not leave?" It didn't look like they had anything to lose.

Alphonse snorted. "How? They're not allowed to use the Green Fey's portals, including the one to Earth. And the other light fey houses are hostile to anyone with human blood trying to settle in their lands."

"There are other portals—"

"Yeah, but even if you can get to one, and that means battling across hundreds of miles of hostile territory, what are you gonna use for money? Slaves aren't rich, and those things are expensive. Not to mention that even if you somehow beg, borrow, or steal your way through, there's a whole world on the other side that you don't know how to navigate, and there's no one to help you.

"Plus, there are all kinds of rumors about Earth, probably planted by the Alorestri, that's got these people thinking it's a hell zone. And the kind of assholes who come here as smugglers don't exactly give anybody a reason to think otherwise. "I tried talking with a few guys in a tavern a week ago, but they didn't believe me."

He thought about it. "Of course, I'm not exactly the poster child for that kinda argument."

"But the dark fey do it all the time!" I said. The casino that housed my court had a kitchen full of refugees from the war, who I strongly suspected didn't get minimum wage. But they did get housing, food, protection, and the ability to slowly assimilate into the magical community.

Why couldn't these people do the same?

But Alphonse was shaking his head. "Some of the dark fey do it, those who can pay traffickers to get them out and have family on the other side who help them get on their feet. But plenty of groups end up being abandoned by the bastards they paid their life savings to and never make it out of Faerie or get killed by those same traffickers as soon as there's any sign of trouble. Cause that's easier than getting sent up on a smuggling charge."

He shot me a look. "Don't you read the papers?"

Not as much as I probably should, I thought grimly.

I stared around the room, seeing again the terrified witches being corralled into pens by Nimue's people back in the sixth century, who I'd been unable to save. I wondered if any of these were their descendants. It didn't feel good to realize that they might be.

It was harder to steal witches now that they'd banded together into a worldwide coven network, but breeding what you needed from former captives was apparently fine and dandy. Because there were plenty here, and I was damned if I'd heard anything about it. And that included in Senate sessions where there'd been plenty of talk about possible allies in the war, but nobody had mentioned a group of humans already living in Faerie!

Maybe because said humans didn't have anything to thank us for.

"Why hasn't the Circle done anything?" I demanded, my

temper rising. "These people are human—"

"Part human in most cases, and don't look at me like that. They're not gonna risk a war trying to drag back a bunch of people who have never even seen Earth and would likely only be trouble—"

"They're magical humans! The Circle doesn't have a choice!"

"Oh, they got a choice," Alphonse said dryly. "And these guys might be magical, but they came from the wrong side of the blanket. Namely, the covens, who don't care much for the Circle in our day and absolutely hated them in the past. You want 'em to risk a conflict with a mostly friendly power over people who would only strengthen their enemies? Not gonna happen. And the Senate don't like mages period and don't want any more on Earth than they already got. Come on, Cassie. You know how it goes."

I was learning.

"Look, let's just get what we need and get out," Alphonse said, scanning the room.

"And what do we need?" I asked, distracted by my thoughts.

"That red-haired waitress."

"What?"

"The one who gave you the fish? She's gotta know something. She delivered the damned poison."

"You think she's an assassin?" I remembered how she'd been low-key flirting with Pritkin, which suddenly took on a more ominous vibe.

"Don't know. But even if not, she'll know who gave her the platter and if she seen anybody adding a little extra "spice" at the last minute. And that might get us a line to somebody working with Tony. But we gotta find her first."

"Do you see her?" I asked because I didn't. She'd been a curvy redhead with dimples, a pretty, slightly round face, a pug nose, and bouncy curls held back by a dark blue scarf to match her tunic. But while there were a lot of people here and a larger-than-normal number of redheads, none looked like her.

"No, but I see the bastard who sent me on a wild goose chase earlier," Alphonse said grimly and darted forward.

And I do mean darted. Vamps could move when they wanted to, which was why a portly cook who must have topped six feet by another foot was soon dangling off of the floor. Because Alphonse had just hung him on a hook.

For a moment, I thought that "hung" might be literal, with the man's tunic threatening to strangle him. But his height saved him, being enough to let him get up on tiptoes to take some weight off his neck. But not to come down because a vamp was in his face.

"You lied."

And, you know, Alphonse might not be pretty, and he might not be eloquent, and he might be a massive gaping asshole when required. But there weren't too many who were better when it came to sheer scare tactics. And it looked like the cook agreed.

"I—I didn't lie—"

Which was when the fangs came out, and like everything with Alphonse, they were more grotesque than usual, being cracked and yellow and with the tip of one splintered into two, like a snake's forked tongue. As if he needed another intimidation factor. The two-pronged fang got very close to the other man's neck before he spoke again.

"I checked every vendor," he hissed. "Every last one, and a lot of the locals who were just milling about. Guess who hadn't seen her?"

"W-well, they're not going to tell you, are they?" the man spluttered. "You're an outsider. They don't trust outsiders here."

"A fact you didn't bother to mention before sending me on that useless chase!"

"What useless chase?" I asked.

"I came here after our lovely meal to talk to the girl but didn't find her. Head honcho here told me she'd run off in a panic. Only nobody saw her where he said."

"That's why you had all that food," I guessed.

"Merchants talk better if you buy something," he agreed. "And I hit up every one."

"Perhaps they missed her?" Honcho volunteered, which was a bad move. Something he realized when the fang was back and scraping his skin this time. But he kept on babbling anyway.

I wasn't sure he could stop at this point.

"It's dinner time," he said, his voice shrill. "Everybody goes to Fountain Court! It's the cheapest place to eat. The fishermen give their unsold catch to the vendors for a song, and they sell it on to the crowds—"

"Shut up!" Alphonse hissed. "The passage from here to the city comes out right in front of them! And a fleeing, half-drowned redhead is memorable. So, she didn't go that way—"

"She did! I swear she—"

"—and now the trail is cold, and you're going to warm it up for me or be the main course at the next meal. With an apple in your mouth."

Alphonse never raised his voice, but he didn't have to. The man shot a look at a nearby spit, where some small, goat-sized animal was roasting. It didn't have an apple, but I thought he got the idea.

"Tell me!" Alphonse said, grabbing the guy's neck and causing his protestations to descend into incomprehensible gurgling.

I glanced around. People were still steadily working, most not even glancing this way. That could have been the heat, sapping the life out of them because the designer of this place must have been a sadist. Yet you'd think their boss possibly being dinner would raise at least an eyebrow.

But no. How often did this sort of thing happen, I wondered. 'Cause it was looking like the answer might be daily, to the point that nobody bothered to take notice unless their workstation was close enough to risk getting sprayed by blood.

One of the workers was a young woman making meat pies at a nearby table. Pritkin had said that the Alorestri had the best food in Faerie because they pulled from both sea and land and had elements from two worlds' cuisines in their own. I'd been looking forward to trying some local dishes but was now more interested in the person preparing them.

Everybody else was red-faced and sweating, but she looked cool as a cucumber, with her clear skin not so much as flushed. She also bore a slight resemblance to the waitress, although she was way better looking, and the other girl hadn't been ugly. I wondered if they were related and wandered over.

And she noticed, although she quickly looked down at the filling she was spooning into the pastry. It looked good, and a platter of finished pies being loaded onto a tray for baking looked even better. My stomach, still neglected and complaining about it, grumbled fiercely, and the girl glanced up in surprise.

I grinned at her. "Missed dinner," I said, and she looked startled before abruptly hitting the floor.

It happened so fast that, at first, I thought she'd slipped. But a check under the table showed her body in something that wasn't a curtsey or even a bow. It was full-on prostration, and the floor was in no condition for it, being full of muddy footprints, pieces of squashed vegetable, and raw sausage.

Without thinking, I grabbed her hand to pull her back up, and she immediately started screaming.

I let her go and stepped back, but the screaming didn't stop. It wasn't crying or even sobbing; it was full-on, high-pitched panic, like a lamb being led toward a stump covered in blood and with a bunch of other lamb's heads scattered around it. And I had no idea what to do with that.

"Um," I said brilliantly as Alphonse looked over at me.

"What the hell?"

"That's what I'd like to know."

"Maybe we should switch spots," he said. "You take bitch boy here and I'll intimidate the girl."

"I wasn't trying to intimidate her! I just wanted to get her off the floor."

And before I'd even finished my sentence, she scrambled up, still screaming.

I blinked at her and then around at everyone else, who had finally stopped work to gape at us. They think I'm a fey, I realized. One of those nobles who were apparently a giant bunch of dicks. I'd put up the hood on the cape as we walked here since I had too many enemies to count, but it wasn't helping now.

And neither was that, I thought, when I pulled it down, and then everybody started screaming.

I stared around in confusion as they dropped whatever they were doing and ran for the exits, fighting each other to get through the doors. Except for the redhead, who caught one glimpse of my messy, air-dried hair and unmistakably rounded ears. And fainted.

"Do you fucking mind?" Alphonse said to me, shouting to be heard over the din. "I'm trying to interrogate someone here!"

"I was just trying to get a meat pie," I said, bewildered.

"Tell them that," he said as I knelt to check on the girl.

I figured it couldn't hurt, and enhanced my voice to be heard over the crowd. "I don't mean you any harm; I just wanted a pie. And can I get some help here? I think she knocked her head."

The panic did not noticeably subside, but the man Alphonse had been trying to question unhooked himself and knelt, his eyes twitching from me to the hulking vampire. When neither of us did anything, he bent to examine the girl and frowned.

"She's bleeding," he said, looking up. "May I get her some help, Lady?"

I stared at him blankly because hadn't I just asked for that? "Yes?" I said when he just squatted there, letting her bleed. And giving the impression that he might have let her bleed out if I'd said so. Which caused a rash of goosebumps to break out on my arms.

What the hell kind of place was this?

But once permission had been given, he snapped into action. Some shouted commands, none of which my translator understood, halted the desperate flight, and some more had several burly men rushing over, one of whom picked up the girl and took her off through an arched doorway. Neither looked at me, keeping their heads down and averting their eyes.

And giving the impression that they thought I was going to go for them fangs first, like a hungry vamp.

Instead, I was just a hungry human who understood exactly nothing.

And then Pritkin showed up.

"Well, that's just jolly," Alphonse said bitterly before I could. Although I probably wouldn't have commented, being too busy noticing something weird. Namely that none of the fey seemed to be afraid of Pritkin.

They were gathering around him instead, talking rapidly in the strange speech that my translator didn't know, even though it was supposed to know them all. And hanging off him with pleading faces and grasping hands, with the clear implication: please save us from the terrible monster. Suddenly, I knew how the Kraken had felt.

"Okay, what did you do?" Alphonse asked me.

"I didn't do anything! I was admiring the pies and—"

And suddenly, I was inundated with them, heaps and heaps of them, on multiple trays held aloft by kneeling people with their faces turned away. Like ancient worshippers making offerings to a . . . vengeful . . . goddess. . . And, okay, I got it.

"Look," I said, and everybody pulled back, almost as one, getting as far as their bodies would let them while still offering up the requested snack.

"You should probably take a pie," Alphonse said dryly, although he looked somewhat sympathetic, probably at whatever was on my face.

I took a pie.

It was too hot and threatened to burn my fingers, being just out of the oven. But I was afraid to say anything lest the woman offering it killed herself or something. I caused a glove from my armor to appear underneath it, hoping nobody noticed.

"Thank you," I whispered, which did nothing. I was still ringed by pie bearers.

But the head honcho said something rather sharply to the mass of people around me. Who scattered on the winds, back to their stations to fill the orders that the throng of younger types in clean, mostly sweat-free clothing, were waiting to take to hungry diners. Pritkin's crowd abruptly deserted him, too, and our eyes met across the crowded room.

Well, shit.

CHAPTER FIFTEEN

Well, I didn't know you were a friend of Prince Emrys, did I?" Honcho said, striding down a corridor that branched off from the back of the kitchen. He was talking to Alphonse but kept shooting me little looks over his shoulder as if he didn't enjoy having me behind him.

Or maybe he was looking at Pritkin, who was scowling from beside me. "Damn it, Rhosier," he said. "I've told you a dozen times to call me John."

"I'm not calling you that!" the man almost shrieked before getting hold of himself. "They'd have my head."

"Rhosier?" I said because that was Pritkin's dad's name.

"Welsh form of Roger," Pritkin said. And then he noticed my expression. "No relation."

"We mostly choose names from Earth, Lady," Rhosier said, averting his eyes from mine. "Or choose dark fey ones. We are not permitted to call ourselves after the light fey."

"Why would you want to?" I muttered, which won me a surprised glance.

And then I guessed he decided that comment deserved something more and stopped dead in the middle of the corridor. But not to look at me, which seemed to genuinely pain him. But at Pritkin, who he pulled aside without the fake cravenness he'd been showing us.

"Why did you bring her here?"

"I didn't." Pritkin's voice was flat.

"Do you know what they say?"

"Heard some rumors."

"She's dangerous!" That was whispered.

"You have no idea."

"Can we go see the girl already?" Alphonse said, and he wasn't talking about the poor thing with the bonked head.

Honcho had been hiding his waitress, something he'd readily admitted to Pritkin, who seemed to be everybody's fair-haired boy. But he didn't like the idea of letting me talk to her. Which was rich, considering that he didn't have the same problem with Alphonse.

And the day that I was seen as scarier than Mr. Sinister over there...

Well, I guessed that day had come.

"They say she's mad," he said after dragging Pritkin down the hall a little further. He'd also put up a silence spell, but I'd aged it out of existence without him being the wiser.

"She isn't mad. Usually," Pritkin amended, shooting me a glance. Because he'd noticed what I'd done.

"They say she brought down Issengeir's shield all on her own! They say she wiped out an entire legion of Aeslinn's men, powdering them away into nothing and eating their souls! They say she wields the power of Artemis and has increased it in unholy congress with a fell beast of a vampire and..."

He abruptly stopped.

"And?" Pritkin said archly.

The man glared at him for a moment, then squared his shoulders and manned up. "And you! The things they say about the two of you—"

"What do they say?"

"I won't repeat it! But they're horrible—"

"And you don't think that might have something to do with the fact that I'm here, competing for the throne, and everyone hates it?"

"Of course I do!" The man shoved limp blond bangs out of his eyes. The rest of the shoulder-length cut had been scraped back into a sad little ponytail, I guessed to keep it out of the food. "But some of the rumors began before that—"

"Imagine," Pritkin said dryly. "A court who feared, admired, and hated Nimue in equal measure, gossiping about another demigoddess. One that none of them have ever even seen before today. One who is on my side—"

"Is she? Is she on your side? Or does she want the throne for herself?" And then Rhosier went *off*, to the point that the passion and venom in his voice were literally spine-tingling. "You know how they are! All of her kind—not just some of them, *all*. They see us as nothing but tools to snatch up when they like and throw away when they choose. They don't care about us, about *you*, any more than their creatures do, those with but a drop of godly blood in their veins but all their cunning, their greed, their *treachery*.

"They and the gods are the same. They will toss you aside when you are old and broken in their service and never even bury your bones. You'll be lucky if they don't feed them to their dogs, who they treasure more than you! So, I say again, how sure are you that this isn't a play to put a crown on her head and make another Nimue to scourge us? I won't help with that! Do you hear me? I won't help to enslave another generation of —"

"Why don't we ask her?" Pritkin said suddenly, cutting him off.

"What?"

"She's been listening this whole time. Cassie?"

I swallowed pie, which I'd been scarfing down while I had the chance. "I don't want the throne," I told the horrified man, who had turned to look at me with the dawning realization that his silence spell wasn't so silent. "Well, crap," I said when he suddenly hit the floor, prostrating himself just as the girl had done.

Alphonse looked at Pritkin. "That wasn't funny."

And when the resident fiend tells you that, you know you've gone too far.

But Pritkin was already helping the shaking guy up, who hugged the wall across from me with the look of someone headed to slaughter, just any second now. And goddamn, was I already sick of that! "I'm not going to hurt you!" I told him. "I'm sorry; I shouldn't have been eavesdropping, but—"

"W-what?" he looked gobsmacked.

"—it's the only way to find out anything around here. When people won't even look at me—"

"Looking at Nimue was death! At least for one of us!"

"I'm not Nimue! I didn't even *like* her—"

"And you apologize? To *me*?" He stared at me some more.

"Well, Alphonse was right," I said awkwardly. "I shouldn't have done that, and I'm, uh, I'm sorry. . ." I broke off because the guy had collapsed again into a huddled heap and was doing something that sounded like sobbing.

I looked at Pritkin, who was leaning against the wall, arms crossed, watching his friend but making no effort to help him. And then I realized the guy wasn't sobbing; he was laughing. Or maybe it was half in half; I couldn't tell.

It looked like he'd lost it, and Alphonse was running out of patience. "Should I slap him?" he asked seriously.

I honestly didn't know. But I guessed not, as Pritkin was helping him up and bringing him over. And sticking out the guy's hand because he was as limp as a ragdoll and seemed incapable of doing it himself. "Remember what I told you about shaking hands?" Pritkin asked him.

"I—I—I—" The man seemed incapable of talking suddenly.

So, I took his limp hand because Pritkin was making little gestures with his eyes, and I didn't know what else to do. "Hi," I said, feeling like a fool. "I'm Cassie."

"Cassie," he gasped and then stared around fearfully.

"God damn, does everybody have PTSD around here?" Alphonse asked.

"They won't behead you over me," I pointed out to the guy, who I really didn't want to call Rhosier or any variation on that.

Along with the blond hair and fey height, he had a muscular build if you looked past the chef's paunch and handsome features that seemed familiar, or maybe I was imagining things. Since Rosier's kids had all died in the womb after draining the life out of their mothers, that seemed a safe bet. Pritkin was the only one who had survived.

And, thankfully, this guy's eyes were brown. "They don't like me around here, anyway," I reminded him.

"Don't like you," he wheezed desperately and then kept repeating it like some kind of mantra. "Don't like you. Don't *like* you. Don't—"

Pritkin slapped him.

It seemed to help.

Rhosier put his free hand over his eyes for a moment, then took it away to stare at our still joined hands. Mine was worse for the wear, it having been a while since my last manicure, and was also greasy from the pie's buttery crust. But he didn't seem to mind.

In fact, its less-than-perfect state seemed to reassure him. "I—it's an honor," he whispered and bent over it.

Right before someone started screaming.

He promptly forgot about me and tore down the hall, and we followed. It wasn't that far of a run, but it felt like ages, especially with us scrambling together in a relatively narrow space. Except for Alphonse, who wasn't with us anymore but had slipped away during all the drama.

Which was why I was only slightly surprised when we showed up to find him facing off with two redheads, one of whom had caught him in a spell that had him splayed against the wall of a small storeroom as if a giant, invisible hand was holding him there.

Surprisingly, it was the kitchen maid, who I hadn't taken for a badass. But I guessed so because she threw another spell at us a second later, some kind of shield, and screamed something at the other girl. Something that my useless translator didn't know but which was probably the local vernacular for "run."

Another door was at the back of the small room, but the

waitress didn't run for it. Instead, she helped to fortify the shield while arguing with her friend. But then Pritkin took their protection down with a flick of his wrist, and all hell broke loose.

I got clocked by an invisible fist to the jaw, sending me reeling backward; Alphonse hit the ground snarling, jumped up, and shoved me behind him; and Pritkin swore and yelled something that the girls weren't listening to because they were busy pummeling me.

Or they were trying to. But the blows landed on an already pissed-off master vamp instead, and that wasn't good. He was gonna go off any moment if they didn't—

Yep, right on cue.

Alphonse threw himself into the fray, ignoring the hits like they weren't even there, and snatched the waitress away from her buddy. And got a hand around her throat, squeezing hard enough to make her yelp and causing the kitchen maid to go ballistic. A human would have been dead under the hurt she put on him, and why the hell was someone that strong a kitchen maid?

But she had clearly never met a master vampire before because her eyes got big as the long, bloody, knife-like rents that another spell put in his body closed up almost as fast as she could make them.

Alphonse grinned at her. "I can do this all day."

"What are you, Captain America?" I asked, picking myself up. And keeping Rhosier between me and the girl because I couldn't heal like that.

"Don't know. Always thought I had the ass for it—"

"And don't hurt her!"

"I ain't planning to hurt her. But the more I gotta heal, the hungrier I'm likely to get," he said, and those terrible fangs re-emerged.

They made even me shudder, and I'd grown up with vamps. But what they were doing to her was . . . nothing. What had happened to the delicate flower that had passed out in the kitchen?

I was beginning to suspect that that had been an act to get out of there quickly and find her friend, since the only thing that happened when Alphonse got scary was that she snarled back at him.

"Touch her and die, vampire," she spat.

He looked at the waitress, who he still had in one hand. "I'm already touching her."

"Then let her go, and perhaps I will spare your miserable hide!"

"Miserable?" Alphonse looked down at himself and then glanced back at his ass. "That why you were 'mirin' earlier?"

"What?" she looked confused.

"You were checking out the bod when you had me splayed up there on the wall. Which good one, by the way. I couldn't move for a second."

This time, she was the one blinking, as if she didn't know which of those statements to answer first. "I was not!" she finally said.

"Was not what?" he asked, like they were having a casual conversation over coffee. "'Mirin'?"

"That—that's not a word," she said, looking flustered.

"Is so."

"It is not! I know your tongue!"

He grinned. "Not yet, but maybe we can work something out later."

Pritkin cleared his throat. "I hate to interrupt—"

"Then don't," Alphonse said and widened his grin at the girl, who did not appear to know what to do with that. Since he hadn't retracted the fangs first, I wouldn't have, either. I decided to get involved because I hadn't done anything stupid in a couple of minutes now, so I was due.

"We don't mean you any harm," I told her, peeking out from behind Rhosier and pushing him forward a little. "Go on. Tell her."

"They . . . may be trustworthy. Lord Emrys vouches for

them—"

"And how do I know that he isn't under a spell?" she demanded, her eyes flashing.

And I suddenly understood why Alphonse was flirting, even in the middle of a fight: she really was a beauty. Her sister was cute in the same way that I was. Nobody was likely to kick us out of bed, but we wouldn't be gracing the cover of *Vogue* anytime soon, either.

But in another world, this one might have. Intelligent hazel eyes were set in a face that a Renaissance master would have loved: a pale oval with high cheekbones, full lips, a perfectly straight nose, and teeth that looked like someone had photoshopped them. I couldn't see the hair very well, as everything but a few tendrils had been stuffed under a mob cap to keep it out of the food, but I didn't need to.

She would have been stunning bald.

Considering how superficial this bunch of fey were, I had to wonder why her sister had been serving and she had been relegated to the sweaty kitchen. And, of course, my stupid mouth had to ask. "Jealousy?" I guessed before I could stop myself.

It was just one word, but she understood immediately. And in a second, so did I, when the glamourie she'd been using fell. Guessed I knew why she hadn't looked flushed in the kitchen, I thought, gazing at what happened to anyone prettier than the highborn fey they served.

I sucked in a breath, I couldn't help it, and she smiled bitterly. "Does this please you, *goddess*?"

"No," I whispered.

"Lady Adira caught her husband looking at me a little too long. I was twelve. The scars were bad then, but they stretched out as I grew, becoming even worse. She said they would, that they'd get prettier right along with me. But that nobody would ever see them, nobody who mattered, as I'd be in the kitchens from then on."

I didn't say anything, still trying to take in the ruin of that perfect face. Her glamourie had been flawless—I hadn't seen a crack, even this close—but I guessed she'd needed to get good at it. The right half of her face was a mass of scars, ones that looked like they'd been made by someone's nails slashing first in one direction and then in another, over and over until deep ridges had formed in the flesh.

"I'm sorry," I whispered, but my apology didn't seem to have the same effect on her as on Rhosier.

"Answer me!" she yelled at him. "How do I know the prince isn't under a spell? For that matter, how do I know that *you* aren't? I told you this wouldn't work! I'm taking my sister and going." She shifted her glare back to Alphonse. "Now, get out of our way!"

To my surprise, he did as she asked after releasing the waitress. And with the added flourish of a gesture that he must have picked up from one of the old movies he loved. It looked like the motion a courtier would have used with a queen, including a little bow.

She regarded him suspiciously, but his gaze never wavered, and his eyes showed something like respect. Alphonse had been born with a face like the one she'd been given. He knew what it cost a person.

"You won't make it out of the castle alive," Rhosier told her, grabbing her arm as she passed. "These aren't the only ones looking for you. I had no less than three sets of visitors tonight —"

"What visitors?" Pritkin asked sharply.

"Lord Sǽþórr—"

"Sǽþórr?" Alphonse interrupted, pronouncing it Sigh Thor. "That prick?"

"—Lady Véfreyja, and Prince Æsubrand—"

"Æsubrand," I said. Because I'd thought he would have had better things to do. Like bind up that broken nose he'd gotten when he hit the floor. "What does he want?"

"Generys, like everyone else," Rhosier said. "He declined to say why."

"Who's Generys?"

The waitress slowly raised her hand. And then, to my surprise, she looked me straight in the eyes. "I didn't try to kill you, Lady—beg pardon, I do not know what to call you."

"Cassie."

"You can't call her that!" Rhosier broke in while her lips were miming the unfamiliar name.

"Of course, she can," the kitchen maid spoke up. "Goddesses don't have titles. They are above that sort of thing," her lips twisted. "Would you call Freya "lady"?

"Well, yes. That is what her name means," Generys said, looking confused.

Her sister rolled her eyes. "Then pick another! The point is, they don't need titles! Everyone already knows who they are."

The bright hazel eyes turned on me, and they weren't friendly.

"What's your name?" I asked suddenly, realizing that I hadn't heard it yet.

Those perfect eyes slitted. "Why?"

"Stop it," Rhosier said to her. "She isn't going to spell you—"

"How do you know that? How do you know anything about these people? You met them the same time I did!"

"Not him," he nodded at Pritkin. And then he paused, sniffing, and his face crumpled up in a by-now-familiar way. "What is *that*?"

"Oh, no," Alphonse said, getting a whiff. "Oh, hell, no." He looked at me. "Send them back!"

"Enid," Generys gasped, looking at her sister. "What *is* it?"

"You just told her my name!" her sister raged.

"Send them back!" Alphonse said to me. "I am not dealing with that shit again!"

"Shit would smell better," I gasped, my eyes watering, but I did nothing. I was out of juice, being between cycles of the portal, so I looked at Pritkin.

"You fed them," the infuriating man said. "Now they're attached to you."

"Fed who?" Enid demanded, looking about wildly.

"I'll introduce you," I said dryly, facing up to it. "In here, Pinkie," I called, and a moment later, someone came through the door.

But it wasn't Pinkie.

CHAPTER SIXTEEN

Alphonse jumped in front of me just in time, as half of a silver sword was suddenly sticking out of his back. I stared at it, having no choice being only inches away, with the dark blood of a master dripping off the end pointed directly between my eyes. And then I was backing up, and Alphonse was pulling the sword out with a growl and attempting to stick it into the fey who had tried to skewer me.

Only I wasn't sure which one that was as there were suddenly a lot of them. Alphonse's new sword rang on no less than three others, and there were plenty more muscling into the room behind them. It felt like another tide was swamping us, this one made out of flesh.

Alphonse was shoving me toward the rear exit while slashing at whoever tried to get behind him. But the door I'd glimpsed earlier was blocked by a bunch of what looked like beer barrels. They were full and heavy, but I was motivated and started shoving them aside to make an exit, and nobody got past Alphonse, possibly because Pritkin, Rhosier, and the kitchen maid Enid were lighting up our attackers.

The invading horde found themselves met by a barrage of spells that it didn't look like they'd expected, as some of them hadn't even had shields up when they came in. And when you're dealing with the kind of magic that Pritkin was able to put out, that was ill-advised. As demonstrated when one of them went up like a Roman candle, burning to death inside his expensive suit of armor.

Within seconds, liquid fat was gushing out of the joints, the acrid smell of burning meat filled the air, and shields bloomed everywhere. And I moved the last barrel, grunting in effort before turning around to yell at the others and tell them to fall back. Fall back and let's get out of here!

Only I didn't get the chance. I was abruptly shoved against the still-closed door by the blue surface of a ward, hard as glass, which had pushed past my defender and pinned me to the wall like a bug on a pin. It barely gave me a chance to breathe, much less to get the damned thing behind me open!

"Get out!" Alphonse yelled as I was squeezed so tightly by the ward that fighting was impossible. "Shift! Shift!"

Yeah, only I couldn't right now, but I had no way to explain that to him as I also couldn't drag in enough air to speak. Just as he couldn't reach me past the shield between us. Which the fey who had cast it was now walking through because it was his shield; it didn't bind him. He had a naked sword in his hand, and I was unable to move or even turn my head enough to get a good look at the guy who was about to kill me.

Desperate, I tried the first spell I'd ever mastered back when I was at Tony's. It drew on my magic, not the Pythian variety, and it still worked. A rune floated up into the air, almost in the fey's face, causing him to grab at it as if it was a tangible thing.

And at the same moment, a burst of strength hit me, flooding down my arms to my fingertips and making me feel like I could run two marathons back to back. And I had better. Because when its effects wore off, I would be out of it for days, as the spell concentrated every bit of energy I had into one short-lived burst.

That meant I was screwed for tomorrow's challenge, but if I died in here, I wasn't making it anyway. And it looked like I still wouldn't because, even after putting everything I had into it, I didn't budge! And then somebody started shrieking.

It wasn't the fleshy candle guy who had never had the chance. It wasn't our waitress, who had been screaming since the horde came in, although at a much lower decibel level. It wasn't even human.

And it was preceded by a stench so bad, so eye-watering,

so throat-closing and head swimming, that the fey who was about to gut me looked back for a second in disbelief. And my hand, which had been fumbling around the door behind me, finally grasped the latch. And slid the bolt back, feeling like I broke my wrist in the process, but not caring because it worked!

I stumbled into a small stone hallway so quickly that my butt hit the floor. The fey could have followed me, but he was too bust scrabbling at his gorget with a mailed fist, like he couldn't breathe, either. And then it got worse.

The familiar reek of the Horror Twins hit me, causing my eyes to flood and my throat to seize up. And to keep on doing it to the point that it felt puckered because they'd cranked the stench up to eleven. Alphonse had been right, I thought, as my attacker and I clawed at our necks almost in unison; that stench was a bioweapon, and one he was suddenly way more worried about than me.

I scrambled back, heart thudding, lungs screaming, eyes watering so much that I could hardly see. So I didn't know what was going on in there, just that a bunch of people had started hitting the walls, very fast and very hard. I also learned that what I'd thought of as Pinkie's shrillness was nothing to what he could do when really pissed off, as it sounded like a few dozen soprano air horns were going off in my ears, increasing the confusion.

Then Pritkin grabbed my hand while I was still trying to get back to my feet and towed me down the hall, just ahead of a rolling tide of fey, demons, and what appeared to be a bunch of the kitchen staff, all trying to fit through the door at once.

I didn't recognize the fey from dinner, and I should have if they'd been there, as they were hard to miss. Their dark hair was stained purple in a wide swath along the bottom as if they'd dipped it in a bucket of paint, and they wore flashy purple robes over expensive-looking dragon-scale armor. But the kitchen help were a lot more familiar, still in their stained aprons and sooty loincloths.

But instead of trying to grab the redheads and flee as I'd have expected, they were actively attacking the startled-looking light fey, who didn't seem to have expected that any more than I had. I also didn't expect it to work because the kitchen help were armed with pots, pans, and old carving knives against people in elite-tier protection. But there were a lot of them, and they seemed unusually strong, magically speaking, just like the kitchen maid had been.

They also weren't taking prisoners.

"Kill them! Kill the bastards!" Rhosier was yelling like a maniac, and they were damned well trying.

I saw a group of five gang up on one of our attackers as Pritkin dragged me down the hall, and recognized him as the half-asphyxiated fey who had attacked me. And whose armor now ran in a rainbow of sizzling colors. He screamed, having had to drop his shield to fit in here, as the hallway was very narrow.

It hadn't been a great idea, as demonstrated when he collapsed to his knees, a mountain of attackers on top of him. Yet the kitchen staff were taking hits, too. I saw one of the breadbakers hit the floor and hoped she was dead by the time she did so, as a spell was literally eating her alive.

In a couple of seconds, she looked like a filleted fish, with nothing but ribs and a smoking spine still identifiable. I stared at her in horror for a second until a welt of warm, sticky blood hit me as one of the spit-turners staggered back. He collapsed, his torso slashed to pieces, even though he had had a shield up, but the fey's blades were enchanted and had carved right through.

I slipped on someone's blood and went down, and a forest of those enchanted blades followed me. But they were stopped inches away from my head by the ward Pritkin threw over us. Instead, the same sword that had gutted the spit-turner bounced off with all of the wielder's momentum behind it, sending him staggering back into a group of others and spilling them to the ground.

And the spells his friends behind them threw in retaliation did the same, ricocheting off our protection and dropping half of them. It didn't look like they'd dealt with demon armor before. Or knew what to do with it now.

But I didn't know how long the shield would last, as Pritkin had to be drawing on some of that stolen power he'd absorbed from the fey who had kidnapped me. He'd drained them dry, carving a path for me out of that infernal camp. But he was facing what looked like a platoon and had to stretch his shield to cover two.

I should have stayed put, I thought blankly. I should have done what he said and kept my ass in the room and trusted him to know more about this place than I did. Instead, I'd been too busy trying to prove that I could be an asset and had only managed to turn myself into a major liability.

If he died because of me. . .

And he very well might because the fey were still coming.

They'd trampled their fallen underfoot and kept advancing, maybe out of courage or because they had no choice. Not with the Horror Twins pushing into the chamber behind them and unwittingly shoving everyone this way. They were stuck choosing the lesser of two evils, and I guessed that was us because they were coming and coming hard, their weapons ringing loudly on our protection as they hacked away at the ward's surface.

And then we were jumped by three more fey coming from the other direction that neither of us had seen, being too busy looking at the ones pursuing us.

I had a wild cascade of images hit me all at once: Pritkin under a brutal assault, with his shields up but thinning quickly; Alphonse down the hall with a fey under each arm, one of whom was stabbing him in the back repeatedly with a wicked looking knife; Enid fighting several fey at once and looking terrified and exhausted and furious, all at once; and her sister, being thrown over a guard's shoulder, her body hanging limply.

Blood was everywhere, the metallic smell of it in my nose, the sight of it splattering the walls and flying through the air to splash my shield, the warm, sticky feel of it sliding beneath my bare feet. And the fact that I could feel it against my soles meant that Pritkin's shield was dangerously thin. He was going to kill himself protecting me, and that wasn't the plan!

At least it wasn't mine, but it looked like someone else's.

I stepped through the disintegrating shield, allowing it to shink closer to his body to protect him better, and was immediately confronted by the front dozen or so fey coming from the storeroom. Who, for some reason, suddenly weren't attacking anymore. They threw up shields instead, despite there being no room for them, why I didn't know.

Until it hit me: they thought I'd come out from behind the shield because I was about to attack. I wasn't; I just didn't see any reason for us both to die when he might be able to survive without me, but the fey didn't know that. It was a shock; the idea of being considered scary by our enemies was still new and strange, but it must have been the case.

Because when I abruptly raised a hand, they collectively flinched back.

It wasn't a complete bluff. I had a bracelet with two ghostly daggers I'd taken off a dark mage once, which I unleashed as I had nothing else. They were usually too dangerous to use, as they didn't always follow orders very well, if at all. But right now, that didn't matter.

Right now, buying a couple more seconds was good enough.

My blades started sparking off the fey armor all in a line, zigzagging back and forth in front of me like the manic things they were. They couldn't get through the shields plus armor and wouldn't last, as Earth magic rarely did for long in Faerie. But they'd spooked the fey, who were used to the kind of magic Nimue could summon, and suddenly, there was panic all around.

The ones in front were suddenly fighting like hell with

their brothers to get out of the way. They'd clearly decided that the tip of the spear gets blunted and that they'd prefer to be farther down the blade. Or out of the hallway entirely, in this case, where there was nowhere to go.

But their brothers-in-arms thought the same, and the panicked fey were getting pushed back at me like the fight behind us was hemming me in. And was growing as more soldiers had joined from that direction, leaving us caught between a rock and a death place. But then Pritkin looked around wildly, spotted me hugging the wall, and realized why his shield was still up—

And took out his fury at me on the fey.

A moment later, half a dozen fey were dead courtesy of a couple of spells that burned through them, armor and all, and took out two who were either braver or dumber than the rest and were lunging at me. But he'd had to drop his shields and use their remaining strength to do it, and it didn't look like he could raise them again. Which was a problem since somebody had just thrown a spell that took out half the ceiling.

And suddenly, here they came, everyone still on their feet. Whether trying to dodge the rock fall, because shields were suddenly getting smashed by giant falling boulders and debris, or just panicked, I didn't know. But it was all the same to us because we couldn't handle that.

With no shields, we were about to be ground underfoot by friend and foe alike.

And we would have been, except that my power took that moment to come surging back, engulfing me in a glittering wave I could feel in every frantic heartbeat. I dragged it to me, hugging it like a cloak in a snowstorm for a second before sending it back out again in a blast that rippled down the corridor like a sound wave. Only it wasn't just sound that froze as solid as if a new Ice Age had arrived.

Abruptly, everything cut out: screams chopped off halfway through; raised, bloodied fists stopped partway through their arc; falling boulders arrested in the air along with a great billow of dust; and wild eyes gleamed in the sudden stillness with no thought behind them.

Because the brains they were attached to were on pause like everything else.

Even the smell had mostly cut out, as the air molecules weren't whizzing around carrying it anymore. I gasped in a breath I hadn't even realized I was holding and stumbled backward out of the spell, my ears ringing in the sudden silence. Which was why Pritkin's shouted "Cassie!" almost deafened me.

I didn't answer.

I couldn't answer.

My knees wobbled, and I would have fallen, the punch of using that particular spell after the day I'd had immediately wiping me out. Only the artificial strength that my human spell had bought me kept me upright and had allowed me to cast the thing at all. But it was fighting the nausea of that much exertion all at once like somebody suddenly deciding to race halfway up Everest.

I found myself having to fight to breathe, with my heart about to beat through my chest and spots whirling in front of my eyes. My knees buckled, and I staggered against the wall, feeling like I'd taken a punch to the gut. Pritkin grabbed me as he wasn't frozen, having been behind me when I cast my spell, along with a lot of dead men.

And a lone fey, pretending to be dead, waiting for his moment to strike.

I guessed he decided that was it, only to encounter a magically enhanced blow from my companion hard enough to knock him out, even through the dragonscale helmet he wore. He went down, and I just stared at him, the room pulsing around me and threatening to telescope right out of existence. But Pritkin wouldn't let it.

He grabbed me, yelling something I couldn't concentrate on with my blood roaring like Niagra Falls in my ears. And then while I puked my guts out all over the floor, gasped for breath, and did it again. So much for the pie, I thought blearily, as Pritkin yelled, "—*how long?*"

Because yeah, we weren't out of this yet.

"Not long," I gasped because even enhanced strength wasn't much when I was already sitting on empty. "Maybe . . . a couple of minutes?"

"Fuck!"

He waded into the frozen tableaux, which looked like something from a Renaissance painting. I leaned against the wall, exhausted and barely conscious, watching the people on the peripheries of my spell start to move in slow motion. A fist connected with a jaw, sending ripples through the flesh and splitting the lip, causing ruby droplets to spill out into the air; an older kitchen maid, one with salt and pepper hair and a rolling pin, cursed a fancy guard so hard that his face cracked as I watched, like the dirt in a long dry lake bed, with red lines blooming between pieces of flesh; and a spray of blood slowly fountained outward from a knife plunged into a neck.

They were already throwing off my spell, and the rest would follow soon. We needed to go. Only I wasn't sure if I could even manage a stagger.

Pritkin dragged over Rhosier, who had a knife in his side and a bloom of blood on his clothes. I didn't ask what he wanted; I already knew. I gathered what strength remained to me, took the cook's hand, and looked at Pritkin.

"He's going to be . . . in a world of hurt . . . when he comes out."

"We all will be if he doesn't."

It was grim enough that I didn't ask what that meant; I just tightened my grip on the guy's arm and *pulled*. It felt like the threads of my spell pulled back for a moment, fighting me. Or maybe my grip was just that weak. I renewed it and *jerked*, and yanked, and dragged the cook back into real-time what felt like bodily and—

And that was it, that was all I knew, with a sea of gray fog rolling over me like the tide.

CHAPTER
SEVENTEEN

I slowly returned to consciousness thanks to a blast of stench and the strangely familiar sensation of being eaten. Someone else had not yet had that pleasure and was kicking and screaming and panicking beside me. Either because the two of us had ended up in Pinkie's belly or because we were suddenly racing down a series of corridors like our lives depended on it.

And maybe they did.

I couldn't tell. I was woozy, and Enid, my current belly-mate, was hysterical, and her antics were throwing Pinkie off, causing him to hit walls. Or maybe that was the blasts coming from behind us, making colors bloom against his translucent skin.

Or semi-translucent. A piece of digesting octopus floated through the thick membrane around us, confusing my already screwed-up vision. It made me wonder if we were in his stomach or just something adjacent to it, like joeys in a kangaroo's pouch. And then to ask why I cared when I had more pressing concerns here.

But I was drifting in and out of consciousness as oblivion kept trying to drag me back under, and nudging the bit of octopus along was about all that I was up to right then. It obscured the view behind us, but there wasn't much to see, even when it was gone. Just what appeared to be miles of hallways dug out of the mountain and almost pitch dark except for where an occasional lantern flashed by, leaving streamers of light across my vision.

It was strangely hypnotic, except for the fact that we were going stupid fast. To the point that the lanterns were almost a continual blur in the darkness, giving me no idea where Pinkie was taking us or much of anything else. Except that it was really tight in here.

I tried sitting up but had no room, maybe because Pinkie's form had been squashed outward by the burden of carrying two. Making his top, for lack of a better word, push downward, threatening to crush us. It was stupid uncomfortable.

"Can I get a window?" I gasped, pushing against his mucous-covered hide. He opened it up easily enough whenever he wanted to screech at someone, eat something, or tuck a person away in his middle. So, I had the idea that maybe his body was more malleable than a human's and did whatever he —

Yep, that worked.

A porthole opened under my searching hand and widened enough for me to stick my head out. Uh-huh. Yeah.

People were shooting at us.

A lot of people. A lot of very pissed-off, fey-looking people. One of whom suddenly hit a wall and dropped behind when somebody started shooting at *them*.

"What is it?" Erin demanded, fighting with me to be able to see. "What is happening?"

"I think Pritkin is behind them," I slurred, although it was hard to tell.

The fey following us seemed to be riding on something because nobody ran that fast, and they kept zig-zagging back and forth along the corridor, getting in the way of the view. I squinted, and sure enough, their feet weren't moving at all. Instead, something clear and rippling was tearing across the gorgeous tilework while they balanced on top.

There were surfboards, I thought blearily, only there wasn't any water under there. Unless the "board" itself was made out of the stuff. Which wasn't as crazy as it seemed.

The fey could make manlikans, which, in the case of the Green Fey, were man-shaped creations composed of water encased inside an outer ward. The ward also directed the creatures' actions, allowing the fey to use them as servants, ammunition mules, and spies, the latter because they could transform into almost any shape, including one flat enough to fit under a door or between the slats on a shutter. A surfboard seemed child's play next to that.

Only these surfboards were allowing them to catch up—fast.

"Get out of the way!" Enid was beating on me now. "Let me see!"

"Make your own porthole. This one's mine," I said, only to have to pull back inside anyway, because a spell tore by almost close enough to set my hair on fire.

Enid took the opportunity to poke her head out, red hair flying because she'd lost her cap somewhere, and then abruptly ducked back in. She looked at me with wide, shocked eyes as if she hadn't understood any of that, either. So much for getting an explanation, I thought, before she snapped out of her shock and grabbed me.

"That is Prince Emrys back there!"

"Is it? I thought I glimpsed him—"

"They're going to kill him!"

"Are they? Then why's he chasing them?"

More shaking and then a slap across the face, which I was pretty sure I didn't deserve. It did clear my head a little, though. I took another peek.

Yeah, that was Pritkin, and yeah, he was chasing a whole group of fey down the hallway, like Han Solo on the Death Star racing after a bunch of stormtroopers. And like Darth Vader's guys, the fey hadn't noticed that they only had one pursuer or, indeed, that they had any at all. Maybe because they were too focused on killing us.

And then the lights went out.

I blinked in the darkness for a moment, slowly realizing

that it wasn't just the lights that had disappeared. It was the corridor, too, since we were currently traveling through a blue-black tunnel with a low, ominous thrumming sound. It was underwater, something I could tell because the sides were all but invisible, composed of wards between occasional pieces of round, metal scaffolding.

It looked like it should have been on the Nautilus as an observation corridor, only there wasn't much to observe. A few crumbled-looking columns shone ghostly pale in the distance, shimmering behind a watery veil. A school of yellow fish, vivid enough to show up even against all that dim water, flitted by like brightly colored birds soaring through a dark sky. And a bunch of merpeople turned from a sand bar a little way off to watch as we zipped by in our crazy ride.

They were on the left-hand side, where they'd been working on what appeared to be more tunnels through the deep, which were dimly visible as they snaked off into the distance. I stared at the builders, and they stared back, their necks absurdly oversized because their gills were fully open instead of tucked against their skin as they had been in the dining hall. Now they were wafting about like the translucent ends of their fish tails. . .

Snap out of it, Cassie!

I tried to wake up, but it was a struggle, with exhaustion clutching at me like spectral fingers. I concentrated on the metal flooring underfoot, which made slight ringing sounds as Pinkie scurried across it and the occasional lights set into the metal scaffolding. There was nothing else to focus on except the endless indigo water—

And that, I thought, as another spell bolt screamed past us, exploding against the side of the tunnel and taking out one of the lights.

And spooking Pinkie, who was already spooked enough. Causing him to veer off the expansive main tunnel into a smaller side one, part of a scrawling network that resembled a rollercoaster track more than the flat, pedestrian pathway we'd just left. Enid must have thought so, too, because she immediately started clawing at me again.

"Get us out!"

"I don't even know what we're in," I said thickly, pushing at Pinkie's yielding flesh to make myself another convertible. Because I couldn't halfway see like this.

"It's the path for an upcoming challenge! That," she gestured furiously back the way we'd come, "is the passageway into the city from Fountain Court. But this is not and they're not finished with it yet. It isn't stable!"

No kidding, I thought, poking my head and shoulders out of the hole that Pinkie had obligingly made. Enid popped up beside me, breathing hard because, yeah. It was ripe down there.

But it was terrifying up here, with us racing along wobbling corridors that resembled less the transparent, glass-like structure of the main tunnel's wards and more the Jello-like consistency of Pinkie's flesh. They were also moving the same way, with disturbing ripples as we passed.

They looked like they were about to collapse onto our heads—along with thousands of gallons of water—just any moment now. Yet a glance behind showed that it was too late to turn around. A boiling mass of hate was headed our way, and even though Pritkin was still picking off stragglers from behind, the rest—

Were almost on top of us.

"Do something!" The redhead yelled, practically in my ear.

"Why do people keep telling me that?"

"You're the goddess!"

"Why does that only get brought up in times like these?" I snarled, and then I shut up. Because I'd noticed that these walls were not only unsteady, they were porous.

I didn't know if that was because they weren't finished yet or if the Challenge was supposed to involve drowning, which seemed to be a theme around here. Either way, Pinkie was sloshing through water a couple of feet deep that hadn't been there a moment ago. Which turned the crazy course from rollercoaster to the world's most diabolical water slide, with Pinkie less running and more sliding desperately down rollercoaster-worthy angles and taking us with him!

And then I got a phone call.

I didn't notice immediately as we were falling down a ski-slope-like drop, which was also twisting us around like a corkscrew. But the cursing in my ear was too familiar to ignore. "Pritkin?"

"Can you . . . damn it . . . me!"

It sounded like he was breaking up, which would have made sense except for one smallthing: I had no phone.

"How are you doing this?" I asked as a fey, who appeared to have lost his surfboard, went slip-sliding beside us on his back and got zapped by a half-crazed kitchen maid for his trouble.

A burst of static that threatened my eardrum gave me a clue, even before Pritkin's voice came again. "Tapped into . . . translator! Now answer the bloody. . ."

"What?" I said, holding my ear to hear better and being cut off anyway because a bunch of fish hit me out of nowhere, along with a ton of water from the rapidly disintegrating sides of the slide.

"Get out! Get the . . . out!" Pritkin was screaming, and I was gasping and coughing, and Enid was trying to get up a shield to act as a makeshift umbrella, but she must not have been able to concentrate well enough because it kept going down, deluging us again.

I didn't know what Pritkin expected me to do, as I wasn't even sure which way was up. I was awake now, thanks to getting slapped repeatedly in the face by all that cold water, but could barely see anything, as nobody had put lights down here. The only illumination was coming from the dazzling spellfire exploding around us. It wasn't hitting us very often, but that was probably because the fey couldn't see shit, either, and because of the track, which remained the water slide from hell!

Out of other ideas, I reached for my power, even knowing

it was futile. And it was. There wasn't so much as a twinge of magic under my fingertips, either because the portal was turned away at the moment or because I was flat out of the energy needed to channel it.

Either way, we were screwed.

So, I used the only weapon I had left, sending my ghostly knives back to torment the fey some more, and it seemed to help. Maybe because they couldn't half see, making them easy targets, as the water was spurting in everywhere now, to the point that Pinkie was swimming instead of running. That was good as he was faster in the water than on land and bad because we were all about to drown, so none of this mattered!

That must have been what Enid decided because she suddenly let loose on the fey behind us with a storm of magic that had less fury than desperation. It was impressive, to the point that she might have been a war mage in another life had she not been born a slave to the fey. And she wasn't about to go out with even a shred of magic left, as she let it all loose in a glimmering cloud around her, grabbing and binding pieces of it to spells as she went, like an archer pulling arrows from a quiver.

I'd never seen it used that way, not even by the Earthly covens, and for a second, I just stared around at the suffusion in the air. It engulfed us like a haze, following its mistress along the crazy, twisting course like a sparkling, beautiful, magical mist. I held out a hand, still half out of it mentally, and watched it glimmer on my fingertips, like something else I'd seen once, something familiar. . .

And then it sank into my skin, a little piece of power, causing a pulse to go through me.

No, not just magic, I realized; it was her *life force* because that was what human magic was. That was what set them apart from everyone else. Their bodies made magic, the substance that the gods lived off of, and the very thing that I'd recently discovered I could absorb in the same way that my mother once had—

So, I ate some more, pulling it out of the air as I once had back in my court in Vegas, where a strange-looking goat creature had shed enough power to fuel a small star. This wasn't nearly that potent, as the gods had tinkered with him to become something powerful enough to slake even their thirst, but it was something. Something that might save our lives if my power would return, if I could take in enough of her energy to use it, and if I didn't get fried in place before either of those things happened!

I ducked again, feeling heat radiate past me as someone cast blind. They must have; none of us could see a damned thing with the darkness and the water falling and gushing and splashing everywhere, like a midnight ride through the rapids on a furious river. But they threw anyway, probably just hoping to hit something—

And they did.

Just not us.

A section of the ward beside us blew out just as we passed, so I didn't see what happened. But I felt the wave pick Pinkie up and throw him down the tunnel. Although what it was carrying us through, I was no longer sure.

The water slide, or what had been one a second ago, now resembled a limp plastic bag floating in the sea. The only reason it had any shape was the water pouring in and filling in out. We couldn't even reach the surface like this, being trapped by disintegrating wards like the remnants of a spider's web, one that was hauling us down to our doom.

My power took that moment to return, but it was too late to help us this time, especially as I still couldn't use it. Enid's power had been like a sip of cool water in a desert—wonderful but useless to someone dying of thirst. I couldn't shift us back to our rooms; I couldn't make it to the surface; I doubted I could go three feet with how exhausted I—

Three feet.

Three feet.

Three goddamned feet. Damn it, Cassie, think! Why was

that so important?

Because it was ringing through my head like a bell. But said head was also doing loop-de-loops down a disintegrating track while Pinkie's screams echoed in my ears, Enid shook me and yelled something in my face, and fey spells lit up the darkness. And yet, all the while, even my heartbeat was thumping out *three feet, three feet, three feet.*

Or how about three inches, I thought, as that looked like all the width the remaining wards had left. Get to the other side, even if the strain of it knocked me out, and Enid could get us back to the surface. Or Pinkie could before we all drowned.

"Close up," I told Pinkie and pulled Enid back into the stinky cavern.

"What are you doing?" she screeched, which seemed to be her preferred tone.

For once, I didn't mind.

"Something called a Hail Mary back on Earth," I said, watching the skin over our heads heal together as if there'd never been a rift there.

Demons.

You had to love them sometimes.

"What?" she was shaking me again.

"I'm going to try to get us to the open ocean," I explained. "But it will take everything I have left. That means—"

"Open?" she screeched. "You can't break through a Margygr spell! That's why they were given this task—so there can be no cheating on the course!"

"Well, the course seems to be disintegrating pretty well on its own right now—"

"Because it's not finished yet!"

"—and I'm not going to break through it; I'm going to avoid it."

"What?"

"Just get us to the surface, all right? I won't be able to help you after this."

She just stared at me because, yeah. Kind of a lot to ask

of a kitchen maid. But then she surprised me, set her jaw, and nodded.

Well, okay then.

You're up, Cassie, I thought, grabbing for my power and hesitating because this was going to be bad. Bad enough that I could almost hear the Pythian power yelling at me, telling me not to try it, warning me without the words it didn't have by a deep thrumming that echoed through my soul. But I wasn't going out like this, without even attempting to save myself; I'd rather die the hard way than drown like a freaking fish in a net, and so I shifted.

For a moment, there was nothing, just a blinding light and an echoing silence, with every sense I had cutting out simultaneously.

If this was death, it wasn't so bad, I thought.

Not like last time.

And then I didn't think anything except, oh, God. Oh, God. Because the lost senses had returned, all at once, and—

"Oh, God!" I screamed.

I didn't know if I'd made it.

I didn't know anything except pain, the soul-deep, bone resonating, I'd-throw-up-if-I-had-the-energy pain that said I had pushed it too far, that even an inch didn't matter as much as carrying three, that I might have just done like a couple of the old Pythias I'd had to learn about at Gertie's who had disappeared after channeling too much power and were never heard from again.

Probably because they were in little pieces.

"Oh, God," I whimpered.

Someone was yelling at me, but I couldn't tell who, couldn't think, couldn't see, couldn't concentrate on anything except pain—

Until suddenly I could, and realized with a stomach seizing lurch that that had all been for nothing. Because we were out in the dark ocean all right, but ringed by the fey, who had escaped the disintegrating course, too, because they understood this stuff better than I did. And because they'd been rending the half-made spell just fine earlier.

Like they were about to rend us, and I guess they wanted us to see it coming because they'd called up balls of spell light that glimmered over their features like the torches a medieval mob would have carried. I could see it spangling their skin and evil, mirth-filled eyes. They were going to enjoy this. . .

Or not, I thought, as Pinkie lashed out, plunging one of those soft little tentacles straight through the nearest fey's chest.

It emerged from the other side in a cloud of blood and the approximate shape of a spear, his still-beating heart suspended on the tip of it. Triple points for style, Pinkie, I thought dizzily. But it wasn't going to matter in a minute.

And it wasn't. And neither was Pritkin, behind them and letting loose a barrage against the shields the fey casually threw up that seemed to do nothing. I saw his face, staring at me through Pinkie's wavering hide; I saw Enid, searching my eyes, hoping against hope that I had one trick left; I saw my haggard face in the shiny reflection of all those lights and knew I didn't.

And then I saw something else.

I wasn't sure what it was, but it was boiling up from underneath us like a black cloud from an undersea volcano. I couldn't see any flashes of fire or golden, molten rock. I couldn't see anything but a spreading miasma that made the dark water around it look as bright as day.

And then I didn't see anything at all.

CHAPTER EIGHTEEN

The first time I woke up, it was to the smell of something wonderful wafting around my nose. I tried to reach for it, but my hand didn't work. Or rather, it did; it just felt like it couldn't get out from under the boulder that was sitting on it.

And my chest.

And my legs.

And my face.

I also had the impression that my mouth was hanging open at an unflattering angle, but I couldn't seem to close it or stop drooling.

God, whatever that was smelled good!

It tasted good, too, when a spoon of it touched my lips. Like some kind of rich, spicy fish stew, which I could really get into right about now if my mouth would cooperate. It seemed to be having problems, maybe because my brain was still fuzzy, but my stomach was not, and, as usual, my stomach won.

"Don't swallow so fast," Pritkin's voice came to my ears as I got the initial spoonful down and then practically face-planted into the bowl.

I didn't care; it was delicious. I found that my hands did work, if shakily, at least well enough to upend the bowl and gulp down the contents, sight unseen. It tasted amazing, and my grumbly stomach, which hadn't shut up in longer than I could remember, suddenly mellowed out and almost purred.

Warmth and contentment spread through me, and I

clutched the warm, muscly body holding me like I would have a man-shaped teddy bear. He was fuzzy enough. I could tell since my cheek had landed on his chest, which was still bare.

I approved, I decided, and drifted back to sleep without a worry in the world.

The second time I awoke, my man pillow was missing, and I was cold. I was also being talked to by someone I couldn't see because my eyelids were all gummed up. I flailed around ineffectually for a minute.

"They say you're a goddess," someone said almost accusingly.

I tried to say not even close, but my throat didn't cooperate. After several tries, I managed to sit up and sprawled against a rocky wall behind me. It was rough and added a few bruises to my collection, but I didn't care much right then.

"Not even close," I finally got out, rubbing my goopy eyes.

God, I felt like death.

"Then what are you?" the voice asked grumpily. As if someone had pulled a bait and switch on her, and I was not delivering on the promised wow factor.

What else is new? I wondered, shoving limp blonde hair out of my face and looking around for the first time.

It was a real disappointment.

The damp wall behind me was due to my being in a cave, like the one where Pritkin and I had first entered this crazy place. It was big and black and had a mostly smooth floor that rippled out in both directions, with what looked like more caves branching off from either side. I couldn't see much, as I was in a depression with a rocky overhang, but the bits I could make out had clumps of stalactites hanging down menacingly from the shadows.

The cave also had a river or canal running through it a little way in front of me, which was where the voice was coming from. Only no. It wasn't coming from the canal, but from what was floating in the canal, and that . . .

Wasn't right. I blinked at it, and it blinked back out of a

large, fishy eye. The eye was dark blue, like the fins on the highly arched, ridged neck and the ones wafting around a curled tail poking out of the water and...

And I just sat there for a moment, like a broken doll, staring at what appeared to be a gigantic seahorse bobbing nonchalantly along the side of the canal.

I did not know what to say to a giant seahorse. It didn't say anything else, either. It just breathed at me, not out of its elongated face but out of the many small mouth-like things on its neck.

Gills?

They were probably gills. At least, they fluttered a lot. They didn't help my confusion.

I couldn't see the bottom of its body as it was hidden by the side of the canal, which was built up like a quay. But what I could see was enough. And considering that all the other oversized/mutated fish things I'd encountered since coming here had been lethal, I think I can be excused for the small mewl that escaped my mouth when my brain finally woke up enough to panic.

Where was Pritkin? Why had he left me on a damp quayside all alone? And what was that *smell*?

I got the answer to that last one when Pinkie muscled his way in front of me, not liking my sound of distress. Which was how I noticed belatedly that the horse-sized seahorse had a rider. A small, very non-threatening rider, who jumped off onto the quay looking pissed.

Pinkie made a small screech of defiance and blew up to about twice his usual size, obviously ready to throw down. It was somewhat like watching the hackles rise on a dog only it was slimy fat instead, which was why I took a stubby tentacle to the face. But I fought free of it, got my hands on the mass of gelatinous hide, and pushed.

And went nowhere because Pinkie wasn't budging. That was a problem since his squashy backside had glorped into the slight depression in the rock that I had been stowed in and all but filled it up. Leaving me suffocating under a mass of stinky pink blubber that appeared to have forgotten that humans need to breathe.

"Come on, dude, I'm dying here," I gasped and pushed some more. The small pissy creature, who I could vaguely see on the other side of Pinkie's semi-transparent ass, was getting pissier by the moment, watching a "goddess" wrestle an overly protective demon for freedom.

And losing.

That wasn't entirely my fault. Pinkie had gotten two good meals into him since we arrived and possibly more if he'd been snacking on a fey, and I would not put snacking on a fey beyond him. He did not appear to be picky. And it had given him additional strength.

I, on the other hand, felt like an elephant was sitting on me, and most of that wasn't Pinkie's fault.

After my recent forays into magical brinkmanship, I was going to be wiped out for who knew how long, and that meant I wasn't going anywhere, regardless of whether my power came by to say hi or not.

I sighed and gave up, making myself a small pocket to breathe through by pushing away the nearest chub with my outstretched arms and resigning myself to looking at the world through a bunch of lard.

My conversation partner, however, did not. "You heard her," she said, sounding less like the woman I'd initially taken her for and more like a girl. "Move!"

Pinkie did not move.

"He's, uh, he's kind of dangerous," I said. "You should keep your distance."

A snort of derision was all I received back. "I wrestle things far more dangerous than him every day," she said and started pushing.

And to my surprise, this time, Pinkie went. Maybe because he'd gotten a good look at the kid and decided I wasn't in danger after all. Or maybe because the seahorse took that moment to give a high-pitched shriek worthy of Pinkie himself, who got curious and headed over there. But anyway, I could breathe.

"Why does it still stink?" the girl demanded.

She was pretty and did not look like she belonged here except for the ears. She had a head full of cornrows as black as her eyes, a light brown face, and a slight grin as she watched me attempt to struggle to my feet, covered in goo. Put her in jeans, a t-shirt with some band's name, and a knitted cap, and she could be a freshman at any high school.

Instead, she was wearing a tight-fitting, bluish-gray tunic and trousers, almost matching the color of her ride, and made from some material that looked like it had subtle glitter embedded in it. She'd accessorized with some scaley gauntlets and enough necklaces to make Mr. T jealous, although that counted as casual wear around here. She was also barefoot, but I was getting used to that.

I finally slimed my way to a more-or-less upright position, dripping, and tried to slough off some of what Pinkie had shed all over me, but mostly failed. Now, I had two forms of protection: dragonscale and a stench worthy of a large pile of rotten meat. Great.

And then what the girl had said registered.

"What do you mean, still?"

She shrugged. "I hit it with a spell, the one I use on the stables when they get rank. It should have helped."

"Pinkie, uh, exudes stuff all the time. So that sort of thing doesn't work."

"Well, I've smelled worse," she said, eyeing our two companions. They seemed to be getting along famously, the giant wad of demonic phlegm and the oversized seahorse, and were happily screeching at each other.

The noise echoed around the cave, but nobody came running. Unless they were going in the other direction. Couldn't blame them there.

"I'm Cassie," I told the girl and stuck out a hand before

realizing that it was dripping, too.

She rolled her eyes. "I know. I'm Rieni. I was sent to fetch you."

"To where?" I asked a little apprehensively.

"Grandmother wants a word."

"Is that . . . a good thing?"

"No."

I sat back down.

"Prince Emrys is with her," she said wryly and had the fun of watching me clamber back to my feet again.

And then onto her seahorse, which appeared to be the only way through the chambers of interlinked caves, some of which hedged the canal pretty tightly. Only that wasn't nearly as easy as mounting a horse. As I discovered when I almost fell into the canal.

Rieni grabbed me at the last minute, but that still ended with me back on the pier instead of on the beast, which was eyeing me with the same disdain as its master.

"I've never done this before," I told her, although that was pretty obvious.

"You're a *goddess*."

"Half and I mostly got the human stuff."

She watched me with dark, disbelieving eyes. "And yet you came to this court?"

"Didn't get the smarts, either."

She huffed out what might have been a laugh—or a snort of derision, the jury was still out—and then jumped back onto the quayside and pushed.

My dragonscale-covered backside wasn't as limber as I would have liked, my currently noodle-like arms weren't as strong, and the damned seahorse kept bobbing about, making itself a moving target. And sometimes moving away and forcing Rieni to leash him while also shoving at me. But I somehow got onto what could in no way be called a back because it was either that or face plant into the water, and I'd had enough freaking water.

And then I just stayed there, clinging to the long spine, because there was no broad back to provide an easy perch. Instead, the creature was essentially perpendicular, leaving me hanging on desperately, like balancing on the side of a ladder. A moving ladder.

"No, no, not like that! You're covering his gills, so he can't breathe," Rieni said as I and the seahorse drifted away from the dock again.

"That part's in the air!" I said, panicking because the quayside was getting too far away. And because I was pretty sure that seahorses couldn't breathe air.

Only to be proven wrong, at least where these were concerned.

"They breathe both air and water, but not with your hand there. Now move it!" she said, and I moved it because she was a little drill sergeant in the making.

And then almost fell into the canal.

Again.

Rieni muttered something before pulling my ride back over by the reins, settling my butt onto a shelf-like seat I hadn't noticed because I'd been too busy holding on, and strapping my legs into knee-high stirrups. The saddle that I finally realized the creature was wearing had two short seats that protruded outward and, along with the stirrups, did give some stability. But it took work to stay on.

Especially when the beast started forward at just a clicking sound from Rieni, who had jumped onto the seat above mine with effortless grace. It was something that her mount shared and began taking us down the canal with an undulating, smooth glide that would have made an actual horse green with envy. I was green, too, but for a different reason.

The world we were passing through was entirely underground but not dark. A sparkly emerald ribbon ran along the cave's ceiling that I hadn't been able to see from under the rocky overhang at the quayside, except for some shifting light. But now daylight speared down in stretchy fingers from high above, tinting us vaguely green and causing my armor to run as if it had been dipped in paint.

Only it wasn't paint; it was daylight filtering through a suspended river.

"Runs all the way to the throne room," Rieni said, glancing back and noticing my awed expression.

"Is that where we're going?"

"No."

I didn't ask anything else. She didn't seem interested in conversation, and I was too busy staring upward. It looked like a Chihuly art fixture but was far more beautiful. I'd seen something like it once at the Circle's HQ in Stratford, but it had been a pale imitation, as if someone had seen a Michelangelo sculpture once and tried to reproduce it from memory. The Circle might have found someone with fey magic—they even had a few part fey in their ranks—to do the spell, but this. . .

No, they hadn't replicated this.

It was equally breathtaking and terrifying, as the magic holding it up also held back a lot of water. Having almost drowned repeatedly at this point, my body tensed up at even the thought of all those millions of gallons falling on top of us, especially when I couldn't shift. It was enough to make me wonder if Nimue's people were able to swim up under an enemy and just . . . jerk them down.

I was beginning to wonder why anyone in their right mind would attack this place, between the water and the scary things in the water. Then I looked around at the passing sides of the canal and doubled that thought. Because while I'd been daydreaming, the scenery had changed.

I guessed we had entered the stables Rieni had mentioned because they did reek a little. Or maybe that was Pinkie churning up the water behind us. I didn't care either way because both sides of the canal had open-sided stalls built into them like boat docks, only what was in them. . .

Wasn't boats.

"Oh," I said loudly enough that Rieni looked back over her

shoulder. And, for the first time, appeared vaguely approving.

"They're magnificent, aren't they?"

"Beautiful," I murmured, trying to look like the towering creatures on both sides of the suddenly narrow seeming canal weren't scaring me crapless. But at the same time, I meant it. Giant seahorses, each two or three times as big as our current mount, reared up on either side of us, and they were much more flashy and raucous than the comparatively small and demure version we were clinging to.

I couldn't even imagine riding one of them. And not just because of their size, which would have left me a small lump hanging off the great hide like a remora. But because of that, I thought, as one of them turned and snapped at us, biting the air just above my face.

I didn't bleat that time. I just stared—at huge, wild, golden eyes; at a zebra-striped hide, black and off-white and with the pattern going everywhere in a wonderfully epic scrawl; at the massive bony protrusions spearing out of its neck that looked like bare tree branches, so many and so thick that I didn't see how anyone could ride him if they would even dare to try; and at the aggressive way he tossed his head. And that was before the deceptively tiny-looking mouth opened unbelievably wide, showcasing pointed teeth that I was pretty sure seahorses weren't supposed to have.

But this was Faerie, where everything could and would kill you at the first opportunity, so of course they did. They would have been eaten long ago otherwise. But Rieni didn't appear impressed.

"Shut it, Golygus," she said, smacking the great neck. "He knows how pretty he is," she said, rubbing the spot she'd just made and laughing. "That and being our champion makes him high and mighty."

Golygus took this rebuke better than I'd have expected, maybe because of the handful of shrimp that accompanied it, pulled out of a bag at Rieni's waist.

"Your champion?" I asked.

"Fastest ever, three years in a row," she said proudly. "Only no one can handle him but me. I raised him from a fry."

I assumed that meant a baby but didn't have a chance to ask, as the champion was trying to eat Pinkie. But all that got him was a punch in the nose from one of the little tentacles, which seemed to work much like Rieni's slap. The aggrieved-looking monstrous creature tossed his neck wildly and postured but didn't try to tear Pinkie a new one, to my surprise.

And most of the rest of the high-spirited creatures seemed more interested in the shrimp than they did in me or my smelly companion. Rieni tossed a few here and there as we passed, mainly to the best behaved, and soon, all of them had settled down in the hope of a treat. I stared at two-story-tall giants hunkering down and trying to behave themselves so that the tiny fey child might bless them with a shrimp and wondered if I was dreaming.

But no, one even leaned down to nuzzle Rieni's shoulder affectionately as we passed. It was a bright neon pink specimen with soft-looking protrusions that wafted about like delicate scarves instead of the thorn-type that Golygus had boasted. They were blue shading to pink at the bottoms, and I found myself wanting to touch one to see if it felt as soft as it looked.

I didn't.

I'd learned a few things over the past month in Faerie.

But it was hard to keep that in mind as the procession continued. If this wasn't the royal stables, it should have been, I decided, staring at the beauty on display. That included a gorgeous iridescent green with bony orange protrusions; several more of the flashy zebra-striped ones, with eyes of sapphire, gold, or emerald green; and a burnt sienna, super bumpy one, with skinny, off-white stripes running across the nobby hide and a "mane" that looked like a little girl's ponytails gathered up and down its spine, where the skin had pulled into tufts that ended with hair-like filaments.

I tried to pick a favorite but couldn't. I loved a dark purple one with lavender on its belly, a brilliant neon blue with a pale green underside, and an eye-searingly yellow with delicate blue fins. Of course, they all had fins, with some on their heads like mohawks that perked up as we floated by and others on their backs and along their curled, prehensile tails. A few of the latter reached up from underwater to hesitantly stroke Pinkie or me as we passed, obviously as curious about us as we were about them.

"They're amazing," I told Rieni, with awe that I didn't try to conceal, which seemed to mollify her a bit.

"I'm glad you think so. You'll be riding one soon enough."

"I'm already riding one," I said, half disbelieving, as a pale green reached out a tail to brush filmy fins over my extended hand. I closed my grip slightly as the softer-than-silk mass trailed over it, like a handshake from another world. And grinned, pleased to a ridiculous degree and equally enchanted.

These creatures were amazing!

"No, I mean in the race," Rieni said, tossing the last of her shrimp to the green one who had greeted me so nicely.

"What?" I asked.

"The next challenge," she said impatiently. "If you and the prince are competing, you'll be riding. It's a *race*."

I just sat there, or clung there to be more accurate, staring at her. Until she harrumped like an old man and turned back around. And kicked our ride into high gear.

"I hope you're a quick learner, goddess," she shouted as we tore through the water like a speedboat. "They're a bit hard to control!"

I would have had a reply to that, but my brain was busy screaming.

CHAPTER NINETEEN

T he journey ended in a rush of water that surged onto a dock ahead of us like waves crashing onto a pier and splashed a group of dignified-looking types who were slightly less so after being drenched. Seahorses stopped on a dime, but the wave didn't and also soaked me pretty well with the backwash. Maybe it'll help the smell, I thought, as I labored up some stairs after Rieni.

Who was being roundly chewed out by someone.

The people here looked more like the polished perfection of those in the palace and less like the beaten-down workhorses in the kitchen. I didn't see anyone who couldn't have bought a house with what they were wearing. A big house.

The robes that weren't drenched were in fluttering silk so gossamer-fine that they looked like a captured breeze. Gems, rings, and shiny things decorated the robes and the people wearing them, including enough strings of pearls to make a jeweler weep. And there were elaborately braided hairstyles on men and women alike, which had weathered the dunking pretty well and made me wonder if that's why braids were preferred here.

People did seem to get soaked pretty often.

But none of them looked happy to see me, making me wonder if taking rides with random nautical babies had been my best move. But then I spied Pritkin. He was heading for us down a wide corridor to the left and being trailed by the Brain, who had flushed a darker shade of blue than usual and was all puffed up like a pissed-off bouncer.

That probably explained why everyone was giving them a wide berth.

Pritkin looked like he'd just come from the fight himself, with the blingy scuba pants torn, his hair rumped, and what looked like slashes of dried blood on his bare chest. I hoped they were someone else's and weren't covering wounds, but I didn't get a chance to find out. Because I was suddenly swamped by more people I didn't know coming out of the same girthy tunnel.

They'd exited alongside Pritkin, but I'd been too relieved to see him to notice. Until they surged ahead, flying at me like overdressed bats all in black, and had me backing up toward the edge of the pier and Pinkie lashing out and thumping them wildly with his stubby "arms."He hit pretty hard, I thought, as a couple of courtiers who had gotten in the way went stumbling backward.

A voice cut through the din, saying something in a low but penetrating tone that my translator didn't know, and the black-clad army peeled off. And reformed into a muttering wad a little way off that I couldn't see too well because the darkness of their robes seemed to absorb the light around them, leaving them looking like a bunch of fey-shaped black holes. But, judging by the occasional flash of weapons, they were probably guards.

"Well, you shouldn't have been standing on the edge, should you?" Rieni was saying to someone, her voice matter-of-fact and unperturbed by the chaos. "You know how Starlight is."

"Starlight," the tall man standing near her huffed. "I know how *you* are, and you took your sweet time!"

"She wanted to see the stables," Rieni said before being led off by the ear.

"Are you all right?" Pritkin asked, coming up alongside me.

"Think so." I managed to keep my voice level. "Where are we, exactly?"

"Long story. Don't kneel."

"What?"

But that was all the help I got before being sized up by a woman I immediately understood was A Big Deal. At her arrival, everyone else fell silent and got out of the way, even when having to move faster than dignity allowed. And then they all went down on one knee, except for me and Pritkin, which made me feel awkward and somewhat ill-mannered.

But if I'd learned anything since arrival, it was to do what Pritkin said.

So, I stood there, dripping in my smelly armor, and wondered if smiling was also off the list.

I decided against it since she wasn't.

She looked like someone who didn't use those particular muscles too often, but I had to admit it worked for her. She was tall, slender, and darker skinned than Rieni, almost like the beautiful face had been carved out of a piece of ebony. Her features were lovely, but it was her hair that really drew the eye, being drawn back from her face in tiny braids that were grouped into a ponytail that cascaded to the floor.

All the way to the floor.

And then some.

I had never seen hair that swept the ground, especially not after being braided, and found myself trying to figure out how long it must be for that to work before snapping out of it. Damn it, Cassie, this isn't a joke! Her clothes alone told me that much.

They were beautiful even for this place, although there were no elaborate, seed pearl bedecked robes here. Or even the diaphanous, only sort-of-there gowns I'd seen at dinner. She was wearing armor of the tightfitting, leather variety I'd seen on fey archers who wanted protection that didn't impede their range of movement.

That type was usually spelled for added protection, which I assumed was true here, as little round cabochon stones of a milky hue decorated the suit at the joints and around the collar, all of which abruptly flashed red when she approached me.

She glanced at some near her wrist and then back up at me. "Stand away from her," she told Pritkin, and to my surprise, he did, backing off about ten steps.

The lights didn't change, except to start blinking rapidly as she approached.

I held my ground, knowing a test when I saw one but not knowing what it was. Other than freaky when she put out a hesitant hand and paused. And then, as if steeling herself, she grasped my shoulder firmly.

The lights abruptly went solid gold, and the crowd gasped theatrically as if rehearsed. The woman, however, did not. If anything, she looked resigned, as if she'd expected that.

Her hand dropped, and she shot me a look that could only be described as venomous. "You don't look like your mother," she said, then abruptly whirled and walked away.

* * *

"We don't have a lot of time," Pritkin said, his voice low, as we were hustled down the same wide tunnel in the rock that everyone had come out of. "Lady Bodil didn't like your mother. Don't bring her up."

"I wasn't planning—wait. She knew my mother?"

"She knew them all, the gods, that is," Pritkin said grimly. "She's one of the oldest here at court."

"She doesn't look it."

"She has god blood, but not Nimue's. She can't vie for the throne as a result. She has a champion, but he isn't doing well, and nobody thinks he'll win. We're up for his replacement."

"What?" I asked, startled. "Why?"

"I've been able to talk her into considering the idea—"

"*You* have?" I said, slightly startled, because Pritkin had many gifts, but diplomacy wasn't one of them.

"—but the outcome is still in the air. We have to—"

But I didn't find out what we had to do because we were suddenly there, branching off the hallway into an expansive room that not only wasn't a throne room but looked more like a stable. Only without the straw on the ground because these horses bedded down in the canal outside. Yet everything else was pretty much what you'd expect.

A row of the unusually long seahorse saddles was hanging on the wall, and another was either under repair or in construction on a tall wooden frame. Rough wooden tables held leatherworking tools, piles of bridles and reins, and lengthy, fishing pole-type things with shiny crystals on the end that I couldn't name and that nobody felt like explaining. Stalls were scattered about the walls, why I didn't know as I didn't see any land animals here, except for an Earth-like cat in a corner who couldn't be bothered to do more than yawn at us as we all streamed in.

And went toward a small area in the back with a beat-up-looking desk, a couple of chairs, and a small wooden half-wall separating it from the rest of the room, like an office for the stable master. Who took her place behind the desk and attempted not to glare at me. She mostly failed but I was used to that by now.

"We have to come to an understanding," she began, but I wasn't having it.

I'd just woken up, I was exhausted, still hungry, fairly cold, and very uncomfortable in my smelly armor, not all of the stank of which was Pinkie's fault. Not to mention that nobody had explained a damned thing! I was also wondering why we needed to risk our lives to put a woman on the throne who I didn't even know when we already had Pritkin.

But I decided to start with something a little less combative.

"Where are Rhosier and the others? Are they okay? And how did we get out of the kitchen? And who were those men who attacked us? And why did they attack us? I thought challengers were supposed to be off-limits!"

Bodil looked at Pritkin, and he looked back. "I said that it would simplify things if she was here when we talked," he commented, pretty mildly for him.

"You know damned well why she wasn't!" Bodil's hand hit the desk hard enough to make a baby bridle slide onto the floor.

"I'm not my mother," I said, forgetting Pritkin's advice. And immediately regretted it when her dark eyes flashed fire.

Like, literally. They went red momentarily, and I didn't back up only because I was sitting down.

Shut up, Cassie, I told myself. Just shut the hell up.

"And I know that how?" she hissed. "From what I hear, you may as well be!"

"And what does that mean?" I asked because my mouth wasn't obeying my brain's frantic signaling. My mouth had woken up and chosen violence. My mouth was going to get us killed because there was no way I could shift us out of there.

Pritkin must have thought the same because his hand clenched in warning on the one I had resting on the chair arm. But to my surprise, Bodil just answered the question. "You look like a human," she said, her eyes raking me up and down. "Soft, weak, young. Not much older than my daughter's daughter, yet all dressed up in dragonscale like a warrior. How many years have you?"

"I've already told you," Pritkin said. "That doesn't—"

"It matters to me!" she turned on him fiercely. "What you're asking—"

"Wait, you asked for this?" I said, looking at him. "Why?"

"Why do you think?" Green eyes blazed into mine, showing that he wasn't as calm as he appeared. "You were almost assassinated—what? Five times in less than a day? We need protection! Bodil can guarantee our safety—"

"Outside of the challenge," she specified.

"Which is all we could ask," Pritkin said as if this was a done deal.

"Five?" I frowned. "It was twice—"

"It was more than that just in the damned ballroom! Not to

mention that creature when we came in—"

"You can't count the Not-Whale. That was a challenge—"

"The what?" That was Rieni, coming in with a large brown leather bag held loosely in her arms and sitting on the edge of the desk.

"The thing we fought in the first challenge," I said, glancing at her. And then watching the bag she held, which, disturbingly, appeared to be moving. "Or when I came in, Pritkin was already here—"

"Who?" she looked confused.

"Uh, Prince Emrys, and why is that . . . squirming?"

"Babies," she said, as if that explained anything. "And are you talking about the Cetus?"

"The what?" It was my turn to be confused and disturbed because something was peeking.

I scooted my chair back a bit.

She laughed and plopped the bag in my lap. "It's okay. You can babysit for a while."

"Rieni!" her grandmother—at a guess—snapped.

"It's okay; she likes them," the girl said, skipping out.

I was getting the impression that Rieni did whatever the hell she wanted and got away with it because the fey had children approximately once every millennium and tended to spoil them. Although the Green Fey had rigged the system with all the humans they'd imported as breeding stock. Only maybe she wasn't half and half.

Those didn't tend to dress so well.

"Some do," Bodil said, sitting back in her chair and not even trying to hide that she could hear my thoughts. "And yes, I can read you—partly. One of the perks of being a half-breed," her lips twisted.

"Didn't get that one," I said distractedly because the "babies" were squirming on my lap. I was never so glad to have armor on, I thought, wondering if they were venomous. And then wondering how I could have thought so when one stuck out a tiny, adorable snout.

"They're dangerous," Pritkin warned.

"Not at that age," Bodil said, watching as a dozen more little faces joined the first, having pushed back the bag's flap and begun peering out curiously.

They couldn't have been more than an inch or so tall, to the point that I could have wrapped one around my finger as a ring. But they were every color of the rainbow, colorful baby seahorses that I was pretty sure should be in water somewhere, only nobody seemed bothered about it. Or about the fact that they were now climbing all over me, hopping from the pouch to my armor, where they paused to stare at their reflections curiously.

"Um," I said. "A little help?"

"You want our army," Bodil said. "For your war against the gods."

It came out of nowhere, although she had warned me that she was a mind reader. Having spent plenty of time with Mircea, who was far more proficient at that sort of thing than he let on, it didn't surprise me. But it was annoying.

"Aren't they going to dry up or something?" I said a little desperately. I did not want one getting under my armor. I did not!

"She's using the diversion to read your thoughts, Cassie," Pritkin said. "It's easier when you're distracted."

"So, get them off me, then!"

But he was too busy staring down the ancient fey. "This war will come to you, sooner or later. Better that you have allies when it does."

"So says the man desperate for troops he can use as cannon fodder!"

"Don't put your sins on us," Pritkin snapped. "And you know your people cannot stand against what's coming. If the gods return—"

"They're already here, it would seem," she hissed, staring at me. I was too busy scooping little runaways back into their rather slimy pouch—and why was everything slimy—to look up, but I could feel the weight of those eyes on me. "You expect us to gamble everything on a war led by one of their spawn—"

"Careful," Pritkin warned.

"—when there's no way of knowing she's any better! Her mother wanted to rid herself of the competition, too, so that she might rule alone, queen of all she surveyed! Why should I believe the daughter to be any different?"

"Because you have eyes?" Pritkin said, disbelieving. "Look at her!"

They both did.

I looked up, more than a little frustrated, with a tiny seahorse dangling off a curl in front of my eyes because the things jumped like baby frogs! I tried to look harmless, which shouldn't be too hard at the moment. But Bodil wasn't convinced.

"Good camouflage," she told me with a vicious smile. "But your reputation precedes you. Killer of great Apollo, of even mightier Ares, and now of Athena, or so I hear. Oh, yes, whispers from the dark fey lands reach us, even ones from the outer world. They tell stories that I did not know whether to believe until I met you."

"I thought I was a child playing dress up," I said because she didn't get it both ways.

"So did I until I peered into your mind."

"Then you should know—I didn't kill the gods, not any of them—"

"Not directly. But a general doesn't strike the final blow, does he? He makes the battle plan and leaves it to others to bear the risks—"

"I don't ask other people to fight for me!"

"Yet you're asking us," she snarled. "Or expecting to command us when the fey princeling you've found and wrapped around your finger wins the kingdom for you. But he won't. My champion will—"

"Your champion will get himself killed!" Pritkin said. "Out of the water if not in it—"

"He hasn't been targeted!"

"Because nobody thinks he's a threat! I wouldn't target him, either!"

Those amazing eyes flashed red again. "But you would target me. Suborn me to get the help you need to win it all, and then what? Tell me, Pythia," she turned on me suddenly like a striking viper. "Where are those who did kill the gods for you? What happened to them?"

I blinked at her but didn't try to lie. I wouldn't have anyway, but it was impossible with those eyes on me. They held something, a weight, a power, or maybe just so much pent-up emotion that they were hard to meet.

"Ares killed Apollo," I said. "Or was in the process of it when a man—a human—sent one of his own spells back at him. As you should know."

And she should; the Green Fey had known the man in question well. Old Wales had been one of their favorite hunting grounds for slaves, where a lively magical community provided seemingly unlimited witches for their breeding program. And where a king named Arthur had been trying to stop it and failed, although he *had* stopped Ares.

One could argue that that was worth his legend alone.

"I did," she said dryly. "And now he's dead—"

"That was hundreds of years ago!"

"He was taken down by members of his court years after the battle," Pritkin added. "You know that—"

"What I know is that I do not intend to share his fate or that of others who have helped this sweet little thing to cut a swath through her enemies and paid the price for it. Take them."

That last was said with the same cold indifference of most of her conversation, even when furious, to the point that I was surprised when the black-robed guards swamped us.

Not again, I thought, right before the lights went out.

CHAPTER TWENTY

I woke up on a hard, furry chest for the second time in one day, and it was still not fun. My mouth was dry, my body ached, and I felt like I'd been drugged. Or hit in the head repeatedly with a large, padded hammer.

I felt something else, too.

"Have to pee," I gasped, and the chest underneath me moved around before my hand was placed on the side of what felt like a wooden bucket. Opening bleary eyes, I saw that, yep. Bucket. "Seriously?" I asked Pritkin, who was sharing what looked suspiciously like a cell with me.

"Fey accommodations for prisoners are not luxurious," he confirmed.

That was an understatement. The little room was about the size of a large bathroom, which was ironic considering that it didn't have a toilet. It did have a rocky floor to match the walls and all of it was in the local black stone, which left it dark and foreboding.

That wasn't helped by the fact that there was only a single window set high in one wall with bars across it to provide light, but that mostly just striped the darkness. And another, smaller opening in the door, although it seemed to face a dark corridor because nothing was coming in that way at all, and nobody had left us a lantern. They hadn't left a cot, blanket, or water source, either, just a plain, slightly damp, black room with some straw on the floor and a bucket.

Goddamn, I hated the fey.

"Prisoners or captives?" I snarled. "What's her name kidnapped us!"

"Lady Bodil, and so it would seem."

"What's the point?" I demanded, stumbling to my feet and finding a corner where I could use my bucket. "Locking us up so we can't beat her pathetic champion? Like somebody else won't?"

"I assume that she is planning to cheat," Pritkin said, leaning his head against the wall and closing his eyes. "And doesn't want us interfering."

"Obstructing a champion is supposed to be off-limits!" I said, only to have him snort derisively.

Because yeah.

Faerie.

"So, are you going to get us out?" I asked when I'd finished and walked back over. The stone walls looked pretty thick based on the amount of rock visible on the window ledge, but Pritkin had an app for that.

Or, to be more precise, a fey ability that he'd inherited from his mother, who'd stolen it from his father before imprisoning him in a tree and running off to Faerie. Where she'd been sure that her command of all four elements would cause her to be welcomed with open arms at court. Spoiler alert: it hadn't.

She'd been a mongrel mix of human, fey, and god blood since her mother, Igraine, was Nimue's child with a human. Nimue had wanted a leader to manage the slave trade she'd started on Earth but didn't have confidence in any of her courtiers. So, she'd given birth to one and sent her to Earth with lofty lies about earning her place at court through her devotion to the cause.

Once there, Igraine had married another human, and their twice-mongrel daughter Morgaine was therefore considered beneath contempt at court regardless of who her grandmother was. But she'd had ambitions, and they hadn't included dying on Earth like her mother. Ambitions that had made her an abomination as far as the fey were concerned.

To improve her status, she had co-opted their abilities by stealing them through sex magic with a demon lord. Who had stolen them in turn from the various part-fey women with whom he'd knocked boots through the years. And the half-demon child that had resulted was something the fey didn't even have a name for.

"Abomination" fell seriously short in Pritkin's case.

So, prince or not, he'd been left to struggle and hopefully die on Earth. And the few times he'd made his way here through the years, being eager—at first—to learn about his fey heritage, had not gone well. It looked like nothing had changed.

"Enchanted," he said briefly.

"What?"

"The walls. And the window. And the door. This is one of the storerooms for the stables, but they've held fey here before. The entire room is warded."

"But what about demons? Or mages?" I squatted down and poked him. "You must have something!"

That won me a vivid green look. "And Pythias?" he said pointedly.

I sat down on my metal ass. "I'm tapped out. Even if the portal gods favor me, I'm going nowhere for at least a day."

"Then that is a problem."

I felt my suspicions rising. He sounded entirely too Zen for Pritkin, who was not known for his patience or his ability to sleep in the middle of a crisis. Yet he appeared to be dozing off again.

"And you're perfectly fine with this because?" I demanded.

"I'm . . . conflicted."

"Meaning what?"

"Meaning that, in here, you're likely to survive. Bodil isn't entirely benign, but she isn't likely to murder us. She was the one who helped us get away from that massacre in the deep."

"*She* helped us?" She'd looked more likely to stick a knife in us to me.

"Her people did," Pritkin clarified, his eyes still closed, and I wondered if that was what that ominous-looking cloud had been, some of Bodil's black-robed guards. "Rhosier called them, but they didn't have time to check with her first." His lips twisted. "Probably just as well."

"A cook called the guards of a noble house?" I asked, not understanding anything. And when he didn't answer, I poked him again.

Damn it, wake up!

Pritkin sighed and sat up, realizing that I wasn't going to let him sleep. "She hit me with an extra dose of Somnolence," he said, rubbing a hand over his face. "It's starting to wear off but keeps trying to pull me back under."

"Can't you do something to negate it?" Counterspells were drilled into war mages until they were almost automatic. I'd have expected him to have used one already.

He pinched the bridge of his nose for a moment and then shook his head as if trying to clear it. "No. You're not the only one who's tapped out."

I felt my eyes widen. "But . . . all that energy, all that magic that you took from a whole camp full of fey—"

"Gone. I'm surprised it lasted this long."

"But there were *hundreds of fey*—"

"And hundreds more harrying me the whole way here and ever since I arrived. It's gone, Cassie. I used the last of it, along with most of my own magic, in the fight in the kitchen."

His head slumped back against the rock again, and I sat there for a second, feeling stunned. Pritkin didn't run out of magic. The demon blood he so deplored had made him far stronger than any war mage I'd ever met.

Even on a bad day, he was a *tank*.

But it looked like the tank . . . was pooped.

And then the rest of what he'd said hit me. "Wait. *Wait.* You were chasing down a couple dozen fey *on your own* while practically out of magic?" He cracked an eye and just looked at me. "*Why?*"

"You know why."

Yes, I did! Which only made it worse. If they hadn't been

so dead set on taking me down, that little stunt would have gotten him killed! And it wouldn't have even helped me and—

And then I was hitting him, which didn't make much of an impact as I was currently as weak as a kitten. And found my wrists captured after a second anyway, which only increased my fury. "You could have *died!*"

"So could you." The green eyes were practically neon, never a good sign. "And as you said once to me, why is it all right for you to risk your life every moment of the day, but I can't risk mine to save you?"

"There were three dozen fey! You weren't going to save me! You were going to die alongside me!"

"And you think I wouldn't prefer that?" I abruptly found myself on my back, with an angry war mage on top of me. And, okay, I couldn't complain about sleepiness now. Pritkin looked like he had when he'd burst into that kitchen, having tracked me down after our last fight.

And yeah.

We hadn't had a chance to talk that out, had we?

"You think a crown means a damn to me if you aren't there to share it?" he demanded. "What do you think I'd do if you die? Have you ever considered that? *What do you think I'd do?*"

"You'd finish this," I said, staring up at him, my anger dissipating in the force of the heat coming off him.

Pritkin said a very bad word. And I guessed it felt good because he chased it with a few more. "We are *through* with this, do you understand? I don't know what the hell I was thinking, even talking to Bodil. As if she could somehow protect us!"

"I don't think that's too likely after the impression I made," I confessed. "I'm sorry; I should have listened—"

But he was already shaking his head. "It doesn't matter. I had time to think about it while you were out, something this place didn't afford me before. And we're not going to be her champion; we're not going to be anything. When we get out of here—*if* we get out—we're done. We're packing up and—"

"We are not—"

At which point I didn't get hit back, but I did get shaken hard. Which wasn't much better as the back of my head impacted the floor a few times before he noticed, grabbed me up, and cradled the bruised item in one strong hand while hauling me against his chest. Which was going a mile a minute because Somnolence or not, remembering that awful moment in the watery death trap had woken him up.

And set his resolve.

"Pritkin," I began after a moment as he rocked us back and forth, but apparently, it wasn't my time to talk.

"Do you think I care about any of this?" he whispered against my hair. "Crowns and thrones and power and wealth —" he spat another curse. "That's what my father lives for. Not me!"

"But you're a *war mage*. You took an oath—"

"To protect the Pythia, which is what I've damned well been trying to do!"

"It's a little more comprehensive than that," I said softly, but he wasn't listening.

"And I *used* to be a war mage. Something I took on after my wife died to give some meaning to my existence. The Corps was hemorrhaging mages whenever they faced a demon, so I stepped in to help, and maybe I did. Or maybe that was a lie I told myself since what else was there to live for?"

His voice grew rough. "The fey were right. I never should have been born. But I was and can do one good thing with my life. I can get you out of here!"

Somehow, I didn't think he meant out of the cell.

"And go where?" I asked.

"The hells."

That had been a rhetorical question, so I hadn't expected an answer. Especially not that one. "What?"

"The answer is the hells." He pulled back to look at me. "We can go there, Cassie—"

"But . . . you hate the hells—"

"I hate most of them; there are a few exceptions. And they make up an entire universe, which even the council doesn't know the full extent of! We could travel for years, centuries, and never see everything.

"And maybe, somewhere, find a place for us. Something beautiful in its way, and strange and different, possibly enough to accept a couple of vagabonds without too much fuss. . ."

He trailed off, but I could see it in his eyes, the first spark of hope he'd shown in a while. And it completely creeped me out because Pritkin . . . no. Just no.

He *hated* the hells and everything to do with them.

But maybe he hated this place more. He'd come here expecting to lose, knowing far more about Faerie than I had. And expecting to die shortly after that, which was something he had long ago come to terms with.

But then I'd shown up, the fey had freaked out, and he'd had to watch me in danger on almost an hourly basis ever since. No wonder he wanted to flee and take me with him! It wasn't like the thought had never occurred to me.

"You know what I used to daydream about?" I asked him. "Sometimes in Vegas, after a particularly close call, but especially at Gertie's. After one of those days when I'd had my ass handed to me by Agnes a dozen times, and I was sure I'd never figure this out. That the only thing I was proving was that I wasn't worthy of my title?"

His jawline alone said that I wasn't getting through. But it didn't stop me because he needed to hear this and to understand—he wasn't the only one who'd ever been caught in a pit of despair that seemed to have no way out. I'd *lived* there for months, maybe years; I didn't even know anymore.

But long enough to recognize it on someone else's face.

"I thought about *you*," I said. "About picking you up and just . . . going. Somewhere, somewhen, where nobody would find us. First as a vacation, and God knows we've earned one! And then. . .

"Well, it's not like anyone would know we were gone,

would they? Or if I extended it for a little while, maybe even a long while. Time enough to have a life—"

"What's wrong with that?" Pritkin rasped, even though I saw the truth in his eyes. He knew what was wrong with it, just as I had every time I'd looked at myself in the mirror. Which is why I hadn't much, not wanting to meet my own eyes.

Because I could have done it. My God, I could have! So many times.

Even with the risk that somebody, maybe Gertie herself, would come after me, because what was that next to the dangers I faced every day? And perhaps she'd have had pity, even let me stay. After all, if there was no future, what was there for me to go back for?

"To make sure that there is one," I could hear the words in her voice and see her gimlet eyes boring a hole through my soul.

Gertie had never let me get away with anything. Gertie, who had given up everything to be Pythia, understood the price she'd paid, that we all had. And she'd made sure that I did, too.

And why.

"Because if I did that," I said softly. "I might never come back. Might not be able to; the Pythian power might desert me. But even if it didn't . . . after years, after a child or two —" Pritkin closed his eyes as if in pain. "After what we have becomes all there is, could you give it up? For the war, for everyone else's good, while knowing the *cost*—"

"I could give a fuck about the war!" he said savagely, those green eyes flying open. "I'm here for you. Not Faerie, whoever the hell she is, not the human realm, who never accepted me and never will, and not the damned demons. They and the fey can all burn, but not you. Not you!"

And then he kissed me, and it was all there, every word he'd said written in another language, a harsher, darker, more primal one, that raised something similar in me. Something dangerous because he could talk me into this; oh, yes, he could.

Not because it was right—there was nothing right about it. But because it was easy, like kissing him, like falling into his arms and never looking back.

So easy that it took everything I had to wrench away.

"And what exactly would be the point in having that life," I demanded harshly. "Those children, that future—when we'd know, every single day, that it was a lie? That we weren't building something lasting, something *real*? Just living on borrowed time until it all fell apart, for us, for them, in a blaze of hate and retribution from a bunch of divine monsters we weren't willing to fight?"

"To fight, but not to defeat," Pritkin said, his face white and terrible. "If we can't even take a bunch of fey—"

"Fuck the fey!" I said, because yeah, he knew. John Pritkin was a lot of things, but stupid wasn't one of them. He wouldn't be human if he didn't get lost in fantasy sometimes when the reality felt so very bleak. But he knew everything that I'd been saying.

He just didn't see a way out.

I took his hands. "You keep saying that they're winning, but so far, there's only one point on the board, and it's ours. And yeah, they've been trying their best to kill us ever since we got here, but *we're not dead yet*. It seems like they're the ones who are losing, and they know it. Why bother to risk so much to take us down if we're not a threat?"

"They know exactly how much of a threat you are—"

"And they're right." I looked at him steadily. "But they're underestimating you. Prince of two realms, holder of all four elements, commander of three forms of magic—"

"When I have any to command."

"—and all-around badass. They *should* worry."

"So should I," Pritkin muttered and pulled me down.

CHAPTER
TWENTY-ONE

His lips were warm in the cold cell, even though his flesh was as chilled as mine. And even more so when my armor, which had steadfastly refused to morph back to its alter ego even to sleep, sensing danger everywhere here, suddenly vanished in a cloud of silver silk. Because there was nowhere I felt more safe than in Pritkin's arms.

We were both sweaty and grubby, and the surroundings were the least romantic I could think of, and none of it mattered. When incubus energy swirled around us, the dirty room became almost beautiful, the black rock glittered in the slanting light through the bars, the cool, slightly musty air turned clean and fresh, and the straw pallet underneath us became as comfortable as a feather bed. Not that I cared.

The hard arms around me were all I wanted, the harder lips on mine, the scrape of stubble as he kissed my neck, my chest, my breast. I was tired of fighting with him; I hated fighting with him! I wanted us to be in sync, working together, fighting together. That's what I'd envisioned when I came here.

But that wasn't what I'd found. Something had been off ever since I arrived, something strange, something wrong. And it still was.

"What is it?" I gasped, breaking away.

"Nothing."

"Tell me," because it wasn't nothing, and we both knew it.

His eyes met mine, and there was no deception in them, but there was none of the hope I wanted to see, either. "I know what you want," he said, his voice rough. "And I would give it to you. But you have to understand, this time, that may not be enough. *I* may not be enough."

"Then . . . maybe we need some help," I said slowly.

He shook his head. "Bodil made it clear—"

"No, not Bodil. One of ours. You're allowed a team—"

"A team who could win here?" A blond eyebrow raised.

"I could call on the Pythian Court. I didn't want to bring them into this, but—"

"And you shouldn't. Rhea is the only one whose magic would work reliably in Faerie, and she's your heir."

No, not Rhea, I thought, seeing my beautiful, kind, and still only half-trained heir. My whole being revolted at the idea. She'd been in Faerie exactly once, and if I had my way, that would be the last time. And not my acolytes, either.

Their power wouldn't be any more reliable here than mine, and they were all about two hundred, which was old even for a magic user. They'd been heroes recently, every single one, but channeling the Pythian power was hard, and they had enough on their hands keeping my court safe. I needed young blood.

"The covens," I heard myself say, seeing the three impressive witches who had joined my court to help watch over the little coven initiates that a few well-disposed Great Mothers had entrusted to me.

They'd been needed, as half of the covens were part fey these days. It was a type of magic that few others knew, including the various magic workers at court. But it would be perfect here!

Especially as they were not only powerful but crafty and inventive. They'd had to be to survive the best that the Silver Circle could throw at them all these years while also keeping their people safe from raids by the fey. Unfortunately, the covens weren't exactly my friends.

We'd had a run-in recently when some of the more radical leaders had decided that the war gave them a perfect opportunity to get some payback on the Circle. I'd stopped it because the last thing we needed right now was to fight each other, but they hadn't liked it. They'd always suspected me of being a little too much in the Circle's pocket, as most Pythias had been, and that had only increased their doubts.

I'd stopped a war but gained few friends, and those I had. . .

"Would not be welcomed here," Pritkin said as if finishing the thought for me. "We have to persuade, not just win, and bringing in an outside army to fight for us, particularly that army—"

"Assuming I could even convince them." Because that had always been the problem with the covens. They'd sacrificed the best of themselves fighting the Circle all those centuries ago. The ones who had survived were those who had stayed out of it, who went to ground, who took care of their own and let the world hang.

And ever since, that had been the model they'd followed.

They wouldn't come, not at my call, and even if they did, an army made up of the very people the Alorestri had enslaved and vilified all these years wasn't likely to gain us many votes.

"War mages then," I said. "The Alorestri have treaties with them; they can't claim them as slaves! And they're supposed to help the Pythia—"

"They're supposed to *protect* the Pythia," Pritkin corrected. "Protecting you means getting you away from here, not helping you win."

"But Faerie said—" I stopped myself. Because explaining that the spirit of a planet had been giving me orders might not help. That was why Mircea hadn't given the consul a precis of what he was doing before he took off for the dark fey capital. He'd known how well that was likely to go over.

And while Jonas Marsden, the acting head of the Silver Circle, was a little easier to deal with than a two-thousand-year-old paranoid vampire queen, his forces had also taken some beatings recently. He wasn't likely to endanger them to get us an army he didn't trust. Not with half of the fey court on the other side!

"The demons!" I said, getting desperate. Because this place was far worse than I'd expected, and I'd expected it to be bad. But how were we supposed to win when we had to fight for our lives just to make it to the challenges?

"Even assuming that you could persuade the Council to send any here," Pritkin said, "and that their magic worked well enough to help us, *and* that the fey wouldn't rebel harder at a demon army than one made up of their slaves, we would have to take the chance that they weren't working for our enemies."

"But they're on the damned menu! The gods want them more than us. It would be like a cow working for a butcher!"

"Yes, but most aren't very fat cows and wouldn't make much of a meal for their new overlords. But they might be useful in rounding up others who would."

"God."

"That's how the world works, Cassie, every world. Including this one."

And yes, it was.

And that didn't change a damned thing.

"I'm still not going," I told him flatly.

"I know."

He kissed me again, and I didn't have to ask the obvious question because it was all there. He wouldn't go without me. He wouldn't leave me here.

Which meant that my blind faith in an alien goddess might get both of us killed.

It had already gotten Mircea lost in another world, and I wasn't sure I could get him back. Yet I'd sent his daughter there after him. Had I sent her to her death, too?

I didn't know, just like I never knew anything anymore. Gertie, what if you were wrong about me? I thought desperately. What if we were both horribly wrong?

"Don't do that," Pritkin said, pulling back. I guessed that what I was feeling was in my kiss, too.

And then it was in more than that. A chill shot down my body, making my hands shake, my teeth want to chatter, and tears leap to my eyes when I couldn't afford them, when I couldn't be this weak! Not now, maybe not ever, but it never seemed to end, not just the war but the *pressure*. The doubt. The ever-present and all-consuming fear that I was getting this wrong.

What if Pritkin was right?

"Maybe we can win without the army," I whispered.

And without warning, the world fell away.

I assumed an attack because, of course, I did. That was all we'd had here! But this didn't feel like one.

It took me another moment to say what it felt like and to realize what was going on, even though I'd been on this ride before. But if this was the Common, the collective consciousness that Faerie shared with her children, it was more chaotic than last time. A lot more.

Usually, most fey experienced it as a flashback: they'd be at a centuries-old tavern and suddenly recall what the local wine tasted like or how bad the stew was, even though they'd never passed that way.

But an ancestor had, and had accidentally "uploaded" the memory to the Common, the hive mind that all fey participated in whether they liked it or not. From what I understood of their religion, they believed that all of them were pieces of Faerie's soul that had been broken off and given bodies to go out and experience life. And that, after death, they would return to her with the knowledge they had gained.

In the meantime, they were still attached to her on some level and communicated back what they were feeling, seeing, and hearing. And, sometimes, it went both ways, with individual fey getting flashes of memory that wasn't theirs. They would suddenly know directions to a place they'd never been, recognize someone they had never met, or taste that wine their ancestor had drunk a millennium ago. For them, such flashbacks usually lasted a few seconds or less, but Faerie was like the mainframe of this particular computer, and she got it all.

And was now showing some of it to us, as she had a few times before.

Only this wasn't the crystal clear version I'd seen on those occasions, which had felt almost like being there. This . . . I didn't know what this was. Other than dizzying, since we were rocketing through the palace, tearing down misty corridors and passing through indistinct walls and ceilings like they weren't even there.

And then through the kitchens again, along that same suffocating corridor cut through solid rock, and now scarred with spell-blackened patches on the walls and what looked like drying blood splatter on the floor. And finally, down a dizzying staircase, through a warded wall that I could swear I felt on my skin, rough-hewn and rock-hard with a biting electric veneer, even as we were dragged through the middle of it. And out into—

I wasn't sure. But it looked like another of those rock-cut storerooms that had been turned into a triage center. Some of Rhosier's people were on cots groaning by the walls; others were getting bandaged up by some of the bread bakers from earlier, stoic-looking women with nimble fingers who wrapped bandages as quickly as they'd kneaded dough; and some were in a corner with sheets covering their faces, being sobbed over by what I guessed were family members, who must have just been told what had happened.

I saw one woman launch herself onto a soot-covered man, screaming and beating on him, trying to force him to wake up when he never would, and having to be dragged back by others while yelling and clawing at them—

"He's fine, he's fine, I know he's fine—"

It was horrible everywhere I looked, not least because the visual wasn't the only part of this feed having problems. The voices echoed oddly, with parts weirdly loud and others almost silent. I saw a woman screaming but could barely hear her while a man's body being dragged over to the pile of corpses scraped deafeningly loud on the floor.

Another person's heartbeat was sluggish in my ears and getting weaker until I held my breath, waiting for it to stop altogether.

Right before a piercing wail so loud that it felt like it punched through my head had me yelling and covering my ears, half bent over, almost mad with it in seconds. Before it suddenly cut out, everything did, except for Pritkin's cursing.

And then Faerie skewed the scene, not letting me see anymore, not letting me hear. Except for what was happening in a corner where Rhosier was talking to Enid. And, suddenly, everything went from hazy to high-def.

"We have to go back for them!" Enid was in the cook's face, or as much of it as she could reach. His height allowed him to tower over her, but it didn't look like he was managing to intimidate her much. Possibly because he had to divide his attention between the furious redhead and organizing the chaos of what was essentially an overflowing emergency room.

A couple more people ran in, supporting a groaning man in between them, and Rhosier snapped his fingers and pointed to a space by a wall.

"Over there, someone will see him in a moment," he said, right before Enid lost her shit and slammed a ward around them, cutting the two of them off from the rest of the room.

But not from us. Faerie didn't get locked out in her world, so the only thing that happened was that our view rippled a little as we moved forward and through the shield. And then clarified with us up close and personal because the shield was small, Enid being low on power after that crazy chase.

"You know damned well why we can't!" Rhosier told her, looking furious. "I won't risk—"

"Anything!" she spat. "You never do! It's always tomorrow, and wait, and be patient—I'm tired of being patient! If they hadn't been there, Generys would be dead!"

"If they hadn't been there, she wouldn't have been in danger in the first place. You forget why the guards came—"

"I forget nothing!" Enid snarled, those tawny eyes suddenly looking more like a tiger's. "Nothing. Not the years of abuse, the constant fear, the certainty that nothing will ever change, no matter what we do. We get out a few hundred a year if we're

lucky. More than that are born each year, born into slavery and deprivation and pain—a lifetime of it."

She dropped her glamourie and got in his face, and I had forgotten just how bad it was. That mangled visage stood out starkly white against the rest of her skin, the scar tissue no longer able to flush. And it was awful, ridge after ragged ridge of a jealous woman's fury that nothing would ever erase.

"You think I forget when I have to look at this every day? You think they left me that choice?"

"I think you need to calm down," Rhosier told her flatly, his voice hard. "Or risk angering our patron and cutting off anyone's chances of getting out. Lady Bodil risks a great deal for us, and your fear doesn't give you the right—"

"The right?" she laughed, and it was ugly. "What rights do you think any of us have? Even our pathetic excuse for a rebellion depends on one of them!"

She threw out an arm that passed through me, causing me to stumble back into Pritkin. And then to keep on going because we were suddenly snatched up by an impatient goddess and sent rocketing onward. Or downward since she'd just jerked us through the floor.

We passed through a succession of them, flashing by my disoriented eyes in an instant like we were riding an out-of-control, glass-sided elevator. I had a brief flash of more storerooms, of a bunch of guards in what I guessed was a wardroom, playing cards, of a boudoir where a woman was moisturizing her face and a man was walking out of the bathroom in his birthday suit, heedless of the Peeping Tom goddess and her posse. And then they started to slur together, blurring across my vision into a sickening sludge.

What happens if you throw up in the Common? I wondered and was trying to choose between that and passing out.

Or both—because they seemed an equal possibility right now.

I didn't know what was wrong with me. I'd previously spent what felt like hours in the Common as Faerie caught me up on what was going on. As she wasn't human and couldn't speak, she'd had to show me instead and let me experience it myself. And I had, but not like this!

I writhed in her grip, feeling like my brain was liquifying inside my skull. But not so much that it couldn't shoot me out a reason: Lover's Knot. Or, to be precise, the absence of it.

Pritkin had given me the ability to access the Common through his fey blood while we were linked. But Mircea had invalidated that when he disappeared into another universe. So, how was I seeing anything?

I didn't know, but whatever Faerie was doing to compensate, it wasn't working. The corridor we were flying down darkened perceptibly, leaving me looking at a drunkenly skewed cell striped with dim light through the middle. It was a double exposure, as if two movies were trying to run simultaneously, each jostling for space and just managing to obscure the other.

For a minute, until they both grayed out, and I was left not seeing much of anything, with my vision going dark, my body going cold, and my heart thudding in my chest as if it was about to beat right out of it. And flop around on the floor, only it felt like it was already doing that. And getting ground under someone's heel into a little bloody lump that was going to stop, just any . . . moment . . . now—

And then we were out, tumbling back into our cell as if dumped there. It left me sprawling on the rough stone floor, breathing hard and clutching the ground underneath me because the whole room seemed to be rotating. Exiting deep immersion in the Common was never fun as a non-fey, and judging by Pritkin's breathing, for anybody else, either. But that had been especially rough, as if Faerie had lost her grip on me.

Or as if I'd nearly died, which. . . yeah.

And then, my body finally made its choice, and I passed out.

CHAPTER
TWENTY-TWO

I didn't know how long I was unconscious that time, but it wasn't long enough. I wasn't chilled when I woke because Pritkin was draped around me, but I still felt like hell. I decided to just lay there for a while.

"What did we just see?" I croaked when I could.

He didn't answer for a moment, but when I turned over, he wasn't asleep. He had that look on his face instead, the one that said that he was debating whether to reply, which wasn't okay. I needed answers, and I'd been getting basically none of them all day.

"If Faerie showed us that, she had a reason," I rasped, wishing I had some water. Or an aspirin. Or a stiff drink.

"The reason seems to be to kill you," he whispered, but it was savage, and the hand on my arm clenched harder, just to the edge of being unpleasant. "Which this damned fool quest of hers has almost done a dozen times!"

"Yeah," I agreed, trying to push myself to a sitting position and somehow missing the floor. But I didn't have time to lie around, so I tried again, slower this time. And for a wonder, the room behaved itself. "But that can be fixed," I added.

"Fixed? Fixed how?" Pritkin's tone said he already knew he wouldn't like the answer.

"I'm not connected to you anymore," I reminded him. "I can't borrow your link to Faerie, and she seems to be having trouble communicating without it. But if you put Lover's Knot —"

"No."

"—on us again—"

"No!"

"Why not?" I asked, confused. "You can cast it on just the two of us, and while it won't give us access to Mircea's power, it will help in other ways. I can borrow your link to Faerie and you—you could even use the Pythian power when it cycles around again and get us out of here!"

I wondered why I hadn't thought of that before because, yeah! That would work. I knew it would as he'd borrowed it before, as had Mircea.

I might be too tired to channel it, but Pritkin—he was drained, but he was stronger than me, and it was a short hop. Just getting us to the other side of this damned wall might be enough!

But he looked at me as if I was crazy. "You know damned well why not! If I die, and we're linked, so do you!"

"Pritkin, we're in a *cell*. We're not going to die—"

"We're in *Faerie*, so you can't know that!"

He abruptly got up, leaving me colder and bewildered on the floor. "I'm talking about a few minutes," I said. "You can take it off right after. We just need long enough—"

"For that fey bitch to give us more marching orders," he seethed, making me blink again. Because yeah, that was the idea. Faerie knew what was going on around here, who we could trust, if anyone, and who was gunning for us. She probably knew all kinds of information that could give us an edge, and she *wanted* us to win.

"She'll be back anyway," I pointed out. "She wasn't done; she just lost her grip—"

"And if someone comes in here while we're both mentally absent? And butchers me as they've been trying to do since I arrived? Tony might be after you, but the rest are after me. If we're linked—"

And for a moment, he really did look demonic: red of face, dark of eye, and with bunched fists sparking with little tendrils of power that curled up his arms as if searching for someone to throw it at. He looked like he could eviscerate said person from here by sheer force of will, which was when I started worrying. Because sure, Pritkin was overprotective sometimes, but not like this.

He had never been like this.

"No one is coming," I said softly as if speaking to a mad bull. "And Faerie needs us. She's not going to let anything happen—"

"And when she doesn't?" It was savage.

I frowned. I didn't like trusting a vengeful goddess any more than he did, but what was the alternative? Because without her and the information she'd provided, we'd have already lost.

She had given me a lot of help getting out of Aeslinn's camp of horrors, help that had allowed me to make it to the portal and then through it. And the information she'd provided after that had let me stop Zeus' plans and live to tell about it. I doubted she cared for us, as we weren't her creatures, even Pritkin, whose fey blood was thin.

But the enemy of my enemy was a friend or at least an ally, and I'd take that.

But he wouldn't.

It was in every line of his body, in the way he was pacing when he never did, in the contour of that jaw, which, if it got any sharper, could cut something. I'd thought we'd settled this; he'd even been talking to Bodil about us replacing her champion. Which might keep the assassins off our butts in between challenges but would still leave us vulnerable in the contest itself.

That was a risk I was willing to take, and he had been, too, just a little while ago. But all of a sudden. . . It was like I was talking to a different man.

I decided to change the subject and let him calm down since I still had about a thousand questions he could answer, assuming he would.

"Okay," I said, and he looked at me in surprise as if he'd expected an argument, one that he probably had the answers for already prepped. So I asked one that maybe he didn't. "Why did it look like a cook was leading some kind of rebellion?"

Pritkin narrowed his eyes at me, but I guessed he preferred this topic to the other because, after a moment, he came back over and sat down.

"Rhosier isn't just a cook," I was told. "He and Bodil have been working together to get some of the humans out of here and back to Earth for years. The servants in the royal household act as his eyes and ears so that he knows who has incurred the wrath of someone important, and she has access to the portal. They've sent through many hundreds at this point without anyone being the wiser. The rumor is that the missing people ran away to join the dark fey, which has happened occasionally."

"But instead, they ran to Earth?"

He nodded. "Bodil never agreed with Nimue's practice of capturing or luring human women here. Although I think that was initially more about the purity of the fey bloodline than any moral misgivings. But over time, as she saw what was happening to them—"

"Like Enid," I said, seeing that half-beautiful, half-destroyed face again.

"Like Enid," he agreed. "They are treated like cattle and abused as easily. It's one reason their hybrid children are taken from them early and sent to the frontiers to be raised as warriors, so they don't get attached to their mothers and cause trouble. But Rhosier's magic came in late, causing the fey to suppose him weak.

"They discharged him from military service, and he became a spit-turner at the palace instead. He moved up through the centuries to head the kitchens, having inherited a long life from his father."

"And found a hobby?" I guessed.

"A dangerous one." Pritkin grimaced. "He started using

the portal, sneaking people through with the help of some of the guards on duty, who were also part human. At first, he concentrated on those who had incurred the wrath of someone powerful enough to cause them trouble—which, for a slave, could be almost anyone. But later. . ."

"Later?"

"I told him it was foolish. But he was determined, and he's extremely difficult to reason with—"

Like somebody else I knew, I thought.

"—and has been telling the slaves, not just here but those in the villages as well, to have their children fake incompetence. He's shown them how to fail the tests they used to vie with each other to pass."

"What tests?" I asked because I still knew so little of this place.

"The guards on the frontiers live well—for as long as they do live—and have some status in fey society. The part-humans who can't pass do not. As a result, the slaves' children do everything possible to be taken by the army. Their mothers even encourage it, knowing what their lives will be otherwise."

"I thought they were returned to Earth otherwise," I said because that was how all those part-fey children had ended up dumped in old Wales.

"Once, but not for centuries. When the Silver Circle, with Caedmon's help, shut down the slave trade and most of the portals making it possible, the Alorestri retaliated by refusing to send back any more part-humans. I think they planned to use the threat as a bartering tactic, but the Circle readily agreed. They didn't like the trouble the Returned made and were happy enough to leave them here—"

"That's why you said Jonas wouldn't help us," I said, understanding a bit more.

"Among other reasons. But the covens were willing to take them in, as it was largely their blood, their sisters, who had been stolen. And thus, the children were their descendants."

I nodded, remembering when I'd visited one of the witches'

hidden enclaves in the desert outside of Vegas.

They'd established a small network of such places as a defense against the Circle and its laws in the 1500s when the two groups had been at war, but it had grown through the centuries to span the globe. The enclave I'd seen had been filled with strange and wonderful magic—and fey, lots and lots of fey and part-fey hybrids. I remembered their candy-colored hair and peculiar clothing but hadn't thought much about it then.

The covens regularly traded with Faerie to evade the Circle's prohibitions on the import of various potion ingredients. Those hit the covens harder than anyone else, as their magic was derived from that of the fey, and they needed their resources for many spells. I'd naturally assumed that the people I saw there were traders, and maybe some of them were.

But not all, it seemed.

"Rhosier managed to sneak out a dozen or so at a time," Pritkin added. "Mostly children, the ones the fey didn't care about as they had already been passed over in the selection process.

"They were seen as fit only to till the fields or serve in the great houses; no one much cared if they ran away to join the dark fey, died of an illness, or were attacked by wild animals—all of which were excuses he made up over the years. The only problem was that there weren't many guards willing to risk helping him, and those who would were rarely stationed together. It caused a bottleneck, and then Bodil caught him one night red-handed. Fortunately, they reached an agreement."

"Lucky him."

"Yes, he has always been that, which is needed considering that he is also reckless, stupidly brave, even foolhardy—"

"Pot, meet kettle," I said.

"What?"

"Nothing. Who did you say his father was again?"

"I didn't," Pritkin shot me a look.

"Does that mean you don't know, or—"

"His father was a fey nobleman named Leiknir, a giant of a man even by fey standards, which is where Rhosier gets his height. He had many human mistresses before his death in battle against the Svarestri."

"And his mother?"

"Was born here. She did not have her son's longevity and passed some time ago."

"His grandmother, then?" I persisted. "Or great-grandmother?" Because Pritkin knew an awful lot about some random cook's background.

"His great-grandmother was brought here as a pregnant slave, and yes, the timeline fits. But that doesn't mean—"

"The timeline fits? Meaning that she was brought here in the sixth century?" I said. Because Pritkin's dad and Rhosier's possible namesake had been prowling around Wales right about then, looking for part-fey, part-human women who might be able to bear him an heir.

He hadn't had any luck with demons, whose infertility eclipsed even that of the fey, and had switched his attention to humans. But none had proven able to survive the birth of a half-demon child, who had sucked the life out of them from the womb, killing both mother and fetus. Until Rosier met Morgaine, whose mixed heritage allowed her to carry Pritkin to term.

But what if there had been another? One who had been carrying a child whose magic had also come in late, thus allowing the mother to survive? If she'd stayed on Earth, Rosier would have found her again, as he had carefully tracked the births of his children. But what if she hadn't?

What if she'd been grabbed by the fey, who were snatching up witches left and right since their magic made their offspring stronger? Nimue's people wanted the most potent blood they could find to produce their battle fodder, and they needed guaranteed fertility. A pregnant witch would, therefore, be a prize, one that might have found herself kidnapped to Faerie before the demon lord she'd had an affair with could return and take the child.

Pritkin looked like he was following my train of thought and didn't like it. "We're not related," he said flatly.

"You sure about that?"

"And it wouldn't matter even if we were. You heard what Rhosier said to Enid. Bodil is his patron; he won't risk angering her and jeopardizing their arrangement."

"Not even for you?" I tried to cock an eyebrow, but as usual, both went up. "The servants in the kitchens seemed pretty darned fond of you, almost like they look on you as a savior."

Pritkin gave his short bark of a laugh. "Hardly."

"Could have fooled me!"

He leaned his head back against the wall and stared at the ceiling. "Everyone is worried about what happens when a new ruler takes the throne. That's as true of the servants as it is of the loftiest courtier. There hasn't been a change of power here for time out of mind. The only force to be reckoned with that most people remember is Nimue. And while she was as changeable as the sea, there were certain rules she didn't violate."

"Such as?"

"Such as those that govern the servants. They don't have many protections, but she wasn't going to risk her precious breeding stock to a noble's whim, and she came down hard on anyone who attacked them."

"But Enid—"

"Was disfigured, yes, but not killed, not blinded, not maimed."

"That's a damned low bar!" I said, outraged. "Beat them all you like, scar them for life, terrorize the hell out of them, just so long as they can still work and have babies for the war machine!"

"Essentially, yes." Pritkin's voice was quiet but steady. He seemed more his old self, as if the conversation was calming him despite its subject. "It's a brutal system, and its protections may seem barbaric to you. But they *are* protections. And to people who have no others, they are important ones."

"Yes, but—"

"And the servants are afraid to lose those protections if the wrong heir wins. As I told you, most have no way out if conditions here worsen. Rhosier and Bodil send through a few at a time, the ones in greatest need, because laws can be disregarded, and a slave can be killed quietly. But thousands? Much less tens of thousands, as the laws also govern those on the frontier?"

"Tens of *thousands*?"

"This has been going on for centuries, Cassie, and the fey have been actively trying to breed more soldiers. I don't know the true number, but it must be at least that. In any case, the servants hope I will win and protect their limited rights, hence the reception you saw. They don't see me as a savior so much as a maintainer of the status quo. They don't dare to hope for anything else."

"Then they should! This isn't the Middle Ages!"

"In Faerie, it may as well be. When people live for thousands of years, social change comes at a crawl when it comes at all."

Great.

"And they trust you just because you're human?" I asked.

"They trust me because Rhosier trusts me. I put him in touch with the covens after he and I met on one of my early trips."

And okay, that made more sense. Pritkin's mother had died trying to stop the slave trade on Earth; I couldn't see her son not getting involved in this somehow. He liked to pretend, even to himself, that he was a rule follower and a stickler for a sane, sensible course of action.

He lied.

He was usually more reckless than I was; he just had the power to get away with it most of the time. And helping a rogue cook smuggle kids to the humans in a reversal of the fey stealing them from us? Yeah, that sounded about right.

"Why didn't you tell me?" I asked.

"The walls have ears, especially here, and it didn't seem relevant."

"Not *relevant*?" I stared at him. "When there are tens of thousands of soldiers who—my God, maybe we really don't need the army! I mean, we already have it, right? If all those kids are being sent to the frontiers, the long-lived ones, the powerful ones, we could just—"

"Do what?" Pritkin said. "Undo hundreds of years of conditioning? Persuade them to go against every oath they ever swore? And throw in with us against literal *gods*?"

Okay, it didn't sound as good when he said it.

"We have to try," I insisted. "Give them a chance, and us, too. Trying to win this way is—" I caught myself, but not in time.

"Foolish?" And there went that damned eyebrow again. "In other words, what I've been telling you?"

"Then why are you here?" I said, exasperated.

"Because you asked me." It was stark. And looking into his eyes, it was also the truth. "I owed you that much, at least, after what I put you through. And I didn't think you were coming—"

"Yeah! Because I'd just leave you here!"

"—which was foolish on my part. But now that you've been here, you must see—"

Nothing. Because the world abruptly fell away again, and we went tumbling through the void. Right into the middle of—

Feltin's office.

CHAPTER TWENTY-THREE

I didn't recognize it at first since my body was still shuddering as if I had fallen from a height and because I'd never seen this place before, having only been allowed to kick my filthy human heels in the atrium. But I was pretty sure of the location anyway. There was an elaborate table serving as a desk, gorgeous floor-to-ceiling windows looking out at the undersea world, and enough sumptuous carpets, fine paintings, gilt mosaics, and expensive spell light to do a king proud.

If there was any doubt about Feltin's pretensions, one look at that office would have dispelled them. Not that I needed it. Because he was talking.

"What do you mean they missed them?"

It would be more accurate to say that he was yelling, although he didn't need to; the guard with the purple-dipped hair in front of him was only about a foot away. He looked like one of those who'd attacked us, to the point that I felt my fist clenching and Pritkin's hand on my arm tightening. But this soldier wasn't splattered with red like the one behind him, with his shiny armor streaked like someone had thrown a bucket of paint over it.

Or had bled out in his arms, because he was looking furious.

The guy at his side, the only other occupant of the room, wasn't looking like much of anything except half dead. His pretty complexion was burnt all along one side, making me think of Enid and how he'd match her soon if he survived. Only that didn't seem to be likely, especially as he'd just sank to one knee.

"He needs a healer," his blood-splattered buddy said, only to *recoil slightly when Feltin got in his face.*

And there was something about that movement, like a bird of prey swooping down on a mouse, that made me blink. I'd seen someone else move like that not so long ago. Someone else . . .

Who shouldn't be here.

Or maybe I was finally losing my mind, I thought, staring at Feltin's surfer-boy good looks. They were draped in a royal blue robe glittering with embroidery and open at the front to show off the finely sculpted lines of his chest. A pair of matching long, silky trousers, barely clinging to his hip bones, completed the look, which was topped off by a mane of rumpled blond hair that appeared to have air-dried after having agitated fingers run through it.

He looked like he'd just rolled out of bed, but he hadn't been to bed, had he? He'd been here, drying off after getting dunked in the ballroom and pacing the floor in his bare feet, waiting for the news that we were dead. This must have occurred hours ago, but Faerie was just showing it to us now.

Because Alphonse had been wrong.

Tony wasn't the problem, or if he was, he had help.

And then I saw it again, not a glimpse this time, but a ghostly face pushing out of Feltin's. A very familiar ghostly face. And, suddenly, a lot of things began to make sense. Zeus, I mouthed at Pritkin as my heart started to slam in my chest.

I didn't think that anyone else could see him. Two of the fey didn't react, not even by a finger twitch, which you'd expect if they were having a divine visitation. Only the leader flinched, and that was because Feltin was back to spewing spittle in his face.

"I cursed him myself!" Feltin snarled. "I know it took!"

"That may be, but he fought like the demon he is," the wounded man gasped, beyond caring about things like diplomacy. His long, dark brown hair had come unbound and fell into his dead white face. "It felt like we were facing an army—"

"We were," the leader said, glancing back at him as if worried about his condition. "Some of the kitchen staff helped him."

Which . . . was probably not the best thing he could have said. Or maybe Zeus-as-Feltin wasn't used to having anyone look away when he was screaming at them. The next moment, the leader found himself grabbed by the neck hard enough that the metal gorget protecting his throat was slowly indented.

"The kitchen staff?" Fletin said, his voice starting low and getting louder. "The kitchen staff? Are you mad?"

"They were powerful," the bloody man insisted, looking from the angry pseudo-king to his captain and back again. "Far more so than they should have been. Only the weak are supposed to be sent back, but those weren't—"

"Shut up!" Feltin all but screeched, causing all three men to stare at him as if he'd sprouted horns. I guessed that sort of thing wasn't considered kingly. But Feltin wasn't looking much like a king at the moment, except possibly a mad one.

He reminded me of Aeslinn when Zeus was in residence, or Nimue when she was under the influence of a piece of Ares' old armor, which had been infused with a bit of his corrupt soul. I guessed having a god ride you wasn't fun, but Aeslinn and Nimue had had more power to help handle it. Feltin didn't.

But he looked better than I'd have expected, as the other of Zeus's little puppets were a powerful demon lord and a few demigods. How was Feltin even still on his feet? And why was Zeus's indistinct face suddenly wavering like a bad phone connection?

Because it was, and then it blipped out entirely, leaving Feltin panting and stumbling back against the table, appearing dazed. And then livid when he caught the side eyes the others were sharing. "Are you elite troops or not?" he roared.

But the leader was made of sterner stuff than I'd thought. "We were," he answered flatly. "But now a quarter of my men are dead, and more are missing—"

"Burnt to death," the injured fey gasped. "Turned to powder."

"It happened in an instant," the third man said."The goddess cursed us, like she did the Kraken in the hall. I know she did!"

Considering that I hadn't done anything of the kind, I didn't know what he was talking about until Pritkin spoke low in my ear. "Bodil's people helped us in the deep but couldn't get to the kitchen in time. Rhosier and I immolated half of the fey in the corridor before the rest broke through your time spell. Most of those remaining chased after you, but a few retreated toward the kitchens and must have gotten away.”

“You mean the ‘goddess’ you were supposed to kill?” Feltin screamed before I could respond.

“It wasn't that easy!” the leader said, looking flushed. He was a tall, attractive-looking fey with dazzling blue eyes. His hair was still up, if only barely, and strands were falling into his face that he pushed back angrily. “You said she would be exhausted, that they both would. You said she’d be easy prey!”

Which got him a backhand hard enough to send him to the floor. Because Feltin’s muscles weren’t just for show, and he was more than furious; he was afraid. I saw it in a flash of those baby blues, in the way his other hand clenched at his side, and in the spittle-soaked reply. “I want them found! I want the woman dead and the ‘prince’ captured. I want whoever is helping them tortured —”

And, okay, I was starting to see why Bodil was so pissed.

“—to find any more! And I want to know why my damned spell isn’t working!”

“He’s a demon,” the injured fey said, looking up with fury because he didn’t seem to like Feltin mishandling his officer. “Who knows if it even took—”

“It took. Barne-Mora always takes! He should be fleeing in terror right now. He should be overcome with it—right now!”

I felt Pritkin stiffen beside me, but he didn’t say anything. Possibly to avoid us breaking deep emersion, which led back to that hazy, echoing place we traveled in when going from one vision to the next. Or because the third man was speaking.

“She is likely shielding him,” he said. “The goddess, I mean. She was there beside him the whole time—”

“That ‘goddess’ is a woman!*” Feltin spat. “A frail, human woman no different from our slaves! And I want her dead—along with the damned traitors on our staff!”*

“We don’t know where they are,” the leader said from the floor. Unlike his men, he was carefully expressionless, and his voice was

neutral and calm—dangerous. If I'd been Feltin, I would have been worried.

But I guessed when you had an elder god riding your ass half the time, it put a different perspective on things.

I suddenly wondered who, exactly, had let the assassins in here that had almost killed Nimue. Forcing her to run away to save her life and somehow end up dead at the hands of Aeslinn's estranged wife, or so the rumors said. Because it had to be somebody in charge, right? With enough knowledge about this place and enough ambition to decide that he was tired of playing second fiddle?

If so, he didn't seem to be enjoying his power all that much at the moment, nor did he seem to notice that the soldiers were still armed. Or maybe he was just past caring. He grabbed the leader by his sensible ponytail and jerked his neck back, causing the wounded soldier, weak though he was, to growl and grab for his dagger.

But the leader put out a hand, stopping him.

Feltin never even noticed.

"Then you find her, you find both of them and finish your task. Or I will finish you. Do you understand me?"

"I understand."

"Then do it now!"

And I guessed that was all we needed to see because we were abruptly jerked out of there. However, I couldn't see where we were headed this time because the lights had just gone out. And because our speed was so dizzying that I started to wonder if this sort of thing could do permanent damage.

Then we came to a stop, hard enough to give me whiplash if I currently had a neck, and I stopped wondering about anything. I felt nauseous and unwell, although not as bad as before; Faerie must be compensating. And I still couldn't half see, just torchlight splashing on rough-hewn stone.

My eyes slowly adjusted enough to make out the vague outlines of a tunnel full of the same group of slaves from the makeshift hospital.

This must be later than the previous vision with them, as they were on the move, with people being carried on stretchers or limping along, helped by their healthier friends. And were almost shoulder to shoulder because the tunnel was narrow, and the poorly excavated walls had plenty of pointy bits that would tear your skin if you got too close. That left everybody bunched in the middle, obscuring my view, and I guessed Faerie must have realized that.

Because she started pushing us forward, even through people's bodies at times, as if we were the ghosts that this place didn't have. Until we burst through the last of the crowd, and I spotted Alphonse up ahead with a heavily bandaged arm, although not because he was injured. Masters heal faster than that, even relatively low-level ones like Alphonse, but he was swinging a torch around in that hand and didn't want to risk the sparks hitting his skin.

The light it and the few other torches shed bounced unevenly off his face, which was tilted upward like master vamps do when on a scent. Alphonse wasn't as gifted as some, but he was a master, and their noses were as good as a bloodhound's any day. And his was twitching.

"This way!" he called after a brief pause, and we were off again, down a branch in the tunnel to the left.

Everyone followed him even though Alphonse was as much of a stranger here as I was. Enid seemed confused about that, too, and quickly caught up with him. And grabbed the arm with the torch, its radiance turning her hair to flame and causing him to curse and whirl on her.

And then his features softened.

Maybe because she hadn't bothered to reapply the glamourie since nobody else down here looked any better. Or perhaps she didn't have the juice. She appeared exhausted, with pale, pinched skin beyond the vicious scarring and wild eyes.

"Don't grab the torch," Alphonse told her just as Faerie plunged us out of the gray haze of transit and into full immersion.

"How can you smell anything past that thing?" she demanded. "And are you sure we're going the right way?"

"Pretty sure—"

"That isn't good enough! Nimue's personal bodyguard is hunting us as we speak!"

"Yeah, I kinda got that."

"So, what if you're wrong? Nobody even knew this place existed!" she gestured around wildly at the tunnel, almost hitting me in the face again, only this time, I ducked.

"I'm not wrong."

"Then what is that?" she demanded, pointing at the floor, where a thin stream of water was sloshing underfoot.

"A good sign," Alphonse said and was off again.

But Enid didn't like that answer, although, at the moment, she didn't look like she'd like much of anything. They were presumably running from the bastards Feltin had put on their trail, which was absolutely the right move, but she disagreed with it. She might have been exhausted, in pain, and almost out of magic, but she wanted to fight.

She reminded me of those witches I'd seen back in Wales and their resolve, their courage, and their fury. It seemed that the best part of the ancient covens' blood had ended up in Faerie. I could see it in every line of her body, in the shape of her jaw, and in the way she caught up to Alphonse again and—

"Don't grab the torch!" he told her, pulling it away just in time. "Unless you want your guide to go up in flames!"

"You're a vampire—"

"Exactly. And we're flammable."

She stared at him. "Then why are you holding the damned thing?"

"To see that," he said, pointing ahead with it.

I peered through the darkness but didn't have a vampire's vision. But a moment later, I didn't need it when the crazy cavalcade burst out of the side of a hill and into brackish-smelling *air. It wasn't exactly fresh, but after the suffocating tunnel, it felt that way.*

Alphonse quickly extinguished the torch in the muddy ground and called back a warning for others to do the same. For a moment, all I could hear was the hissing of torches and people's panting breaths. But I realized that I was straining for something else: the sound of pursuit, a shouted warning, an attack—

Which didn't come.

"Where are we?" Enid demanded after a pause as if she'd been listening, too.

"On the left of the Myrgard, near the Black Tower," Rhosier said, coming up from somewhere behind us. "You can see the old watchtower there, to the left, through the mist."

"How? There aren't supposed to be any tunnels here!"

"No, there aren't." He glanced at Alphonse. "How did you come to smell it, vampire?"

"Easy," Alphonse said, still scanning the landscape, half of which was forested, and the rest was water sparkling under a crescent moon. "A guy I know came through it recently."

And just like that, Pritkin and I were out, falling back into our cell with no more warning than when we'd been snatched out of it. As if Faerie was saying, now that you know what's happening, do something! Only I didn't.

I didn't know anything.

But I was damned well going to.

"What's Barne-Mora?" I asked Pritkin because it seemed the most pressing.

"Nightmare," he croaked.

I turned to see him looking like he'd just woken up from one, with his face pale enough that the blond scruff looked dark by comparison. And then the eyes changed, from wide and shocked to livid, the green flooding them so brightly that they almost glowed in the darkness. And, okay, I thought.

That was more like it.

"A nightmare," he repeated savagely. "With the 'mare' or

'mora' in that term a demon thought to torment people with frightening dreams. Some have confused it with a visitation from an incubus. I suppose Feltin thought it fitting to curse me with a spell named after my own kind!"

He got to his feet even though there was nowhere to go, even after he slammed a fist into whatever shield protected this place hard enough to rattle it and make the whole room shiver. And groan as if the rocks themselves had woken up and were unhappy about it. As one demonstrated by shocking the hell out of him.

"Are you okay?" I scrambled to my somewhat unsteady feet because he didn't look okay. His hair was smoking! But he waved me off and then just stood there, vibrating because he was so furious.

"Curse you how?" I asked after a minute.

"Barne-Mora is an Old Norse curse that magnifies someone's fears a hundredfold," he grated out. "Making their worst nightmares stalk them in the waking world."

"Nightmares like us losing?" I said, starting to see where this was going.

"Nightmares like me losing you!" He grabbed my upper arms as if to reassure himself that I was really there. Because the spell was still on him, wasn't it? It had been all along, which explained a whole hell of a lot.

Like why, every time we fought, it seemed to clear his head. But as soon as he had some time alone, when no one was reminded him of the stakes, the damned curse took him again. Damn it, I *knew* he'd been acting weird, but I'd never thought of that.

Pritkin had always seemed immune to such things.

But not when a god was casting it, Cassie!

"Feltin cursed you," I said. "That must have been step one, even before the attempted poisoning. That's why I haven't been able to get through to you, why you were so eager to walk away, even if it meant walking into the hells. You're *cursed*."

Pritkin didn't say anything, but his stance—wide-legged,

stiff-backed, and closed off, told me the answer to my next question before I asked it. "Can you break it now that you know it's there?"

"No." It was stark.

"But when you rest up a bit? When you're stronger?"

And okay, that got a reaction. "Stronger than who?" he demanded, eyes flashing. "Feltin, *or the one who rides him?*"

I crossed my arms. "Zeus isn't here, Pritkin."

The won me a laugh, and it sounded shrill. "Isn't he? It feels rather different! Like barbed chains that bind me and dig deeper whenever I try to—"

He broke off, red-faced and furious. He knew what the problem was now, but he couldn't throw it off. He couldn't break it.

"I still want to run," he told me, the words sounding forced. "To pick you up, throw you over my shoulder, and sprint for the nearest portal out of here—*and I would.* Even knowing—" He broke off and glared around our cell. "Even knowing what it would do, the price we'd pay, I still would. If not for these walls, Feltin and his master would get what they want. It's been building since you came, and no matter how much I reason with myself or tell myself that it's a lie, it *grows.*"

He looked at me, and his eyes were back to that startled look I'd seen before, as if whatever magic this was, he didn't know how to counter it. For perhaps the first time in his life, he didn't. And it terrified him.

"I can't guarantee that I won't do exactly that as soon as we're free," he said. "If it worsens, I can't guarantee *what* I'll do."

I looked at him for a moment and felt my own eyes narrow. Because, yeah, I knew the feeling he was describing, knew it intimately, as those barbs had been inside of me once. After Zeus and I met for the first time when he was riding his other puppet, Aeslinn.

We'd battled on the Thames after the All-Father grabbed hold of one of my shifts and followed me to Gertie's, where we'd had a colossal fight that I'd barely survived. And only because I had absorbed some of the godly aura surrounding Aeslinn and used Zeus's own power against them. But tricking an elder god has consequences, as I'd quickly discovered.

Once he realized what I'd done, he used the remnants of his power in my body to start tearing me apart. Literally. And yes, it had felt exactly as Pritkin described—barbs in my skin, shredding it, shredding me, and the worst part had been that I couldn't do anything about it.

But Zeus wasn't here. I knew that as certainly as I knew my name, and not only because I'd seen him wink out when he lost whatever tenuous link he had to Feltin. But because if he had been, Pritkin wouldn't be writhing in the grip of some curse; he would be dead. Just as I would have been in London if he and Mircea hadn't saved me.

And not just them, because there'd been a fourth person there that night when we battled for my life, hadn't there?

"I need to see the other guy," I said abruptly.

CHAPTER TWENTY-FOUR

Pritkin didn't look like he knew what I meant, but someone else did. The brilliant green of the eyes, almost neon bright a moment ago, darkened, flooding with black and starlight, like a beautiful night sky. The face changed, too, not in features but in attitude, in how he carried himself, in a thousand things that told me before he spoke that I wasn't facing the same man.

And that the man I *was* facing was not happy. "No."

"I haven't even said—"

"Oh, forgive me," Pritkin's incubus said with a sneer. "I was under the impression you were about to ask me to fall on my sword!"

"Not for me—"

"I would hope not. As I recall, I don't owe you anything."

"—but for him—"

"My dear jailer, you mean?" He lifted an eyebrow in a deliberately provocative move, then flopped onto the straw pallet with the air of a man who had no intention of ever leaving it. And he probably didn't. Feltin's men were out there, so the safest place for us was in here.

"You have the rest of the power that Pritkin absorbed in that camp, don't you?" I asked, coming to the point. Because I wasn't going to outthink Pritkin or outcharm an incubus. The truth was all I had to work with here; luckily, it was compelling.

"Bollocks," he said succinctly and got up again as if he

would like to get away from me, but there was nowhere to go. I sat down because chasing him around the little room wasn't likely to help his mood, and it was already pretty foul. Only I didn't know why.

"I thought things were improving," I said. "Between the two of you—"

"So did I!"

I waited, but he didn't say anything else.

"He took responsibility," I added. "That night in the forest, he told me—"

"I know what he told you!" He walked over to the door and jumped up to peer out of the small, high-set window, although he had to grab the windowsill to do it since it was at fey height. But I guessed he didn't find anything helpful because he jumped back down.

And turned around, leaning against the door and looking frustrated. Maybe because Pinkie and the Brain were nowhere in sight. I assumed that was who he was looking for, but I didn't expect them. Bodil wouldn't have attacked us if she didn't already have a plan for dealing with them.

But she better not have harmed them, or there would be hell to pay, I thought, thinking of Pinkie's loyalty.

"I need a cigarette," the incubus said abruptly, making me blink.

"Does Pritkin know you smoke?"

"I *don't* smoke," he said savagely. "I don't do anything. And I don't have what you want, so leave me be!"

"But you do," I insisted. "You wouldn't have been able to surface just now if you didn't. And there's been a ton of other indications—"

"There has not!"

"You're not as good of an actor as you think you are," I told him dryly. "Pritkin would have never worn that crazy get-up to dinner, court protocol or not. He'd have worn what he liked, which would have probably included a lot of weapons—"

That got a snort of laughter, at least, because it was true.

"—and if others didn't like it, they could lump it. Yet last night, he dressed like an *Aquaman* extra, a particularly sexy one, and didn't think twice about it."

"Around here, that get-up, as you call it, is positively monkish," the incubus informed me. "You saw what the rest were wearing."

He looked envious, as if he'd have preferred to go to dinner looking like Lord Bling and outshining everyone. I, for one, was glad he hadn't, but still. My point remained: he *had* influenced Pritkin's choices to a degree at least, which meant he had more power than he should have.

A lot more.

"That wasn't the only thing," I said. "He also doesn't flirt, even mildly, with pretty waitresses. He doesn't even flirt with me all that much unless you count sword practice—"

"And knowing him, he probably does!" the incubus said scornfully, but he returned and sat down.

"—and yet last night it was almost automatic," I continued. "Pritkin also doesn't stroll along with feline grace. Or pull admiration from a pissed-off fey woman who'd just had her stuff raided by a giant wad of snot—"

That got another small snort.

Well, at least I'm funny, I thought, my temperature rising.

"—or try to charm a ten-thousand-year-old demigod and almost succeed! Bodil was going to recruit us until she met me. Until I reminded her too much of my mother, and she threw a fit. And Pritkin never did that, never charmed someone like her. *I'm* more charming than he is, and I'm not charming at all —"

"You have your moments," he said dryly.

"—so, yeah, you've been surfacing a lot. And that takes power, power you didn't have before but do now, and I need to know *how much*."

"Not enough." He started to get up again, but I pulled him back down. And he let me, even though he didn't have to. My skinny arms weren't trapping him; knowing how much trouble we were in was doing that.

I just had to get him to admit it.

"I thought you two were reintegrating!" I said. "Pritkin told me he took responsibility for what happened with Ruth and knew you weren't at fault. He said—"

"A lot of things!" As it turned out, black eyes could flash, too. "He was feeling horrified over what happened to you in that camp and was beating himself up over it—as usual. But in the light of day, nothing changed. He still doesn't trust demons, especially me. He still doesn't listen to anyone, especially me! And he isn't going to."

I started to speak, but he didn't let me. I'd forgotten how much this version of Pritkin liked to talk, and now that he was on a roll, I was getting a lecture. I supposed that was better than nothing, so I shut up.

"If I had the power you seek—and I'm not saying I do— giving it to him would only trap me again. Leaving me at his mercy when he doesn't have any mercy, not for my kind! And I'm not doing that, you understand? I *can't*.

"It was hard enough when I thought I deserved it, when I was doing penance for my part in that bitch's death. But now?" He shook his head violently. "No, just no."

I scowled because that had sounded pretty final. "Look, I get it. I'm asking a lot—"

"You have no idea."

"—but that curse could drive him mad if it's anything like the one we battled in London. And as you told me once, you *are* him—"

"Like he's ever admitted that!"

"—so it threatens you as well—"

"So does he!"

"—and you've helped me before, several times. Maybe I can help you now—"

"You can help by leaving me the hell alone!" the incubus snarled. He threw off the hand I'd put back on his arm, leaned his head against the wall, shut his eyes, and looked asleep. Or like he wanted to be.

And maybe he did. Maybe Bodil's Somnolence was still active on him, too. Or perhaps he just wanted to forget I was here.

I stared at him, but he had that same mulish look I knew so well, that set-jawed, stone-faced stubbornness Pritkin got sometimes that never boded well for me. Or anyone else trying to reason with him. For such an intelligent man, he could be really stupid sometimes.

Especially about anything to do with demons.

His incubus half and his human/fey half had had their own little war going on for most of his life. That hadn't been true when he was younger, growing up quite happily among humans and human/fey hybrids in old Wales. I'd met his previous self there and had been astounded at how easily he laughed, at how mischievous he was, at how at home he felt in his skin.

I'd never known that man.

Pritkin's incubus half had been repressed for over a century, ever since it got carried away on his wedding night and drained his wife to death. That had sent Pritkin into a tailspin for years, filled with grief, guilt, and self-recrimination. For the first time, he had truly felt like the monster everyone thought him to be.

But that explanation for what had happened to Ruth hadn't told the whole story. Pritkin's wife had been part demon, too, and had wanted to increase her status and exchange her crappy life on Earth for a much more powerful, luxurious one in the hells by hitching her star to Rosier's only son. But not simply by marriage.

She had wanted power in her own right, which was why, on their wedding night, she had instigated the power exchange that demons view as sex and which the incubus royal house was particularly adept at.

Unlike other demons, who could give or receive some of their partner's energy in coitus, the incubi royal house could multiply it. Many, many times over, thus making an already pleasurable act a very lucrative one for both parties, as power was the only real currency in the hells. Rosier had made it the foundation of his wealth and influence, picking his partners carefully, as the power boost he offered was something the great demon lords would give almost anything for.

But great demon lords already had power to burn, which they needed as the process took before it gave. And it took a lot. More than a reckless, greedy, half-demon girl had had.

The result had been a shocked Pritkin suddenly holding the shriveled corpse of his wife in his arms while power surged through his horrified veins. He had blamed his demon half, but it had had very little to do with it. Ruth hadn't told him what she'd planned, and it happened so fast that no one had had a chance to react before it was over.

And she was dead.

With her had died a big part of Pritkin. Or should I say, with her death, a big part of him had been imprisoned, for he'd never trusted his demon half again. They'd already been at odds over some of the things that Pritkin had seen in the hells after his father came to Earth to claim him, and that had put paid to any reconciliation that might have happened over time.

Instead, he'd locked his incubus away, pretended it didn't exist, and denied himself the massive power boost it gave. And that was where things had stood for something like a century. Until I was being tortured in that camp, helpless and alone, and there was only one way to get me out.

Sex to an incubus was a conduit to someone's power, just as blood was to a vampire. And the sexual torture those silver-haired freaks had put me through, and the sick lust it had raised in them, had been all the access that Pritkin had needed. He'd used it to grab hold of their life essence, doing to them on purpose what he'd done to his wife accidentally, and drained them of every bit of their power. Until they tumbled lifeless to the floor or puffed away on a breath of wind.

I'd used the chance to escape, while his incubus had used it as a way out of his cage.

Pritkin usually would have been furious about that, but in some of the memories Faerie had shared with us through the Common, we'd seen another side of his wife. She hadn't been just a down-on-her-luck part-demon desperate to escape a life of poverty and powerlessness. She'd been an assassin, doing a job.

And guess who she was doing it for?

Enter Zeus, who had a problem. He was plotting to circumvent the protection spell that Mother had cast millennia ago, blocking the gods from Earth. And also blocking them from the hells and all those fat demon lords full of power that were waiting to be feasted on.

He needed the gods to hold this place against said demons, who disliked being lunch. But having the pantheon return risked a repeat of the situation he'd faced with Mother: a mad scramble among the gods for power, with anyone who turned out to be better at it than him trying to unseat him. She had done that after killing Rosier's father, the previous prince of the incubi, and absorbing his ability to multiply magic.

She'd used the gift to greatly expand the power that all those demon lords she'd been hunting had given her, then turned it on her fellow gods, killing or vanquishing them from this realm. If she hadn't been drained so low in the great battle for Earth that she nearly died herself, she could have fed using that same gift, replaced the magic she'd lost, and ruled here alone as she'd always wanted. But to receive you first have to give, and give a great deal, as Ruth had discovered to her cost.

And mother hadn't had enough left.

But Zeus did.

Mother might have slain the great king of the gods, but she hadn't gotten all of him. Wiley old Zeus had become suspicious about her frequent hunting trips into the hells and the power she was amassing. He had, therefore, persuaded a demon lord to carry part of his soul into those realms, where Mother's gift for traveling between worlds allowed her to easily go but where he and the other gods had struggled.

And what he'd discovered there, too late, was that she'd found a way to make war on them all—and to win.

He couldn't save himself from her wrath, but that small piece of his power, disguised in the demon lord he'd overwhelmed, had endured. He leeched off the creature's power until he found Aeslinn, a more willing puppet, and jumped ship. And began trying to recreate Mother's success, only with the incubi grandson this time.

Ruth had been paid to trap his prize for him, but one of Aeslinn's functionaries had changed the order at the last minute, knowing what would happen if his lord obtained all that power. So, Pritkin had become her target instead. And she'd almost succeeded where far more powerful enemies had failed, by serving him poison after he helped her get home following an attack by some street thugs.

But the demon lord who had carried Zeus all those years also knew of his plans and got there in the nick of time. He proposed a different outcome to her: watch Pritkin, get close to him, and only kill him if one of Zeus's operatives found him again. He had plans that involved the incubi and wanted Pritkin alive—and soon, so did Ruth.

After a while, she realized that no matter what she was offered as payment, it was nothing to what she could gain from Pritkin himself. So, she, too, had tried to emulate my mother and use an incubus to magnify her power. And had died for it.

Once Pritkin found out all of this, and his incubus helped save me from Zeus and then the fey camp, I'd thought they would mend their relationship. And work together as they'd been meant to all along. Reintegrating into one man of unimaginable power and far more peace. Only apparently not.

But perhaps I had one card left to play.

"What if I could give you more power?" I asked idly. "Like a lot more?"

The incubus cracked an eye at me because that was the one word that always got their attention.

"Won't work," he said flatly.

"What won't?"

"Waiting for the Pythian energy to return and using my abilities to magnify it, thus breaking Zeus's damned spell and getting us out of here in one fell swoop."

I blinked at him. "Why not?"

"You know damned well why not! Every time we do that, it gets out of control. We burnt a pub down—"

"We burnt a *god* down!"

It was true—or close enough. We'd helped defeat Ares by engaging in the same activity that had drained Pritkin's wife. But I was not a half-demon with barely any strength; I was a half-goddess with the added boost of the Pythian power.

And for the first time, Pritkin's incubus had been able to *feast.*

First on my power, and when he was sated, he had magnified and expanded what he'd taken a hundredfold and fed it back to me. And then fed again on *that*, over and over, in a cycle of creation that had left the two of us glowing like a star. And feeling like we were about to be ripped apart because Pritkin hadn't known how to handle it.

But his incubus did.

I was sure he did because he'd eaten the life essence of hundreds of fey without a burp! Like he'd helped me to send all that glowing power we'd made in Wales into the battle with Ares, directing it to rip open a portal in space-time and release another god onto the field. He was a Prince of the Incubi; he was born for this!

"This room is sealed, Cassie, not just warded," he said harshly. "It means the wards are ancient, to the point that they've seeped into its very bones. If we call up that kind of power, there's nowhere to send it if it gets away from me. The wards could reflect it back and immolate us both!"

"Or it could save us both, as it did in London—"

"In London, we had Mircea's help. His family took the load, dispersed it among themselves, and acted as a safety valve.

And in any case, you were locked in a battle with the king of the gods; there was nothing to lose. There is here!"

"Yes, there's you!"

But the chin stayed mulish, the eyes closed again defiantly, and the head went back. Saying without uttering a word that he wasn't budging on this. He wouldn't risk my life trying to make more power, and he wouldn't give what he already had to a man he didn't trust.

And the fact that the man was him made no difference at all!

The incubus wouldn't rely on someone who had imprisoned him all those years, and Pritkin wouldn't trust the demon who probably reminded him too much of his father. That also explained why he didn't want to acknowledge his maybe nephew, for fear that Rosier would come for his namesake if he knew and drag him off to the same hell that Pritkin had endured.

And I didn't know what to do about any of it.

CHAPTER TWENTY-FIVE

I just sat there since there was nothing else to do, waiting for Faerie to provide some inspiration—only she seemed to have gone off somewhere—and trying to find the calm I didn't have right now.

Seeing Zeus again, even as a bad TV-type broadcast, had been terrifying. I'd told Pritkin the truth; the old bastard wasn't here, probably couldn't be, considering that he and his current avatar were facing invasion by Caedmon's forces. I wondered how that felt, being besieged by your own son.

Of course, with Zeus, it probably wasn't the first time.

But he had a thousand tricks up his sleeve, and with someone like Feltin, he probably didn't need to be on site. He could play puppet master from the other side of Faerie, dangling rewards and punishments as a carrot or a stick for his latest donkey. And doing a bit of mind control when that wasn't enough.

And the fact that he wasn't even having to break a sweat to ruin our plans was just—

"There she is," the incubus said, watching me through a crack in his lids. "Your mother, peeking out of your eyes. I saw her in London, and I'm seeing her now. The difference is that you're starting to see her, too. And that scares the hell out of me."

"I'm not my mother."

"Yes, so you keep telling people. But has it occurred to you that most of us would be gibbering right now? You've just seen

Zeus for the first time since that complete debacle in Romania, where you *literally died.* If you had any sense, you'd be looking for a bed to hide under—"

"I'm done hiding!"

"So it would seem," he murmured, and I suddenly realized that I'd swooped on him like Feltin had that fey in his office.

For a second, both of us froze, barely breathing. Then, I slowly crawled backward and sat down, working to get myself under control. It didn't go so well.

Yeah, I should be scurrying away and searching for a bolthole, but I already had one. It was buried somewhere under the stables, where nobody ever went except for the demigoddess who ran this place and her stooges. I was as safe as anybody could be in this world, but I only wanted to get out.

And put Zeus's head on a goddamned *pike.*

"You sure your mother is dead?" the incubus asked dryly. "And not doing a little puppeteering of her own?"

"She's dead," I said harshly. "This is all me."

He thought about it. "Why doesn't that reassure me?"

I crawled back over, getting into his face slowly this time because I wasn't Zeus and wouldn't act like him. But I wanted Pritkin's alter ego to *get this.* And we didn't have time for subtleties.

"We will *die* in here," I told him. "Not our bodies, maybe, not yet, but our chances. Any hope of beating this bastard is ticking down with the clock. And if we don't win this, he will come for us—me, you, everyone we care about. We're at the top of his hit list, and you know it. So get over whatever this is, right freaking now, and help me!"

The incubus's eyes narrowed to the point that I could barely see the stars anymore. And his expression blurred the lines so that I wasn't sure who I was talking to or if it mattered. Because on one thing, at least, both men agreed.

"I *am* helping you, even if you can't see it," he said shortly.

"Martyring yourself is not helping me!"

"Martyr—my *dear.* I am an incubus. That word isn't even in

our vocabulary."

"Then what the hell is this?"

"Demon practicality. Humans always see things in black and white, with no shades of gray. It's been your problem all along and is one my "brother" unfortunately shares."

"So, how should I be seeing it?" I demanded.

"Simple. We miss the race. Bodil is satisfied. Winning two out of five challenges would make us the odds-on favorite and upend everything. But not even bothering—or daring, as it will be believed—to show up will effectively tank our chances. The main thing the fey look for in their leaders is courage.

"So, she comes to let us out, either then or at the end of this farce. I explain what that bastard Feltin did and that if she will be so good as to use her demigoddess abilities to lift the curse, I will show my gratitude by retiring from her lands forthwith —"

"And then what?" I demanded. "Watch the world burn? Two of them?"

He rolled his eyes. "Oh, give it a rest. Do you remember that camp? How close it was? Or Romania, where you—at best —managed a draw? And that only because of an ability the Pythian library had that Zeus didn't know about, coupled with your unparalleled ability to piss people off.

"If he'd been thinking clearly, you would be dead, permanently." He made a sound of disgust and grabbed my shoulders. "Listen to me, and listen well. You've done better than anyone could have expected, but you were right before— you *aren't* your mother. And I am not some demonic god or whatever storyline you have my brother believing. We are not going toe-to-toe with the king of the gods and walking away, not again. We're going to die, or we're going to run, that's the truth—"

"And leave the job to *who*?"

"Who cares?" It had an edge of shrillness to it. "When the hell did this become our responsibility? We're two very small, very insignificant players on a huge cosmic stage! You sound as if—"

"You're a coward." I stared at him. "I thought after London —but you're a *coward*."

"You're damned right," he said, with no embarrassment at all. "I'm a bloody coward. In a case like this, anybody with a brain would be!"

I felt my eyes narrow. "Are you calling me stupid?"

"Well, if the high heel fits—"

He'd let me go during that exchange, so I took the opportunity to grab him. And to shake him as hard as I could, only that amount of muscle doesn't shake. All it got me was another raised eyebrow, and I swore to God—

"I'm calling you young," he said flatly. "And naïve. And brainwashed—"

"By who?"

"By any number of centuries-old people, putting more and more of the burden for this war on your fragile shoulders and not caring when they inevitably snap. But I *do* care—"

"If you cared, if you loved me as you once claimed, you'd *help*."

"Help you kill yourself?" The mulish chin was back. "That I won't do. I won't endanger you or let you endanger yourself by giving you power. And that's not the spell talking. Fey magic has a limited grip on me; unlike my other half, demon blood is resilient—"

"Then help yourself!" I interrupted because the damned man could talk all day! "Zeus is still looking for you. He wants to strip your soul and gain your power—"

"He'll have to find me first."

"And you think he won't? That he can't? The only safety for you is if we beat him!"

"Nice try, but my father has eluded that old bastard for centuries, proving you wrong—"

"Centuries when the gods *weren't here*. They had to work through intermediaries like Aeslinn and that demon lord we saw in the Common who regularly erased his memory. But if they come back—"

The incubus smiled. "If. So far, everyone who has tried it has died."

"Because we beat them!" I practically screamed. My God, and I'd thought Pritkin was hardheaded! His incubus made him look positively easygoing, and I was running out of arguments. "Do it for Pritkin, then—"

"Who will then help you, thus putting you in danger? No. Bodil will be back eventually, and I can wait for her."

"Can *he*?"

"Who knows? Who cares?" the familiar face darkened. "My dear, foolish brother can look out for himself, as he left me to do for so long. And who knows? If Zeus's spell destroys him, perhaps it will leave me in charge for a—"

I don't remember moving, don't remember anything until his head snapped back, with the shape of my handprint livid on his cheek. "You wear his face," I hissed. "But he was right all along. You're not him! *And you never will be!*"

Retreating, I went to the corner with the damned bucket and sat there, my back to the room, because I didn't want him to see my face. Demons only respected power, and right then, I didn't have any. I never did unless it was borrowed from someone else.

I sat there for a long moment, almost shaking with rage. But it didn't last. I felt myself deflate and grow almost perceptibly smaller, just a tiny, insignificant thing like the incubus had said.

And a grubby one.

I'd been wearing this gown for a while, being too afraid in Faerie to take it off. And although it had been laundered a few times, it looked the worse for wear. Augustine was going to have a fit when he saw it. . .

If he saw it.

I stared at the toes peeking out from under the hem, visible now that the armor had retreated, and tried to push thoughts like that away. It was stupid, and I always did this, and it wouldn't help! But I didn't know anything that would.

The toes didn't look any better than the gown. The chipped paint was in all colors of the rainbow, courtesy of my little initiates, who loved painting anyone they could find. My big, strong vamp bodyguards fled in terror when a mob of them came hunting their latest victim and still ended up with sparkly nails more often than not. But the last time they'd caught me was before my foray into Faerie, which was beginning to be a while ago.

So long that I wondered if I'd ever see them again. Like Tamsin, with her vibrant red hair, a coven hallmark. It was a Little Orphan Annie bush most of the time and long, Victorian-era sausage curls when anyone had the time to fix it up.

But what she lacked in hirsute management, she more than made up for by a precocious ability with the Pythian power. She was *four* and already calling it to shift things to her that she couldn't be arsed to get for herself. Annabelle, one of my acolytes, had started to whisper that she'd be shifting herself soon, and how would we keep up with her then?

Or Betty, an old-fashioned name for an old-fashioned girl who liked having tea parties with our resident ghost, the Pythian librarian, whose hairstyle she'd recently copied. I was starting to suspect her of being a ghost magnet because there had been a lot more ghosts around my court than usual lately. And most of them hadn't come to see me.

Or Mira, our artist, she of the epic 'fro and the ratty pink bunny suit that she wore everywhere, although it was starting to look as bad as my gown. Rhea had given up enchanting her drawings, which Mira insisted be animated, and had started enchanting the crayons used to make them instead. Resulting in epic Cassie pics—Mira's favorite subject—showing up everywhere.

They usually depicted me putting a beat down on one of the gods, with a couple of golden whips—which I didn't have the power to manifest most of the time—flashing. Or facing down Ares with an emerald green thunderbolt, which she'd carefully spread some glitter on to make it clear that it was *magic*. Or dressed in one of Augustine's ridiculous gowns, which she always managed to make even more outrageous. . .

I stared at my ratty-looking nails and felt tears well up in my eyes, and I didn't care enough to brush them away.

It was too much, suddenly, that little reminder of a better world. One that I'd thought I was almost back to, with Pritkin in tow, and could put this damned land and its goddess and its stupid, endless problems behind me. I could go home. . .

Only I couldn't, and even if I could, without an end to this, would home even be there for much longer? Would my court? Would my *girls*?

No. It wasn't even a question. Zeus played the part of the avuncular All-Father, but he was a bastard. He'd hunt them down, one by one, not because he needed to; they were no threat to him. Even Rhea, the oldest, was only nineteen and half-trained. But because he'd enjoy it.

He'd killed two of the three Graea, old demigoddesses who had been acting as my protectors since I got this crazy job. Unlike everyone else, they'd known who my mother was as soon as they saw me and had signed onto team Cassie. And like Bodil had said, that didn't improve anyone's longevity.

He'd almost killed the previous Pythia, Agnes, and her mentor and mine, Gertie, until she sent me away in sheer self-preservation. He had killed thousands of war mages and vamps, who had been bearing the burden of this war largely alone. He'd cost me my ghost companion, Billy Joe. . .

I was sobbing in earnest now and didn't care. I couldn't do this! Not alone, not with Pritkin spelled and possibly dying, and everybody else off limits or lost or . . . or something. I couldn't even say the words, that Mircea might be dead, too, and that it was my fault because I could have saved him—and I should have, even if it made him hate me!

I should have figured it out, made better decisions, done *something*. But I hadn't because I wasn't good enough for this job, and all my bravado and "badass" this and "goddess" that didn't change that. And now I was truly alone, and I couldn't think, didn't know, *wasn't enough*...

Billy's necklace bumped my hands when I bent over and put my face in them, and I felt my breath hitch. He'd died defending and believing in me, and it had all been for nothing. Because it ended in a dank cell in Faerie that I was too stupid to get out of!

I felt arms go around me, and someone pulled me back against a hard chest. I knew it wasn't Pritkin, or at least not the right Pritkin, but it felt so good I didn't care. This man had said he loved me once, too, but I didn't know what that meant to a demon.

Not enough, apparently.

We sat silently for a moment because I guessed there wasn't much left to say.

And then there wasn't anything because the room winked out.

"What the—what is this?" the incubus demanded.

I didn't answer because I didn't know. I couldn't tell whether this was another hint from Faerie or something more sinister because I hadn't felt the transition into the Common. Of course, I hadn't always before, but it had been a lot more abrupt since losing the link to Pritkin's fey blood.

But this transition had been so effortless that if I'd had my eyes closed, I wouldn't have noticed it at all.

I put a hand down to the cool marble floor I was sitting on, so different from the dank stone of a minute ago. It was a massive, white, polished slab with gold veining that ran halfway down the wide corridor we were in before being paired beautifully with another. And so seamlessly that it was almost impossible to tell where one began and the last finished.

There was also light here, faint but like actual moonlight, not the dim, underwater world of Nimue's mountain. It was flooding over the marble from a window at the end of the hall, where diaphanous curtains were being tossed around by what smelled like an ocean breeze. But that was the only sign that we might be near water.

"What is this?" the incubus demanded again. He grabbed me when I didn't answer, but it didn't help because I still didn't know.

But when I slowly, carefully got to my feet, they felt solid underneath me, not the hazy, not-actually-there sensation of my recent trips into the Common. Where I hadn't even needed to walk, with Faerie towing me along like a kid dragging a balloon behind her. Only that was not nearly as reassuring as you'd expect since that meant I might not be in the Common at all, but then what was this?

Illusion? Some shift that couldn't be happening because I was the only person in Faerie who could currently do that? A trick?

And if so, a trick by who?

I'd started to break out into a cold sweat, as the answer to that last question was obvious, when the incubus grabbed my chin. "Look at me!"

I looked and immediately crossed incubus trickery off the shortlist because he looked as spooked as I did. "What? Is. This?" he demanded and then didn't allow me a chance to answer. "No, do you understand? I said no!"

"No to what?" I asked, which was hard as he was pushing my cheeks together to the point that my lips were pursed.

"No, I am not doing this! I am not being drawn into another of your weird, metaphysical adventures! I am not!"

"Okay," I said through duck lips. "Then how do you suggest we get out?"

"You take us out!"

"I didn't take us here, and keep your voice down!"

"Why?"

"That's why," I said, dragging him through an open doorway as the sound of booted feet rang down the hall.

CHAPTER
TWENTY-SIX

*M*y attempt to hide didn't work, as the soldiers followed us in, and there were a lot of them. First came a bunch of Nimue's impossible-to-miss peacock guards, their distinctive armor looking even stranger outside a watery setting. And then the purple-dipped guys, with the shiny, breathtakingly expensive armor and the velvet cloaks hanging from their shoulders. And finally, Nimue herself, her long, dark hair floating around her head in defiance of gravity, as if born outwards on the tide.

Damn, I'd forgotten how beautiful she was. She didn't seem real, with the uncanny valley effect kicking in hard whenever my eyes tried to look at her, making them want to slip off the other side. Only to come immediately back because beauty like that attracted as much as it repelled.

Her face was a pale oval without a flaw, her lips red as coral, her body clothed in what looked like liquid seafoam. It may have been that amazing fey silk or, knowing her, the real thing magicked up to swirl around her. But either way, it made all the ridiculous pretensions of her court seem like what they were—bad copies of her effortless perfection.

Yet it was the eyes that stunned.

They were blue, but that description totally misses the point. They were blue—and green and gray and all the colors of the ocean. And right now, they were angry, so much so that I could swear I saw the colors change and slur like the ones in waves that the light was shining through.

A storm was coming, only I didn't know at who.

Until I turned my neck and saw who Nimue was looking at. She was standing on the opposite side of the room behind us, holding a baby in her arms. A baby . . .

Who I recognized immediately.

It was the hair that did it. Pritkin's hair could lay flat as an adult if he wasn't messing with it and his magic wasn't surging. But if it was . . . well, I'd often wondered if that was why he favored spiky hairstyles, because they covered up what happened when he got mad.

Like that, I thought, watching as the baby's scant blond whisps suddenly started wafting about like Nimue's. Or like Jonas Masden's, the most powerful mage I knew, who had white tresses that drifted about his head like a sea anemone's tentacles. And got progressively more spiky as he became more annoyed.

The baby's short strands were almost perpendicular because he'd recognized danger, even if he didn't know the word for it yet.

"What is this?" the incubus asked, his voice suddenly quiet.

"Shhh," I told him, even though I was pretty sure no one could hear us. No one had even glanced our way, and there was nowhere to hide. So, this was either the Common or—

Okay, that would be interesting.

"Morgaine," Nimue's voice, often as melodious as a babbling brook, was flat today.

The woman holding the baby looked up, and strangely enough, considering all the soldiers, she smiled. "I suppose I should be flattered," she said. "You sent so many of your best soldiers to fetch me from Earth that I wondered if they were meant as an honor guard for your grandson."

"He is no grandson of mine!"

"Great-grandson, then, if you wish to be precise. And as everyone knows, you are always precise. . ."

Amazingly, she sounded amused.

I remembered that about Pritkin's mother, how she'd even gone into battle laughing. And how much she'd favored Nimue, especially now when dressed like a fey. But while she was beautiful, with long dark hair highlighted by a dress the color of sunlight, it wasn't half so active as her grandmother's, and her blue eyes were lovely enough but merely . . . blue.

You could really see the human in her, and it made me like her more.

"Give me the child," Nimue said, never one to beat around the bush.

"No." It was mild, and the sunny smile on Morgaine's face never wavered.

"I will not play these games with you," Nimue snapped. And there was power behind the words, enough that I could feel it ripple over my skin all these years later.

Power that Morgaine turned aside with a gesture as casual as brushing a speck of lint off her pretty yellow skirt.

"Do not test me!" Nimue thundered, and the room shook. But Morgaine ignored that, too, with an insouciance that felt foolhardy under the circumstances.

"I'm beginning to see where he gets it," the incubus said, his words light but his expression. . .

Because yeah. I supposed seeing yourself as a baby would be attention-getting. Only he was looking far more interested than even that would warrant.

And he wasn't looking at the baby.

"She's beautiful," he whispered, staring at Morgaine.

Because she was his mother, too, wasn't she? He'd known her back in old Wales, or rather, Pritkin had when they were more intertwined. But neither had known who she was to them. That had been kept quiet to protect them, as plenty of people in Wales hated the fey and Nimue's line in particular.

So she'd died there as nothing but a passing acquaintance. I'd told Pritkin the truth after that little adventure, but this was his first time seeing her as his mother. And he was soaking her in.

"Give me the child!" And okay, that command had felt less like a ripple and more like the storm I'd been expecting. Nimue had seemed fond enough of Morgaine when the woman was doing as she was told, which was basically never. But she had not enjoyed *being crossed.*

But to my surprise, Morgaine didn't crumple to the floor or even noticeably react—other than to broaden that cheeky grin slightly. Something that did not falter even when the array of guards lunged for her at a gesture from their mistress, only to run into something halfway across the room. Judging by how hard they hit, it may as well have been an invisible wall.

Nimue began to frown.

"How are you—" she began and then stopped herself. Maybe because Morgaine had gestured to something that had appeared hovering in the air between them.

"Your court wasn't impressed by my new abilities," she pouted. "But they do come in handy, at times. Times like these, to be precise."

"Take it down." And, for the first time, there was real menace in Nimue's lovely voice.

"Oh, you don't like people using magic you don't know against you? Fancy that."

"Take it down!"

I was starting to worry about the room's integrity, as that last thunderous command had caused little siftings of dust to shake down from the rafters. They highlighted Morgaine's creation in the center—a ward, I assumed, although not one I'd ever seen. It looked vaguely like a compass, being round, with symbols at each cardinal point, and was starting to glow a bright, almost electric blue.

Probably with the magic that Nimue had started throwing at it.

"You can do that all day and only exhaust yourself," Morgaine said casually, picking up a fuzzy yellow blanket and wrapping it securely about her bundle. "It's like a key, you know. You only have three tumblers, grandmother.

"And it takes all four."

"Stop this immediately!" Nimue thundered.

"Or what? Will you come after me? Or send your guards to jerk me and your grandson back again? You're going to do that anyway, but this time, I've made plans. I made a deal with the devil, you

might say—"

"Traitor!"

"You're not going to kill my son, Nimue."

"Your abomination, you mean! Do you realize what you've done? Do you have any idea—"

"Made someone amazing?" Morgaine asked, bouncing her baby slightly. And looking at him with such love that I felt a pang under my breastbone. Had my mother ever looked at me that way?

Why didn't I think so?

"You put our power—all our power, including that of the gods —into the hands of the demons!" Nimue raged. "Do you not think they'll use it?"

"I think Emrys will use it," Morgaine said. "But not on their behalf."

"Then you're even more of a fool than I thought! They care for nothing but power. They are selfish, self-aggrandizing, cowardly animals, every one—"

"Not cowardly, surely," Morgaine said, sounding amused again.

Which, yeah. Not the time, I thought, as her grandmother flushed puce. And somehow made it look good.

"Yes, cowards!" Nimue spat. "They fled deeper to the hells when the gods pursued them, refusing our offers of alliance. They left whole worlds to burn—their worlds—rather than defend them. They died by the hundreds of millions, by the billions for all I know, fighting and scrapping among themselves like wolves over meat—"

"Instead of what? Cooperating with their overlords as we did?" Morgaine hiked an eyebrow and, for a minute, looked so like her son that I blinked. "You act like it would have changed anything to stand together. They'd have died all the same."

"No, not the same!" Nimue hissed. "Our people died fighting them, as you seem to have forgotten—"

"Some did. In time, when it became obvious what our fate was to be otherwise."

"—and we did it facing them, not fleeing into the night! We did it on our feet, like fey, not on our knees, like vermin! There is a

difference in how we face death, Morgaine, and it says everything about who we are as a people."

"Perhaps," Morgaine cradled her son, who had calmed down and was giggling as his mother tickled his tummy. "Fortunately, my boy has fey blood, too, doesn't he? Your blood. Do you think that someone with your blood could be less than courageous?

"If so, you don't know yourself half so well as I do."

"Have a care, Morgaine. For I will find him."

"I don't think so. Not this time. But if you do, hopefully, it will be when you've had a chance to cool down. And your decency has overtaken your panic, as it always does. And you have thought on the fact that the worth of a man isn't entirely down to bloodlines. Who he is and what he does with his life is up to—"

The room wavered again, but not because of Nimue this time. She was suddenly as frozen as if I'd cast a time spell or a TV had been paused. The whole scene was.

"What is it?" the incubus demanded, looking around. "What did you do?"

"I don't run the Common," I reminded him. "Faerie does."

"Then why did she pause it? If she brought us here to see this—"

"Lover's Knot," I said, wincing slightly.

"It's not on you!"

"Yes, that's the problem." I staggered slightly before I caught myself. "Without access to Pritkin's fey blood, I keep . . . coming unstuck. . ." I gasped, and the room darkened slightly. "That's why she had to . . . drop me out of it . . . the first time. . ."

"But we went back in after that," he said, sounding almost panicked. He really wanted to see this. "And you were fine!"

"I wasn't fine. Nothing changed on my end, but I think she . . . compensated . . . by pushing more power into the spell. . . But she's carrying two of us . . . and it's getting . . . tiring. . ."

"She's a goddess! They don't get tired!" I shot him a look and didn't say anything because I didn't have to. My bedraggled state said it for me. "Then put it back!"

"What?" I gasped.

"Lover's Knot!"

"I can't. I don't know the spell and . . . don't have the power . . . anyway. And I think . . . we're about to get thrown . . .

"Out," I finished, just as a wave of magic hit me.

It was as refreshing as a drink of water in the desert, as powerful as blood rushing back into half-collapsed veins, and as comforting as warmth after bitter cold. I almost gasped in shock, not having really expected this to work. Because Pritkin was smarter than me, but right now, he was also distracted.

Which gave me a minute to act, or however long this vision had left. Because that's what we were in; not the Common, but a vision of my own, like the ones I used to have all the time growing up. But which I'd had very few of since becoming Pythia.

The Pythian power sought formidable seers to work with because our union was a symbiosis. It gave me the ability to shift and use its godly power in various ways, while I . . . gave it my eyes. At least, my metaphysical ones.

It used my ability to peer through the centuries to patrol the timeline. And in doing so relieved me of all those nasty visions I used to get, very few of which had ever been positive. And neither was this, I thought, as the vision slowly restarted, showing Morgaine finishing her sentence with a defiant "—him!"

Then she made a gesture, and her compass flew through the air to hit the wall. And a moment later, there was no wall. A tunnel opened up for her, spiraling out from the middle of her compass as I'd seen the stones at Aeslinn's court do for his fey, creating an exit where none had been before.

Earth magic, I thought, something that Nimue didn't have. And although she sent her fey leaping across the room after Morgaine, they only ran into what was once again solid stone. Just that fast, Morgaine was gone.

Meanwhile, I had barely kept up with what was happening because I was focused on something else, specifically the black claws biting into Pritkin's flesh. They weren't inside it, not yet, but they were bleeding him dry spiritually. I could see the weeping wounds now, trace the tiny streams of power leeching out into the air, and almost feel his pain as I hadn't been able to a moment ago.

Because a moment ago, I'd been powerless, almost bone dry. Before tricking a demon into giving me access to the vast reserves he held from draining all those fey. Because putting Lover's Knot on me to steady the vision had steadied something else, hadn't it?

Like my hands, which had been trembling a moment ago and were now rock steady as I started to unwind all those horrible barbs.

He was going to notice, just any time now, which was why I was careful. And not just about the incubus. But also about my safety because there was no way I wanted to experience Zeus's power again!

That was why I'd wrapped my hands in triple levels of protection before starting this, layering ward on top of ward. And it was lucky I had, because the barbs on all those strands, like thorns on a vine, bit deep. But not deep enough, and I used the leverage they gave me to pull them slowly out of Pritkin's metaphysical flesh, freeing him by degrees.

But the main event was over now, with nothing but an empty nursery to hold the incubus's attention. And some of the thorns were buried deep, having had plenty of time to work their way into Pritkin's spirit, getting a good grip. I was almost out of time and hadn't managed to free enough—

Until Nimue saved me.

She'd had her eyes closed while her men beat uselessly on stone, standing as still as a statue. Then those amazing gray-blue orbs opened, and her finger pointed. "The Myrgard! She's made her way out of the tower!"

The soldiers, their knuckles bloody from their useless fight, turned gratefully toward the window. And the incubus's attention focused, as did everyone's, on the tiny, fleeing figure of a woman, her dark hair flying out behind her as she ran easily over the top of the marshland, as I'd seen her do to plain water back on Earth. Because Pritkin's mother held all four elements, didn't she?

But she was on Alorestri turf this time, and they tore after her. Like I took the reprieve and ripped the remaining barbs out of Pritkin's flesh. Enough of them, at least, that it was too late when *the incubus finally caught a clue.*

I jerked them free, like pulling a heavy, stubborn vine off a house that it had been growing on for decades, and it required an alarming amount of power. The incubus's power, to be exact, something he realized when he saw those dark barbs dissipate in the air, letting go with a hissing sizzle. And then he started fighting me.

And he wasn't just grappling metaphysically. We crashed back into our cell and went rolling across the floor, kicking and screaming and hair-pulling—at least I was—until the incubus scrambled up my body and pinned me to the floor, panting and furious. "What did you do?" he screamed in my face. "What did you *do*?"

"What you should have!" I stared up at him defiantly. Which was not bright as he already looked like he could have strangled me. But he settled for shaking me instead.

"You *mugged* me!"

"Yeah. Sucks to be you."

That, of course, prompted some more shaking. "*How*?"

"Lover's Knot. You put it back on us—"

"To steady you!"

"I didn't need steadying. That wasn't the Common. It was a vision—one of mine."

"But it *dimmed*. It flickered—"

"Yeah, because I dimmed it."

He stared at me for a moment, but then his head shook violently. "Why are you lying to me? *I can't see your visions!*"

"Yeah, that stumped me for a minute, too. But you, Mircea, and I . . . got close . . . in London, back when we were battling Zeus. And in the incubus version of sex, sometimes traits get passed over." I saw his eyes widen. "My guess is that you absorbed some of Mircea's mental powers and kept them. I don't know how many, but I didn't bring you into that vision, so you must have brought yourself."

"I was trying to calm you," he said slowly, those pale lashes blinking. "To reassure you, when the vision hit—"

"And sucked you in alongside me. I just let you think it was the Common because I needed access to your power. And because you were the only one with enough juice to put Lover's Knot back in place."

I saw when it truly hit him—that he'd been played, and by a human no less. And for a second, he looked more surprised than outraged. "What the hell . . . do you call that?" he asked in wonder.

"Demon practicality," I said, and sucked down the rest of his power.

CHAPTER
TWENTY-SEVEN

O f course, it wasn't that easy.

Damn incubus! I thought a short time later. Because Pritkin's other half had had far less power than I'd expected. Regardless of what he said, he must have been helping his counterpart on the way here, and by the time I finished freeing them from Zeus's curse and shifted us out of the damned cell, we'd used up most of that.

Which was a problem, as Bodil's fey were everywhere, and it looked like they'd been warned that we might find some way out of our cage. They were on us before we'd gone ten yards. And I do mean on us.

One took me down in a flying leap before Pritkin pulled him off, and another dropped on top of us from a hidden perch we'd never even seen, all while bellowing for backup. And as soon as we took care of one group, another appeared. And Pritkin didn't want to immolate them because these were the good guys!

Or as close as this place ever got.

So, that made shifting them necessary, or trapping them behind power-sucking wards, or doing Somnolence spells that, as it turned out, weren't much easier on our power reserves. All while on a mad scramble through a maze of tunnels with more guards launching themselves at us at seemingly every turn. And I now understood why they wore those black outfits, as they were almost impossible to see in the dim lighting.

It was like fighting off a bunch of damned ninjas that

appeared out of nowhere every time we looked. Another grabbed me on an incline, and Pritkin slammed him into the wall with a sticky, white, spider-silk-looking spell I'd seen him use a few times before. And then we were scrambling up an area that absolutely should have had stairs because it felt like my ankles were bent totally the wrong way.

And, of course, there were more guards at the top, firing down at us. And some we'd missed or new ones that had come up behind, doing the same. And us shielding like bastards in between while I shifted whoever I could see through the spell fire and thought about shifting us back to the room, but we could hear the trumpets echoing even down here, announcing the start of the next challenge. Pritkin said we were almost there, and so we kept going.

He lobbed sticky spell after sticky spell at the mob outside our shield, which the crazy bastards were grabbing the sides of and jumping on top, trying to slow us down with their weight alone. And it was working. Cursing fey ended up dotting the walls, floor, and, in one case, the ceiling, as Pritkin caught one halfway through a leap, yet still, they came.

You had to give them points for resilience, I thought, and shifted half a dozen into the canal.

But it was getting harder. We were battling a whole platoon on our own, and while it appeared to be working since we were still on our feet, it was draining us—fast. This needed to end!

Pritkin finally dropped the shield and we ran for it, having finally cleared the fey in front of us. But more were coming on little cat feet from behind, and they were barefoot. There were no boots to ring out here and give us any warning.

So, half the time, I didn't hear them before some spell tripped me up and had me face-planting. Or a numbing curse clipped my shin on the way past and had me dragging that leg for what felt like half a mile. Or a web came spiraling out of the darkness and grabbed my hair instead of my body.

That last one had been fired too high because the fey weren't used to aiming at someone my height. But it had enough momentum to rip me off my feet and drag me down the hall before affixing me to a protruding bit of stone overhead, like a circus performer dangling from her ponytail. Only I wasn't one, and it freaking *hurt,* not to mention that I couldn't get down!

Pritkin caught up with me, released me on the fly, and dragged me further up the corridor, my scalp aching, my deadened foot stumbling, and spell fire we could no longer shield against hitting the walls on all sides. The only good thing was that they didn't seem to be trying to kill us, which was a nice change. But it was still infuriating!

And then we were out, stumbling from the dank, dimly lit tunnels through a door and into—

I couldn't tell. I'd just been hit by a wall of heat, sound, and sunlight so bright that it completely blinded me. It felt like a slap to the face, and the roar accompanying it was like the follow-up punch.

My ears crackled, my eyes fought to adjust, and my translator spell gave the hell up and shut down, leaving me with no idea what anybody was saying, shrieking, singing, or laughing about.

But they were doing a lot of it.

I was momentarily stunned, but it didn't affect Pritkin the same way. He yelled something at me that I couldn't make out even this close, grasped my hand, and started forging a path through a crowd so thick that it felt like a solid wall of people. He also jerked the hood of my borrowed cape over my face even though his was still out in the open.

Only it wasn't the one I was used to, I realized, as my vision slowly adjusted.

I found myself in a dazzlingly sunny day amid a smear of color, vibrancy, and life, surrounded by what looked like all the people in the world, and holding the hand of a pop-eyed fey with bright blue hair and a goatee. It took me a second to realize that Pritkin had flung a glamourie over himself but was conserving magic where I was concerned as I had a hood.

I shrank back into it because there were a lot of guards in the colorful crowd, not to mention over the top of it.

The latter were perched on overhangs and rocky outcroppings above a great open space that reminded me of a canyon. The more or less level ground area ran through and around giant black rock fingers erupting from the soil and spearing six or more stories into the air. And the surrounding cliffs were even taller.

Patches of what looked like sailcloth had been stretched between some of the former to provide shade to the many merchants with stalls underneath, although that wouldn't be the case for much longer. Some of the purple-haired guards were going around, cutting the ropes holding the sails in place, despite the protests from sellers and buyers alike. The guards ignored them because they weren't interested in people's comfort.

They were interested in us and wanted a clear field of vision.

And they were getting one.

A larger-than-average sail, maybe because it was anchored to some of the cliffs, collapsed without warning onto the crowd below, causing shouts of anger from the people trapped underneath. We edged around, staying in the traffic flow as hundreds fought their way free, and were pushed toward one of the black rock columns in the process, like a couple of leaves being born downstream in a gale. Fortunately, one of the leaves had some magic left and managed to forge a path for us back toward the line of stalls hugging the cliffs.

The crowd was thicker there, but the pace was slower as people waited in long lines to be served. I barely noticed, being too busy watching the watchers, which included four fey on top of the huge pillar we'd just missed, sitting under their own shelter. The wind was up and whipping the brown material of their tarpaulin around, along with their hair, causing one to pull his back into a ponytail.

They didn't appear to have binoculars, but those were fey

eyes; they didn't need them if they were paying attention. And they were, their grim faces contrasting with the laughing, excited throng. Probably worried about what Feltin would do if they didn't bring our heads back on a platter, I thought.

Since I liked mine where it was, I put it down and hoped my height wouldn't give me away.

It didn't seem likely.

This crowd wasn't the usual seven-foot-tall willowy type I had become used to in the lands of the fey. It was of all sizes and varieties, including some I'd never seen before. And some that I was pretty sure nobody had ever seen before, with the combo of dark fey, light fey, and human genes making a hell of a soup.

A trio of giggling, three-foot-tall women with pointy ears, big noses, and wild green hair pushed past, looking almost exactly like the troll dolls sold in gift shops. They were eating stuffed squid and using their sharp elbows to cut a swath through the crowd. And they didn't get so much as a glance from anyone, except for some of the people they jostled out of the way.

Because cotton candy hair was everywhere, in pinks, lavenders, blues, and greens, and in every style from afros to wild tufts, and from sleek, silky braids to elaborate updos. The facial features matched the hair, ranging from the delicate elfin variety to the bulbous and ogre-ish and everything in between. I saw a nine-foot-tall shaggy creature that could have doubled for Big Foot; a couple of stocky, lizard-headed guys like the ones I'd seen on a recent trip to the realm of the dragon lords; a lovely blonde woman with bright green skin, a slim build and delicate ogre's tusks; and a swarm of pixies flying overhead, collectively carting around a large paper spill of spicy red shrimp that they were sharing between them.

Again, they attracted no one's attention but mine, possibly because, around here, that was perfectly normal behavior or because there were a hundred other things to see.

Pritkin towed me through the crowd, taking the brunt of

the work himself and leaving me to gape around in wonder. At the huge waterfall at the end of the ample open space, cascading over a cliff so high that I couldn't see the top from here and misting the nearby crowd as if a light rain was falling; at the mass of vendors calling out their wares, which seemed to consist of every type of seafood imaginable prepared in every kind of way, including some prawns as big as my two fists being grilled over an open flame that looked delicious but the seller was mobbed; at the musicians on a dias, tuning up some instruments I didn't recognize; and at the streamers and banners snapping in the wind, with what I guessed were the different challengers' emblems on them, although I didn't see ours. And then I realized that I didn't even know what ours was supposed to look like, and started to ask Pritkin, when he shoved a spill of small, fried, soft shelled crabs into my hands.

I had no idea how he'd managed to acquire them but didn't care as they were warm and smelled sweet and spicy and—

"Eat," he yelled. "It distorts the face!"

He didn't have to tell me twice.

I ate, stuffing my cheeks with the little things, and they were amazing, or maybe I was just starving. And so were some shrimps like those the pixies had had, a spill of which was tossed to us by a vendor after Pritkin lobbed him a coin in passing and which were hot enough that I thought the top of my head would come off. But instead, we picked up a cold brew from a wandering giant-sized seller with massive kegs on each burly shoulder and found it to be pink, punchy, and vaguely beer-like, as if a nice wheat beer had been mixed with Kool-Aid.

I'd have eaten and drunk more, but suddenly, we were there, having traversed the length of what I guessed was Fountain Court, although I had yet to see a fountain. The great waterfall was on one side of us, its roar almost deafening this close, filling up a large round pool or a small lake. On the less spray-filled side, the pool was surrounded by an amphitheater-type setup composed of a cascade of sweeping, black stone seats.

More seats were on the other side, where stands packed with the fey nobility hugged an open space between the cliffs, with a backdrop of the palace in the distance. I'd never seen it from the outside and wasn't seeing much of it now, as it looked like a mountain had eaten it. A few towers stuck out here and there, surrounded by gardens, waterfalls, and pagodas, which I guessed were for lounging as a lot of people seemed to be doing that, with spyglasses trained this way.

I supposed they were the ones who hadn't managed to secure a ticket to the stands.

Between them and the mountain we were on was a chasm, as Nimue's kingdom seemed to be like Rome and built on hilltops. Only in her case, they were more like islands, sticking out of the water that shimmered all around. Including the waterfall's pool, where a bunch of seahorses were bucking at the traces in stalls on this side.

But I could see no connection between the waterfall pool and the open water, which was down a pretty steep drop anyway. The pool only covered maybe an acre and a half, and no river ran out of it. So, what were we supposed to do? I wondered. Circle the pond like a bunch of rubber ducks in a bath?

I couldn't figure it out, maybe because I could hardly think. Tens of thousands of people had gathered on the steps surrounding the pond that cascaded down toward the water, and those who hadn't gotten a perch had crawled onto the surrounding rocks to wave pennants and scream. Since I didn't know any fey languages and my translator wasn't even attempting to sort out the babble, I had no idea what anyone was saying.

Then the musicians started up, and it didn't matter anyway.

They drowned out what some official-looking type in a glittery robe was trying to announce in front of the stands of the beautiful people. He tried to wave the musicians off, or at least get them to shut up, because even enhanced speech wasn't good enough to cut through the din. But it didn't work, and he finally gave up, and some of the shell-shaped trumpets sounded again as they'd been doing about every five minutes, deep and resonate, and whipping up the crowd even more.

And finally, here they came, out of a tunnel in the rock under the falls, a troop of the wildest-looking people imaginable. The challengers, of which there seemed to be about twenty, had all dressed for the occasion, and to give them credit, they managed to stand out even in this crazy mix. I recognized Æsubrand, still keeping to his brilliant white arrogance and ignoring the resounding boos that met his appearance, as it looked like Aeslinn's son wasn't any more popular than his old man.

But most of the competition wasn't so austere. The jewels flashing under the brilliant sun, the crazy plumage decorating headdresses that would have made a Maya proud, and the crystals, sequins, pearls, and iridescent cloth had me squinting my eyes as the panoply passed below. It reminded me of the opening of the Miss Universe pageant, but if the various completely over-the-top outfits had any symbolism, I didn't know enough about Faerie to recognize it.

Pritkin yelled something I couldn't make out, snapping my attention back to him.

"What?" I looked at him.

"I'm going to join the race! I'll steal down in disguise, then throw it off just before the start!" He nodded at a black seahorse without any other color on the extreme right-hand side of the pool, under a pennant of bright green with a stylized sun in the middle that was rapidly getting drenched.

Our colors, I guessed.

"Okay, let's go," I said, swallowing the last of my drink.

"No! You stay here!"

He started to pull away, but I held him back. "What are you talking about?"

"You don't know how to ride!"

"I'll learn!"

"This is not the time—

"This is exactly the time! You said it yourself—they're going to cheat. Bodil, definitely, and everybody else, probably. And cheating around here involves blood—"

"I'll be all right, Cassie—"

"You'll be dead!"

Pritkin snapped a silence shield around us because we were attracting a few glances, even though we couldn't afford the power loss.

"We just went through this!" I said, not bothering to lower my voice, even when he winced. "What the hell?"

"It's not what you think—"

"Then what is it?"

"I need someone to replace me if I fall," he told me. "You have the right to contest for the throne—"

"What the—"

"—and you don't have my handicap. You've no demon blood, and one of your parents was a senior god, just like Nimue—"

I stared at him. "Have you lost your *mind*? I only told you that to keep you from leaving!"

"I know, but it doesn't make it wrong. And you saw what Faerie showed us. If we don't get this army, Zeus will. He already has Feltin and who knows how many others—"

"Then we'll take them down together!"

He shook his head. "I don't intend to die today, Cassie, but if I do—"

"Shut up!"

"*If I do*, you still have a claim. A blood right to the throne, and you've been here since the beginning. You don't even have to challenge; you're already part of my team, so mine covers you."

I stared at him mutely for a second, and then the words bubbling up in my throat spilled out of my lips. "I can't. I *can't*. Not just stand here, and you don't even have your magic, and those *bastards*—"

"Then you're making the same mistake I did when under Barne-Mora," he said quietly. "I didn't want to risk you, to the point that I was willing to quit and walk away. I was wrong then, and you're wrong now. Are we partners, or will our personal desires keep getting in each other's way?"

"*Are* we partners?" Because lately, it hadn't felt like it.

"We always have been."

I looked up at him miserably, knowing he was right. It made me want to vomit.

"I *will* be back," he said and kissed me hard and fast.

And then he was gone.

CHAPTER TWENTY-EIGHT

P ritkin moved so quickly that it almost looked like he'd cloaked, only he didn't have the strength for that. Or for this, I thought, as the challengers mounted their rides, some of them making come-on gestures at the crowd as they did so as if asking them to be even louder. And the onlookers obliged, with shouts that would leave them hoarse after this and with noise from the various ungodly instruments they'd brought with them, all of which made a vuvuzela sound like a softly whispering brook.

I couldn't hear a damned thing as a result, and thanks to the pennants people were waving everywhere, I couldn't see much, either. Except for one thing: maybe a minute after Pritkin left, the royal guard did, too. Jumping down from their perches high over the crowd and surging ahead.

All in the direction he had just taken.

Shit.

He'd had to drop his disguise because no rando from the audience would be allowed to participate in the royal race, which was what they'd been waiting for. And he couldn't hope to win if they assassinated him before the pistol went off or whatever the fey were using to start this thing! I tried to shift because I could feel the Pythian power surrounding me—

But I went nowhere except staggering forward a few feet from the pain, as if I'd sprained my whole body.

So I began doing what everyone else was, not that I had much choice. The crowd was suddenly on the move and sweeping me along with it, right across the people who had been here all night, judging from the makeshift encampments scattered around the stairs. But their seats were getting overrun, with fights breaking out on all sides, orders that no one could hear being shouted across the crowd by the authorities, and people getting trampled if they weren't impolite enough to climb over everyone else the way I was. The only good thing was that the crowd was impeding the royal guard, too, who were lashing out, beating everyone around them with clubs and fists and trying to throw them out of the way.

I was getting battered, too, only not by them. The crowd was doing that well enough on its own, and with so many tall people surrounding me that even looking down from a height wasn't helping anymore. I couldn't see Pritkin; I couldn't see anything!

And then I felt the Pythian power leave me, not that it mattered since I couldn't use it anyway. I'd used up my part of the pilfered power on the way here. Only . . . it didn't just vanish.

It spiraled overhead instead, a glittering golden scarf that only I could see, shimmering against the vivid blue sky like a stray sunbeam. I didn't know what it was doing, but it hadn't been cut off. The portal was wide open and pointed at Earth, giving it all the power it needed.

But to do what?

I followed it across the sky, as difficult as that was as I was being carried down the hill now as everyone rushed toward the pool where something was about to happen. But through the forest of heads, I saw it circle overhead once, twice, three times, and then dive—straight at Alphonse. Who I'd almost forgotten about, but of course, he'd be here—it looked like the whole city was.

Only he wasn't fighting the crowd along with me. He had found a perch on top of another outcropping of rock, this one in the middle of the stands, leaving him a couple of stories above everything else with an excellent view. But he wasn't looking at the racers.

He was scanning the crowd instead, and he had someone with him.

"Radu?" I said aloud, and the handsome brunette, who looked so like his brother Mircea that it broke my heart, jerked his head.

Impossible, I thought, staring. He couldn't have heard that. *I* couldn't even hear it.

But then, I wasn't a second-level master vamp, either. Radu wasn't as powerful as his brother, but he wasn't the weakling he liked to play, either, the inoffensive, eccentric, somewhat flamboyant Basarab that you didn't need to worry about.

You worried about all of them if you were smart, but many people weren't. Even people hundreds of years old who ought to know better. For myself, I'd learned a while ago never to underestimate that family.

"*Radu!*" I screamed and saw his head whip around and those dark eyes get closer, but they were still sweeping over me because—

Because I had the damned hood up!

I tore it off and screamed again, at the top of my lungs this time, to the point that I could feel my vocal cords being stripped raw, but I didn't care. And it worked. A second later, Radu's eyes met mine across the crowd, and he gripped Alphonse's arm and pointed.

And then they were jumping down, I assumed to come this way, although I couldn't see them anymore. And no, no, no, I didn't need them here! I didn't want them here!

"*Go to Pritkin!*" I screamed loudly enough that a fey beside me gave me a dirty look. Although why his eardrums weren't already ruptured, I didn't know because mine were. And now I was being swept off course!

Pritkin's ride had been bobbing gently in a stall to the far right of the pool, but the crowd was carrying me to the left. There was more room to maneuver there because it was a little too close to the drop-off into the surrounding sea than most people were comfortable with. And that included me!

But people had busted past the safety ropes and were surging ever closer to the edge, pulling the crowd that way. And I couldn't change direction because my feet weren't touching the ground but maybe half the time. I was shoulder to shoulder with everyone else and being dragged along by their momentum, and if I tried to change that, I was afraid that I'd disappear into the human tide and possibly get crushed to death.

And then those damned trumpets sounded again.

The blast was the same as before, but the reaction from the crowd was even more intense. They all but leaped forward and, in doing so, shook me free. I hit the ground then, whether I liked it or not, and was immediately battered on all sides as the whole mountainside made a push to reach the pool.

It looked and felt like a fleshy avalanche. I screamed because someone had just kicked me in the ribs, then had it cut off abruptly when the same thing happened to my head. Or maybe I took an elbow there; I couldn't tell, but the whole world went swimmy.

And then somebody grabbed me.

I looked up, fearing a guard because I'd been less than subtle, yelling my head off. But when my eyesight cleared, I realized he was far too pretty for a guard, even a fey one. Radu, I thought, as he lifted and carried me through the crowd, the people almost magically getting out of his way.

Or maybe that was because of Alphonse, up ahead, beating the heck out of anyone dumb enough to provide an obstacle.

I watched him lay waste with what looked like one of the guard's clubs, which made sense as he also wore one of their uniforms. This was likely why nobody was making a fuss about the beatings they were taking. Radu was wearing one, too, I realized, a purple and gold tabard over a shiny set of armor he didn't need because vampire.

I didn't know what those two had been up to, but it looked

like they'd been having their own adventures. Only I couldn't ask because I couldn't hear myself think! But I could suddenly hear Radu doing so straight into my head.

—*from Mircea*, he was saying when I managed to focus.

"What?" I yelled, and he winced slightly.

I can hear you without that, he reminded me. *How much did you manage to hear from me?*

"Not much. Someone kicked me in the head."

Radu sighed and tossed his own. His silky dark hair, at least as long as the average fey's, shone in the sunlight. It wasn't purple dipped, but other than that and being a paltry six foot in height, he could have passed for the guard I assumed he'd disposed of somewhere.

I'm sorry I didn't reach you sooner, he said, *but I only arrived last night. There was some trouble finding the thing, you see, as Mircea thought he'd put it in the safe at our Paris house, but it wasn't there. Or the one in Rome or the chateau in the Alps. I finally found it in a desk at Hawk's Nest—*

"What?"

—and then had to make my way from the Cascades to Upstate New York the old-fashioned way, as the Senate blocked the portal system after that raid on the Circle's HQ—

"Radu—"

—and then once I finally arrived, the damned—excuse me—our lovely consul wouldn't let me go through. Her portal is still open, of course, but she's angry that Mircea disappeared into Faerie and isn't taking her calls—

"He's lost in another world!"

Yes, so Dory tells me. I contacted her when I finally won through and heard all about her adventures. And now you and Mage Pritkin seem to be having a spot of bother here. I told him, nothing ever goes according to plan in this infernal—

"Radu!"

I guessed I finally yelled loudly enough to get his attention. *Cassie, I already said you don't have to scream.*

Yeah, only I did; I really, really did. "What. Are. You. Doing.

Here?"

What? Oh, didn't you hear that part?

I gritted my teeth. I'd forgotten what talking to Radu was like. "No."

Oh, well, just a moment. He began searching in a silk and velvet purse he wore clipped to his swordbelt, which didn't look to be of fey make. But then, it didn't look like the motheaten, tattered old relics in museums back home, either. It was a legit Renaissance-era purse that Radu had probably had in his wardrobe because he wore whatever the hell he liked.

I don't know why men ever stopped using purses, he told me, casually reading my thoughts. *They're so useful. Pockets*, he sneered. *You can't fit anything in those.*

"Satchels are starting to come in for guys. Basically man-purses," I told him, surrendering to the insanity.

Oh, yes, I've seen them. Huge, bulky, crossbody things, or else the dreaded "fanny pack," he shuddered. *Ruins the lines of any outfit you're trying to—ah, here it is.*

He held something up.

It flashed in the sunlight so brightly that, for a moment, I didn't know what it was. And then I did, but I still didn't understand. "What is it?"

The Ring of Water, Radu said, as though I should know what that was. *Mircea sent it to you, or more accurately, to Mage Pritkin. He said it should help.*

"Help how?" I asked, watching a sizeable sapphire glint in the sunlight. It was a pure, bright blue with no inclusions that I could see, and probably worth a mint, being set in a heavy gold band. But it meant nothing to me.

I'd never seen it before.

He didn't specify. Just that he came across it long ago in England, and that it was one of the great relics of the ancient covens there. Oh, and there was something about stealing it from a vengeful witch; I don't know. But it's supposed to give the wearer great facility with the water element, which seemed appropriate here.

He looked around with some distaste.

At any rate, he called me mentally some time ago and asked me to locate it and bring it to mage Pritkin. But as I said, there was a spot of bother—

"Did he say how to use it?" I interrupted as it hit my palm because Radu could go on forever. It was as heavy as it had looked but just lay there, as inert as any other ring.

That likely wasn't a good sign. If a talisman was powering it, I should have felt something, if only a background hum. But there was no sign of magic at all.

I tried to get more information, Radu fretted, *but it's difficult to communicate between worlds, even for us, and I assumed he would mention it when you were together at that dark fey city. You know, the one that blew up?*

"He didn't."

Well, I suppose that was understandable. He thought you were going to stay with him, didn't he? But that was before he went through the portal to that other place. What was the name again?

"Jotunheim." I felt the usual hand around my throat whenever I thought about it.

You'll see him again, Radu told me kindly. *We both will.*

"You sound sure."

It's Mircea, the shrug was in his voice as well as on his shoulders. *Now, don't you think you should get that ring to the mage?*

"How?" I asked, and it was a question. Even with the help of Radu's height, I couldn't see anything over the crowd or much ahead of us except for the swath carved by Alphonse's viciousness.

Which had just been joined by that of someone else.

A bunch of people were abruptly raised into the air and tossed aside like Moses carving a path through the Red Sea. An invisible path that people washed up against on both sides in a working mass of limbs and furious faces but didn't break through. Maybe because this path led to a witch who specialized in shields—and fury.

I wondered briefly what Enid looked like when she wasn't pissed off and if I would ever find out.

Not today, it seemed.

"Where have you been?" she demanded, screeching loudly enough in my face that I had no trouble hearing her, even through the sustained trumpet blast deafening everyone in sight.

"Trying to find Pritkin," I yelled back. "Where is he?"

"There!" she screamed and pointed to where the riders on their strange mounts were circling the middle of the pond like rubber duckies around a drain.

It must have been a really big drain because, suddenly, there were fewer of them, as several popped out of sight. I could see them briefly under the water's surface, like vague, rippling shadows, for a moment, and then even that much vanished. And they didn't come back up again.

"What happened?" I asked, grabbing Enid as Radu let me down. "Where did they go?"

"To the race! But they're not alone! The Queen's Guard went too, supposedly for security—"

Yeah, the security of their master, I thought furiously, catching sight of some of the purple-haired assholes.

Enid kept talking, and from her expression she was thinking the same thing I was. But I couldn't hear her because the damned horn sounded again, drowning her out. And giving me a migraine because we were almost on top of one of the trumpeters.

But several more riders had just disappeared, and they were all speeding up. Round and round, like racing in a bathtub, but at every revolution, another one or two vanished from sight, including one of the Queen's Guard. Leaving no fewer than four more, all jostling for position near Pritkin.

"Grab him!" I said to Enid as the latest blast cut out. "Don't let him go!"

"I can't! No one can enter the pool on pain of death save for the challengers—"

"And their crew?" I demanded because some of those strange mounts were carrying two.

"Yes, but—"

"Can you ride?"

She looked at me like I was mad. "What does that have to do with—"

I shook her savagely, which was likely not a wise move considering her hair-trigger temper, but I was past caring. "Can you ride?"

"Yes! But what difference does—"

I held the ring up in front of her eyes. "I need to get this to him if you want him to win or even survive! So, are you with me or not?"

She stared at me wide-eyed. "I—I—I'm a *slave*. I'm not part of your team—"

"You are now." I looked at Alphonse. "That's all it takes, right?"

A huge shoulder shrugged. "As far as I know. But you won't catch him, not carrying two. And not on that thing," he added, nodding at the stall where Pritkin's mount had been a few moments ago.

It held another, although it was obviously a case of the palace being funny. Or maybe they thought that, given my lack of expertise, it wouldn't matter if they gave me an old, decrepit-looking nag that even my inexperienced eye could tell was on its last fin. That thing wouldn't catch Pritkin swimming alone, much less carrying two.

But there was no other choice. I couldn't ride and Enid wouldn't be allowed in the race without me. So we were going to have to figure out a way to make this work, although I didn't see—

And then I did.

"Come on," I told her, because another mount had been left behind, one which had just thrown off its rider.

Her eyes got even bigger as she followed my line of sight.

"You can't be serious!"

She was actually backing up until Radu, who hadn't said a word in all this, proved that he was a Basarab, after all. "I can't blame you," he said diffidently. "I wouldn't touch that thing, either, and I'm freeborn." He looked at me. "You expect too much from a slave, Cassie. Alphonse will go with you."

"Alphonse will?" the man in question asked.

But Alphonse didn't. Because the next thing I knew, a furious redhead grabbed my hand and dragged me over the railing, through the middle of a bunch of startled-looking, peacock-armored guards, and over to the stall where Galygos was tossing his pretty head.

His pretty huge head, because damn. I'd forgotten how large he was, even compared to the other mounts. Which, for the record, was a lot.

Well, here goes nothing, I thought grimly and grabbed the reins.

CHAPTER
TWENTY-NINE

T he shrimp saved me. To be precise, the spill of firecracker red shrimp that I hadn't finished because they were too hot for me. But not, it seemed, for Galygos.

After tossing his head in outrage over anyone daring to try to control him, and lifting me about four feet off the ground in the process, he abruptly stopped. And sniffed. And started nuzzling me all over before zeroing in on the spill of shrimpy goodness that I was somehow still clutching in one sweaty palm.

"Get on!" I yelled at a frozen Enid, who had been watching this display with something approaching horror.

I guessed she expected to be eaten next.

But I made some shooing motions with the arm that wasn't halfway down a seahorse's gullet, and she snapped back into action, mounting the great creature as several guards ran at us, thankfully part of the peacock brigade. Maybe because the last of Feltin's guys had just disappeared after Pritkin. Damn it!

"She's with me," I told them breathlessly, and they just stared as if they couldn't believe we were planning to ride the giant bastard.

"What about me?" the former rider demanded, clambering back to his feet, with his wetsuit barely concealing a sizeable paunch.

It matched his ego if he'd demanded Galygos for a ride, I

thought, finding my feet again. And grabbing the forearm that Enid extended before scrambling up the horny hide. And even though the great beast was mostly submerged, it wasn't easy because he was still as tall as a house!

But I felt a subtle force field under my foot, helping me, and I managed to clamber up behind her.

"Did you hear me?" the paunchy fey demanded, his lard jiggling with outrage. It made all the bling on his wetsuit flash in the sunlight, but bling didn't matter here, only skill. And I thought he should be grateful.

Galygos would have killed him.

Of course, there was a better-than-average chance that the same thing would happen to us as soon as the shrimp ran out, but it was a chance I had to take.

"You can have that one," I yelled, gesturing at the nag the palace had seen fit to give me. Then we were off, not bothering with the pretty prancing-around-the-drain thing that everybody else had been doing but diving straight into a vortex of bubbles that was going to drown me any second now if it didn't pull me apart first!

It did neither because I'd picked the right racing partner. Enid wrapped a ward around Galygos's middle, covering the area around the seat and shielding us from some of the turbulence, although I still got battered about like a stone inside a maraca. Probably because she wasn't exactly flush with power right now, either.

And then the drain, or whatever was down there, caught us and felt like it was launching us at approximately the speed of sound, only I couldn't see where. There was nothing but thrashing water, frothing bubbles, and whirring fins. I concentrated on holding on for dear life, clutching the horny hide until I lost feeling in my fingers, my cheek pressed hard against Enid's back, and my legs already crying out for mercy because the saddle was all but useless.

And then we were through and out into something different but no better. No better at all, I thought, as we found ourselves racing down a "track" with transparent sides, like the one the merfolk had been working on and which I had very bad memories of. Especially now, as the tubes were flooded, with water filling the inside as completely as the ocean we were racing through.

I didn't see the point of having a track if the entire thing was just a water-filled tube! And then I did, watching a competitor get thrown into one of the walls and be zapped as if hit by a lightning bolt. Wards, then, and punishing ones.

Okay.

I couldn't tell if the guy was dead or not, but he was definitely out of the race, with his body going limp and he and his seahorse getting all but mowed down by several more riders. He vanished into the darkness, and Enid steered us into the center of the course, which, yeah. Good job, Enid!

Or it would have been, only Galygos had finished his shrimp and had it register that there were freaking seahorses in the water ahead of him.

And how very dare they?

He *shot* ahead, and I mean that literally. I now know what a bullet feels like, I thought, trying to scream but not being able to as hitting the back of Enid's shield forced all of the air out of my lungs. And then I hit it again and again as we dodged this competitor and that one, trying to get ahead, where Galygos clearly believed he belonged.

"Do up the straps!" Enid was yelling, and for a moment, I didn't know what she meant—and then I realized that I hadn't strapped my legs into the thigh-high stirrups. And sure, I was going to be able to manage that now!

But I tried anyway because this was unsustainable, and she couldn't help me. She looked how I felt, with her face white, her eyes huge, and her glamourie glitzing, showing glimpses of the ruined flesh beneath the perfect veneer. Maybe because it was taking every ounce of concentration she had to steer with Galygos not caring if he ran over the competition.

In fact, he seemed to prefer it.

And then, so did I when we started getting attacked on all sides. Some guards had noticed that we'd joined the race and reined in to allow us to catch up, only to start trying to force us into the walls as soon as we did so. Only, yeah, I thought dizzily.

Have you met our ride?

Apparently not.

The next moment, one guard and the pretty gray-green seahorse it was riding were flung into electric hell, courtesy of Galygos' mighty tail, and another mount disappeared in a sea of red after getting a sizeable piece torn out of its neck by those vicious teeth. And then Galygos demonstrated another way in which Faerie's children differed from their Earthly counterparts, by opening some bony plates covering his stomach.

And launching a bunch of knife-like spikes into the guard right in front of us, who had been attempting to slow us down.

They popped his shield like it wasn't there and then tore apart what was inside. And that was enough for the remaining guards' mounts, who scattered in a storm of panicked fins and churning bubbles while we tore through the bloody remains. Just in time to see Pritkin up ahead, battling with the remaining guards, who were also targeting—

"What the *hell*?" I asked Enid breathlessly. "What is *she* doing here?"

She didn't bother asking who I meant. "Bodil can't compete!" she yelled back, to be heard over the water rushing on all sides.

"I know!"

"So, she must have a champion—"

"I know!"

"—who she doesn't trust to take this! She must have joined his entourage to win it for him!" A lot of weird fey curses followed this pronouncement because Bodil ran the stables and had for basically ever.

What chance did we have against her?

Maybe better than I'd thought. Because the purple-haired

guards seemed to be splitting their time between trying to kill Pritkin and trying to knock Bodil out of the race. Probably to help Feltin's champion get ahead, whoever that was.

But while the beautiful black and silver seahorse she rode had the delicate features of a female, it fought like a male—and a vicious one at that—matching its rider's skill and aggression. As a result, the two of them were holding their own, even though there had to be a dozen guards boiling around her and Pritkin, like vultures around a carcass. Until he broke open a hole in the line by expanding his shield and scraping a guard along the wards of death until there was nothing left but a smear of red, even though the fey in question had been warded and clad in dragonscale.

I stared at the wards and vowed to stay very far away from them, which was what everyone else was doing. Except for Pritkin, who skimmed along the surface of one, what must have been a millimeter away, enough that the deadly thing started sending little tendrils of lightning outward, trying to rope him in. Until he'd bypassed the remaining guards, then he broke for open water, with Bodil right behind him, along with the guards, peeling off from their formation and shooting spells through their shields.

One of the curses set another champion on fire, and even though we were all submerged, he kept right on burning. The guards seemed to have forgotten that Feltin had said to capture Pritkin, not to kill him! But it looked like he'd really managed to piss them off.

The man had a talent.

And right then, they wanted payback for all the people they'd lost in the kitchen fight more than they wanted rewards. He needed additional power, but he'd removed Lover's Knot as soon as we'd escaped Bodil's trap, so I couldn't send him any. And that was assuming I had any to spare, which I didn't!

But they did, I thought, noticing a couple of royal guards who were lagging behind slightly to allow them to lob spells from a safe distance. And just like Enid on the merpeople's unfinished track, they'd released a cloud of magic around their heads to speed that process up. A cloud that looked like every meal I'd been missing for the last week.

"Get me closer," I urged her, pointing at them, and got a wild look over her shoulder in return, but it didn't matter. Because it appeared that there was something Galygos liked better than shrimp, and she was straight ahead and being attacked.

And, okay, forget the bullet; now I knew what a missile felt like. I hit the back of the ward again, and this time, I didn't climb back up against Enid. Because she'd just slammed into me after our sudden surge broke the straps on her stirrups.

For a moment, there was nothing but thrashing limbs, a twisted saddle, and pressure, like an extra atmosphere or two. And the knowledge that now no one was driving—except for the dangerous, half-crazed monster we were trying to cling to, who had an agenda all his own. And who was hunting guards all by himself.

A second later, he caught them, racing up beside his lady, only I might have been wrong about which one that was. Bodil's beautiful black and silver mount was bleeding, with a haze of red spreading in the water around her, and she looked up at Galgygos with desperate, pleading eyes. And we suddenly had a furious savage on our hands, going to town on the guards and their mounts surrounding her.

Which would have been great, except that Pritkin was speeding away with half a dozen guards on his magically bottomed-out ass!

It was something that Bodil seemed to realize, and the next moment, a furious demigod had somehow stepped through Enid's shield and—

"What are you *doing*?" I demanded as she grabbed Galygos' reigns.

"Stealing your mount," I was told savagely right before she elbowed me in the gut.

And not on my watch, bitch!

But before I could retaliate or even remember how to breathe, we were off, although less, I suspected, because of Bodil's skill and more because the guards and half their mounts were now dead, and Galygos and his lady friend were chasing down the rest. Seahorses seemed to be vengeful little bastards. Or make that vengeful, two-story bastards, or closer to three in Galygos' case.

And if I'd thought he was tearing through the water before, it was nothing next to this. It seemed that his little seahorse mind had figured out that the guards were bad, m'kay? And decided that what he really wanted to snack on right now wasn't more shrimp, but rather a whole boatload of Queen's Guard ass.

And since that was what I also wanted, I decided to forego revenge on the bitch who had jailed and now assaulted me and find a perch. *Get ready*, I mouthed at Enid because after Galygos finished his main course, we needed to retake control of our mount. All I got back was a terrifying "Are you kidding me?" look that said that fighting demigods wasn't in our agreement.

But I didn't have time to argue because we were already crashing into the guards hammering Pritkin.

Galygos swerved to take out the closest competition, and I screamed at Enid to "Drop your shield!"

For once, she didn't argue, or else it popped on its own as we were already getting strafed by the spell fire zipping around. I felt a bubble slam into place around my head, and then a wave of water hit me, rushing in to fill the void where the shield had been. It would have knocked me off my seat, except that I didn't have one, and at the same time, I grabbed hold of the sparkling clouds around the nearest two fey.

And *jerked*.

And, oh, what a difference that made!

Their power tasted thin, like Enid's, because I was comparing it to a god's. But while it might not have had the heady rush of Zeus's energy, it still packed a punch—and could hopefully deal one as a bunch more riders had just crashed into us, turning the race into a free-for-all.

Bodil shot a barrage of spell bolts at our attackers, Galygos savaged three mounts at once, and Enid screamed at me from inside her bubble. And I shifted the nearest guard outside the track and reached over to grab his mount. Because Galygos wanted to fight more than he wanted to race, and Pritkin and his personal gaggle of guards were getting away!

I dragged myself over there less than gracefully, grabbing the dropped reins and just holding on until I could crawl up the horny hide. But I got the job done. My new mount wasn't on Galygos's level, but it wasn't crap, either. An immense, black beauty with flashing red eyes that matched Bodil's right now, as Enid joined me, and we left the stable mistress behind.

She and Galygos didn't look like they needed the help.

Pritkin did.

And this time, he was damned well going to get some.

"Take the reins!" I yelled at Enid, who clambered onto the higher-level driving position without even pausing her rant at me. It was almost Pritkin-worthy, but I'd heard all that before, and—

There!

"What are we doing?" she demanded as we shot ahead.

"Island hopping."

"What?"

"Get me close to every damned guard you see!"

She had a lot to say about that, but again, it didn't matter. Because our latest purloined ride was trying its best to get back to its pack, or whatever you call a family of seahorses, all of which were being ridden by other guards. Which was why the next few minutes were a heady mix of panic and exhilaration.

Panic because Enid and I were doing the equivalent of Pritkin's Han Solo run from earlier. Exhilaration because every time we caught up to someone, I got fed by another cloud of magic. I ripped them off of fey after fey, like stealing a bunch of glittering cloaks, and by the time I reached numbers six and seven, I had practically a whole wardrobe.

That fight didn't last long as a result, and Enid and I quickly left them behind, one seahorse bleeding out in the water, the other hauling ass back the way it had come, and the two fey floating in our wake and looking stunned. Maybe because a glimmering golden whip had uncurled from my hand, causing the water to bubble and hiss and their wards to give up the ghost. And, suddenly, things got a little easier.

Make that a lot easier, I thought, as we sped through the middle of a sizeable group of guards. It should have been a death sentence, as no one had instructed them to bother with capturing me. But I was lashing the ones on my right-hand side before they realized what had happened and draining those on the left so that I didn't lose power in the process, and Enid was cursing those in front of us to clear a path.

Allowing us to plow through a dozen of Nimue's elite troops as if they weren't even there. I laughed; I couldn't help it. Power was singing in my veins, my movements had evened out and become fluid, and I could breathe for what felt like the first time in days.

No wonder everyone had feared the gods so much!

Including me, when I glanced behind us and saw the red-eyed fury right on our tails.

Well . . . shit.

"Hurry up!" I told Enid, whose head jerked around to tell me off, only to see the same thing I just had.

"Aggghhhh!" she screamed, because if I'd ever seen death on anybody's face, it was on Bodil's. Guess that whip had brought back memories, I thought, but I didn't reabsorb it, even though it was boiling the water to our right and obscuring our view. I had a feeling I would need it again in a second.

And I did, but not for Bodil.

We suddenly surfaced again, breaking into the air without warning, leaving me confused and seriously battered. Because what we'd surfaced into was an all-out gladiatorial match. One that was quickly spreading red all over the churned-up surface of the water.

The same water we'd left from, I realized through the steam my whip was sending up. The track must have looped back here. This would explain the roaring crowd, the blaring music, and the announcement from someone's enhanced voice that my translator decided to wake up and feed back to me.

"—yes, indeed! It's anyone's race, lords and ladies, anyone's at all, as we wait to see which of our bold challengers will cross the finish line first—"

"What finish line?" I asked Enid, who was cursing the crap out of someone. I didn't get an answer as she was pulled under a second later, until I shot my whip into the churning waves after her captor and dragged her back out.

"My thanks," she spluttered as I shook her hard enough to get her attention.

"What finish line?"

"That one," she said, looking off to the right, and then she threw up.

But for once, I didn't join her. For once, I had my eyes on the prize and the silver-haired son of a bitch who was about to cross the line ahead of us. Æsubrand had lost his mount, parts of his armor, and a good chunk of his hair, which appeared to have been burnt off, probably by someone's spell. But he was wading that way and not a chance in hell!

My whip reached out and curled around one armored leg, and I jerked. And forgot that the power I was momentarily wielding made everything easier. Æsubrand came flying into me from halfway across the pond, and we both went under; my whip went out because that sort of thing eats power like nobody's business and I was bottoming out; and then we surfaced and the bastard got me in a neck lock, trying to murder me.

Bodil pulled him off, possibly because she wanted that pleasure for herself, which was how the three of us were watching when Pritkin and his mount tore away from the snarling pack and darted across the finish line.

The crowd went crazy, and I screamed and yelled along with the rest, caught up in the adrenaline of the moment. That and being half-strangled is my excuse, anyway, for not seeing what happened next. Although, in retrospect, I don't know how I could have possibly predicted it.

There was a crack like thunder; there was a fat, familiar face; there was an eye-widening second of recognition—

Then a time spell grabbed me . . .

And it wasn't mine.

CHAPTER THIRTY

I hit the ground hard as if falling from a height and landed in what felt like a bowl of cold mud. As stunned as I was, I couldn't tell much more than that, but I wouldn't have been able to anyway, as it was also dark. A second ago, it had been broad daylight, with a raucous, shouting crowd in every color of the rainbow under a brilliantly blue sky, but now...

My eyes registered only pitch black, and my ears, still ringing from all those cheers, picked up nothing past the echoes except eerie silence. I swallowed, my mouth strangely cottony, and stayed put, trying to get my bearings. I thought I heard a faint trickle of water from somewhere, along with the sound of the wind.

That was it.

That was all.

It didn't help.

And neither did this, I thought, as I started squelching around, trying to find purchase on the spongy ground and mostly failing. The mud felt like it went all the way down, with no firm bottom anywhere. That left me less crawling than swimming, although that might have had more to do with the state of my head than the muck.

Something was wrong with me—something was wrong, period. I could feel it, shuddering through my body like the grip of a giant's hand. An evil giant who was squeezing, squeezing, squeezing all of the air out of my lungs, making me squirm and thrash and beat against what felt like a skin on the air.

I had a sudden image of a baby, caught in an intact

amniotic sac, staring out at a world it couldn't touch. Only I could, I *would*, whether this spell liked it or not. I was Pythia, damn it!

And the spell had a name.

Illusion, I thought, growing furious. Pritkin had said that the water fey were better at them than anyone else, but I'd been trained for this, as a Pythia who couldn't tell the difference between reality and illusion was a danger to everyone. That was why I'd spent the better part of two weeks stumbling around from one illusion to another as Gertie and company tried their best to trip me up.

And had me screaming in terror when my bed was suddenly floating on a rising tide despite being on the second floor of the London court. Or stopping, dropping, and rolling because my ugly lace gown was abruptly on fire. Or shifting a dozen snarling Weres, who raced into the front hall one night just after I returned from a mission.

Fortunately, I'd been too exhausted to send them far because they'd turned out to be real and were less than happy about their sudden relocation to the roof. Especially since it was night, rain was bucketing down, and lightning hit the rod designed for such things above their heads a moment later, hard enough to make their hair stand on end. And continue to do so while everything was sorted out, leaving them looking like murderous puff balls.

Gertie had been in a long-running feud with one of the local clans, and they'd decided to visit in force without an invitation, which was a no-no. So I didn't get in trouble. Other than for being unable to tell the difference between illusion and reality.

"But you will," she'd said, an evil glimmer in her eyes.

And I had, the hard way. Which was how I did everything, it seemed, but hard times make hard women. So no illusion . . . was going to . . . hold me . . . goddamnit!

And it didn't. One second, I was punching my way through what felt like eighty layers of plastic wrap, feeling like a suffocating mummy drowning in mud. And the next—

I was still drowning in mud because I had somehow buried my face in it.

I came up gasping, expecting to see water, light, and color after shattering the illusion, or at least the shins of the people fighting around me. Instead, I saw . . . nothing. Or nothing different, at least.

It was still dark, the mud was still gritty, and the night was still cold. Except that it suddenly felt more real somehow, more solid, more *there* than a minute ago. And the suffocating sensation had been replaced by the sweet feeling of air rushing into my lungs, filling them up with an almost heady surge of—

Someone else was there, too.

I froze, all that wonderful oxygen catching in my throat. One of my senses—I couldn't have said which one—had picked something up, enough to shout a warning. But now there was nothing, just more wind whistling overhead but not hitting my skin as if it was being blocked somehow.

But not by a ward. Most of my stolen power had gone into the race, and what I had left wouldn't fuel any protection for long. Not against the kind of magic the fey could manifest.

But damn, did I wish it could!

I stared around, not understanding anything. But at least my eyes were adjusting a little, allowing me to see a few scattered stars overhead. And the fact that they were blocked in places by what might have been cliffs. The cliffs were indistinct voids cut out of the starscape, but as I concentrated, the faint, silvery light from above highlighted pieces of their craggy surfaces.

There was nothing farther down, toward what should have been the base of the cliffs, and I slowly realized why. The silvery threads of an almost dried-up waterfall were dribbling into a basin—one that had been a pool a few moments ago but was now a mud pit with its sides blocking the view beyond. Because I hadn't changed locations, had I?

I'd changed *times*. And then it all came rushing back, the

desperate fight inside the churning pool, the exhilaration of seeing Pritkin defy the odds and cross the finish line first, the glimpse of Tony's fat face. The time spell that hadn't been mine but which had caught me anyway—

My head jerked around, hearing the sound of light, running feet in a place that shouldn't have had them—that *couldn't* have them if they were human, as this mud wouldn't hold one of us up. And then I was floundering more quickly, trying to get to my feet before that son of a bitch finished me off. Only to get taken down a second later—

By an enraged prince of the light fey.

I'd expected Tony for obvious reasons, but the starlight was glimmering off of silver dragonscale, long hair almost the same color, and a beautiful, furious face. Æsubrand—I'd nearly forgotten about him. But the same wasn't true in reverse, as he demonstrated by flipping around like a monkey and getting me into another headlock.

That would have been it, but I'd had those few seconds of warning thanks to the squelching mud and used them to manifest my whip. Which I flung backward at the bastard imprisoning me because I'd never been all that great at defense. Not that offense worked much better, with my opponent having the reflexes of a cat on steroids.

But so did my whip, and it seemed to have a mind of its own.

He released me after the third time it gouged his pretty armor deep enough to crack it and lunged backward, his breastplate falling off and the glowing tip missing his unprotected chest by millimeters. And then he dodged from side to side as the lethal golden stream slashed out again and again, like the tongue of a massive snake. Anyone else would have run for their lives or at least for cover, but did he take the wise course?

Oh, hell no. He ducked and darted, dodged and zigzagged, and somehow returned to his feet in the middle of all that. And kept.

On.

Coming.

But others were coming now, too, a bunch of them drawn by the sounds of battle and the flashing light that my whip gave off. It was strobing the ugly, muddy scene, highlighting the churned-up soil, the fury on Æsubrand's face, and the flash of red in the eyes of the woman who took him down, even while glaring daggers at me. Bodil, I realized, wondering why she kept saving me and who else had been sucked into this.

And then somebody grabbed me, vampire quick, only to have Pritkin come out of nowhere and tackle him. The two combatants fell into the mud, beating the hell out of each other, while Æsubrand elbowed Bodil in the gut and tore free. And came straight back at me.

Only to splat face-first onto a shield I hadn't put up and didn't think that Pritkin had, either, as he and a hulking shadow I finally recognized as Alphonse were still trying to kill each other. Until someone lit a wand, showing them that they were fighting the wrong guy. And lighting up a familiar redhead with a scarred face, who I guessed was my most recent savior because she grabbed me.

"I was in the water," Enid said frantically. "And then I was here, but I couldn't move! I could barely breathe and thought I was dying! That someone had spelled me—"

"Yeah, I thought the—"

"—but the paralysis vanished as suddenly as it had come, and I was on my way back to my feet when I heard—"

She broke off suddenly, terror flooding those usually staunch features, and I didn't have to ask why. Something echoed through the night, a stuttering, haunting cry that was horribly familiar and no, no, no! I hadn't even dealt with the current crisis yet!

But I had a new one, ready or not. And everyone else seemed to sense that, too, their heads jerking up. And freezing in place, even Æsubrand, who looked confused, probably wondering what he was feeling. Had I dared to speak, I could have told him: the same thing a mouse felt when a hawk glided overhead.

"Shhh!" I hissed, extinguishing my whip, but nobody shhhed.

Quite the contrary. Once their paralysis broke, right about the time that terrible cry petered out, they all tried to talk at once. And that was a problem—that was a big problem—because someone else was out there.

Or make that some*thing*, I thought, my spine crawling as another stuttering cry tore through the night, closer this time. I knew those sounds. They'd featured in my nightmares often enough.

"Shut up!" I hissed, and we all hunkered down. Even Æsubrand, although he was breathing hard and trying to maneuver his way over to me, probably to gut me while we hid from what was out there. Which would lead them right to us because—

"They scent blood," Pritkin whispered before I could, probably hoping it would cause the princely idiot to pause and think for a minute, something he seemed to have trouble doing when enraged. And it might have—if it hadn't been Pritkin speaking.

I guessed Æsubrand hadn't noticed his chief rival before, probably being too focused on me. But he saw him now and immediately launched himself at him, a wicked-looking dagger glinting in the starlight for half a second. Until Pritkin and Alphonse took him down, although he fought like a tiger.

A seriously stupid one who was about to get us all killed!

"Muffle him!" I whispered and I guessed they did because I didn't hear anything else.

Except for that, I thought, as several somethings from different directions gave a combined cry that echoed off the sides of the old lake bed and etched its way down my bones. I couldn't see them as the steep embankment still blocked my view. But a recent memory gave me an image anyway.

Not of what they looked like because they could look

like anything. But of what they were: eldritch monsters that everyday demons called "Ancient Horrors" because they didn't have a better description. And because it really, really fit.

The Ancient Horrors were old demons, powerful ones, practically primordial ones who the Demon High Council had long ago locked away on some barren worlds and left to die. Only they hadn't died. They had gotten seriously pissed off, however, and once Zeus showed up with an offer of alliance, they'd taken it gleefully.

Most recently, they'd possessed the bodies of some vamps in old Romania, where Zeus had intended for them to ravage the world's vampire senates in the past, thus winning him the war before it started by drastically weakening our side. My court and I had denied him that, and Adra and the council's demons had killed the Horrors he had selected for the mission. We'd already killed some of them at the battle for Issengeir, Aeslinn's southern capital, where they'd been stuffed into the bodies of rock-like manlikans to help with the city's defenses.

I'd hoped that, together, those battles had gotten them all.

Guessed not.

A silence spell clicked shut around us, and it must have been Bodul's work because a second later, she was in my face. "What is that?" she demanded. "Where are we? How are we here? *What did you do?*"

The rapid-fire questions reminded me of the ones I'd asked her back in the stable, none of which she'd answered. I would have been more obliging, but there was no time. The predators after us sensed magic as quickly as blood, as I'd learned the hard way once.

And preferred not to learn again!

"Drop the spell," I told her. "Do it now."

"Are you mad?"

"No! And do what I tell you, or we're all about to die!" And unlike Æsubrand, she appeared to be able to think past her anger because she dropped the spell. "No magic," I whispered. "No blood. And do what I do."

I ducked into the mud, rolling to get it over the few parts of my face, hair, and neck that were still clean and shedding scent. And then I started crawling—fast. The others followed because more and more sounds were echoing through the night, horrible, skin-ruffling noises that were like nothing on Earth.

Or in Faerie, either, I assumed, since Bodil was also taking a mud bath while we crawled. And looking around with a furtiveness that she probably hadn't shown in a few millennia. I just crawled faster because we needed to get away from where we'd been, and we needed to do it now.

I'd no sooner had the thought than something with brilliant yellow eyes peered over the edge of the pool. I couldn't see anything else except a shadow against the night, and I was good with that. If I never saw another of those things again—

But I was going to because one person hadn't followed my commands. One person had stood up, his silver clothing shining in the starlight like it was made out of the stuff, and pulled out a sword. A sword that would do exactly nothing, no matter how pretty it was.

I'd seen one of those creatures gut an ancient demigoddess who was a hell of a lot scarier than him. Only one thing worked on them, and he didn't have it. Son of a *bitch*!

"Get them away," I whispered to Pritkin, who had crawled up beside me.

"Do you know what those are?" he hissed because, yeah, I didn't have to explain it to him. He'd gone with Adra to check out the demon prison worlds and found their population largely missing.

"Yes! And I can't shift you all!"

"Leave that fucker!" Alphonse growled at me while glancing back at Æsubrand, but I couldn't.

Fey bodies were almost as resilient as vampire ones, and I knew his fate if they caught him. He'd be lucky if they just ate him. Really lucky, I thought, my mind flashing back to the vampire bodies I'd seen in Wales, which the Horrors had invaded and then fused to make themselves even more deadly forms.

Some of the bloated results had looked like a rat king by the time they'd finished, only far more terrible. I still had nightmares about a pair of horrified blue eyes floating in a prison of flesh that had once been his body and was now just part of a demon construct. One that wasn't reversible.

The demons would use their fleshy tanks in battle then discard them and find new patsies. But he was trapped like that permanently, along with whoever else's bodies had been commandeered and morphed out of all recognition. And as bad as Æsubrand might be, no one deserved that.

"Go!" I told them, and for a wonder, they went. And dragged Enid and Bodil along with them, just as something hideous and multilegged was silhouetted against the starlight as it jumped into the mud.

And was met halfway through the arc by my whip, which was thinner now and not nearly so impressive-looking. But which nonetheless spilled the creature's guts all over the haughty fey prince. Who turned on me savagely.

"I don't need—" he began right before the wounded creature lunged for me, trailing half its entrails through the mud but not caring. And allowing me to see it clearly for the first time, only my eyes couldn't quite manage to focus.

Maybe that was a self-defense mechanism because what I could see was so hideous that it broke my brain. I realized I'd never seen one of them in their natural state unless you counted a snake-like version that Pritkin and I had fought what felt like ages ago and which must have been the beauty pageant winner. Because this. . .

"Augghh!" I whispered, the visceral *No!* having to come out somehow. But it was pitifully inadequate because the thing was . . . the thing was . . .

The thing was on me.

CHAPTER
THIRTY-ONE

I shoved the guttering remains of my whip into the creature's maw because I couldn't think of anything else. Or think much at all with its teeth trying to bury themselves in my flesh and its blood splattering and hissing against my armor. All while Æsubrand hacked at it with no effect from that impressive-looking sword.

He finally realized that and paused, looking at his weapon in confusion while the creature's insides burned, its eyes became even more fire-like, and the golden light I was shedding poured out from under the scales that covered it. Until I ripped my acid-etched armor out of its mouth, its saliva hissing and dancing on the surface as it fought to consume me, even as the creature it had come from writhed helplessly in the mud. And then I grabbed a foolish fey prince by the leg and *shifted*.

Or rather, I tried.

But several more somethings had just torn through the air, leaping down on top of us. I could feel claws raking me even as we started to disappear, could sense them opposing my spell, trying to throw it off, and could tell when my already tenuous concentration started to wobble. Which would be bad since I didn't think I had enough juice to try this again.

I wasn't even sure I had enough to finish this spell, not carrying two—including the idiot who was currently fighting me! He didn't understand that I was trying to save his stubborn hide, and I didn't have the strength to explain it right now. I didn't have the strength for anything, which was why my spell started to falter, the thread beginning to vanish like smoke in my hands without enough power behind it—

Until someone sent me some.

Pritkin must have re-engaged Lover's Knot because I felt a hit of energy flow into me through the bond. It wasn't much— I doubted he had much—but it was enough to tip the balance. The spell caught, flinging us across the lake to the concave side of the far wall.

It was deeper than I'd thought, arcing far overhead like a frozen wave of dirt. But it cast a shadow so dark that even Æsubrand's silver magnificence couldn't be seen. But he could damned well be heard if he didn't *shut up*.

I shoved him face-first into the mud at the first intake of breath, then managed to get a hand over his mouth. So, of course, he bit me and put enough force behind it that I could feel it through a dragonscale gauntlet. I hope you break a tooth! I thought right before he got me in yet another chokehold because he was a bastard, but he could fight.

Only not well enough to defeat the things that were hunting us. Something he must have finally realized because he stopped moving as a dozen more shadows leaped down to the spot where we'd just been. And started savaging the creature I'd disemboweled, heedless of the fact that he was still alive and one of theirs.

It was over in seconds and probably could have been even faster considering how quickly some of those things moved. But it seemed like they were enjoying the carnage and their former ally's desperate cries more than the meat. Blood, viscera, and body parts went flying, and the sounds, the horrible, laughing, gobbling sounds, were enough to make me dizzy.

They must have affected the haughty bastard choking me the same way because he made another mistake.

"Pah," he exhaled, barely a breath on the air.

But that was enough.

A few of the creatures looked up, having locked onto that tiny sound despite all the noise they'd been making. One of them had huge, bat-like ears that stood up from its head and turned this way and that while it sent out weird little clicks in all directions from its bloody maw. Clicks I could feel as a tangible force as they swept over us—

And bounced back.

The thing's head turned, eyes redder than Bodul's looked straight at us, and it started screeching, loud and piercing and echoing through the night.

And then they were coming.

"Here!" I heard Pritkin yell just as something hit me in the face.

It was dirty and scraggly and I didn't know what the hell, just that it had come from above. As if the rest of our crew had somehow managed to find a way up there, not that it mattered. Because the creatures were as fast as a blur.

Æsubrand, the complete madman, shoved me behind him like he hadn't just been trying to kill me a second ago. And like that was going to help! But *that* might, I thought, as somebody suddenly appeared in front of what had been the great waterfall.

They must have been small since the embankment still blocked my view, even at this angle. But the sickly green illumination they shed cast a hell of a light shadow on the cliff face behind. It extended almost the full height of the towering slope, painting it in leaping shadows that were monstrous enough on their own.

But then some ungodly screeching began emanating from it, like rusty hinges magnified a hundred times over, until I thought my head would burst or my heart explode.

It was the worst thing I'd ever heard, and the creatures hunting us seemed to think so, too. Because they paused, turned, and snarled, their attention momentarily diverted. And a moment was all Æsubrand needed.

He looped what I'd vaguely decided was a woody vine

around his arm and grabbed me, all in one fluid movement.

"Pull!" he yelled because it was the only way to be heard over all that.

And he was, both by those above us and the creatures down here, who realized that their prey was about to get away. Which was why, as we were dragged through the air and up the clifflike side of the embankment, the snarling, furious pack was leaping across the lakebed. And jumping up, screaming defiance as fetid breath blew over my feet, as my heart tried to leap out of my chest, and as I did my best to climb up Æsubrand's body while more claws raked over our dragonscale.

I glimpsed some of the shapes below as they tried to drag us back down. One had fur but was bird-beaked, with a body that didn't make sense, but mercifully, none of the tangled-up limbs seemed to include wings. Another looked like a giant amoeba, formless and hairy with grasping, pale, sliver-like tentacles longer than my body that shot out from its edges, trying to wrap around us.

And that took Æsubrand's boot repeatedly to what I guessed was its face instead. And when that didn't work, the prince snarled, "Hold on," at me and pulled his sword again. He carved his way through half a dozen whipping white strands, including four that had grabbed his foot and tethered us in place.

The white goo they contained splattered us in the process and burned like phosphorus, glowing in pale patches on our armor and eating through his sword blade, causing him to curse and drop it. But the goo was defeated by our dragonscale, although mine had to build up my breastplate to keep it from getting through. Causing my gauntlets to disappear, as their strength was needed elsewhere.

And that was just one monster!

Others were down there, but my brain was too freaked out to register them as anything but claws, strange appendages, and teeth. I realized I'd started giving off some half-strangled screams, which would have been stupid, except they already knew where we were. And it would have made me feel pathetic if Æsubrand hadn't been doing it, too.

The perfect fey prince was making what he would probably describe as manly grunts if we survived this, but which sounded more like the shrieks of a little girl. And I was not going to say a goddamned thing about it, not if I lived to be two hundred, which was looking freaking doubtful. Because he was shrieking and fighting, and I was just shrieking.

I couldn't do anything else as I was dead out of power, except to hope those things couldn't leap this high!

And they couldn't, maybe because six-foot-deep mud is a crap launching pad. Or because this side of the little lake was taller than the other, making it a big jump. Or because Pritkin and whoever was helping him were pulling like their lives depended on it, or at least like ours did.

We finally topped the rise after what felt like hours but was probably only seconds, and I found myself snatched up and thrown over Alphonse's beefy shoulder. The light was a little better here, allowing me a quick flash of some ruined stone steps, cracked and broken and vine-strewn, of a dilapidated raised platform that looked like the one the musicians had been using but obviously wasn't, and of a single, rusted sword, lying on a step and half buried in dust. And that was all I saw, as Alphonse was *motivated*.

I didn't know if Pritkin had had time to tell him what was back there, but he certainly ran like all the demons in hell were after him.

"To the right!" Pritkin called as the strange green light went out, and a pack of braying somethings tore around the side of the lake—the rest of the bastards who hadn't jumped in, I guessed. But now, they were after us.

"I will hold them off," Æsubrand said because he apparently had not been paying attention.

"Yeah, for half a second. You'll be eaten!" Alphonse snarled, and I nodded vigorously.

It was all I could do, as the bastard had half choked me.

"You have a better idea?" the prince snapped.

"Run faster," Pritkin said grimly, and they did, with magic enhancing their already impressive speed to the point that we were practically flying. Only that wasn't as easy as it sounded.

There was stuff in the way everywhere: a mountain of tumbled rocks and dirt where it looked like an avalanche had descended from the heights above; pieces of wood from the nicer seating for the nobles, or whatever it had been used for in this time, which was half tumbled down and had a single ragged banner blowing in the breeze; and vines growing everywhere and covering the half of the lakebed closest to the water source, which looked like a dark jungle.

Even worse, some of the vines had climbed the surrounding stone pillars and hung in festoons, draping themselves between columns. And while many were as thick around as my arm and easy enough to see even in the darkness, others were deadly little rope-like things that could catch a neck if you weren't careful and, at this speed, hang a person in mid-air. Like that, I thought, as one snared Æsubrand, who was saved from decapitation by his gorget but who lost his footing, tumbling to the ground.

Pritkin pulled him back up while simultaneously sending a fireball ahead of us. I couldn't understand why he didn't send it the other way, and then I realized that it was too small to do us much good on offense. But it could burn through the hanging mass ahead, clearing a path.

And it did a pretty good job. Vines went up in garlands of fire before crumbling to dust, while others on the peripheries continued to burn, lighting us up for our pursuers. However, that hardly mattered now that they had our scent, and at least we could run. Only I didn't know where to until I spied something up ahead that looked familiar.

"We're headed . . . back there?" I croaked. "To the tunnels?"

"It's Bodil's fiefdom," Pritkin reminded me. "She said she could hold it."

Well, I damned well hoped she was right! Although it didn't

look like we were going to find out. The creatures chasing us moved like the wind and were almost on top of us already, prompting Pritkin to yell, "Go! Get her out!" and turn back around.

And me to start fighting, and Alphonse to start cursing, and Æsubrand to spin on a dime to join a helpless cause because they could not win this! Or even buy us enough time for their sacrifice to matter! And they couldn't have, at least not alone.

But they weren't alone; they were on the territory of a seriously pissed-off demigoddess who had decided to show what she could do. And I guessed that all those tunnels Pritkin and I had fought our way through must have been directly beneath all this. Because suddenly, it was as if they were trying to come out of the ground.

All of them.

All at once.

What felt like an eight on the Richter scale hit, causing the dirt to crack and the massive stone pillars to calve, splinter, and break. And topple over to meet the cascade of boulders bouncing down the surrounding cliffs to join the fun. Only it wasn't.

It wasn't fun at all.

Alphonse fell into a fissure that opened under his feet and only grabbed the edge at the last second, allowing him to launch us back out again before a pillar slammed into it, filling it up. Æsubrand flipped over a boulder almost as large as he was, dodged another, and was nearly taken down by one of the creatures until a rock the size of a car crushed the life out of it. And Pritkin must have found and enchanted some more discarded weapons because a sword and a wicked-looking knife were now fighting a rearguard action on their own.

None of which would matter in a moment because the mountain was about to come down on our heads!

Or go up, I thought, blinking, as a mass of stones and dirt took that moment to erupt from the newly created fissures, spewing multiple stories into the air. And making me wonder how the hell this was supposed to be helping us, Bodil! Only it was.

I wrenched my abused neck half off, looking behind us, and saw something that resembled a beaded curtain explode out of one of the longer fissures. Only those weren't beads. They were jagged pieces of rock blasting outward at bullet-like speeds, and they took a toll on our pursuers, the leaders of which foolishly tried to run straight through.

Limbs were slashed, bodies were pierced, and although these things healed quickly with demon magic behind them, it wasn't quick enough. Not when the leaders had just run into what was essentially a meat grinder, although how Bodil was doing this, I didn't know. She wasn't supposed to have earth magic!

And then I understood when the rock eruptions suddenly changed into something else. I realized it wasn't the tunnels causing the explosions after all but muddy geysers flooding through every fissure with enough force to send the soil and rock above them flying. And then came the water, in sparkling vertical rivers that were clean now and shooting up twenty stories or more into the air from the immense pressure behind them.

I felt spray hit me from the rain created when all that water started pelting back down, and it was hard enough to sting. But I barely noticed through the cracking sounds going on everywhere, the boulders falling from the cliffs above and bouncing around us, and the leaping, scale-covered thing that came at us from the side, screeching. Only to encounter a razor-thin fissure that opened up beneath its feet—

And cut it in half.

It fell neatly into two horrible pieces, and my mind started gibbering. Shut up! I thought because this was no time to lose it. Not with blood and rain falling everywhere and thin blades of water spurting up without warning, doing what steel could not and slicing and dicing through the horde behind us.

But they didn't slice enough. Or maybe there were just too many creatures back there. Despite the roar of the water and the rumbling of the stone, I could hear them howling, chittering, and screeching from all directions as more came running.

Not that they needed more, as the dozens pursuing us had barely broken stride, ignoring their losses and staying on the hunt.

The moon took that moment to come out from behind some clouds and flood the scene with light. Giving me a clear view for the first time: of toppling black pillars, each larger than the biggest obelisk, shattering against the ground; of shooting silver geysers, now spearing skyward all around us; of what looked like every demon in hell being slammed by the first and bisected by the second. And in one case, shot straight in the face by a geyser that erupted sideways from the cliff face and sent something with scales and bat wings flying over the lakebed, like a belt from a giant's fist.

And yet, it *still* wasn't enough. They kept coming, dodging, twisting, and trampling the sundered bodies of their kind as if they were just more debris on the field. We were almost to our goal, but suddenly, we were out of time.

Until a crazy redhead jumped out of the mouth of the tunnel that Pritkin and I had escaped from and threw up a shield.

It was a shitty one because she was drained, and it had to cover a lot of territory. So it didn't repel the thousand jagged pieces the cliff was shedding or the bodies slamming into it at top speed. It trapped them instead, leaving them to punch inward at us like a bunch of heavyweight boxers fighting through a cloth.

But it was heavy-duty cloth, and Alphonse was an old hand at dodging blows.

He ducked and whirled and danced through the line-up and then threw the two of us into the tunnel entrance and utter darkness, so hard that we tumbled halfway down the incline before I managed to free myself and start back up. Because Pritkin was still back there! Only to have that son of a bitch grab my ankle.

"Let me go!"

"Make me."

Goddamnit!

But then everyone was coming, Enid running past with her long hair streaming out behind her, looking like a gray ghost in the eerie light from outside. Pritkin supporting Æsubrand, who was bleeding from a head wound but somehow still alive. And then a crap ton of dirt, rubble, and larger stones came bouncing in behind them, enough that they had Alphonse throwing himself over me as what felt like the entire mountain finally did what it had been threatening.

And came down on our heads.

CHAPTER THIRTY-TWO

I didn't pass out, although I kind of wished I had. The only thing less fun than spiraling into unconsciousness under a suffocating mountain of dirt and vampire flesh was lying awake under said mountain, waiting for rescue. Which wasn't coming because everybody else was in the same position!

"Okay," Alphonse wheezed from on top of me. "I got this."

I sincerely doubted that. But since he was the only reason I wasn't currently a corpse, I didn't point it out. Alphonse wasn't Atlas and couldn't hold the weight of the world on his shoulders, but he was doing a pretty good job of keeping a large chunk of it from crushing me.

But digging us out of here at the same time was going to be tough.

That was something he seemed to realize because a lot of huffed curses followed, as every time he tried to move, the mountain moved with him. Or at least the crap ton of it residing on top of his back, which sent cascades of sand, rock, and dust down into the little cleared space we had left. And while he didn't need to breathe, I did!

It was getting harder. The enclosed area had no ventilation, and I didn't know where to dig to change that, as there was absolutely no light. But the air was warm and getting warmer, and my chest was tight and getting tighter.

I had to move.

I was lying face down so I could crawl forward a little

under Alphonse's arms and feel around, hoping to locate an exit hole or enough loose pebbles that maybe I could make one. But smaller rocks and dirt had collapsed into the crevasses between the larger stones, sealing us in. And leaving me scraping bloody fingertips over what felt like a solid wall and making no progress at all.

Which was about the time I started to panic because I didn't want to die like this!

"It's okay," Alphonse said, probably sensing my heart rate speed up.

"How . . . is this . . . okay?" I gasped.

"I hear something."

I froze. "Some of those . . . monsters?"

My brain conjured up a sudden, horrible image of things with whipping tails and bat wings crawling all over the rubble, waiting for us to poke a head out so they could bite it off. I stopped breathing altogether at that point, and Alphonse wasn't doing it anyway. Which I guessed let him hear better because he suddenly chuckled, an almost obscene sound under the circumstances.

"Nope. One of ours."

Then it came again, magically enhanced this time, and I heard it, too: Pritkin yelling from what sounded like a mile away, probably because his voice was filtering through solid rock. *"Cassie!"*

"Over . . . here," I croaked, pretty sure that was useless. But then Alphonse started bellowing, and everybody heard that. Including the mountain, which began sending tricklings of dirt and stones onto our heads.

And then more of them, and more, but not because of another collapse, but because somebody was moving them. Tons of earth and rock were being blasted off us and sent flying back down the tunnel. I couldn't see them as I couldn't see anything, but I heard when they hit what sounded like solid stone.

"Getting close!" Alphonse yelled. "Don't blow my damned

head off!"

They didn't, but more boulders met more rock as layer after layer was peeled away, loudly enough that it resonated even down here. The passage behind us must be pretty well blocked by now, I thought, and perked up slightly. But I was considerably less happy by the time I was dragged out from under the remaining mountain of dirt, bleeding and filthy and gasping for air, and was immediately beaten soundly on the back.

Which I was about to insist I didn't need when I started hacking up half the damned hillside.

And once I started, I couldn't seem to stop, coughing and retching until I was pretty sure that I was going to lose my breakfast, only I didn't. My deprived stomach clung to it like it was the last meal I'd ever get, and maybe it was. And my lungs finally stopped trying to throw themselves up, too, although less because they were clear and more because I was exhausted.

I rolled over onto my back when the beating stopped to see Pritkin, who had cursed every time he'd had to hit me. But his face was stoic in the watery ball of light that Enid was holding, and his eyes were focused and assessing. They were less like a lover's and more like a soldier's evaluating an ally in battle, and for some reason, that made me feel better.

Or maybe it was just the fact that I could *breathe*.

"Are you alright?" That was Enid, looking really invested in my answer for some reason. I couldn't imagine why, as teaming up with me hadn't gotten her much. Except almost drowned, eaten, and pulverized.

I remembered what Bodil had said about people who worked with me and hoped that wasn't a prophecy. But I nodded because Enid looked rough, and it seemed to reassure her slightly. And then Pritkin turned my face towards his again.

"Cassie. I need to know what happened. Can you tell me what happened?"

I licked dirt-covered lips and tried to speak, but my whole

throat was coated in dust, and nothing but a vague wheeze emerged.

"Move," Bodil said, pushing through the small group of people surrounding me and crouching on my other side. She held something out, which my dust-filled eyes finally identified as a globule of what appeared to be pure water. It was the size of a softball and just sitting there, wobbling on her palm.

It was suddenly all I could concentrate on.

I grabbed it clumsily, only to have it fall apart as soon as it left her hand, soaking me everywhere except for my throat. I mewled in distress, and she sighed and magicked up another one. And it was magic; I saw her that time, looking like she plucked it out of thin air.

That was probably exactly what she had done, drawing together the surrounding water in the air and merging it into drinkable form. Something that I finally managed to get down with her help, letting her hold the ball to my parched lips before attempting to swallow. It was warm and slightly dirty from the dust in the air, and I'd never tasted anything so perfect in my life!

God, that was wonderful!

After a moment, I lay back gasping, and Bodil gave the rest to Enid. The kitchen maid was still staring at me out of a dirt mask, with only her long, dust-covered hair and hazel eyes allowing me to recognize her. I probably looked just as bad, if not worse, but I didn't care.

I was just grateful to be alive.

"Cassie," Pritkin said again.

"It was Tony," I gasped, finally answering his question. "I saw him . . . in the pool . . . for a second."

"Tony?"

"He appeared . . . right beside me. Did a time spell—"

"A time spell?" That was Bodil, although why she sounded shocked, I didn't know. After what she saw outside, what did she think had happened?

"That wasn't you?" Pritkin sounded disturbed, and for good reason. Tony couldn't do spells of any kind, which was why he had dark mages working for him. And he sure as hell couldn't use the Pythian power!

"It's true," Alphonse backed me up. "He appeared out of nowhere, right beside Cass. I saw him through the waves—"

"How?" Bodil demanded. "I was there and couldn't see anything through all the water being splashed around!"

"'Cause I was looking for him," Alphonse said heavily. "I been haunting Cassie's steps since she got here. I knew he'd come for her, and that was the perfect moment to strike. She'd just towed that one," he hiked a thumb at a filthy looking Æsubrand, whose previously shiny armor was caked with mud and whose face was set on a thousand-yard stare, "back from the finish line—"

"Alphonse," I said, sitting up and backing off a little because I didn't want to get stabbed by an enraged fey. Only Æsubrand didn't even blink.

He must have seen his fair share of battles, but that one seemed to have knocked some of the stuffing out of him. Know the feeling, I thought grimly. And he didn't even flinch when he looked at me, only not with anger, for a change, but with bewilderment.

"What . . . were those things?" he whispered.

"Demons," Pritkin answered for me.

"Demons?" Æsubrand looked like that didn't compute. "Like the ones the two of you brought?"

"No. Not like them."

"Old ones," I croaked. "Bad ones." It wasn't much as explanations went, but it was all I could manage, or he would likely understand. If the fey knew little about Earth, it was nothing to the gaping void of knowledge they held about the hells.

And I wasn't up to a lesson.

Although he looked like he could use one because his face scrunched up in disbelief. "Demons . . . in *Faerie*?"

Bodil didn't say anything, but she looked grim. And poked Alphonse to continue, even though one doesn't poke a master vampire. But after what he'd just seen of her power, he didn't object.

"I leaped for him from the side of the lake," he said, his lips drawing back into a snarl in memory. "It was what I'd been expecting, so I had the stake and knife all ready. It wouldn't have taken but a sec—"

"Then why didn't it?" Enid asked.

She didn't sound angry. She didn't sound like much of anything, her voice almost expressionless with shock. But Alphonse flushed.

"You know why! Right before I could get my hands on that bastard, there was a flash of light and . . . we were here."

"And where is here?" Bodil demanded. She was covered in mud and dust like the rest of us but somehow made it look regal. And furious. "What happened? This isn't the city I know!"

"It isn't the city that any of us know," Pritkin said, looking at me. And then came out with the question we had all been thinking. "What year is it?"

I shook my head. "I don't know."

He frowned. "What do you mean, you don't know? Pythias have an innate time sense—"

"Yeah. It isn't working."

"And why not?" That was Bodil, sounding as impatient and imperious as if she were talking to one of the slaves. I would have given that the reply it deserved, but I was still relearning how to breathe and didn't have the energy.

I settled for answering the question instead, as it was relevant.

"Best guess? The portal . . . is turned away. My power . . . doesn't work unless it's . . . pointed at Earth—"

"What?"

"—where it was tethered . . . by the gods . . . all those centuries ago. But when it cycles . . . back around . . . I should get an answer."

Bodil just stared at me, her eyes back to black but no less hard to meet—even when looking gobsmacked for some reason. "You mean to say," she said slowly, "that you've been making yourself a target—*the* target of the entire Challenge—and your power only *occasionally* works?"

"Is that true?" Alphonse demanded and then didn't give me time to answer. "That's why you were hiding half the time against the Kraken, isn't it? You were waiting for your power to come back!"

"Do we . . . have to talk about this . . . now?" I asked. There seemed to be more pressing matters, like finding out if I could walk.

Which was a no, I thought, as I got dizzy halfway to my feet.

"Sit down before you fall down!" Alphonse growled, and a heavy hand descended onto my shoulder.

Which I didn't need, as my ass had already been headed back to the floor. It hit the dirt, and the room slurred wildly around me. God, I felt rough.

I lay back against the rock fall and let the conversation wash over me for a minute. And there was a lot of it, as people were recovering from the initial shock and beginning to get scared. And pissed.

"You're damned right we have to talk about this now!" Alphonse said. "You're supposed to know what you're doing—"

"She's been handling things better than you, vampire!" Enid said, with a little of her old spirit coming back. "We won that race, in case you've forgotten—"

"And what did it get us?" Alphonse said, throwing out his arms.

"A chance! This may be a game to you—"

"It's not a game." That was low and menacing, but she didn't seem to hear. Or care if she did.

"—but it's deadly serious for us! Do you know what happens to the slaves if someone else wins? We can forget about any hope of freedom!"

"Freedom?" Pritkin repeated. "I thought this was about maintaining the status quo—"

"Why? Is that what Rhosier told you?"

"It's what he believes—"

"Which is why he isn't told everything!"

"—and a reasonable conclusion from the available evidence. In a revolt, you'd be slaughtered. You must know that —"

"You might be surprised!"

"And so might you," Bodil said dryly.

"This isn't your fight!" Enid snarled. "It's ours, and we want a chance!"

"At what?" Alphonse asked.

"The things you already have and take for granted," she said passionately. "A life we can call our own, a chance to live where we choose, do what we like, and marry by our choice. Do you have any idea—"

She broke off. "No. Of course, you don't. And those who do, like Rhosier and our betters," she glanced at Bodil, and it wasn't friendly. "Want us to accept that this is how things are and will always be. But I, for one, will not accept!"

"We have been getting your people out," Bodil said, frowning at her.

Enid laughed scornfully. "Oh, yes. A handful at a time. Should I thank you for that?"

"Yes." It was flat. "I have risked much—"

"You have risked nothing!" Enid was suddenly in her face, making Alphonse start looking worried because Bodil wasn't someone you wanted to piss off.

But Enid had the bravado of someone who had almost been killed half a dozen times today and had officially reached fuck it. She was telling truth to power, and power had best sit down and listen. Or lose it and kill us all, I thought, exchanging a glance with Alphonse.

"Hey," he said, but Enid wasn't listening.

"Do you think I don't know what you're doing?" she said fervently. "You serve the system just as much as Feltin and the rest!"

"Be careful," Bodil warned. "Do not speak my name and his in the same sentence."

"Or what? Will you have me beaten? Or do even worse? At a word from you, I could vanish, never to be heard from again—"

"If I acted in such a way, which I do not!"

"No. They have enough people to terrify us. You act as a pressure release, like the valves on the cooks' pots. Shuffle out the troublemakers, the dissidents, the ones willing to fight. Get them to Earth before they cause too much unrest and influence others. Keep the docile ones, let them continue to breed for you, die for you—and raise more just like them. A perpetual slave class to preserve your power—"

"Is that what you think?" Bodil demanded.

"It's what I know. Rhosier can believe what he likes and tell himself he's a rebel, so he can channel his rage and not explode when they grind him under their collective heel. But I know the truth—"

"You are an angry child who understands nothing," Bodil said calmly.

"I understand that your 'help' is why we haven't fought before and continue to suffer this! You who so value children, do you know what it's like to give birth, to suckle a babe, to see him grow—

"And to watch him go off to war to die for his jailors and yours? Or to watch your daughter be taken by one of those fine lords, to be 'selected'—what a lucky girl! To be ripped away from her family and—" She stopped with her face crumpling as if she couldn't go on. "It's you who doesn't understand," she whispered.

I put a hand on her arm because I didn't know what to say. I didn't understand all that, either, and I was grateful for it. Sometimes, it was easy to resent my life until I met someone like Enid and got some damned perspective.

Enid looked from my hand to my face, and her eyes were flooded but resolute. "I wanted to fight for years but couldn't," she told me. "I never had the chance. Everything was the same no matter how much we tried to change it—until you came."

"I thought you hated her," Alphonse said.

"I hated her when I thought she was the same as all the rest. But she's like . . . like that earthquake out there—"

"Which I did," Bodil said sourly, not appreciating the love fest.

"—and changed everything in an instant! Suddenly, the world looks different!"

"Considering where we are, I wouldn't say that's a plus," Alphonse pointed out, but Enid wasn't listening.

"Thank you for that," she said to me, her voice wavering. "No matter what happens . . . thank you for letting me fight!"

I blinked at her, feeling a hundred different things, but mostly shame. Because I hadn't been doing any of this for her. Or for any of the slaves.

This was a power struggle for everyone in the contest. Some wanted the power for good, some for self-aggrandizement, and some for evil. But all of us were reaching for the brass ring as hard as we could.

Except for the slaves. They were just fighting to survive without many people in their corner. Or anyone, if Enid's take on this was right, and she knew this place better than I did.

So yes, I felt ashamed.

"Enid," I began when Pritkin shot me a look I didn't understand and cut me off.

"We need to get moving," he said tersely. "We're being hunted, and they'll find a way in soon enough."

"They won't," Æsubrand argued, blinking and returning to life. Maybe because hunting was something he knew a bit about. "They've lost the scent—"

"Not them."

"—and there must be easier prey—"

"They don't want easier prey," Pritkin said flatly. "They

want to test themselves against the strongest. It's in their nature."

But Æsubrand was shaking his head. "Animals don't think like that—they don't think at all—"

"These aren't animals!"

"Then what else would you call them? Filthy, hideous, corrupted beasts who—"

He cut off, perhaps belatedly remembering that he was talking to someone who was half demon himself. And currently looking like it. But Pritkin didn't press the point.

"They'll be coming," was all he said.

"Yeah, and Cassie's power don't work!" Alphonse seemed hung up on that fact. "So how do we get back? Because this ain't our time—"

"We don't know when it is—"

"Well, we know it's not right!" And okay, that had been a little shrill. Which was not a sound I'd ever heard from Alphonse. But looking around the tight, dirt-filled tunnel into blackness, I understood.

"You heard her," Pritkin said. "We wait for the portal to come around again."

"And if it doesn't? If it *can't*?"

"Then we wait some more."

Alphonse didn't like that answer. But before he had a chance to explain, in detail, exactly why he didn't, Bodil intervened. "I can make it work."

Alphonse turned on her as if glad to have somebody new to yell at, as neither Pritkin nor I were giving him much. "It may not be a case of flipping a switch! If the portal is in the same shape as the rest of this place, we're *boned*—"

"Get yourself together, vampire," Bodil snapped.

"Get my—" Alphonse stared at her. "I'm the only one talking sense! We're stuck in a horror movie with monsters chasing us. And I'm hanging around with the goddamned blonde!"

"What is wrong with that?" Æsubrand asked, looking

confused, perhaps because I wasn't the only one with that hair color.

"It means half of you are red shirts, and I'm starting to wonder about me!"

"Red . . . shirts?"

"Never mind," Pritkin said, standing up. "Lady Bodil will get the portal running, and Cassie will get us home."

"How the hell do you know that?" Alphonse demanded.

"My people and I created the damned thing," Bodil said, rising back to her full height from the crouch she'd been using to talk to me. Which left her eyeball to eyeball with Alphonse, even when he straightened up. "Now get a grip, vampire, as your people say, or I'll do it for you."

"I'd like to see you try!"

"Right now, so would I," she said grimly and swept down the tunnel.

And that ended that.

CHAPTER THIRTY-THREE

I tried to stand, but it didn't go any better this time. The room did its shaky-shaky thing, and I stumbled into Alphonse. Who I guessed didn't want to wait for me and my pathetic human recovery time because I was snatched up, flung over a beefy shoulder, and carted down the sloping tunnel like a sack of beans.

I'd have preferred Pritkin's shoulder, but he was up ahead, taking point, and as laser-focused as usual in a crisis. Everyone else flowed after him and Bodil, leaving me and Alphonse to bring up the rear. And to watch the passage trundle by, as there was nothing else to do.

Enid's light source was ahead of us, possibly leading the way considering how dim it was here. But it nonetheless lit up the walls with a faint, shifting radiance, like looking at the moon from underwater. And showed me glimpses of rubble extending much farther than I'd expected—piles of it.

In places, it half obscured the tunnel in slanting mountains of rock and dirt, forcing Alphonse to clamber over. He didn't get winded because vampire, but I heard some huffing and puffing up ahead, probably from Enid. I felt for her, as there was a ton of stuff in the way, making the walk an obstacle course.

Much of it was unexpected, such as the shattered pieces of wood propped against the walls or reinforcing the rubble in spots as if somebody had tried to make barricades. There were also a bunch of crates that had once held magical weapons and were now mostly empty and dust-covered. And the few potion bombs still in place, like eggs in their cartons, were sunken in and looked decayed.

There were also a few discarded hand-held weapons here and there, primarily broken spears and pikes and one sword half covered in dirt. Alphonse bent over and pulled it out of the rubble. Like the pikes, it was almost new-looking.

Of course, this part of the tunnel was bone dry, unlike the area outside, where vines and mildew had taken over, and further down, where the river ran. So that might explain the state of the weapons. But it didn't explain why they were here at all or why the rest of this place looked so unfamiliar.

I glanced around, wondering just how far back we'd been sent. Because the tunnels that Pritkin and I had made our frantic escape through hadn't looked like this. Like most of this place, they'd been tall to accommodate fey height and black and glittery.

They had not had huge chunks of rock missing, as if a backhoe had carved them out or the walls had been mined to provide rubble for the nearby barricades. They had not had giant cracks scrawling like black lightning everywhere and a half-collapsed ceiling as if someone had tried to seal themselves in after the barricades fell. I would have thought I was reading the signs wrong, but Alphonse saw them, too.

"You can see where they put charges," he said, his voice low and his finger pointing up at the fractured ceiling, the ruins of which we were slowly clambering over. "Brought it down in big enough chunks to impede a tank."

But it hadn't been enough. Because we were traveling a path carved through the wreckage, and while it wasn't easy, it was doable. And seemed to go on forever.

"Wasn't enough," Alphonse agreed. "Looks like whoever was defending this place brought down half the mountain, and whoever was attacking just kept going."

"Who was attacking?" I asked. "Those things out there?"

"Dunno." He kicked something with his foot, which I

guessed he'd been able to smell despite it being buried under dirt. A human skull peeked out at us, but there was no body attached. And the skull. . .

My thoughts petered out, but Alphonse wasn't so squeamish. "Whoever it was, they were hungry," he said and crushed the gnawed-on bone under his boot.

He walked on.

Alphonse stayed busy ducking under pieces of rock or climbing over debris. It was bad enough that he was continually cursing in places, but nobody shushed him. I even heard a few competing phrases from up ahead after somebody jostled a precarious slab and almost got crushed.

"Everybody okay up there?" Alphonse yelled as the rockfall sent reverberations along the tunnel.

"All right," Enid called back. "But be careful. This part is not stable!"

"Like everything else in this damned place," Alphonse muttered over the echoes of the fall, which were loud enough to wake the dead, only nobody seemed to care.

Maybe because, while a battle had happened here, it hadn't been recent. Drifts of dust in the crevasses glittered in the low light, highlighting those jagged scars instead of being suspended in the air. Like the coating on the weapons, it had been here for a while.

Alphonse edged closer to the right wall to avoid another unstable area, and I reached out and touched the pole of a pike that had been propped against the stones for who knew how long.

"What do you want that for?" Alphonse demanded. "It's broken. The end was snapped off in someone's hide."

Or something's, I thought.

"I don't want a weapon," I said. "I want to touch it, but it's coated in dust."

"You gonna do something?" he asked, putting me down on some fallen stones.

"Gonna try."

"Okay." He looked around but couldn't find any part of us that wasn't just as dirty as the pike. So he shook it instead, then rubbed a big palm over it to get it, if not clean, at least less filthy. I took it gingerly, hoping for a flash of something.

I wasn't the best touch telepath out there, but sometimes, it worked.

And sometimes it didn't. What it did not do was to shoot a skin-crawling frisson straight up my spine. Along with a sense of wrongness so dizzying that I'd have probably fallen over if I hadn't been propped against the rocks. I dropped the pike and clamped my teeth on a scream I didn't understand.

"You're freaking me out right now," Alphonse said.

"Sorry."

He shrugged. "S'okay. I'm used to it. You were a creepy kid."

"I was not."

"Big, blank blue eyes, looking like they stared into a guy's soul. And that was when you weren't busy talking to people who weren't there or laughing at jokes nobody told."

"I was talking to ghosts—"

"Yeah, 'cause that makes it so much better. You want that thing or not?"

He gestured at the pike.

"No."

"Okay." He threw me back over his shoulder and walked on. "You gonna tell me what you saw? 'Cause I remember that reaction. You used to scream for no reason all the time. I thought you were going nuts 'till Sal said you got pictures sometimes."

"Sometimes," I agreed, wishing he'd drop it.

He did not drop it. "She said you can touch stuff and see who owned it or what they did when they used it. So, what did you see this time?"

I shivered slightly and knew he felt it. "Nothing."

"You wanna explain that, or do I gotta keep playing twenty questions?"

I struggled to find the right words, but it didn't go well.

It reminded me of the first few moments after I arrived here, when I'd felt a scrim across the world. As if it wanted to reject me as being wrong somehow.

That didn't make sense as I'd been to plenty of different times and never felt that way, although I had always been a visitor who didn't belong, like one of those stray leaves stuck to the bottom of a dark witch's shoe. I rubbed the fingers that had been clutching the pike together and felt the grittiness of the dust again. The pang was less now but still there, and not just on the pike.

Now that I concentrated, I could feel it everywhere, in the dirt clinging to me or the breath in my lungs. There *was* something wrong, but it wasn't this place. It was me.

I was the displaced thing, and this world knew it. It sounded ridiculous, but I could feel it as clearly as if I was looking at a "Don't Enter" sign. As if I'd somehow breached a forbidden zone where I was not supposed to be.

Was it because of the Horrors? And if it was, how were they doing this? They didn't have power over time any more than Tony did!

Not to mention that Æsubrand was right: when had demons crawled all over Faerie? Because I'd sat through a lot of deadly dull briefings in recent months, many of them about fey history, and nobody had mentioned that. And he'd probably received far more lessons growing up in a position where he might be called on to rule parts of this place someday.

So what the hell?

"Cassie?" Alphonse prompted because he was relentless.

"There's nothing, and then there's nothing," I said shortly. "I didn't get anything that would help."

"Yeah. Just be certain you mention it when you do."

Sure thing, I thought, trying to concentrate as I bounced along, but it was hard. Maybe because it felt like my brain was sloshing around in my skull, still trying to play catch up. And that wasn't helped when we finally reached the stables again.

The first thing I saw were reflections in the canal, which

had me gasping in thirst with Bodil's brief drink long gone. Alphonse must have heard because he swung me down, where I wobbled a little but stayed up. Causing him to give me an approving slap on the back that almost knocked me into the water.

"Hey," he called out. "Give it a minute. We need a rest."

The others stopped, possibly because the water looked good to them, too. It turned out not to be fit to drink, being brackish from the flow outside, but Bodil filtered out some balls of the stuff that allowed us to quench our thirst. After which, we sat on the steps leading down from the quay and washed some of the dirt off.

The mud from outside had turned into dried chunks that caked everything, including my hair. I shook it as clean as possible, then felt fingers combing through it from behind, pulling free the bits I couldn't see. I glanced up but already knew who was there.

I covered one of Pritkin's hands with mine, and he sat beside me. We just stayed there for a minute, glad to be alive but unsure what this fresh hell was. He didn't ask if I had any ideas— he knew I'd have mentioned them if I did—and I didn't offer anything.

I still had no idea what was going on.

Enid ran past and jumped into the water, splashing us, and came up smiling. I suddenly wondered how old she was, as that kind of resiliency was rare. Not to mention that she looked about sixteen suddenly with that exuberant hair plastered against her skull.

Alphonse sat down on the other side of me a moment later and sighed, his eyes on Enid. "I'm officially a dirty old man," he proclaimed.

"You are dirty," I agreed. "Maybe a swim?"

"Don't tempt me."

"Why? She'd curse your balls off if you got out of line."

He laughed suddenly, a brief bark. "That's half the attraction."

"And the other half?" I wondered if it was just her strange, almost ethereal beauty.

But she looked a little more real now, splashing about and causing the mud in her hair to trickle down her face in dark rivulets. She'd also dropped the glamourie, probably to conserve whatever magic she had left. And when Æsubrand, who had sat on the other side of Alphonse, noticed, I heard his indrawn breath.

"Exactly what you think," Alphonse told me. "Takes lady balls not to have your spirit broken someplace like this, and triple that after what she went through." He glanced at our silver prince. "One word," he told him. "One goddamned word —"

"I am not a monster, vampire. I leave that to you."

"See that you do."

"Or?" Æsubrand bristled. He didn't seem to take orders well.

Alphonse draped a very large arm around his shoulders. "Ask Cassie."

Æsubrand looked at me, appearing startled for some reason. I guessed well-brought-up fey women turned deaf at times like these. Too bad I wasn't one.

"Which story should I tell him?" I asked Alphonse, who had found a toothpick in his borrowed guard's outfit and was picking at his fangs. He shrugged, and I glanced at Æsubrand, who looked like he wanted to throw off the brotherly hug but wasn't sure it was a good idea.

"He has something of a reputation," Pritkin commented idly as if he'd know. And maybe he did. It had been his job to check out anybody hanging around me, and Sal and Alphonse had been at Dante's, the casino where I had my court, a while back.

"So do I!" Æsubrand bristled.

"Yes, but your opponents are usually in one piece at the end."

That took Æsubrand a minute, then he scowled and got up

before huffing off. Alphonse grinned at us. Enid splashed some more.

And Bodil did what she had been doing all this time after quenching our thirst. And stood at the top of the steps, looking around with a frown, maybe wondering where the seahorses were. I didn't see any.

I didn't see much of anything except the canal itself, which looked odd for some reason I couldn't immediately name. Then I realized the shimmering, ever-changing cascade of emerald light from the suspended river wasn't there. I peered upward but couldn't see what was in its place, as the ball of spell light Enid had parked on the pier didn't reach that far.

Whatever it was, it was dark.

Pritkin glanced up, and I saw him noticing, too, but he didn't say anything.

"Why didn't you want me to say anything to Enid?" I asked him after Alphonse went off to smoke a cigarette.

"You were about to tell her the truth."

"And that's bad?"

"It is when we don't know what we're facing here. She saved us out there in the rock fall. Best not to alienate an asset in an emergency."

I frowned, although he did have a point. But then, so did she. "It sounds like she thinks you're going to free the slaves if we win."

"That would be . . . difficult."

"Difficult isn't impossible."

"No, but if they're free, we don't have much of an army. They make up a good percentage of the Alorestri forces."

"So, we're supposed to send slaves out to die for us?"

"It's their fight, too. If we lose this war, none of us may survive. Or they may look back on their time as slaves to the Alorestri as 'the good old days.'"

"Maybe, but you and I signed onto this. We made a choice, one they never had."

"Did we?" He looked at me. "How much of a choice did you

ever have? How much did I? Unless you count the choice to die on our feet or kneeling!"

That last was said in the same low voice he'd been using, giving us some degree of privacy, but there was genuine anger in it. "We're supposed to be the good guys," I reminded him.

"We're trying to be. I'm trying to be." He was quiet for a moment. "Sometimes, it's hard to know what that is."

I lay my head on his shoulder and felt his arm go around me.

"Yeah. There's no manual."

"What?"

"I've been saying since I landed this job that there should be a manual, but there isn't. For a long time, I wondered why no Pythia ever made one, wrote down a how-to guide, a top-ten list, *something*. They left all kinds of other writings, whole libraries full of them, but not that.

"Then I worked with Gertie for a while and started to understand. There's no manual because there can't be one. She told me once to trust my heart, that it was the best guide I'd ever get in this crazy world. I thought that sounded strange, but I'm starting to understand what she meant."

"And what did she mean?"

"That in times like these, you just have to feel your way, day to day. You want to be perfect; you think you have to be perfect, but none of us are. But the fact that you want to be, that it weighs on you when you're not, that you keep on trying even when everything seems hopeless . . . it's what makes you a good person." I looked up at him. "A good man."

"I'm not a good man."

"If you're not, I don't know one."

"Then you don't know one." He got up abruptly and walked away down the side of the canal.

"Pritkin—" I started after him, but Alphonse, standing at the top of the steps and probably eavesdropping, caught my arm.

"Give him a minute. He's had a tough couple of weeks."

Haven't we all? I thought, wondering what the hell.

"And guys like him, who think they're in charge, blame themselves when things go wrong."

"This had nothing to do with him. This was Tony—"

"Yeah, but still. You wanna talk? Talk after the crisis is over. You'll get further."

And it was hard to argue with that.

After a few more minutes, the group reassembled, and we walked on.

The stable office where Pritkin and I had been interrogated was also radically different, with what looked like another barricade thrown up in front of it, this one made primarily out of furniture. I recognized a bunch of sturdy wooden tables and a few broken bits of wood that might have been saddle holders. That seemed like a crap job of barricading for the kind of people who lived here and whose magic should have sufficed anyway.

But maybe the Green Fey hadn't colonized this place, back whenever the heck this was? I didn't know, but looking at the splintered wood gave me a bad feeling. It told a story of shock, unpreparedness, and desperation.

And of failure, as the barricade hadn't held.

Suddenly, I really didn't want to go in there. But Bodil felt differently and pushed forward, squeezing past the hanging shards and blackened stones, and we slowly followed. Annnnnd I should learn to listen to my gut, I thought, finally understanding where all the people went.

And where they'd stayed.

Pritkin, Alphonse, and I had stopped just inside the entrance, with Alphonse's arm flung out in front of me like a parent catching a child in a fender bender. But Bodil was standing in the middle of the room with no expression on that beautiful face. I couldn't blame her.

I didn't know what was on mine, but it might have looked similarly blank, as I wasn't sure what would fit the moment. Because there were bones everywhere as if we'd walked into an ossuary. Only in that case, they'd be in nice little rows and patterns, and nothing was orderly here.

The remains of the defenders were littered across the floor, piled against the walls, and blackened in chunks as if spells had eaten through flesh and bone. Or, in one memorable case, as if someone had been blasted against the wall with such force that he had remained there like a partially excavated fossil. I even thought I saw an expression of surprise on his face or what was left of it.

He was alone, but in other areas, it was impossible to tell how many dead there were, as skeletons were piled on top of skeletons. Their flesh was mostly gone now except to stain their bones, with even the smell of decay long gone other than for a mustiness in the air that I tried not to think about. But their clothes, ragged though they were, were intact, and the robes were black, like the type Bodil's guards had worn, the ones that had given them the bat-like appearance that had so startled me when I first came here.

This had been someone's last stand.

I took in the gouges in the walls, the marks that spell fire had left on virtually everything, and the rotting hulk of some fallen beast in a corner. It was unrecognizable now, its fur covered with a fine layer of black dust. Like the huge pile of the dead that had all but blocked a door beside the stall that Bodil had used as an office.

The black-garbed guys had made a new blockade there, out of their bodies this time, but it hadn't been enough. It had been plowed through, too, leaving heaps of broken skeletons framing the entrance, a few still held together by rotting sinew. I stared at them, wondering what had been in there that was so important.

The only thing I remembered was that it was the door Rieni had disappeared through after saddling me with a bunch of baby seahorses. And then laughing and skipping out of the room, secure in the knowledge that there was little a fey child couldn't get away with. Especially that child.

Which was why it seemed strangely appropriate to see her

again, emerging from its shadow and stepping delicately over the bones, a slender figure clad all in black with a faint green luminescence still clinging to her. It was so appropriate that I didn't even question it for a moment. "That was you," I started to say, recognizing the color of the beast that had saved us at the lake by distracting the demons for a crucial few seconds.

But I didn't.

I didn't say anything.

Because the implication of her being here had just hit, and because Rieni . . .

Wasn't herself.

CHAPTER
THIRTY-FOUR

The face was recognizable—just. The skin, a pleasing creamy brown the last time I'd seen her, was now a sickly off-white, and I didn't think that was because of Enid's ball of moonlight. Because Rieni also had what looked like black mold growing up one cheek and into her hairline, eating across the previous perfection like scorching.

Her clothes were also wrong, as tattered as the skeletons' and barely clinging to her bones, and her hair was singed off on one side as if she'd dodged a spell by millimeters. But it was the eyes that really gave it away. They were as fixed, staring, and lifeless as mine had probably been when fighting Zeus as a bloody corpse.

And I wasn't the only one who thought so. Æsubrand had strode into the room on Bodil's heels, not bothering with Alphonse's caution, but his bravado had gone fast. He had been standing there, looking silently around like the rest of us, but now he stumbled back, making some sign in the air.

Had he been an elderly Romanian woman instead of a hunky fey prince, it would have reminded me of the evil eye. Because that was what you did when confronted with a zombie, I thought, only that was impossible! Faerie didn't have zombies!

But that was definitely what I was seeing here, and Rieni looked like she'd been one for a while. Half of the flesh on one slender arm had rotted away, her eyes were sunken pits that clearly showed the shape of the skull underneath, and her teeth were cracked and partly missing when she suddenly grinned at us, causing her grandmother to make a little sound before going to one knee. But Rieni wasn't looking at Bodil as I'd have expected.

She was looking at me. And coming toward me with an intent that would have had me backing up, too, except that Alphonse grabbed me and let out a roar of challenge before shoving me behind him alongside Enid. At the same moment, Pritkin moved forward, getting in between the zombie and me, but he didn't tell me to leave.

Because where was there to go? And before we could discuss it or even form words in our half-stunned brains, the zombie caught herself and stopped, still partway across the room. I guessed our expressions had been eloquent.

She put out a soothing hand, which would have helped more if it hadn't been connected to the mostly missing arm. I could see the tendons working in the bare spots where all the flesh had rotted away. I could see tendons. . .

"I apologize," she said, her voice a raspy thread on the air as if the vocal cords making it were dried out and dusty, too. "It's been so long, I almost thought you weren't coming. And when you did, it was so sudden that I didn't have time to choose a different avatar—not that many are left intact."

"Avatar?" I whispered.

"I am not the girl Rieni," the thing peering at us through her eyes said. "Her guards fought valiantly for her, dying to give her time to escape. As a result, she was one of the few survivors of the Black Day. She fled but died later when a ceiling collapsed, trapping her underneath." She glanced down at her ruined arm. "I had to shred this to get her loose after she passed."

Bodil made another sound, and this one wasn't the stunned horror of a moment ago. This one was pure rage, and her eyes flooded with flames so bright they stained her face crimson. She jumped at the body of her granddaughter before any of us could react or even register the movement.

But the zombie didn't have that problem, and Bodil found herself suspended off the ground by some spell halfway through her leap. And, okay, no, I thought, staring. Zombies couldn't do that.

A fresh zombie, just hours old, might have enough magic left in their veins for one final curse, assuming they'd been a magic worker to begin with. But not one like that. Not with Bodil fighting it, and looking like she was giving it her all, not to mention that whenever Rieni had died, it had been a while ago.

And that meant. . .

I felt my brain skitter away from the implication for a second time.

"You're not a necromancer," I said harshly and had those dead eyes look my way again.

"No," the creature agreed. "Or I wasn't once. But needs must, isn't that what you humans say?"

This human found it challenging to say anything but decided I'd better keep her talking. We were outclassed, with our magic almost gone, and even Bodil, the most powerful among us at the moment, unable to break that hold. She was still trying, thrashing in mid-air and yelling something I couldn't make out, probably because it was profane, and my prissy little translation spell tended to censor stuff like that.

Or maybe because it was old, specifically old spells that started shaking the room from their power, toppling the skeleton piles, and sending the barely held-together guards falling to the ground. One of them lost a head that went rolling across the floor to land at Enid's feet, causing her to scream and kick the thing. And she kicked it hard, sending it flying against the opposite wall, where it shattered into a dozen pieces.

And yet Bodil had moved not an inch.

"Stop it!" Æsubrand yelled. "You'll kill us all!"

"As long as I kill her, too," Bodil hissed, looking half mad.

But then the thing-that-wasn't-Rieni put out a hand, and Bodil froze, her lips pulled back in a snarl, and her eyes wild and burning with still leaping flames. But nothing else on her body moved. I couldn't have done better myself.

I cleared my throat and hoped my voice wouldn't squeak. "That's . . . what we say."

And I supposed that non-committal answer was good enough since the zombie swiveled those dead eyes back to me. "Yes, I like that phrase. And it is appropriate. I have had to learn many new skills in recent years, and the information I gained from you was invaluable."

"From . . . me?"

Rieni's head cocked as if in surprise. "Yes, I had thought you finished when Zeus's creatures drained you of blood and left you a corpse floating in the water in that other place—what was it called? The cold one with all the ice."

"Wales," I whispered, a strange idea forming.

"Yes, that was it. I was bemoaning trusting you only to have you fail so easily. You did not even put up much of a fight.

"But then you did, rising from the beach where they'd dragged you and laying waste. I did not understand it at first, thinking that I must have been mistaken, that you had not been dead, after all. But the more I watched, the more convinced I was that I had been correct the first time and that this was some magic I didn't know.

"When you finally made your way into my realm and I could see you and your thoughts clearly for the first time, I took that knowledge from you, just in case. I never intended to use it, but a weapon is a weapon. And in this war, needs must, don't you agree?"

I swallowed, the room swimming a little. Because only one person here could have been in my head through all that. Only one had seen me defy Zeus with some of the only magic he didn't know. And only one, with her back to the wall and her creatures dying around her, would have been able to reproduce it.

But I still had to hear it.

"Who are you?" I whispered.

"You know who I am," she said, somewhat impatiently. "I am Faerie and have been waiting for you to arrive for some time. Come. This place is not safe, and we have much to discuss."

* * *

"There is nowhere safe above ground and little beneath it," the zombie said sometime later, chatting casually as the rest of us stumbled along behind her. "But those who share great Poseidon's blood do not like the creatures who prowl this land any more than you do. The waves offer some protection as a result, as the beasts will not go there."

She glanced back at me, I guessed to see if I was paying attention, allowing me to see the maggots churning slowly under the skin of her face.

Yeah, that was the problem with zombies, I thought dizzily. The magic that sustained them slowed down normal decomposition but didn't stop it, and it looked like some serious stuff was going on inside Faerie's avatar. I wanted to ask how long she'd been that way, when exactly we were, how the hell we'd gotten here, and a whole list of other things.

But I only swallowed thickly and didn't say anything for fear that I might start screaming.

"So, we must go beneath the sea. Mind the debris," she added as we entered the throne room I'd expected to see when I first came here.

From what our guide told us, it was the old one, the first seat of power in these lands before the mountain across the water was hollowed out and turned into a fortress. The old palace slowly lost out to the new, becoming first auxiliary housing, then storage, and finally, the stables, as the new digs were expanded and these were no longer needed. But it remained as immovable as ever, built primarily out of stone and timeless in its beauty.

And it was beautiful, as so much was in the land of the fey, although their definition of the term differed somewhat from ours. The people who built this place didn't care if they had others' approval or if foreign ambassadors felt at home. They built what they liked, and it reflected their priority, which, judging by the décor, was to project strength.

It still did.

A line of black stone eruptions had been magicked out of the floor, some reaching halfway to the soaring, cavern-like ceiling and delineating a central walkway. They were in more or less matching pairs on either side and slanted toward us like the huge crystal formations they resembled. Or like the swords a bride and groom ran under at a military wedding.

Only those were held aloft by their friends and well-wishers as a salute. These looked more like obsidian daggers and felt like a threat. "You're here under sufferance," they seemed to say. "Don't push it."

Only someone had.

The walkway between the lines of stone daggers was littered with bones, the "debris" the zombie had mentioned. And as bad as the stables had been, this was worse, with thousands of skeletons visible between the slanted columns of stone, some in piles, and some scattered across the floor like animals had been at them, a few with teeth marks still visible. And while most of the bodies were fey-shaped, some . . . were not.

The latter came in all types and varieties, for the Ancient Horrors were from many species, and they were what Faerie claimed had done this. Which didn't make sense; none of this did! But whenever I tried to focus enough to get some answers, I glimpsed some new horror, and my brain skittered off somewhere as if trying to hide.

But there was nowhere to go and no safe place to look, even though I didn't want to see this now. I didn't want to see this ever! And I mostly wasn't, as all of that was in the dark peripheries, and my eyes kept going to the only source of light around.

The wide, intimidating walkway led to a throne in the center of the room, although it was less of a chair than an eruption of natural rock half as high as the columns, a miniature mountain. A shelf had been carved three-quarters of the way up where I guessed pillows had once been piled for Nimue to sit on. It was empty now and bathed in a slant of faint moonlight from far above, adding to its already eerie air.

Like at the canal, there was no great river. I could see the channel for it snaking across the ceiling, but it was gone, with only the dim light from outside filtering in like spectral fingers. The height of this place ensured that most of the beams scattered and petered out before they hit down, leaving us trudging through almost darkness.

I, for one, was glad of it. The less I saw of this place, the better, but bad lighting didn't affect my ears. And our footsteps rang on the floor, almost shockingly loud in the silence.

"When is this?" Bodil demanded abruptly, cutting off the running commentary that Faerie had been providing.

She might have learned to talk our way but hadn't learned when to shut up. Or any diplomacy, as she stopped and turned obligingly toward Bodil, who had remained silent since being released in the office. She answered her in a friendly tone but with no effort to soften the blow.

"It has been more than fifty years since you vanished. You were in the pool, fighting near each other, then you were gone."

"Gone where? This isn't my city!" Bodil hissed. "This is some sort of . . . of illusion meant to trick us!"

Tried that one, I thought. But the denial phase had been short, as this wasn't my home. How much harder must this be for Bodil, who was seeing the destruction of everything she knew?

And everyone.

Like we were going to do if we went back to Earth. Even the thought made me dizzy again, and my knees wanted to give way. What the hell had gone wrong?

I wasn't sure I wanted to know, which was a bad sign. Like

the fact that none of us had asked any questions on the walk here until Bodil recovered enough to do so. We'd been in shock at the enormity of what we were seeing, and I, for one, still was.

But I straightened my shoulders a little, stopped gazing around like a wide-eyed tourist, and tried to concentrate. There were things we needed to know. And Pritkin seemed to agree because he spoke up.

"This isn't an illusion," he said hoarsely. "I've been trained to see through them—"

"And you think I haven't?" Bodil snarled. "I was here when your pyramids were built, boy!"

"Then you know I'm right."

Faerie nodded along, still giving that vaguely pleasant smile that was creeping me out. It reminded me of Adra, the leader of the Demon High Council, who wore a glamourie so that people didn't kill themselves in terror when they looked at him. But it wasn't much of an improvement, and neither was this.

"It isn't anyone's city," she said placidly. "It is a tomb, like most of my lands."

"*Your* lands?" Bodil said because, apparently, she hadn't understood all that back in the office. Or maybe she hadn't been able to hear in her frozen state. Not that it probably would have mattered.

Looking at her granddaughter must have been excruciating; I doubt I could have focused, either.

"I am Faerie," Faerie repeated patiently. "Your goddess."

"I have no goddess!" Bodil spat.

"No, I shouldn't think you would like that term after the Great Huntress took your sire and husband both in one day," Faerie agreed, and I stopped breathing. "Oh, you didn't know?" she asked, seeing whatever was on my face.

Pritkin got between me and Bodil, like that was going to matter. "She didn't like your mother," I thought numbly. Way to understate it!

Yet she'd saved me more than once.

"Why help me?" I whispered, meeting Bodil's fiery red eyes. "You saved me in the pool, and then again after we came here —"

"My champion turned out to be disappointing," she said, shooting Æsubrand a purely vicious look. "And Feltin was compromised. You might try to drag us into war, but at least it would be on the right side. If I couldn't win, better you and your puppet than—"

"He's not my puppet—"

"We're all puppets!" she roared, passing Pritkin before either of us could react and getting in my face. "It's all the gods know, all they understand! My father was a minor river god, Aliacmon—have you ever even heard of him?"

"No."

"No." Her face twisted bitterly. "Neither have most people. He was nothing, a nobody in the vaulted pantheon, barely acknowledged as a god. One of the ones who couldn't feed as effectively as the mighty and would never have their power.

"Yet she killed him. And when my husband tried to intervene, she killed him, too. My father was a resource to great Artemis, someone with a power she needed. He could travel anywhere, even into the hells, where gods far greater than he struggled to go. And she killed him for it.

"Do you *understand*? Not because he hurt her—as if he could! Or offended her. He was a tool and nothing more. Just as we all are, the only difference is that I know it!

"But I didn't want my family to." She looked at her granddaughter and her face crumpled, with the light suddenly dying in her eyes. "Your mother?" she whispered.

"The Lady Ærindís is dead," Faerie replied, but with a slight frown as if some of Bodil's anguish had gotten through.

"Then they're all gone. Everyone."

She sat down suddenly on the floor and did not look like she planned to get up again.

Faerie's frown grew.

"They are dead in this time," she said slowly. "But not in the other. You can go back. Put all this right—"

"Can we?" Bodil asked, her face expressionless. It didn't help that she was looking at me and that I . . . didn't have good news for her.

I licked dry lips. "I . . . don't understand what happened to us or how Tony did . . . whatever he did," I said. "But . . ."

"But?" Pritkin spoke that time, looking intense. As if he already sensed the truth.

"But Pythias don't deal with the future, as it doesn't yet exist for us. Navigating to it would be like . . . like trying to vacation in a town that hasn't been built yet or moving into a house that isn't finished or even started."

I was struggling to explain as I didn't have the words prepared. This wasn't something Gertie had taught me, as there was nothing to teach. The future was as closed and locked for us as for anyone else.

It was the province of its own Pythia, only here . . . there was none. We would absolutely have met her already if so, as this kind of incursion would have rung every alarm bell she had. And the fact that we were in Faerie wouldn't change that, as there was no division anymore.

It was all the realm of the gods now.

"Cassie?" Pritkin prodded, but I only shook my head. This was why I hadn't been asking questions; this train of thought led to madness. What had I *done*?

I had abandoned my post; *that's* what I'd done, and the fact that I hadn't meant to do it or wanted to go didn't matter. I had left, and a timeline cannot be without a Pythia. So, when my power returned, understood that I was missing and wasn't coming back, what did it do?

Where did it go?

Who had been here, trying to hold everything together, when the gods returned?

"Cassie?" Pritkin prodded more forcefully, and I was glad for it. I couldn't think, couldn't face it, didn't want to know.

"We can't travel there unless taken by someone from that time," I said harshly, desperately trying to concentrate while horror ate at my vision. "So, even if Tony somehow accessed our power, as Jonathan did, there's no way—"

"Jonathan?" Æsubrand interrupted, probably because he knew that name. He should; the bastard had been working for his father.

"A dark mage who used an ancient tool of the gods to graft part of the soul of a Pythian acolyte onto his own, borrowing access to our power," I said and saw his eyes widen.

He appeared to be having a bad day, but unfortunately for him, so was I, to the point of barely staying on my feet. I was in no mood to soft-peddle anything. Which wouldn't help us anyway.

"But even assuming that was the case here, it wouldn't matter," I continued. "I couldn't have gotten us here, and neither could an acolyte. It isn't possible—"

"And yet, we are here," Enid said. I'd almost forgotten her, as she'd been so quiet. She looked like she might regret her earlier outburst, as making an enemy of Bodil wasn't a great idea. Or maybe she was just as spooked as the rest of us.

"But you don't need to take us into the future," Alphonse said. "You don't gotta deal with this at all. Just get us back to where we belong. A jump into the past is all we need!"

He looked at me as they were all doing now, and I looked mutely back.

"Cassie?" Pritkin said quietly.

I swallowed and faced the other half of the problem that had white noise filling my head and threatening my sanity, what remained of it. "We've been here for what?" I said. "A few hours?"

He nodded. "About that."

"The portal's cycle isn't that long. I timed it before, and it seemed to be ten to twelve minutes. Maybe fifteen; I'm not completely sure, but . . ."

"Just say it!" Bodil snapped. "Your power doesn't work here, does it?"

"Well, of course not," Faerie said as if that should be obvious. "When she vanished, it went to her heir."

"Rhea," I whispered, feeling like I'd just been punched in the gut. It was the name I hadn't been able to say or even think. Rhea... An abrupt cascade of goosebumps flooded my body. "Is she—"

"She lives," Faerie said, "but the gods locked down her power so that she cannot use it. She is kept like a trophy in her old court in Las Vegas but helpless. A symbol of their ascendancy."

"Why not just kill her?" Pritkin asked, his hand under my elbow, steadying me.

"They could kill her but not the power, which would merely go to someone else as soon as she died. The only way to rid themselves of it was to consume it, which they were afraid to do as it originally came from Apollo, a powerful source. And it has since learned to hate them.

"It would be like ingesting poison."

"So they imprison it by imprisoning her," Alphonse said, and the sudden enormity of it all hit me—what she must have gone through, what she must have suffered. All alone and only half-trained—

I made a sound—I don't even know what kind—and Faerie looked at me. And this time, the smile faltered slightly. "Rhea cannot use the power, but you can," she told me. "It should return to you once you reenter Earth and it senses your presence. All you have to do is evade the gods, visit your heir, find out what happened to cause all this, return to your time, and prevent it."

"Oh. Is that all," I said blankly.

"Yes. Now, we must get you out of here, all of you. Come with me."

CHAPTER THIRTY-FIVE

O kay, no," Alphonse said.

After what felt like forever, because this cavern was immense, with a ceiling that soared so high that it almost felt like being outside, we'd finally made it to the throne. Only now, I wished we hadn't. This place had been built here for a reason, and it hadn't been the excellent acoustics.

I stared into the black water of a jagged crevasse behind the massive stone chair and felt all the hair on my body stand up.

What the hell was down there?

"This is where the Margygr used to pay court on Nimue," Faerie told us, still playing tour guide. "This was their realm before she arrived and took the area for herself, demanding that they send representatives to her court as hostages for their good behavior. This was where they came and went after she forced the waters back and changed their course."

She gestured at the colossal cavern. "This was all underwater once, but after she finished her conquest, she made it into her throne room. It had been the Margygr seat of power, and I think she liked forcing them to make obeisance in their former great hall."

"Sounds like Nimue," Bodil murmured.

"But it is fortunate for our purposes, as it leads past the Margygr realm and into the new palace complex. The portal was shut down once the invasion began but not destroyed. You should be able to get out that way once you restart it."

I glanced around, but nobody looked relieved. Everybody was looking the way I felt, a combination of shock and alarm. Because there was something wrong with that pit.

There was something very wrong.

"Is there another way?" Bodil asked as she could sense it, too.

"Not one you would survive," Faerie said pleasantly. "You've seen the land route; it is impassable. And even if you did fight your way through, the palace is flooded, a last-ditch attempt by the defenders to hold off the creatures the gods sent against them. It failed, and in the end, no one was left to drain it."

"Okay, but if we gotta swim either way. . ." Alphonse said, speaking for all of us.

"The portal is on the lower levels, leaving you to swim down many floors to reach it, and those floors are filled with perils. Many creatures have taken refuge in the palace now that the land is overrun, and . . . some of them are hungry. This way, you can take the lower entrance and come out quite nearby."

Nobody said anything, but nobody moved, either.

"Maybe we could drain the palace?" I offered, hopefully. Swimming through a pitch-black sea to a flooded labyrinth of corridors to find a portal we might not be able to get working again anyway wasn't my idea of fun. Especially through that water.

God, what was *wrong* with it?

"It has a fell nature," Æsubrand said, kneeling by the side of the pit. It was deep, maybe five feet from where we stood to the water itself, down a craggy gap with large black rocks all around. It forced him to lean over to get close, and I had to stop myself from pulling him back despite the fact that I didn't even like him.

He reached out a hand, making me wonder if he was completely crazy. But just before it touched the surface, he jerked it back, although it was mailed. There were some things that even dragonscale didn't help.

"It's cursed," Pritkin confirmed, staring at it.

"Can you lift it?" I asked because I really, really hoped so. My goosebumps had goosebumps, and I hadn't even touched the stuff. I couldn't imagine going down there, submerging myself under those inky waves, feeling them close over my head—

A shudder went through me, my whole body revolting at the very thought.

Pritkin didn't immediately reply. He just knelt by the crag, but instead of reaching down as Æsubrand had, he hovered his hand over the top as if feeling the heat of a fire. Only there was no fire here. Instead, the closer I got to the water, the colder it felt, like a portal straight to the Arctic.

I backed off a bit because my cred as a badass demigoddess had already been shattered by having to be hauled around over Alphonse's shoulder like a toddler, but Pritkin stayed put. In contrast to Æsubrand, he looked fairly barbaric—shirtless, with muddy spikes in his hair, and a body painted with streaks that looked more pale than dark in the moonlight. Like a pagan priest caught in the middle of a ritual.

One that he wasn't enjoying, as slowly, a strange look came over his face. It took me a moment to recognize it as shock. "I don't know this magic," he whispered.

"I am sure there are many forms you don't know," Æsubrand sneered.

"No," Pritkin sounded bewildered rather than insulted. "There aren't." He looked up at Faerie. "What is this?"

"The Margygr cursed it to protect their realm from the gods' creatures as they did all access points to their kingdom."

"And the gods didn't care?" I asked, staring at the inky darkness.

Unlike normal water, it didn't reflect anything. The serpentine-shaped hole in the roof was letting in a flood of moonlight, but none was dancing on the surface of that stuff, not so much as a ripple. And sure, maybe that was the sides of the crevasse shading it, but I didn't believe it.

I didn't believe it at all.

Faerie shrugged. "The Margygr are . . . temperamental. And as they had effectively trapped themselves, why interfere? It was easier to let them be.

"They also butcher anyone who dares to enter their realm."

"Oh. Oh, really?" Alphonse blinked at her. "You mean the very thing you are telling us to do?"

"We should drain the palace," I said more forcefully.

But Faerie was shaking her borrowed head.

"The controls for that are also in the palace," she told me patiently. "And it would take some time—time you do not have."

"W-why do we not?" Enid whispered. She was looking more ghost-like by the moment, with her now clean but still damp hair straggling around her face and her already pale skin dead white around her scars.

Faerie sighed. "Did you not hear me? I explained this earlier."

"We were looking at the bodies," I said.

Faerie tilted her head. "Why? They are dead."

"Yeah, like we're going to be if we go down there!" Alphonse exploded. "You just said the Margygr kill anyone who comes into their realm!"

Faerie frowned. "Yes, but not you. They should protect you, or at the least, not interfere."

"And why should they do that?"

Faerie looked at Enid, who stared back in shock.

"You told the others that you wished to fight, did you not?" the zombie pressed.

"Yes, but . . . not them," Enid whispered. "Not them!"

Faerie looked like we were giving her a headache. "Not fight them, girl. Fight *with* them. You are one of them, after all, aren't you?"

But Enid was backing away, was shaking her head, was looking like she was about to—

And there she went, running across the dark floor as fast as a fleeing doe. But Alphonse was faster, and he went after her. And brought her back the same way he'd been carting me around.

Only she was beating on his back, kicking her feet in the air, and making it clear in no uncertain terms that she was not okay with Faerie's suggestion.

"Enid," I said, and she stopped kicking for long enough to look at me. "Are you Margygr?"

She didn't look it. There were no gills I could see, and her features were human, not the human-ish ones of the merfolk. The full-blooded ones had huge eyes for seeing underwater, wider-than-normal mouths, and flat little noses that melted into the skin of their faces the way a human's never did.

They also had a variety of skin and hair colors, none of which were found naturally on Earth, and subtle scale designs on their skin when they caught the light just right, as I'd seen on some of those in Nimue's ballroom. And that was in their human form. In their altered state . . . well, then they didn't look human at all.

None of which was true of Enid.

"Are you?" I asked because she was just looking at me, defiant and proud yet somehow miserable.

"Put me down!" she told Alphonse, who obliged, although he looked pointedly at her legs.

"I don't have a tail!" she snapped.

"Just checking."

"Enid?" I pressed. I hated to do it, as she'd been through hell already, as we all had. But if she had any pull. . .

"They hate me," she said shortly.

"What did you do?" Alphonse asked, which earned him a purely vicious look. If he was trying for boyfriend material, he was missing by a mile.

"I didn't do anything!" she said bitterly. "Other than being born. My grandmother met one of their emissaries at court and fell pregnant. She was a servant, of course, and he was one of their nobles. But she regularly cleaned his rooms and . . ." she shrugged.

"And when she told him?" Pritkin asked, although he looked like he already knew the answer.

"He gave her a plant they use and advised her to make tea with it. It took her a while to realize what he meant. He wanted her to kill me, as it would make him look bad to have a part-human child. A disgrace, he called it."

"Here?" I said. Because if ever there was a place that didn't mind that sort of thing. . .

She made a face. "They send their people to court to protect their interests, not for any real loyalty. They look down on the fey, even the highborn, whereas we humans. . . We're nothing to them—less than animals."

"Yet he didn't mind crawling into bed with an 'animal,'" I said, feeling my color rise.

"Men," she and Bodil said together and then looked at each other in surprise.

I guessed some things were universal.

"I'm only a quarter as a result," Enid continued. "And they do not claim me or allow me to claim them. When I fled to them after . . ." she gestured at her face. "They wouldn't help me. They said my grandmother should have done as instructed and spared us all. They had me beaten for daring to enter their halls and threw me out.

"They swore to kill me if I ever returned—and anyone with me."

"Sounds familiar," Pritkin said. He'd had much the same reception when he'd visited his fey relatives and been made to regret it.

"Much has happened since then," Faerie said. "The shocks they have endured may have taught them wisdom."

"And if they *haven't*?" Enid demanded.

The shrug was back. "Then you must decide who you would rather face, your kin or the Horrors."

"Well, isn't this just peachy," Alphonse said savagely.

"I did not say it would be easy," Faerie said. "But the passage between here and the palace was destroyed in the siege, and you saw what trying to go aboveground is like." She paused slightly. "It is a short swim—"

Alphonse had things to say about that, as it seemed that, unlike the rest of us, he had been paying attention. Only he'd thought I could rest up and shift us back, so he hadn't cared. Now that he realized it wouldn't work that way, he was starting to freak out.

No shame, I thought, staring at the inky water.

No shame at all.

"If you're a goddess, how about some help!" Alphonse snarled at Faerie.

"I *am* helping you to the extent of my abilities."

"That I do not believe," Æsubrand said. Suddenly, he looked less like a bedraggled war veteran and more like a prince. The moonlight loved him, turning his hair to silver fire and making his frosty complexion look more alive. Instead of a statue carved out of marble, cold and unfeeling, he had a faint blush on his cheeks and silver flames for eyes.

He didn't seem to like what he took to be blasphemy.

"If you are who you say, nothing should be beyond you," he added. "This is your realm."

"*Was* my realm," Faerie snapped, showing genuine emotion for the first time. "It is mine no longer. I am a fugitive in my own world, forced to hide from beings who would devour me, as they have so many of my children.

"They are lost now, millions of them. Most of them, if truth be told, even in your father's kingdom, young one. Worse, they are not dead; I could recover them if they were merely dead. They are *gone,* devoured by the gods and those things the gods sent as a plague upon me."

"Devoured?" Æsubrand looked like that did not compute. "You lie. We are their servants—"

"Treacherous, deceitful servants," I pointed out. I doubted he'd been planning to use his newfound kingdom to help dear old Dad in his bring-back-the-gods quest. Bodil wouldn't have partnered with him if so.

"Perhaps," the prince said. "But my father is not. He has risked much for his plans, ill-advised as they may be—"

"Which preserved his life, however little he may be enjoying it," Faerie said with an edge to her voice. "But when the gates vomited forth the gods and their beastly dogs, they feasted on everyone else. They were starving after so long, and, well. There are many ways to serve, are there not?"

Æsubrand stared at her in shock.

"She means serving yourself up on a platter, princeling," Enid said, in case he hadn't understood. "I suppose we're all equal now, aren't we? Just food for the gods'... and their dogs."

"Shut your mouth, slave!" he snarled, turning on her, his shock shifting to anger in an eyeblink.

And met the same fire in her eyes. I didn't know what her problem with him was, but she obviously had one. Maybe because he was the pampered son of the king who had been slaughtering all those part-human soldiers for so long.

Or maybe for the same reason I didn't like him.

He always looked like the rest of us smelled bad.

Enid smiled. It wasn't a particularly nice one. And then she repeated what Alphonse had said to me at the mouth of the tunnel. "Make me."

Alphonse barked out a laugh, also getting the reference. "We'll make a human out of you yet," he told her and grabbed Æsubrand by the arm. "Touch her and die."

"I have no intention of touching her!" Æsubrand spat, throwing off his hold. "I do not consort with slaves, much less half-breed bas—"

He stopped abruptly because Enid's wand was in his face, almost touching his nose.

I didn't know she'd had one, as I hadn't seen it before. I guessed she reserved it for when she really wanted to get nasty. And damn it, we didn't have time for this!

And for once, Alphonse seemed to agree. "Kill him later," he advised. "Save your strength."

"Yes," Faerie said. "You will need it." She looked at

Alphonse, and her voice strengthened, echoing around the great space. "I told you the truth, vampire; my people were slaughtered, and with them went pieces of my very soul. The same soul that gives me my power. So, I cannot do more for you than I am. This is your fight, and if you do not win it, all of us are doomed."

"Win it how?" Pritkin asked. "What went wrong? You said we need to find Rhea to tell us. Does that mean you don't know?"

"Yes, I am afraid so. Zeus realized I had allied myself with you and thus made his plans elsewhere, beyond my vision. I cannot see outside my realm unless one of my people is there, or there is a gate, what you call a portal, that gives me a hazy vision for a space around it.

"He well knew this. And when the Black Day came, it originated from beyond—from Earth."

"The place you want to send us to," Alphonse said heavily.

"The place you must go to find out what happened. All I can tell you is this: Shortly after you vanished, Feltin's champion won the challenge. That was followed by many days of feasting and celebrations, but Feltin was not there. He crowned Lord Sæþórr, but even at the ceremony, he was distracted, almost as if it no longer mattered. He immediately left for Earth thereafter and was still there when the invasion came. It was as if something had been decided in that short time."

"It was," I croaked, my throat feeling half closed. I looked up and met Pritkin's eyes.

"Zeus realized I was beyond his grasp," he said.

I nodded. "And got tired of waiting."

"Yes," Faerie said. "I thought it might be something like that."

"Something like what?" Bodil demanded. "What are you talking about?"

"The young one can multiply magic," Faerie said. "It was an ability great Artemis craved and slaughtered his grandfather for." She saw Bodil's shock. "Yes, little one. Yours was not the only family ravaged by the gods' lust for power."

"But . . . but you're with *her*?" Bodil asked Pritkin, glancing from me to him. *"Why?"*

"She's not her mother," he said simply.

Bodil scowled.

"Artemis used demon magic to overwhelm the gods, taking on the entire pantheon by herself," Faerie added. "She could not have done it without those borrowed abilities. They are . . . impressive."

And, suddenly, it was Pritkin's turn to have everyone stare at him.

CHAPTER
THIRTY-SIX

But . . . if you can do that, we don't need the portal," Alphonse said, his whole face brightening. "That's to let you access the Pythian power, right?" He looked at me, and I nodded. "But you got power of your own. You're a witch! Just have him do his thing," he waved a hand at Pritkin. "And top you up. Then we don't have to go through any of this! We can just go home!"

"That would not tell you what happened," Faerie pointed out.

"We know what happened! Pritkin slips through old Zeus's fingers, he throws a tantrum, and—"

"And does what?" Pritkin demanded harshly. "He doesn't have the power to break Artemis's spell without me. Otherwise, he'd have done it before."

"Well, he obviously figured it out!"

"He and Aeslinn were draining god blood from everyone in Faerie who still had any," I said, thinking about the cages full of captives I'd seen in that awful camp.

Aeslinn's people had been rounding them up from everywhere, even Earth, where some of the fey had fled for safety and where he'd set up portals to make hunting them easier. Not to mention scattering more portals throughout Faerie, as his god's appetite was insatiable. And there was little else that could satisfy it.

"Maybe they found enough," I added.

Pritkin didn't look like he thought much of that idea, but

Æsubrand cut him off before he could reply.

"What . . . did you say?" he asked, staring at me.

And crap, way to tell someone that his dad was a butcher. It was a tough conversation, and I wasn't up to it. But I guessed my silence was answer enough because Æsubrand looked appalled.

"Mother said that Father was doing such," he whispered, "but I didn't believe her. I didn't think that even he. . ."

He trailed off, his expression darkening and those pewter-colored eyes shading closer to black. He looked genuinely outraged, making me wonder who the real Æsubrand was: the arrogant, power-hungry son of a couple of dodgy-ass parents or the noble fighter? Or, like most of us, somewhere in between.

But right then, I didn't have time to worry about it.

Only apparently, that wasn't my call because he grabbed my arm, and he wasn't gentle. *"Are you lying to me, witch?"*

"Why would I bother?" I said before Pritkin struck his hand away. It probably wasn't a good sign that Æsubrand didn't even seem to notice.

"To demoralize me, make me believe outrageous things—"

"We're not in the race anymore," I told him. "Nobody cares what you believe."

But he wasn't listening. "Were some of our people among them? Were *my* people?" he demanded, looking a little wild-eyed. And then the hand was back along with its twin, squeezing my biceps hard enough to have broken the bones underneath if not for my armor. Only I doubted he knew it.

Æsubrand was having a moment, and it wasn't a good one.

"Ask her," I said, pointing at Faerie with my chin because my arms were busy. Until Alphonse and Pritkin worked together to pry off Æsubrand's grip.

"This is not the time," Faerie said, which was true but not helpful, as our resident silver-haired prince had lost his damned mind. To the point of turning on her and grabbing her instead. And shaking her wildly, which was not a great idea since I didn't know how well attached that head was.

Pritkin and Alphonse grabbed him and dragged him back, and Faerie looked on, unperturbed except for a slight frown creasing her forehead.

"Answer me!" Æsubrand screamed, struggling with his captors.

"I already have," she reminded him. "I said that your father's machinations did him no good, nor your people, either."

"You did not say that he murdered them!"

"It did not seem important."

Æsubrand stared at her for a long beat, and then he suddenly started laughing. It wasn't any more reassuring than his rage had been, as it was high-pitched and a little crazed. To the point that Alphonse and Pritkin exchanged a glance while keeping him restrained.

"You shoulda let those things eat him," Alphonse told me.

"Oh, no, she wouldn't do that!" Æsubrand said, still laughing. "She's the sweet-faced little human who wouldn't hurt a fly—but would destroy my capitol and murder thousands of my people! She's the wide-eyed innocent who ventures where angels fear to tread—yet somehow survives as she's also the heir of Artemis, the most savage god of them all! She—"

He suddenly decided that he was through talking and made a leap, somehow slipping through both men's grasp before I could blink, with his mailed hand reaching out toward me. Until Faerie intervened, only not in the way that any of us could have expected. Well, shit, I thought, as a slew of images hit me instead of Æsubrand's fist.

Rask's wrists were slick with blood. His skin was thick and resisted tearing, but working all night, rubbing it against the hard metal of the cuffs, had taken its toll. The blood was smearing everywhere now.

That was good.

He was almost free.

"Wake up, elf," he grumbled and listened as the translator spell he used to deal with traveling merchants converted the words into the silver hairs' strange speech.

When that did no good, he lightly kneed the creature who lay beside him on the trundling cart and who, amazingly, had been sound asleep. Yet still he snored on as if he rested on the feather beds he probably had at home instead of cold iron bars covered with straw, and as if he had a full meal in his belly instead of the gnawing hunger Rask felt. He hadn't eaten in three days while watching his captors feast each night by the puny fire they made.

And listening as they joked, after slinging his fellow captive in beside him, that perhaps Rask would eat him. As if his people were the barbarians here! They did not steal women and children, they did not enslave, they did not—

His thoughts broke off because the added outrage had lent strength to his struggle, and he had felt the cuffs pop and loosen. Now, all he needed was to finish the job and wake his companion, who had turned over muttering something and dragged some straw over his head like a pillow. What was wrong with the creature?

Perhaps he had been spelled as Rask initially had, or possibly his sleepiness had more to do with the crust of blood covering one side of his head, where his fellow silver hairs had beaten him. It had formed a dark welt that looked like a skewed hat and had splattered his cheek. But it did not appear to be bleeding anymore, which Rask took as a good sign.

For his part, he hadn't slept in days, as the cage was too small to allow him to lie down without the cold iron of the side bars torturing him. He wondered if that was deliberate, to wear his people out and make them more docile. They would see how docile he was when he got loose!

Fortunately, he could go for a long time without sleep with few ill effects. He had thought the silver hairs could also, but this one seemed to be the exception. He was the exception to many things, as his fine clothes showed.

Most of the slavers came from the surrounding villages and dressed like it. Not in the hides his people wore but in rough homespun and scarred leathers. But this one. . .

He was dirty now, after being hit many times and falling into the muck of the road, but underneath all that were fine clothes of a soft blue. There wasn't a patch on them, and all were woven stuff, not animal hides. There was also pretty stitchwork around the neck hole, as Rask had seen only once before, on the edge of a cloak owned by one of their nobles.

Rask had been just a boy when he came through their village, but he still remembered how it had flashed like silver fire in the moonlight and the awe he had felt just looking at it. He'd edged close enough almost to touch it when the nobleman noticed him. And, to Rask's surprise, swung him into his lap to see it closer up.

It had been Rask's finest moment, not least because he'd been allowed to trace the edge with his finger, feeling the embroidered designs against his skin. He was almost surprised they hadn't burned him, but they felt cool. And slightly rough, as if they truly were made out of tiny filaments of silver.

"Took it off one of their magic workers," the noble had said. "The symbols around the edge are supposed to be a protection spell."

"Didn't protect him, did it?" One of the elders commented.

"No, but the cloak's all right," the noble shot back, and they all laughed.

Rask had made himself a similar garment when he was old enough, although nothing like so fine. Gathering enough pelts had taken many hunting trips, and his mother had tanned them for him and stitched them together herself. The silver hairs had stolen it, leaving him only his hide loincloth.

He supposed he couldn't complain as his people took trophies, too.

And would again, he thought, sensing movement in the trees on either side of the road, movement that the silver hairs seemed oblivious to. His people were quieter than that, moving silently through the forest when they wished, but they wanted him to know *they were there. Wanted him to be ready.*

They would save him if they could or avenge him if they could not. His captors would pay a price for raiding their village. All those with silver hair would die this night, which was why Rask was bleeding.

He had to protect the one at his feet. The one who had been captured for trying to rescue him and the others, although he did not know why. Why put himself at risk for those his people had killed for time out of mind? And fight his kin to do it?

Rask did not understand, but he knew he owed him a debt, one that he would repay, even if he had to fight his own. And he might, for his rescuers were likely composed of many tribes, the scattered remnants of which had bonded together after losing so many fighters, and they might not be ones he knew. He twisted his wrists harder, using the blood as a lubricant to try to slip his hands out of the smallish openings.

They were the largest cuffs the silver hairs had had, as they had been hunting women and children the day he was taken. Those made better slaves, as the women could be forced to accept almost any treatment to save their young, and the children would thereafter know nothing but servitude. The silver hairs hadn't come equipped for the males of his kind, as they were too cowardly to enter any of their cave systems and face them.

They did not like the dark, where his people could see and they could not. They liked even less the many twists and turns in the system, as they provided opportunities for ambush. No, they did not like that at all.

So, they had attacked a group of bathing women and playing children, laughing and splashing in what was supposed to be a hidden pool, and brought only smaller chains.

They had not expected him to be there or understood that, by his people's reasoning, he was only a child himself. But he was older than the others, already knowing how to hunt and fish, which was why he had been there. His young cousin had begged to learn how to search for worms, how to thread them on a hook, and where to drop that hook to make the best catch.

Rask would never teach him that now, as he had hidden him in a bush when the attack came so he would not be caught. He remembered his huge eyes and small hand clutching Rask's cloak, begging him not to go. But no bush was big enough for him, and he would not flee.

He was not yet grown, but he was old enough to know.

A troll does not run.

But he had almost wished he had when the silver hairs jumped him, and he saw the knife one of them held flash in the sunlight. It would have been the last thing he saw, but another had stayed his attacker's hand. "No! Not 'til he's checked!"

Rask had not understood that, not even when a gray-robed figure pushed through the group and knelt by his side as six silver hairs held him down. It was hard for them even then, for Rask had struggled and done so with all his might. But the gray cloak had murmured a word, his limbs had gone temporarily numb, and he had found his face pulled up into the sunlight.

The gray cloak had searched it for a moment, then made a sign over top of him, burning brightly in the air. Rask did not know what it was, but he felt the strangest sensation, as if all his blood suddenly leaped in his veins. The gray robe smiled and looked up at the one holding the knife-wielder's wrist.

"Take him."

And they had.

The shackles they'd used to bind him were so tight that his hands had gone numb. He didn't know how much hide he would lose to slip out of them, but he didn't have long to manage it. Bird calls had started sounding within the trees; the attack would come soon.

He had to be ready.

One final, great effort and the bonds that had held him for so long twisted and broke. One cuff dangled free, and now that he could maneuver, he quickly ripped apart the other, feeling the blood rush back into half-starved veins. He flexed his hands, and they obeyed his commands.

He could move!

And barely in time. He ducked down, covering his fellow captive's body with his own, just as an arrow came whizzing through the night. And took the silver-hair driving the cart straight through the throat.

He didn't live long enough to do much more than raise a hand to it in shock before slumping over onto the bench seat. The horses were unaware that anything had happened and kept plodding on. But the silver hair beneath him had seen.

"What—" the creature said sleepily.

"Stay down!" Rask hissed. "Do as I tell you and say nothing. I will speak for you."

But there was no time to speak or to do anything, for the road did not end in a settlement as Rask had expected. That was what usually happened to his kind who were taken captive. They were sold as chattel to the silver hair's towns, who used them up in fields and mines until they escaped or died.

At least, that was what had happened before his people started fighting back. Now, it was more common for the journey to end in a slave caravan, which would take them so far away from where they'd been found that no one could hope to rescue them. But this . . . was neither of those.

"Get off me, you big lout," the silver-hair gasped. "I can't breathe!"

Neither could Rask, but for a very different reason. But he got up because the arrows had stopped, and light suddenly spilled around their cart. It was so bright that he shielded his eyes, only able to see another silver hair jumping onto the wagon seat, throwing his fellow elf off the side, and whipping up the horses.

"Prioritize the first five wagons!" he heard someone yell. "The king has need of them!"

Rask assumed his wagon must have been one of those, as the horses broke into a gallop and the cart plowed straight ahead, swaying alarmingly in its speed, toward what looked like a descended sun. Rask grabbed the cage bars and stared; it had not been there a moment ago. But now, it was all he could see as it rapidly grew closer, blocking his vision.

It was blinding.

But it did not seem to blind the silver hair who had come up beside him, on his knees as Rask was, as the ceiling was so low. "What is it?" Rask asked, his voice full of wonder.

"Haven't you ever seen a portal before, troll?"

"A what?"

"A gate, a passage to another place, even other worlds."

"Other . . . worlds?" Rask began to wonder just how hard his companion's head had been hit.

But the creature just looked at him with those strange, metallic eyes. "You should come down from your mountains more often."

Rask hadn't wanted to come down from his mountains at all. He had been taken from them. And he wanted to go back right now!

"Hold on," his companion said grimly and got a better grip on the bars, using his tunic sleeves to cover his hands.

"Why?" Rask said, hearing the fear in his voice.

And then he understood why.

It felt as if the light suddenly reached out and grabbed them, jerking them forward as the cage they were in turned upside down, or so it seemed. He didn't know anymore, couldn't tell. Only that he was being tossed around, that the silver hair was being thrown along with him, that they were tumbling any and everywhere while light seared their eyes and somebody screamed.

Rask was very afraid that it might be him.

Then the light was gone, and they were tearing across a wide expanse of pavement in the pounding rain, for the horses were as spooked as he was and weren't stopping. Until something plowed into them from the side. Rask wasn't sure what, but it had been so fast and hard that his cage, already unsteady, toppled along with the wagon, throwing up sparks as it skidded across neatly fitted cobbles.

Fortunately for the silver hair, Rask had landed on the bottom. He felt the creature's body hit him, but it was so light that no damage was done. And he likely wouldn't have noticed if there had been.

He found himself lying on the cold iron bars, feeling them start to burn through his hide, as he had no protection like the hand wraps that had covered his palms or the leather wrappings on the cuffs. But he barely noticed that, either, as he was too busy staring through the bars at what was happening around him. And wondering if he'd hit his head, too.

Rain was everywhere, reflecting torchlight across water-slick stones. Some of the torches were in people's hands, showing their frantic, terrified faces; others were guttering against the cobbles, getting snuffed out by rain or running boots. He didn't know where he was or what was happening—why were the silver hairs in such disarray?

And then he looked up.

CHAPTER THIRTY-SEVEN

Rask just lay there for a long moment, staring at another great sun opening in the stormy skies and spilling out a tornado of beings. Some were huge and godlike, in the form of elves but the size of towering trees and glowing like stars. Their hair floated around them on the currents of their power, and they were so bright that he could barely look at them.

But he tried because the others, flanking them on both sides, were. . . He didn't have words for what they were. As hideous as the others were beautiful and hungry, like a baying pack of wolves.

Suddenly, Rask returned to himself and started struggling, grabbing the cage bars and trying to pull them apart. Not because he thought he could get away, but because he didn't want to die like this, like vermin in a cage. He would die on his feet like the warrior he had someday hoped to be.

"What are you doing?" Someone yelled. "Come on!"

He looked up to find his silver hair staring at him. He'd found a guttering torch and held it up with one hand while holding the back door of their prison with the other. From the outside.

"How did you get it open?" Rask asked, blinking.

"By taking the goddamned keys off the goddamned guard, you big oaf! Now come on, if you want to live!"

Rask came on, scrambling out of the hated iron prison and getting back to his feet. The silver hair hadn't waited on him but had sprung at the rest of the cages, some still upright, others not, from their caravan. He was running about, fighting guards, why Rask didn't know.

The world was coming to an end, and it hardly seemed worthwhile.

But he had nothing better to do, so he helped, pulling off guards who apparently had not yet looked up as they were beating on his ally instead of running. Something that Rask put a stop to by smacking their heads together until they stopped moving. Meanwhile, the silver hair had grabbed more keys and opened more cages, screaming at people to go, go, go!

Although where they were to go, Rask had no idea. He stared around, getting a brief glimpse of a vast expanse of rain-slick stone, where people were running and screaming and smacking into each other or standing and staring upward as if they couldn't believe what they were seeing, either. And of a vast city behind them made of golden stone and topped by massive, bulbous domes like nothing he had ever seen or dreamed of.

Normally, the city would have left him speechless with awe, all on its own, but these were not normal times. The tornado was landing, with some of the strange, terrible creatures close enough now to jump to the ground, hitting with terrible splats, growls, and screeches that hurt his ears. But the fall did not seem to harm them.

They were back on their feet in an instant and tearing into the crowd. Their prey included those still trapped in the cages, some of whom were trolls like him and taken in the same raid. But others had silver hair, just like their captors.

In the end, it didn't matter, as the beasts didn't care; they—

"Stop staring!" his silver hair screamed. "And come with me!"

Once more, he came, dragging some of the wounded they had been able to save under each arm, one a silver-haired woman shrieking her head off and the other a troll even younger than him, who should have been chasing minnows in the pool's clear water.

Instead, he looked around dazed, his eyes reflecting the torchlight yet probably seeing nothing. Rask hoped his mother was among those saved, but no one was calling for him. No one was doing anything but running, seeing gods and demons, for that was what they must be, returning together to destroy everything.

Rask risked a glance behind him just as something huge jumped at him so quickly that it was merely a blur against the darkness. And was hit by an enormous bolt of lightning from somewhere above, just before it could devour them all. Its smoking body slammed into a door as Rask ran through it, already crumbling to ash, and he glanced back again to see crisscrossing bolts of power tearing through the night.

They hadn't been saved, he realized as they ran down a hall; they had gotten lucky. One of the gods' energy bolts had taken out their servant as they were throwing them at everything now. No one was likely to help him here, as the whole sprawling city seemed to be under attack at once.

But his silver hair knew where to go, and the people he had released surged around them in the hall, following his lead as they had no other. Rask kept pace with the fleet-footed throng despite his size, living up to the name his mother had given him long ago when he passed older boys in races when most of those his age could barely toddle about. He had always been fast for his size and had more reason than ever now.

The wall they were racing beside started crumbling around them. It hedged the great stone expanse outside, or rather, it had. It was quickly falling apart, forcing him to jump over huge sections that were failing and falling or being blasted inward even as he tried to run past them.

He dodged as best he could and kept going while parts of the ceiling broke on his back. He did not know why their group did not turn more toward the place's interior, away from the bolts, but perhaps the silver hair was afraid it would collapse on top of them. Although it seemed to be doing that already!

It was getting hard to see, with billowing clouds of dust highlighted by the bolts of energy cutting through and zigzagging across the hall. They were catching some of the runners broadside, evaporating their bodies into scatterings of ash before blowing out more walls farther in. Rask ignored them as there was nothing else he could do and kept moving.

And in moments, his decision to trust his would-be rescuer was rewarded, although he wasn't sure with what. They burst out of the disintegrating hall and into an enormous cave, the biggest he had ever seen, yet more caves were connected to it. He could see some of them ahead in a long line, but they weren't full of trolls.

They were full of silver hairs.

There were so many that Rask just stared for a moment, as he had never seen that many people at one time. Nor had he ever seen the silver hairs, who always seemed so icy cold and devoid of emotion except hate, full of the same panic he felt clawing at him. And holding onto small, mountain-shaped wooden creations, like some that Rask had seen flying over his homeland occasionally, and been told to avoid at all costs.

They could spit fire, he had been warned and were there to search for the locations of his people's settlements from the air. That was why they had to hide their cave entrances carefully and never return home while the wooden birds were in the sky. He had only glimpsed them through the treetops before and hadn't realized how small they were.

Yet multiple people were packed inside them, and more were clinging to the outside and begging not to be left behind.

Some of those were getting towed along the ground and into the air as a few of the strange creations took off, with no flapping of wings as they didn't have any. They levitated how Rask had seen some magic users do to small items back home. Were they magic, too?

He supposed they must be.

But there weren't enough of them for all the people, and some of the desperate crowd didn't know how to operate them. Many of the birds stood idle while people hedged around them, screaming into the crowd for those with knowledge. The knowledge that his silver hair seemed to possess, for he threw a guard out of one and made it rise jerkily into the air.

But those inside were fighting him before he could make off with it, and more were on the ground, jumping up with the springy grace of their kind, latching onto it, dragging it back down.

"Let me go!" the silver-haired woman he had been carrying yelled. "Leave me and go help him!"

Rask let her go and left her with the troll child, who she hugged to her bosom, both of them watching him with huge eyes. He pushed through the crowd to the odd craft, grabbed the edge, and started towing it back across the floor while being hammered by the guards inside and the people around him. But his blood was pumping so hard that he barely noticed, and when he reached his small band, who had gathered together in a defensive knot, he tipped the craft over and watched the guards inside fall out.

They didn't seem to have expected that but were quickly back on their feet and brandishing the lightning spears that Rask had learned to hate from his experiences on the road. They could rupture even his skin, and he wasn't sure what to do about so many until his silver hair yelled, "Drop!"

Rask dropped, and his rescuer activated something inside the craft that had lightning emerging from underneath it, spearing out just above Rask's head and targeting the guards. They fell twitching to the ground, people screamed and ran, and he looked up at the elf.

Who had just attacked his own people to spare a crowd full of trolls.

"Get in!" he screamed, looking half-crazed.

Rask did not get in. He helped the others do so instead, not sure that the craft, which was one of the larger varieties but still relatively small, would hold them all. But they made themselves fit, and somehow, there was room for him to stand in the doorway and cling onto the side, gripping the roof with all his might as the crazy thing went skittering over the floor, knocking people down and causing even more unrest, if that was possible. But not taking off because his half was too heavy and was dragging the whole thing down to the point that it scraped the floor on his side.

But when he went to step off, his silver hair screamed at him incoherently, and some of the women grabbed his legs and would not let him go.

And then they were over the edge of a cliff, plummeting and spinning about like a top as the unevenly weighted contraption struggled to fly. But fly it did, in fits and starts, while other *such craft zoomed past it, heading off into the night as fast as they could. His vessel was more sluggish, and when the silver-hair finally got it to stop spinning, they moved away from the burning city slowly enough to give Rask an excellent view.*

It was not one he would ever forget. The great domes were burning now, as the gods seemed to be concentrating primarily on them. The fires were already so huge that they stained the clouds that the city sat among at the top of a great peak, almost as if it was composed of them itself.

But this wasn't the pretty red-gold of a sunset; it was a bloody hue to match the carnage as everything burned. The city went up like a torch as he watched while the rains beat at him, the light dazzled him, and the terrible beasts feasted on live and burning flesh. And as their tiny band of survivors slowly limped their way into the night, entirely silent.

For what was there to say?

The vision shattered, and I found myself on the floor, unsure how I got there. Probably rolling around with Rask, for the Common's images were so real it was almost as if you were experiencing them yourself. And while this hadn't been as deep of an immersion as I'd felt before, where the lines between myself and the person I was following had blurred, it had been deep enough.

I felt the bruises Rask had taken in my own flesh, smelled the burning city in my nose, and tasted his panic on my tongue. And I guessed Æsubrand did, too, because he suddenly tore up from the floor and launched himself at the first enemy he saw. Which must have been me because all I could see through the still-turning shards of that other time was his face. And if ever anyone had looked like murder—

Bodil dropped him with a word, and he fell flat on the floor. I lay there, still half out of it and wondering what had just happened. And watching a shard of memory showing Rask and company dodging pieces of the fiery city that explosions were sending flying out at them.

I hoped they made it, I thought dizzily; I hoped—

"What the hell—" Alphonse said, jumping to his feet.

"We have to leave him," Pritkin told me flatly.

"What?" I looked up at him, uncomprehending.

"We can't risk bringing him with us. I can't watch him every second, and he obviously means you harm."

I blinked at the fallen silver hair, my mind and Rask's still intertwined enough that that was the only name I could remember for his people. "Did they make it?" I asked Faerie. "Rask and . . . and the others—"

"Yes," she said. "Surprisingly. Their craft was overloaded, but it took them back to the road where the slavers had been. There, they met up with some of his people and, after a discussion, were taken into their caves. They retreated farther into the mountains and remain there, one of the dwindling islands of survivors."

"Cassie!" Pritkin's voice brought me back somewhat, and I felt Rask slipping away. I looked at Æsubrand some more. Svarestri, I thought.

That's what we call them.

"So what do we do?" I asked, looking up at Pritkin. "Tie him up and leave him for those things?"

"There's an idea," Alphonse said. "Anybody got a belt?"

"We aren't leaving him," Bodil said angrily.

"You saw what just happened," Alphonse argued. "And in case you forgot, we need Cassie alive or none of us is going anywhere. So unless you feel like becoming a permanent resident in this little corner of hell—"

"I do not," Bodil said, kneeling beside the fallen man. "But he is young and excitable. And consider what he just learned, what he experienced—"

"None of which is Cassie's fault!" Pritkin said.

"No, but Issengeir was," Bodil said. "And he lost many friends that day."

"So did I!"

"I'll make it quick," Alphonse offered. He made a twisting

motion with his hands about neck width apart that did not improve Bodil's temper.

"You will do no such thing!"

"You know we're right. You just don't want to lose your champion."

"That is part of it," she agreed with surprising candor. She seemed to do that a lot. I didn't know if it was a long-term character trait or if she was simply too old to give a damn. She also seemed to be throwing off the vision better than the rest of us.

I could still hear the wind.

"But he isn't Aeslinn," she added. "He is impetuous and acts on emotion far too often—"

"Something we can't have in a situation like this," Pritkin said. And unlike Alphonse, he wasn't arguing. He was stating a fact and ending the discussion.

Only he wasn't, damn it.

I sighed.

"No," Pritkin said flatly, shooting me a look.

"Yes."

"Why the hell would you want to risk it?"

"I'm not Aeslinn, either?"

"You're also not a fool," Alphonse said. "Get over the bleeding heart shit. This is the third time that moron tried to kill you—once in Feltin's office, once when we first got here, and again now. And in times like these, three strikes, and you're out.

"Only with me, it woulda been one."

"He's right," Pritkin said, earning an approving glance from Alphonse.

"He also saved me in the pool," I said, remembering.

"After you'd just rescued him," Alphonse retorted. "He thought he might need more help; he wasn't doing you a favor!"

"And how do you know that?" Bodil snapped. "I thought I was the only mind reader in the group."

"I know the type."

She gave up on Alphonse and looked at me. "He is a boy. Not that much older in our terms than the troll you saw. But unlike him, who seemed to have had a loving family, Æsubrand grew up with incredible abuse, enough to have turned most others into monsters like his father. Instead, he's tried to do the right thing, advocated for his people, fought Aeslinn on their behalf more than once, and supported his mother in running away from their kingdom, even though discovery meant death for both of them—"

"Oh, boo hoo." That, of course, was Alphonse. "Lots of us got the shit beat out of us as kids—"

He broke off, maybe because the other half of that sentence, "and didn't turn into murderers," wasn't exactly true in his case.

"At least I'm on the right side," he mumbled as our eyes met, and finally shut up.

"—and when she turned out to have more vengeance in her heart than concern for their people's welfare, he left her to come here," Bodil continued grimly. "And risk his life for a force to unseat his father and restore order to his lands."

"The Alorestri have been battling Aeslinn's people for centuries," Pritkin pointed out. "Even if he won control of their army, how could he hope to triumph now when they never could before?"

"He knows his father's kingdom like no other," she said. "Knows who are disaffected and might turn against him given enough help, knows secret ways into the castle—a hundred things! And Aeslinn's forces have been weakened in the war; he is vulnerable. Why do you think I partnered with the son of our oldest enemy?"

"I had wondered about that," I said and was ignored.

"We only end centuries of war by ending Aeslinn, and this boy is our best chance to do that. So, no, he doesn't die. I will talk to him when he comes around—"

"Talk! That's great," Alphonse said.

"—and explain that the girl must live."

"The Pythia," Pritkin said sharply. "And explain it to her."

Suddenly, everybody looked at me as if this was my choice, which I guessed it was as it was my life on the line.

I wondered if there had been a reason that Faerie had shown us what she did from that precise angle. She didn't need a slave being dragged back to Dolgrveginn to be a late-night snack for a god to make her point. She could have shown us the city's destruction through a thousand different eyes.

But she chose that one.

Maybe because he had been saved by someone who was supposed to be an enemy, and only by working together had they been able to survive and help the others with them. Subtle, I thought, looking up and meeting her eyes. Like a brickbat.

But effective.

There were just six of us against ridiculous odds. We needed everyone, even an arrogant fey prince with anger management issues. So, I was just going to have to suck it up.

"Æsubrand lives," I said shortly. "This time."

CHAPTER THIRTY-EIGHT

What felt like a year later, we were all sitting around the floor watching Pritkin work on the black slab that formed the back of the mountainous chair. He was trying to summon his mother's tunnel, which apparently hadn't been just a one-off thing. And which might get us to the portal room without risking whatever the Margygr had put in that water.

I say might, as it wasn't going well.

"So she made a tunnel that just . . . moves around?" Alphonse said, his forehead wrinkling.

He was sitting on the rocky edge of the chasm while Enid paced nearby. She'd handled the trip into a troll's brain better than I'd have expected, maybe because she was part fey and the Common wasn't completely unknown to her. But sitting around while her fate lay in someone else's hands seemed to bother her a lot more.

I could sympathize.

It wasn't exactly doing me a lot of good, either.

Pritkin nodded. "On call might be a better word for it, as she had no way of knowing when or where she might need it."

"But *how*? And that's the back of a chair you're working on. There's nothing on the other side to make a tunnel *through*."

Pritkin shot him a mildly amused glance. "The same way that the Svarestri, whose element is earth, use it to create almost anything they choose, from cities where none should be possible to great stone defenders of their realm."

Alphonse did not seem satisfied with that answer, and I couldn't blame him. Human logic and magical logic were often not compatible. "Okay, but that explains the what, not the how."

"You want me to explain elemental magic while you wait?" Pritkin asked dryly, glancing over his shoulder at the big vamp.

"Well, you know. The crib note version?" Alphonse had never cared much about magic, but now that it was his only way home, it had gotten his full attention.

"The elements stand in for the building blocks of our reality," Pritkin said, returning to his work. "Ability with one allows you to manipulate reality where that particular element is concerned."

"Like to create a tunnel on demand."

"Yes. My mother was weak in earth magic but used it here as the Green Fey do not know it. They have fought the Svarestri for so long that there has been little intermarriage between them. Most do not carry even a shred of it as a result and, therefore, would not recognize what she was doing."

"But you said this thing needed all four elements?"

"She used the others, with which she was more comfortable, to boost the power of her earth magic. And to ensure that no one could interfere with her escape route. Only someone with all four elements can cast or delete the spell."

"And you can cast it 'cause you inherited all four elements from her."

"I'm not trying to cast it," Pritkin said, pausing as some blue sparks appeared against the black rock for a second and then vanished, as ephemeral as fireflies. "I am trying to summon the one already here."

"Your mom's old spell?" Alphonse asked, frowning. "But why not just recast? You don't have the power?"

"Not at present. But it isn't simply a matter of power. My earth magic is weaker even than Mother's was. I do not think it is sufficient to cast that spell."

"But it is sufficient to summon it?"

"Let us hope so." It was grim. "The spell has been sleeping for many years. I have to get its attention, and for that, I need all four elements shouting at once. But my earth magic is more like a whisper. So far, the spell is ignoring it."

"Or maybe it's not there anymore," Alphonse said skeptically. "Ain't your mom dead? I thought spells died with the caster."

"Typically. But she fueled hers by linking it to the defensive network around the capitol, using the city's own wards to power her passage through them."

He sounded impressed as if even he might not have thought of that.

The fey sure hadn't.

"But that defensive network is down now, right? So how's that work?"

"It doesn't," Bodil said, looking like she thought this was a colossal waste of time.

Pritkin glanced at her. "You know as well as anyone that this place is built on a ley line sink—"

"Ah, so that's why they chose to build in a swamp," Alphonse said.

"—and it's energy therefore doesn't run out. The wards are nonfunctioning, possibly damaged in the attack. But the reservoir of power they draw from, the same one that Mother tapped into, is still here. And therefore, her spell is, too."

Bodil didn't say anything more, but her expression was eloquent. She didn't think this would work, but she wasn't arguing because she had no better idea. And because she was sitting beside a still-unconscious Æsubrand.

She'd probably be more vocal once her backup was awake.

She also kept glaring at me like I had somehow turned her fair-haired boy feral. As if he'd ever been anything else. So, I figured if I was to get the blame, I should at least get some answers to go with it.

"Aeslinn might have found the power to collapse my mother's spell from the god-blood he was harvesting," I said to

Pritkin, taking up my previous point. "I've been thinking about it—"

"A dangerous occupation," Bodil murmured.

"—and he might not need as much as we think. Athena had an army already waiting on the other side of the barrier when Mircea and I went through. So, Zeus must have been able to communicate with her—"

"How?" Bodil demanded.

"He uses these supersized crows as his eyes and ears, sending them all over Faerie. I saw some at the dark fey capitol. Big as humans or maybe bigger, they had nests all over the place. Anyway, he can see what they see, and the ones on this side also report back to him."

"On this side?"

I nodded. "When Mircea and I went through the portal to Jontunheim, we saw the crows everywhere—"

"They originate from there," Faerie said. "Zeus brought them with him when he came, and some were left behind when the gods were banished."

"Well, they must have been reproducing because there's a lot of them. And the fact that they're on both sides of the barrier gives him a conduit to the other gods. He must use them to communicate."

"How?" Bodil demanded again. And damn, she was getting on my last nerve.

"I don't know, but he must have a way. How else would Athena know to go for that particular portal just when it was about to be opened from our side?"

"So, you think he's getting help," Alphonse said. "Somebody pushing on that side while he pulls from here?"

"That's what it looked like. And while Athena is now dead, there are plenty of other gods to take her place."

But Pritkin wasn't buying it. "Plenty of half-starved gods who can't give him power they don't have. And those poor bastards he and Zeus have been rounding up, like Rask and his group, are getting thin on the ground. And most didn't have much god-blood to begin with."

We paused while he tried another spell. It flared vivid blue against the rock's black surface for a second before petering out once more. But he stayed with it because if anyone could jury rig a solution, it was Pritkin.

And what other choice was there?

"Zeus might have found enough power to heal after his battle with you," he added. "But to overcome your mother's spell? And not just hers. She cast it, but the Circle maintains it. He would have to defeat all of us."

"Maybe he did." I didn't like to think about it, but our forces were damned vulnerable to someone who could feed like I had in the race. That was how Mother had ravaged the hells, only on a whole other level. She'd drained entire armies and turned their power against them; why would Zeus be any different?

But Pritkin was shaking his head. "He doesn't want to risk himself in a straight-up contest. He isn't Zeus the Mighty or Jupiter Best and Greatest anymore. He's a fraction of his old self —"

"And still packs a punch."

"Yes, but he's vulnerable in a way he doesn't like and isn't familiar with. That's why he went back in time, courtesy of his pet dark mage, to weaken our alliance in the past when he couldn't manage it otherwise. Yet he somehow did so shortly after our departure?"

I frowned. "He could have used the Ancient Horrors. They don't have god blood, but they're powerful. If he drained them —"

"It would give him a meal, not a feast. Your mother drained whole worlds and, afterward, multiplied the energy she gained with my grandfather's power a hundred times over, a thousand. The Ancient Horrors couldn't give Zeus anything like that.

"I don't know what could."

"*You* could," Alphonse said. "Like you could give it to Cassie. Then we go back, find Tony, and make his fat ass sing about whatever he did. Ten to one, that little bastard knows Zeus's plans. He always knew everything—"

"But you have to catch him first," Faerie pointed out. "And if he can time shift, that may be difficult. Whereas we already know where Rhea is, and she's a seer—"

"*Cassie* is a seer!" Alphonse yelled, his voice echoing around the great space. The Ancient Horrors seemed to have made an impression.

I wondered what he'd think of Zeus.

"But Cassie cannot force a vision," Faerie said patiently. "And did not live through what happened. Rhea did. She can give you facts—dates, events, methods—"

"Which won't do us any good dead!"

"What is it?" I asked because Alphonse suddenly looked close to panicking, and the big man didn't panic. "What do you hear?"

"What do you *think?* They've started calling to each other; I can hear them through that," he gestured up at the missing river. "And they're all around us, digging. They're coming, which means we need to get going. And you," he turned on Pritkin, "need to get busy charging her up before they get here!"

But Pritkin had a weird expression, one I couldn't interpret. He didn't look enthusiastic about Alphonse's plan, which was starting to sound better all the time. Because yes, using his gift was dangerous, but not doing so might be worse.

"I don't need enough power to take us all at once," I told him. "This reality tried to reject me when I first arrived, but I tore through—"

"So that is what released us," Enid said, looking at me with far too much admiration. It made me uncomfortable.

"—so, now that I've been here, I should be able to return after meeting up with the Pythian power again—"

"Hell, you don't even need to," Alphonse said. "Go back and help old me kill Tony before he can do whatever he did. Then this future," he looked around malevolently. "Never happens, right?"

I stared at him. "You'd make a good Pythia."

"Don't have the assets," he said, grabbing his chest. "But I pick up on stuff fast when it's my ass."

He looked at Pritkin and scowled. Because the mulish look was back, and there was no spell to account for it this time. "What is it?" I asked.

"I can't," Pritkin said.

"What do you mean you can't?" Alphonse asked, getting in his face faster than I could blink.

I could have told him that was a waste of time. If anything, it was likely to have the opposite effect . . . and it did. "You want to take a step back," Pritkin said.

"What I want to do right now, I can't say 'cause there's ladies present. So start talking or—"

"Or what? You'll feed me to those things?"

"I won't have to! They're coming for all of us!"

"Yes, they are," Faerie said, tilting her head. "You are running out of time."

"So do your thing!" Alphonse said and grabbed Pritkin's shoulder.

Only to find himself on the floor—for a second, until he jumped back up. And was met by a hand on his arm, but it wasn't Pritkin's. "Stand down," Bodil said.

"Lady, I don't like hitting women, but you're about to—"

Bodil knocked him out with a word, and Alphonse fell over.

"Stop doing that!" I told her angrily. We had enough problems without lugging two unconscious people around!

But she wasn't listening. "Explain," she said to Pritkin.

"My ability takes before it gives," he told her tightly. "When Cassie has the Pythian power, it takes from that. But currently, she doesn't."

"You do not believe she would withstand the process alone?" Bodil raised an elegant eyebrow. And even though she hadn't washed off and should have looked like a bedraggled mud monster, it was elegant. I would never understand the fey.

"No."

"She is half goddess, and her mother was one of the strongest of them all," she said dryly. "I think we can risk it."

"I don't."

And unlike Alphonse, who had been snorting like a bull but with wide, panicked eyes, there was no fear there. Pritkin's gaze was level and cold, as much as I'd ever seen it. Giving Bodil nothing.

She could knock him out—she probably already had back in the stables—but she couldn't force him to do a damned thing. Which she seemed to realize because she looked at me. Batter up, I thought.

"Can we talk for a second?" I asked him.

Pritkin glanced at me, and then a silence spell clicked shut over our heads and he turned us away from the rest. He even led me off a few yards, I guessed so they couldn't read lips. Not that most around here could understand English anyway, but he wasn't taking chances.

"I'm willing to take the risk," I said before he could start.

"I'm not."

"Pritkin—"

"And even if I were, it wouldn't help us."

I had been formulating a thought, which that comment erased. "What?"

"I *can't*," he repeated.

"But your other half can. And he will; you know he will—"

"Yes, I'm sure he would jump at the chance." It was grim.

"—and yes, it'll reenergize him, but not for long. I'll be using most of the power we generate for the shift. And even if I don't need it all—"

"Cassie—"

"—and he starts to become a problem, well, I tricked him once—"

"And won't again. He's not a fool. He simply made the mistake of underestimating you."

"—and we'll have the time to worry about it later," I pointed out. "If we die here—"

"You won't. I promise you—"

"You can't promise me." I stared at him in confusion. "You know what those things can do! And if you don't, I can tell you stories—"

"I've heard the stories."

"Then what—"

"You don't understand," he said, looking almost. . .

"What did you do?" I asked, feeling my stomach drop. Because shame wasn't in his usual repertoire.

"What I had to. I needed to cross that finish line, but you were in danger. You'd just jerked Æsubrand back to you, and he—the fey aren't like us, Cassie, or even like Alphonse. They don't have chivalry, or if they do, it's of a different kind. He wouldn't see you as anything but an opponent, and one whose magic he had cause to fear—"

"Pritkin." It was flat because this was bad. This was very bad. Pritkin didn't do long, involved explanations. Pritkin explained things in terse, basic terms when he could be bothered to explain himself at all.

Except for now because this was *bad*.

"I had to be in two places at once," he said and waited for me to get it.

Which took a second because—

No.

No!

"Cassie—"

"You—" I grabbed him by those massive biceps. "You *left* him there? You went and left Zeus the one guy he needs to kill us all?"

"What are you talking about?" Bodil asked because the bitch had done to us what I once had to Rhosier and pulled off our silence spell without us even noticing. "What did he do?"

"Chimera!" I all but yelled it. And Pritkin met my eyes with no defiance in them but no apologies, either.

"If I hadn't, you'd be dead," he said simply.

"You don't know that!"

"And I don't know otherwise. Neither do you. I couldn't take that chance."

"So you used freaking *Chimera*?"

"You used it—"

"I'm Pythia! I'm allowed!"

"What does this mean?" Bodil demanded, getting between us. "What is Chimera?"

"A human spell for duplicating yourself," I told her while still staring at Pritkin. It had taken me ages to get that spell right, and he'd never even been trained for this! But when it came to magic, the guy was freaking Einstein. "Or, in this case, separating," I added because Bodil didn't look like she understood.

I guessed that didn't help because she looked at Pritkin.

"I split my soul into two pieces to make two separate bodies," he said hoarsely. "Chimera allows the use of magic as our illusion spells do not. They make it look like my duplicates are casting spells; Chimera allows me actually to do it, which I would need against Æsubrand. And it was on the spur of the moment, with no time to consider the implications—"

"What implications?"

"That my soul was already split, had been so from birth, into my incubus nature and my human one. And thus, when the spell activated—"

"You left him behind," she whispered.

"Yes. I dove for Cassie, which is why I was taken by whatever spell Tony used, but my . . . other half . . . was across the way, having just crossed the finish line, putting him outside the spell's reach. It, therefore, took me and left him."

"Then . . . you literally cannot do what we ask."

He shook his head. "Not even if I was willing to take the risk. My demon half isn't here."

"Then that's how he did it," Alphonse said groggily from the floor. "You handed Zeus the key to our world. You let the bastards in!"

CHAPTER THIRTY-NINE

Give us a minute," I told Bodil, my lips numb, and for once, she obliged.

We walked further away from the group, none of whom seemed to know what to think about what they'd just heard. And, frankly, neither did I. With Pritkin's family trait on his side, Zeus would be unbeatable, absolutely unbeatable.

It was something that Pritkin knew better than I did because, despite his disclaimers, he was looking sick. "I should have told you," he said, facing the far wall. "When we were sitting by the canal. I almost did—"

"That's when you realized."

He nodded. "There was no time before that; everything was too confused. And once I did—"

He turned to me, and his face was terrible.

"We don't know what happened," I began.

He gestured around wildly when Pritkin never did. "I think we do!"

"We know Zeus brought the gods back, but not how. Your incubus is still you; he wouldn't be easy to catch—"

"Are you trying to convince me or yourself?"

"I'm trying to make sense of this!"

"There's no sense to make!" It was savage. "Except for the one fact neither of us has wanted to face: I'm not up to this. I never have been—"

"Faerie thinks you are—"

"Faerie can't even save her own world! She's walking

around in a dead girl's corpse, clutching at straws! Recruiting any and everyone she thought might be able to help her. And somehow, against all odds, you and Mircea completed two impossible tasks. But the third. . .

"That was on me, and I *failed*."

I tried to say something, but the man who never talked was talking now as if he couldn't stop. "What you said earlier about someone who keeps going despite the struggles, the risk? That describes *you*, not me. Do you know what I did, the last time things were this hard? I hid away, became a hermit, then took a job blowing things up. And now—"

He stared at me, and his eyes were terrible. "Cassie. I've destroyed two worlds."

"*You* haven't. *Zeus* did—"

"With my help."

"We don't know that! And even if we did, that's still on him!"

"No, it's on me. I could have taken myself out of the equation, vanishing into the hells or . . . by other means. And I should have as soon as I knew what Zeus wanted from me. But *I* wanted—" His hand came up and clutched my shoulder, but not as he usually did. But barely there, as if he didn't think he had the right. "I wanted you. I wanted a life for us, and I wanted it so badly I made myself blind to the risks. I even came here when—"

He laughed, although there was no mirth in it. "When I knew, if I lost, it might end up costing us the war, and if I won . . . I would get a throne I don't want and responsibilities I can't handle."

He shook his head. "How can I be a good king when I can't even keep you safe?"

I covered his hand with mine and pressed down hard enough for him to feel it. "You're not responsible for that—or for this. And you've done an amazing job ever since you came here, and against ridiculous odds. Neither of us knew how hard this was going to be—"

"I knew. And I have bumbled about, barely keeping my head above water. I would have been trapped by my other half, possibly permanently, if you hadn't come up with a way to free me, and before that, Feltin's men had us well and truly cornered in that hallway. We wouldn't have gotten out of the kitchens if you hadn't bought us time."

"And I would be dead if you hadn't saved me in the dining hall and again in the corridor," I said, frustrated. "It's what I've been trying to tell you—we work better together. We're practically unstoppable together! Only Zeus's spell was working against us."

And Pritkin's insecurities, which were worse than I'd realized. No wonder the spell had taken him so hard. It had had the perfect in, the ideal path through the shields of the most dangerous man I knew. Who inside was still the little boy that nobody wanted, the child who had grown up alone because his grandmother tried to kill him, his mother feared getting near him, and his father was waiting until he grew up to see if he'd be worth his time.

He'd been little better off than the slaves here, maturing on a farm where the house and pigsty didn't look that different, and forced to make a life with little help from anyone—a life that had been jerked away from him time and time and time again. Until suddenly, one day, somebody wanted to put a crown on his head, not because they thought he deserved it, although he did more than the rest of them put together! But in a desperate bid to prop up a failing system.

A system he wanted no part of but which he had braved anyway . . . for me.

"We're better together," I told him tearfully. "We always have been. And we will find a way out of this. But I can't do this alone; I *need* you, I need every ounce of your strength, and I need—"

More time, I thought, but we'd had all we were going to get, because our other problem took that moment to arrive, blowing through the enormous main doors and sending them spinning halfway across the expanse of polished floor.

And ready or not, here they came.

"Into the water!" someone yelled, but it was already too late, although not because of the creatures fighting each other to get in the room. But because of something even more immediate.

Suddenly, bodies were falling everywhere, like a hideous rain. One splatted in front of me, a fur-covered nightmare with five or six rows of teeth in its misshapen jaw that would have had me screaming in horror, except that it was dead. As a doornail, I thought, staring at a mushed-up mass of fur and blood and bone that lay there and bled at me.

I looked up and saw that a horde of the creatures had crawled through the gap left by the now-missing river, clustering along its banks in the hundreds, framing the serpentine opening. Which no one had worried about as it was over an impossible, fifteen-story drop! Only it wasn't impossible for most of the dozens now jumping down on top of us, who shook off the stunning fall and quickly got back to their feet.

Or back to their appendages, which might be a better phrase, as insect-like bodies were as prevalent as the hairy animal type. They were interspersed with more amoeba-type things and others with angles that confused the eyes and broke the brain because they didn't belong in nature. At least not our nature.

And then a sixth sense had me throwing myself to the side as something hit the ground where I'd just been standing. And sprang at me for a split second before being sent rocketing back against the far wall by a blast from Enid, who was screaming hysterically and targeting everything in sight.

"Get to the water!" Pritkin yelled, grabbing my arm. Right before he was jerked away by something with wings and dragged into the air.

"Pritkin!" I screamed, watching as he formed his shields into a shiv as long as his arm and plunged it into the creature's belly, gutting the thing mid-flight.

I saw them fall, started to run that way, and got cut off by a surge from a group of the now rapidly landing creatures. But Bodil had decided that she wasn't going down without a fight and had hopped onto the highest rock surrounding the crevasse and raised her arms. And before I could wonder what she thought she was doing, a roar of water shot out of the fissure, what had to be thousands of gallons of it, formed itself into a wave and bitch-slapped the horde.

They tumbled backward, desperately struggling for purchase on the slick and now wet floor while an ocean crashed around them. It knocked them off their feet and into each other, and then into the side wall as if a freight train had run over them. And there they stayed, splayed against the rocks as the surf pounded, battered, and broke on all sides.

It was an impressive opening salvo and one they hadn't expected. But it wouldn't help us for long because we couldn't escape through the same crevasse that Bodil was using to defend us. Leaving us trapped and waiting on the main force, and we wouldn't be waiting long.

Damn it, we should have taken that swim! But we hadn't, and no way could Bodil handle them all. But she knew this place like the back of her hand and might still have a chance—if she left us behind.

She could get to Rhea even if I couldn't, and Rhea was smart. Maybe together, they could figure something out. And erase all this before it became the end of our story—and everyone else's!

"Go!" I screamed at her over the roar of the water. "Get out of here!"

"Stop trying to be a hero," she seethed, calling up two huge, watery fists from the flow like the golden one Pritkin had used on the Cetus.

They were as big as tanks and hit just as hard, using elongated river-like arms to knock the hell out of anything in the vicinity, even as torrents of high-pressure water spewed out all around them, sweeping away anything they'd missed. Combined, Bodil was laying waste, which was needed as the rest of the overhead squad had started hitting down, just an endless falling curtain of them.

One that was being lit up before they even made it to the floor, this time by Pritkin, who had fought his way back over here. I stared because he didn't have that kind of power. He didn't have any power!

But Æsubrand did, and although he still looked pretty out of it, lying on the floor by Pritkin's side, he was awake enough to cough up a cloud of energy just like Enid had on our chase. Only not just like. He had clasped Pritkin's left leg with his right arm, and a wreath of sparkling silver-white light hazed the two limbs before climbing up Pritkin's body. Where it was absorbed and came out of his extended right hand as a gigantic fire hose of flame.

It lit up the falling Horrors, turning some of them to ash in the air and causing them to flutter down like gray rain. It sent others to the ground still burning, giving me the surreal image of a curtain of living fire, writhing and screaming even as it fell before smacking down and sending sparks flying everywhere. Then Pritkin twisted around and sprayed more flames at the oncoming mass of creatures from the door, which had almost reached us.

Geysers of fire and water mixed and flowed, steam billowed and fought with blowing clouds of ash, and Pritkin yelled with a magically enhanced voice. "Go! We'll hold them off!"

"That 'we' better not include me, white boy," Alphonse growled, ducking under the fist-shaped tidal wave aimed at a flying creature swooping at him. And, when it went screeching into the void, he headed for the crevasse, where Enid was defending Bodil as she defended us.

But reaching her was harder than it appeared, as another of the creatures almost immediately fell onto him. It was one of the kaleidoscoping Horrors that kept changing form, or maybe my brain was just trying to figure it out and failing. All I could see were sharp edges and strange colors I didn't have names for, but it must have had wings, as it and a handful of others had been circling overhead, looking for victims to pick off.

It jerked Alphonse off his feet and into the air, only to get a surprise when the big man tore free of those talons and then used them to somersault on top of it, despite leaving a lot of shoulder meat behind. And reminded me that he was the old-school kind of vamp who preferred jeans to a tux, didn't know what all the forks were for, and didn't have a sophisticated bone in his body. What he did have was a knack for putting a hurting on whatever was hurting him.

As he demonstrated by grabbing the thing at what might have been its middle and *ripping*.

Suddenly, it was a mass of green-tinged weirdness, which I supposed was caused by some kind of blood because it was spewing everywhere. Alphonse dropped ten feet back to the ground, and the creature fell on both sides of him into a puddle of its own ichor floating on the tide. And the circling things abruptly got more distant, screeching at each other in warning.

And watching as their fellow Horror kept morphing, squealing, fighting, and—finally—dying. Because, Ancient Horror or not, nothing survives being torn in two. At least, I hoped not, but I didn't see what happened then because somebody grabbed me around the waist and started running for the crevasse.

It wasn't Pritkin. He had set up a ring of fire around our small area, with the flames leaping five or more stories into the air, I guessed so that nothing could jump over them. But creatures could go through if they had bodies that could withstand the heat, like the one he was currently battling, which was nine feet in height with a hard, turtle-like shell, only what was inside wasn't a cute Ninja.

What was inside was—

My brain skittered away in fear and revulsion as Æsubrand carried me forward while still stumbling from sleep and what must have been a massive magic loss. I wanted to ask what he thought he was doing, but then my train of thought, such as it was, cut out because something was burning me—from inside my armor. Something small and bright enough that I could see it through the silver scales as if a hot coal had been shifted under my suit and was now torching the bottom of a breast.

What the—

And then I remembered something I should have thought about before now.

"Put me down!" I told Æsubrand, who was hauling me bodily toward the fissure while waves crashed all around us courtesy of Bodil.

I think she was trying to clear us a path, but that's a little difficult when you're slinging around the equivalent of a raging river at the end of each arm. As a result, she was hitting us about as often as everything else. Waves slapped us, gushing into my mouth every time I tried to speak; the spray stung me like a thousand tiny needles on any part that wasn't covered by dragonscale; and Æsubrand said something that my translator primly refused to interpret in reply and struggled on.

"Wait," I told him, gasping. "I have to—"

He didn't wait.

"Listen to me!" I yelled. "We have to go back—"

"Shut up!" he screeched, with whatever had been left of his princely calm in tatters. "Shut up, shut up, shut up!"

"Because I'm trying to tell you—"

"Shut up, or I'll *make* you shut up!" he might have said more, but something came flying at us, and he thrust out a pike that he'd picked up somewhere, allowing it to skewer itself on the point.

And halfway down the shaft because its momentum caused it to just keep going. He whipped the shaft around as it clawed at us and tried to bite with a long, deadly-looking beak, even though that caused it to impale itself further. And the hideous thing was too far along the thick wooden pole now to fling off, forcing him to throw the weapon and its shish-kebobed addition away, sending it flying into the waves, still shrieking.

"The demon is right," he added without missing a beat. "You have to survive! You and Bodil can go back, can talk to them, make them understand—"

"Like I could have made you understand?" I yelled. And then we were caught in the wash of foam on the edge of another massive, watery fist, but I was ready when he stumbled free, gasping, dripping, and shaking his head. "No one will believe us when we return—if we do!" I said quickly. "Not without proof—"

"Then make them!"

"Are you listening? They don't trust me! And they hate you! We can't do this, but if you get me to Pritkin—"

But Æsubrand could give a shit what I wanted, although he had finally stopped, but only because we'd reached the crevasse. It was now an upside-down waterfall shooting skyward to fuel Bodil's fight, which suddenly wasn't fist-shaped any longer. It was fey-shaped, as a mass of translucent manlikans sprung out of the crevasse in our faces, looking like seven-foot-tall crystal statues and leaving me staring at the carnage through their watery flesh.

Before they scattered in all directions, taking the fight to the creatures for a change.

And okay, maybe we had a chance!

Or not, I thought, as the Ancient Horrors tore through our new army like it wasn't even there. Æsubrand looked like he couldn't believe that, either, as the fey constructs weren't puny. One could have taken on a human platoon and had a pretty good shot, but not a platoon of these things.

But the manlikans were having an effect, if not the one that Bodil had probably hoped for. Some had trapped slashing appendages inside their watery forms, tightening the ward that encased them enough that the furious creatures could not get back out, no matter how hard they struggled. Others were piling on individual Horrors, six and eight at a time, sealing them off by the watery scrim of their bodies and effectively drowning them in mid-air. But most were breaking against the assault like the tide, exploding on all sides and seemingly useless—until you noticed that the enemy had come to a halt, giving us a brief reprieve.

Which Bodil and Æsubrand intended to use to shove me into the crevasse whether I liked it or not. "Get ready," she told him. "I have to release the spell to let you through. Take her to the portal and thence to Earth—"

"Like hell," I said, thrashing. "They'll kill you as soon as you let go!"

"What do you think is going to happen in any case?" she snapped.

"I . . . am not entirely sure that I know how to repair the portal, should it be required," Æsubrand told her. "We had servants for such things. . ."

"Then figure it out!"

"I will do my best," he said before a watery hand reached out and jerked him up to her face, dragging me along for the ride.

"You. Will. Figure. It. Out!" she yelled. "I buy your chance with *blood*, princeling! We all do! And you," she looked at me. "I hope you're as evil as your mother. You'll need every bit of it. Now go!"

We didn't go. A zerg rush of creatures came at us from the side through one of the steadily widening gaps in the flames, just as the ones overhead swooped down in a combined attack, forcing Bodil to change course.

Instead of releasing all that water, she dropped us and reclaimed her watery fists, sending one to meet the flock mid-air. It slammed into them in a liquid firework that sent them flying in all directions, shedding feathers, fur, and other stuff I couldn't name and sending ear-splitting shrieks echoing around the room. While swiping with the other hand at the force on the ground, throwing them into chaos once more.

Æsubrand abruptly released me and spun to take on something massive and prehistoric-looking, covered in armored plates like a Stegosaurus that God had cursed, that had somehow withstood the onslaught, and I took the only chance I'd likely have to reason with Bodil.

"I'm not leaving without Pritkin!" I told her. "And the rest of you!"

"Stupid child! Stop thinking about yourself!"

"I'm not!" I yelled back, more furious than I could remember. "Listen to me! I can't do this without you!"

"And why not?" she sneered. "You've been managing so far —"

"Because I can't use this!" I screamed and held up Radu's ring, which had come alive in the pocket I'd stashed it in after Bodil started a flood of water magic spilling everywhere, to the point that it had been burning the crap out of me with just the overflow from its power. And was now sending a cascade of bright blue light everywhere that lit up the water with a shimmering, glowing, spectacular iridescence like nothing I'd ever seen.

It was beautiful, I thought, dazzled in spite of everything. It was beautiful! Like the bioluminescent waves on some beaches on Earth.

Only the creatures didn't seem to agree.

Maybe because it was burning them, too. Every Horror that the light touched started screaming and, in some cases, writhing, smoking, and melting, with appendages sloughing off of the bones underneath like shed clothes. Only clothes didn't bleed that much.

It was as if the tide rolling out from us was no longer water but acid, causing bloody pools in different shades to bloom everywhere. But I didn't feel anything. I was getting hit with spray from all sides, but it was just cold, clear liquid, without even its former black color, now that it was outside of the caves.

Bodil grabbed me. "You wait until *now* to show me this?"

she screamed and snatched it.

And I guessed she did know how to use it because a second later, the flow from below suddenly increased, like a Yellowstone geyser times ten. To the point that I was blasted backward, slipping and sliding and landing on my face. I picked up my head to avoid drowning in the madly frothing water and then just stayed there, staring.

The crevasse had become an enormous fountain, now gushing up three or four stories high and causing the flying things to wheel away, back toward the top of the cave and out of its acidic spray. And it was raining death on the demons down here while the surging waves flowed over any who stumbled as I had. But while all that had happened to me was that I'd ended up soaked again, when the water washed past them, it left only more bones behind to join the skeletons already there, with all traces of anything else eaten away.

I stared at the twisted remains of something a few yards off, the bones of which were sizzling despite all the water, and the realization hit hard. Pritkin was part demon, too! I looked around for him for a blank second and then scrambled back up, screaming his name even though I knew it was useless; he'd never hear me in this!

I'd forgotten that he'd linked our translators, something that the curses suddenly flooding my ears reminded me of. And then I spied him coming at a run through the maelstrom of acid-like rain whipping about us like a hurricane because Bodil was getting the hang of whatever the hell was in that ring. And he wasn't burning.

He wasn't burning!

Human blood for the win, I thought dizzily, as he grabbed me, bleeding from a dozen wounds but still on his feet. And tore me off of mine as the furious waters cut out like someone had twisted a spigot. I guessed Bodil had enough liquid to work with up here now. And the next moment, before I could even catch a breath, his momentum had us plunging into that dark, watery hole, which had once looked so forbidding, but now—

Was our only way out.

CHAPTER FORTY

Pritkin had enough juice left for a bubble spell that snapped in place over my head right before we submerged and found Æsubrand already down there. He was clutching a ball of moonlight and looking stunned and fairly pie-eyed from whatever had happened while I hadn't been looking. But he was kicking with his legs like his life depended on it, although he was going in a circle in his panic.

Pritkin grabbed him when he came around again, which made swimming difficult, but what the hell wasn't? I started trying to help, only to stop almost immediately and stare around. Because something was wrong.

"Disorientation spell," Pritkin gasped while struggling with Æsubrand, who was fighting him for some reason. "You have to—"

But I didn't hear what I had to do. I suddenly couldn't hear anything except my frantic heartbeat. And I realized that maybe Æsubrand hadn't been stunned by the fight after all.

Disorientation, my *ass*.

A wave of vertigo hit me so hard and fast that it stripped everything else away, and made the "oo" sound at the end of Pritkin's last word elongate for what sounded like forever. My head started spinning to the point that I felt nauseous, my brain fritzed like a lightning bolt had just hit it, and when the gray static cleared, I was left with no idea where I was. The ball of light and the crevasse were still visible, but they suddenly didn't make sense anymore; nothing did, including whatever Pritkin was yelling at me.

And then it got worse.

For a moment, I thought that the Horrors must have taken the plunge, too, because it felt like the various pieces of me were no longer attached. None of them drifted off with the tide as if something had slashed a path through me, but they also didn't seem like they belonged to me anymore. I couldn't feel my hands; my legs may as well have been someone else's; and my head felt like it had blown up to three times the normal size and was drifting about like a detached balloon.

Someone grabbed me around the waist, and I couldn't fight them, even assuming that I was supposed to. I didn't know what was happening; I didn't know anything! Except that it was getting darker.

Somebody grabbed my face and looked into my eyes, and I could barely see him, although he couldn't have been more than a few inches away. I didn't know who he was; the mixed-up features weren't in the right place, and as I stared, an ear floated off to the other side of the head. But he was telling me that the spell had been formulated against demons, that he couldn't break it, and that I needed to *breathe.*

And yes, yes, I did.

I could feel my chest getting tight despite having a bubble of air right there. But my lungs couldn't recall what to do with it, assuming they were lungs anymore. And not whatever my fingers were becoming, which—agghhhh!

I flapped them in horror, but it didn't help; if anything, it only made things worse. They noodled out in pale, too-skinny appendages, miles long, like thick spaghetti disappearing into the distance, which didn't make sense! But nothing did. Including the face in front of me that was now melting like hot wax and making me want to scream, only I couldn't remember how—

And then somebody else seized me, although not in the usual way. A hand felt like it reached into my chest and fisted, which would have been enough to send me spiraling the rest of the way into a nightmare, except it didn't hurt. And this grip, I could feel!

It was solid and real as nothing else was, making me clutch it in panicked relief. As soon as I did so, a tiny bit of sensation returned, confused and randomly firing from different parts of my body. A toe spoke up to let me know it was still down there somewhere, a bruise throbbed menacingly in my side, and my vision started to clear, only I found myself looking at nothing as I was staring off into the inky void.

And then a voice echoed through my head. "You are a great deal of trouble," Faerie said and *pulled.*

All of a sudden, I could see clearly again, although what I could see wasn't down here. It was up there, where I guess she still was, and things hadn't improved. Bodil was running out of juice, with the ring's light starting to stutter around her; the enemy was regrouping on the sidelines, waiting her out; a circle of bodies where the fires had almost burned down surrounded the throne and was sending up noxious smoke everywhere, which her rain was no longer thick enough to disperse; and Alphonse—

What was he doing?

He had climbed on top of the giant eruption of a throne and was now peering into the darkness. And then yelling back down at us. "I don't see her! I don't see her!"

"Go," Faerie told him, her voice echoing everywhere. "I have one more trick, and once it is done, it is done. You must be well away before then."

I didn't know what she meant and was too busy sucking in oxygen to care—until Alphonse did a perfect dive off the back of the big chair and into the crevasse, which I hoped would treat him better than it had me. And as soon as he was gone, all hell broke loose. But this time, it wasn't their hell.

It was ours.

Faerie did have a trick, and it was a good one. I'd seen it once before when she helped to get me out of that horrible camp. Which was why, when every intimidating creature that she or one of her children had ever seen suddenly came roaring into the room, I barely even flinched.

The demons, however, looked around in terror and confusion, wondering what this fresh attack was, before spotting the force arrayed against them. They didn't stop to wonder where they had all come from or how so many had managed to sneak up behind them. And in their shoes, I probably wouldn't have, either.

Because they were facing an army of ten and twelve-foot-tall trolls, scarred and wearing old, greasy hides and carrying huge clubs; a contingent of ogres that framed them on both sides, armed with crossbows and, in some cases, old blunderbuss-style firearms they must have traded with the humans for once, and modified to be even bigger and more deadly; and an assorted company of dangers that ranged from several massive dragons, gleaming in scarlet and gold, to a swarm of pixies big enough to count as a storm.

The latter group also included an enormous Kraken, peering into the cavern through the missing doors, which didn't look so big next to its enormity, and a group of merpeople, tridents in hand, even though there wasn't near enough water to support them. But nobody was clear-headed enough to consider that when the most cacophonous battle cry ever screamed out of their collective throats, loud enough to shake the very stone around us, and they charged as one. All of Faerie's vanished children coming home to defend her, one last time.

The ranks of the Horrors, so relatively ordered a moment ago, broke and ran. But since there was nowhere to go, they mostly ran into each other, sinking teeth or claws or whatever they had to work with into whoever was between them and safety. The room fell into utter pandemonium, to the point that the Horrors were too busy to notice that the horde descending on them wasn't real.

But for a minute, it didn't have to be, as they were doing a fine job ripping themselves apart.

"I have to send you back," Faerie told me, snapping my stunned gaze back to her. "Your friends are getting as far from the Margygr's spell as they can, and the further they go, the less it should grip you. Go quickly, and remember, you are my last hope. If you don't reverse this, it will be cemented as my future —and Earth's, too."

I stared at her. "Wait. You're not coming with us?"

"I cannot travel outside my realm. And even if I could, I do not have the strength. I spent too much magic holding on all these years and then helping you in the fight, and already feel myself starting to unravel."

"You were helping?" I repeated, trying to catch up.

She laughed suddenly. "Yes, child, or you would all be dead ere this. But I can do nothing else. And it feels . . . strangely liberating . . . not to have to fight anymore. Or to see, as I have every day for fifty years, the piecemeal destruction of my world. Better for it to go all at once, in one great eruption, than to be taken like that!"

"A-all at once?" I repeated, hoping I didn't understand.

But as usual, when it was bad news, I always got it right.

"When I go, my world does, too," she confirmed. "You must be past the portal by then, or there is no saving you. Go—and let us hope that I chose my champion well."

With no other warning, I found myself back under the waves. And saw Pritkin's face emerging from the darkened flood, although it was wildly distorted and frankly terrible, and I wasn't sure whether that was from the spell or the mess we were in. But probably the latter, as he was clutching me against him as he swam, and we were *moving*.

And Faerie was right. The more distance he put between us and that awful crevasse, the clearer things became. I could still barely move but could see straight, and the rest of my senses seemed to be sorting themselves out.

Enough to recognize that the little puddle of light we were shedding held me, Æsubrand, Pritkin, and Alphonse, who was ripping through the water like a dark bullet before catching up to us. And that was it. Until Bodil dove down into the haze of moonlight under the crevasse, ceding the battlefield she could no longer hold and making my heart clench for her.

"Pritkin!" I gasped, getting his attention because he was facing the other way.

He looked back, and we paused to see if the other demigoddess in the group could handle the Margygyr's spell better than I had. And yeah. Being half-fey instead of half-human made a difference, didn't it?

Because instead of freaking out, getting disoriented, and forgetting how to breathe, Bodil shook her head as if to clear it a couple of times, spotted us, and started swimming our way. And unlike Æsubrand had been doing, she swam straight. Even though the blue light haloing her from the ring was stuttering so badly now that it looked like she was being electrocuted.

But she didn't appear to be harmed by it, and then I knew she wasn't when she turned and sent a tide pushing out behind her big enough that I could feel its suction tugging on me, and I was not that close to the chasm anymore.

But, I suddenly realized, someone else was!

I grabbed for Pritkin's shoulder and missed, but he got the idea. "Enid!" I yelled and saw him wince, as voice modulation seemed to be another thing I couldn't control. But then he looked about and noticed the same thing I had.

The beautiful redhead was missing.

"Cassie—"

"I lost track in the fight!" I said, forcing my numb lips to form words. "She must still be back up there—"

"We can't—"

"We have to! We can't leave her!"

"Faerie is with her—"

"Faerie's almost out of power and told me that when she goes, so does this place! We—"

"She told you *what*?"

"She helped us in the fight," I said, gasping because my lungs were still trying to play catch up. "And said we'd have died otherwise. I don't know what she meant, but—"

"She was using something similar to the spell on the

crevasse to disorient the enemy and make it harder for them to attack us."

"*That* was them disoriented?" I said, disbelieving.

"Go back to the stuff about what happens when she runs out of power," Alphonse said, swimming closer. And for some reason, I could hear him as easily as Pritkin.

"I added him to our spell," Pritkin said before I could ask. "Looped in his translator."

"Who cares?" Alphonse demanded, glaring at me. "What do you mean, this place goes when she goes? Like the palace?"

"I think . . . the world?"

He stared at me.

"I didn't get a chance to ask a lot of questions! But it sounded like this whole world dies with her. Like she's vital for its survival, and it can't continue without her."

"Then what the hell are we doing here?" he yelled. "Let's go!"

"We have to get Enid! Did anyone see her?"

"We're not going back," Bodil said, catching up to us. Unlike me, she seemed to be moving fine, and while her voice had a strange, underwater quality, it was perfectly understandable.

"We don't have to," Alphonse said. "Those things'll be on our ass in a second as soon as that plug runs out! We need to *go!*"

"I did a water ward," Bodil explained to the rest of us, which I guessed was what that last push had been. "But it won't hold for long. Or at all if we rupture it from this side."

"But Enid," I said, looking around, hoping to spot that flame-red hair in the gloom. But there was nothing, not even any fish. The water was as empty as it was cold and deep, just an endless dark nothingness.

"I didn't see her and I looked," Alphonse told me. "I climbed that damned throne trying to spot her, but there was nothing. One of those things probably dragged her off."

I stared at him, and he looked steadily back. As a vampire, Alphonse had lost many people through the centuries, including the one who meant the most to him. He'd had to learn how to let people go, but I hadn't. I hadn't!

"We have to go back!" I told him.

"No." That was Bodil. "Nor can we stay here arguing about it."

"You can't—"

"I can." It was implacable. "The ring's power is guttering; it won't last much longer. Decide if you want to save the world—both of them—or a single girl."

"The world," Pritkin said. "She just needs a moment. The disorientation hit her hard."

"Unfortunately, we don't have one," Bodil said, catching me around the waist.

And the next thing I knew, we had left the others behind in a rush that would have made a speedboat proud.

"You—let me go!" I said, trying to fight her. But I could still barely move, and it did no more good than it had with Æsubrand. The fey looked tall and willowy, like a good gust of air would blow them over, but it was a lie. They had the strength of high-tensile steel.

And this one was using it.

"No."

"That's *my* ring!"

"Yes, and I will thank you for it when we have time. Right this moment, we must swim—for our lives."

And I guessed the others agreed because they caught up to us over the next few moments, with Alphonse carrying a still loopy-looking Æsubrand on his back, Pritkin cutting through the water like a blond porpoise, and Bodil swimming as quickly as if she had an outboard motor attached, even when dragging me. And leaving a brave woman behind to face death alone in what was probably the most horrible manner possible.

Thank you for letting me fight.

I felt sick.

Bodil glanced at me, and something shifted in her expression—from an iron-jawed will to. . . I wasn't sure, but she looked different suddenly. "You're not like your mother," she said.

"No. My mother would have found a way to save her."

An elegant black eyebrow raised. "Your mother wouldn't have tried," she said and then twisted her neck around.

"What is it?" Pritkin said.

"They're coming."

And they were. Despite what Faerie had said, the Horrors could go underwater; they just didn't like to. But it looked like we'd pissed them off enough to make an exception in our case because a boiling mass of hate was pouring through the chasm and headed this way.

I couldn't see them except as a frothing wave and then not at all as the light Æsubrand had conjured up winked out. But if he hoped it would hide us, I had bad news for him. The army chasing us came raging on, not needing light as some didn't even have eyes, but the magic radiating off of Bodil's ring drew them like blood in the water.

Which there would be soon enough if we didn't do something!

"Take her and go," she told Pritkin, thrusting me at him. "I'll swim away, and they'll follow me. Don't use magic."

"That's not a problem," he said grimly. "I barely have any left."

"Then swim fast," she advised, and the next moment, she was gone.

Or, rather, she tried. But once again, the best-laid plans came crashing down around our ears, although not for lack of effort on her part. She sent a tidal wave surging through the water behind us, disrupting the horde and causing them to scatter in every direction.

Which might have been enough to let us get away if not for one small problem.

There was another army in front of us.

They came from the palace, I thought, my stomach sinking. To make sure that we really did not have any way out.

And they'd succeeded because we couldn't fight them all. In seconds, we were surrounded.

CHAPTER FORTY-ONE

I looked around, searching for a way out, but all I saw were Horrors of every type and description, and looking worse now than they had up top. The close-up view, because they were maybe forty yards away, allowed me to see the damage the fight had done to them. Some were relatively unscathed—I assumed those who'd been at the back of the pack—but the rest. . .

Half of the ones we'd been fighting were missing limbs or had acid scars or burns sketching patterns across their bodies, and a cloud of blood was staining the water on their side. But they were still deadly, and worse, they were angry. Now, it was personal.

But the ones arrayed behind us were undamaged, having never been in the fight, and they looked eager for a taste of battle. Or more likely of our flesh. Yet, for some reason, neither group was advancing.

Huge tails and other appendages I didn't have names for were whipping up the water behind them in their excitement, causing ripples I could feel from here. But the creatures themselves weren't getting any closer, even though we couldn't do anything to stop them. Including Bodil, whose ring light had finally flickered out.

"What is it?" I asked Pritkin. "What's stopping them?"

But he didn't know any more than I did. Until a few huge specimens moved aside, and someone appeared in the gap between them, but it wasn't Faerie. It wasn't anyone I'd ever expected to see again.

"Feltin," Pritkin breathed, and the name in his mouth sounded like a curse.

The blond surfer dude was looking a little rougher than the last time I'd seen him. Instead of a Liberace-esque robe, beaded and spangled within an inch of its life, he had on scarred leather armor, something like Bodil's if it had been worn continuously for a few decades. His long hair, floating like a cloud around his head, was also longer and shaggier than before and had white streaks among the blond, and his expression...

Wasn't entirely sane.

"Surprised to see me?" he asked, his voice echoing underwater as Bodil's had done, but powerfully enough that there was no trouble understanding him.

"Moderately," Pritkin replied as Feltin was looking only at him. Until his eyes slid over to me, and his expression turned even more mad.

"Still have your little whore, I see. Thought she'd have been killed by now as the monsters are drawn to magic. But this makes things easier."

"Makes what easier?" Pritkin asked, sounding absurdly unruffled under the circumstances. Which wasn't a sign of calm but rather his bad-things-have-hit-the-fan voice, only Feltin didn't know that. Strangely, it seemed to reassure him slightly.

The nervous, jittery energy he'd been giving off, which seemed to have whipped up his troops, calmed. He even managed a smile, although it was terrible. Mad and unpractised, as if he'd forgotten how.

"You're fond of the bitch," he said casually. "If you want to save her life, give yourself up without a fight, and she and the rest can go.

"The gods will deal with them soon enough."

Yeah, sure, I thought, staring at the ranks of his army, which were fanning out to encircle us better. And I do mean encircle, as we weren't on land, where an army would only have four directions to come at us. We were in the water, and they were taking full advantage of that, trapping us in an ugly, snarling, savage ball of hate.

In seconds, we found ourselves in a 360-degree Thunderdome, and I didn't see a gap big enough for a mouse to slip through unnoticed.

Nobody was getting out of here.

"Give myself up?" Pritkin repeated, and again, there was no emotion in his voice, just vague curiosity. While behind him, something sparked in the water.

I wasn't sure I'd even seen it because it was so faint. But it was dark down here except for the glowing eyes of some of the creatures and Æsubrand's pale moonlight. And Pritkin's body blocked most of that.

Then it came again, and I was looking right at it. Blue sparks lit the darkness for a moment, dim and barely staining the water, like the ones that had briefly appeared up top when he was summoning his mother's old spell. He was still trying to get us out of here while keeping the madman talking.

It made me feel a surge of something powerful, gratitude maybe, or affection because Pritkin would struggle to the end. But not hope because, just as before, it wasn't working. And the fact that Pritkin knew that and was still trying said everything about how much trouble we were in.

As if I needed it, I thought, staring at the growling, hissing, and screeching mob. The sounds echoed horribly underwater, to the point that I thought the sheer vibrations, hitting us from all sides, might tear us apart before their claws could. But then Feltin raised a hand, and they suddenly quieted down.

"Why?" Pritkin said. "Aren't we past all that? The challenge is over. You won—"

"Won!" Feltin choked on what might have been a laugh or a snarl. "Won!" he repeated, raising his arms and staring around. "Yes, it looks like it, doesn't it? Behold my glorious victory!"

"Be that as it may, the contest has ended, and we lost. Why

go through all this to pursue us?"

"I have orders!" Feltin spat. "Zeus wants you. He said 'at whatever cost' and would have come himself, but he doesn't dare. That so-called goddess haunts this place, and he's afraid of her."

"So he sent his lackey boy instead?" Alphonse said, and shit.

Alphonse didn't seem to understand that this wasn't a conversation. This was Feltin trying to extricate Pritkin without risking the horde tearing him apart while they savaged us. Anything could happen in battle, and he didn't want to further jeopardize his god's prize.

But why was he a prize? I suddenly wondered. And why was Zeus afraid of Faerie if he already had Pritkin's ability in his arsenal? Pritkin glanced at me, and I stared back, my eyes huge.

He isn't dead, I mouthed, thinking of Pritkin's incubus. But he also wasn't here, so what had happened to him after we left? I didn't know and didn't ask because shock after shock kept hitting me before I could absorb the last, the way Faerie always did.

Only this latest one . . . was literal.

Something shivered across the world, something deep and foundational and coming from all around us. It could have been anything. It could have been a mild earthquake or even my imagination, but if it was the latter, Bodil was imagining things, too.

She looked at me wildly, both of us having been there to hear Faerie's last words. And while I doubted that the Horrors had heard her or understood if they had, they didn't like that feeling. They didn't like it at all.

Pandemonium broke out without warning, to the point that they were screeching and fighting again, and some were about to make a break for it. Before Feltin gave a roar, fisted his hands in reins he wasn't holding, and pulled them back. And it worked.

It looked like he had a mental grip on the creatures the same way he probably had the Kraken when he sent it to attack us. A gift from the gods to their servant or part of his natural mental gifts, I didn't know, but he and the horde were acting almost as one entity. And it didn't seem that the Horrors could break his grip because they stayed in place, although the agitation factor had ramped up to eleven.

"Make your choice, demon!" Feltin shouted, still battling with them.

"What choice?" Pritkin bellowed back. "Zeus wants me badly enough to spare all these?" he spread his hands and looked around at us. "That sounds . . . unlikely."

The last word dripped with sarcasm, but Feltin didn't react to it, maybe because he was already reacting to something else.

"He always has," the gorgeous blond all but spat it. "I gave him everything—Nimue, a kingdom, an army—*everything!* Yet he wanted more. Wouldn't let me just kill you both and be done with it. Oh, no. He must have his prize."

"You betrayed her," that was Bodil, who I guessed hadn't figured things out until now. "You betrayed Nimue to her death!"

"Not her death," Feltin scowled. "They didn't send enough people for that. Even after I told them—but it doesn't matter."

"It doesn't matter?" Bodil's eyes were flames and bright enough that Feltin saw them across the murky water.

"Oh, don't act so grief-ridden," he sneered. "I was there for the shouting matches you two had. You and she never got on —"

"But I didn't kill her!"

"No, but you *should have*. And you should thank me for it. She was going to fight, did you know that? Going to ally with Caedmon to try to take Aeslinn down. I heard her talking about it with his ambassadors one night and knew she was serious. She hated that bastard; their marriage was a nightmare, and he let her hang out to dry afterward. She should have never even given them an audience, but there they were, drinking tea like old friends!

"I knew then that something had to be done."

"So you betrayed all of us," Bodil said, and unlike Pritkin, there was no lack of emotion in her voice. If fury and loathing had a tone, she'd managed to find it.

It enraged Feltin, who darted forward, dragging his horde of Horrors along like a vicious train. Until he caught himself and paused, maybe thirty yards out now, looking shocked for some reason. As if he hadn't even realized he'd moved.

Then he laughed, despite being underwater and without the bubble most of us were using.

"That was good," he told her. "You almost had me. But I know better than to get anywhere near your clutches, Lady Bodil." He sketched her a bow, and some of the Horrors actually bowed along with him, including a huge, scaled monster like something resurrected from the primordial ooze, who nonetheless put a clawed hand on his chest and bent over slightly.

I wondered if I was going mad.

"And for the record," he added, "I saved you—or I tried. The gods were returning, whether we liked it or not, and the only choice was between dying uselessly or joining the winning side. I chose the latter, and because great Nimue was too idiotic to see it, I chose for all of us.

"And I made a *good* deal, a *survivable* deal, do you understand? Give them Nimue and put our army under Aeslinn's control once I assumed power, and no part of what was to come would touch us—"

"You call this no part?" Bodil hissed. "They destroyed us!"

"No! She destroyed us!" he screeched, pointing at me. "I had the deal, and Zeus even modified it once the half-demon showed up for the Challenge. Give him over, and even the army could stand down. *We could stay neutral.* We could *live!*

"But the bitch ruined everything! When she vanished with the god's prize, he was furious! He blamed me, even though I had done all that he asked. He ensured that we were one of the first attacked when the Black Day came, and I could do nothing to stop it, even though I went to beg for forgiveness personally."

"How?" Pritkin said. "We heard that you went to Earth. How could you have seen him?"

I blinked at him, impressed. I was finding it hard to think at all except about the one revelation I'd managed to hold onto through all this. But he was fishing for information. Now, when we were staring down the gullets of the army about to eat us!

But it didn't work because Feltin didn't know anything. "He and Aeslinn had gone to Earth to prepare for whatever happened. I found them there, much good that it did me. And it's of no importance now.

"Nothing is, except that you make a choice. Which is more than the rest of us were ever given. More than me."

"You made your choice," Bodil snarled. She'd been so calm earlier when the rest of us were losing our shit, but she seemed to have reached tilt. Pritkin had the right idea about how to deal with Feltin, but she couldn't emulate him. Not now.

And now was all we had.

But it didn't matter because Feltin was mad. Seeing his machinations destroy his world had broken his mind, or maybe Aeslinn and his godly rider had done that. But he was muttering to himself now, and his creatures were becoming increasingly agitated.

"His control is slipping," Pritkin told me, his voice low. "And when it goes—" He didn't have to finish that. "Go with Bodil when I tell you," he said. "Go fast."

"Go where?" I said as Feltin's creatures lunged for us, and he had to drag them back again. "They're everywhere!"

"I'm going to charge Feltin. He's controlling these things. If I can take him out—"

"He's too far away!"

"—it may throw them into confusion—"

"And get you killed in the process!"

"—and give the two of you a moment to slip away—"

"Now, who's trying to convince himself?" I said, furious.

"I can't watch you die!" The green eyes were wild. "Don't ask me to watch you die!"

"I'm not. I'm asking you to stay with me and keep me with you. *Partners*, remember?" And I held out a hand.

I didn't know if he'd take it. He was a stubborn man, and this whole hellish experience had asked him to grow faster and in ways that many people couldn't, bringing up long-buried things from his past and introducing horrible new twists. Most people would have buckled under its weight or folded at the terror of where we were now.

Most people weren't John Pritkin.

He took my hand, and the eyes were still fierce, but the grip was strong.

And then Feltin was back, only . . . not entirely.

It was starting to look like the symbiosis between him and his allies went both ways, as their agitation was leaking through to him. They didn't want to talk; they wanted to tear, to rend, to taste blood in their mouths, and to visit dire retribution on the people who had hurt them and failed to die as proper prey should. They wanted to *win*, and we were *right there*—

It affected their master, who had his own grievances with more than one of us.

"Didn't have a choice," Feltin said, staring at me again. "*She* did. She could have stayed away, let things run their course, let us *be*. I had it all planned out. You were never going to win; wouldn't have had a single point. All kinds of ways to make sure of that, and I'd used them all. But then she showed up, and I immediately knew it was over.

"Know the type. Nimue was the same. Never stop; no, no, they *never stop*. The gods keep going and going until they win or die, but she wouldn't *die*. And neither would you."

His eyes shifted to Pritkin. "Zeus said I can't kill you. Said he wants you for himself. Threatened my life if I don't bring you back."

He laughed again, and it was insane and furious and somehow strangely tragic, all at the same time. "My *life*," he sneered, followed by a word I didn't know and that my translator wouldn't help with. "Well, he can have it or what's left of it! Which was nothing after you came. And her. And *him*. But I can't kill him, can I, no matter how much he deserves it—"

"*Shit*," Pritkin said.

"—but two out of three will have to—" Feltin cut off abruptly, but not because he was finished, but because—

"Shit!" I said, staring at the bloody trident suddenly sticking through Feltin's chest. And I do mean all the way through, as the entire three-pronged head was visible, along with a cloud of what must have been most of the blood in his body.

He died with his mouth open, ready to pronounce our doom, and I didn't understand anything. I thought at first that one of the Horrors must have done it in retaliation for him being ready to betray their god. But they didn't use weapons like that.

And then I remembered who did.

"Oh," I said as three things happened at once. The Horrors were released from Feltin's control and immediately came at us; a very pissed-off group of Margygr descended on them, coming out of nowhere with weapons flashing; and another rumble, harder than the last, tore through the water, throwing everyone into everyone else.

I'd never experienced anything like an earthquake at sea. And I wasn't sure I was experiencing one now. But something was happening, something that felt like being in a snow globe that was being violently shaken, only without the snow.

And with a lot of terrifying monsters, one of which had kept his eyes on the prize and came churning through the water at us despite everything. And was blasted out of existence before I even got a good look at it by something that looked a lot like wand fire. Maybe because it was, I realized, as

Enid, with the tail she claimed not to have, came shooting up and grabbed me.

And began babbling something I couldn't make out because all hell had just broken loose.

"What?" I yelled and was jerked within an inch of her suddenly much flatter nose.

"They're going to kill us all!"

"I know! The Horrors aren't under Feltin's control anymore —"

"No, not the Horrors! The *Margygr*! I went to them for help, but . . ."

"What?" I stared around. "They're not rescuing us?"

"They're not rescuing us," Alphonse said, grabbing a trident all of an inch from my nose. And then seizing the guy who held it and introducing them to each other repeatedly before glaring back at Enid and I. "Don't just float there. *Run!*"

CHAPTER FORTY-TWO

Great idea, but where? I wondered, staring at a scene unlike anything I'd seen even in Faerie, where impossible sights were an everyday occurrence. But not like this.

We found ourselves in the middle of a squirming, thrashing, flailing ball of blood, flying spells, flashing weapons, and severed body parts. And we hadn't joined the dozens already floating lifelessly in the sea only because the merfolk were too busy slaughtering the Horrors to bother with us. And getting slaughtered back, I thought, as a powerful-looking warrior nonetheless ended up impaled on something's three-foot claws.

I stared as he twitched like a speared fish for a moment before being ripped apart when the creature tore its talons back out. And didn't even know who to root for since whoever won was going to eviscerate us for an encore. And yet, there was no path out of here that wouldn't mean immediate death, something Bodil seemed to agree with as she didn't even try to swim off with me.

There was nowhere to go.

"Human!" Æsubrand said shrilly, appearing at my side. I guessed the current hell had jolted him out of the remains of his disorientation because he looked sane if overwhelmed. And then he cursed as something huge and black darted at us and was blasted back by a wave from Bodil, sending it tumbling head over heels into some of its fellow Horrors, who savaged it in their panic.

Æsubrand stared at them for a second with the same shock that was probably on my face. Then, he turned on me again. *"What is he doing?"*

I stared uncomprehendingly. "What? Who?"

"The demon!"

"Which one?"

"Your one!"

I looked for Pritkin, but at that moment, the whole world shivered again, although that is a wholly inadequate description. It wasn't like the faux earthquake in the mud pit; it wasn't like the previous quake down here; it wasn't like anything I'd ever experienced. The world convulsed and sent the whole sea churning with wild fluctuations that ripped me away from the silver prince and sent me into a maelstrom of teeth, claws, and jumbled-up bodies.

That would have been the end, except our enemies were freaked out about what was happening, too. The battle paused momentarily as we all realized that we had bigger problems. And I felt a surge of hope because was that it? Was Faerie's dying convulsion going to buy us one last chance?

And then one of the biggest creatures roared, a stuttering, mind-ripping challenge that reverberated through the water and into my very soul.

And it was on.

Enid appeared at my side, somehow fighting her way through the carnage and cursing multiple creatures on all sides. Including one I hadn't noticed that had been about to eat my head. And then Æsubrand, who was nothing if not single-minded, grabbed me again. Right before we were all thrown almost back to where we'd started by another convulsion, one bad enough to cause great stones from above to break off their foundations and come speeding down at us.

But since they were in the sea, they weren't speeding as fast as they could have been, leaving me watching huge black boulders, pillars as big as skyscrapers, and small rocks the size of cars tumbling through the battlefield. Where they were dodged by the combatants who kept right on slaughtering each other. It was weirdly beautiful, with the dim light cascading down from above, spearing the dark blue water like the rays through the windows of a cathedral.

Appropriate, I thought, as this was the funeral for a dying world. . .

And then somebody grabbed me hard enough that it jolted me out of my shock. I looked up to see Æsubrand screaming in my face. "What is he *doing*?"

I followed his gaze to see Pritkin inside a shield, probably to keep anything from killing him for a minute while he tried one last Hail Mary, moving his arm in circles as he had in front of the great throne while trying to summon the tunnel.

"He's using elemental magic, isn't he?" Æsubrand demanded, shaking me.

I nodded. "He's trying to summon a spell to get us out of here, but he doesn't have the power—"

"*I* have power!"

"Yes, but it isn't just about energy. It takes a command of all four elements—"

The shaking recommenced wildly, leaving me feeling a bit like a bobblehead doll, one whose neck was about to snap and probably already would have, except for the water cushioning it. But then he said something that made me forget about that, that made me forget everything. "*I have all four elements!*"

I blinked at him. "That's not possible. Nobody has all four except Pritkin—"

"Why do you think my father married my mother?" he asked me hysterically. "For *love*? He wanted a son who could command all four, to help bring back his precious gods, but that didn't work out as he'd planned and—"

He cut off because I screamed my head off into the translator link between Pritkin and me. "*Æsubrand has all four elements!*"

Pritkin turned, his eyes flooding a brilliant, blistering

green. And a moment after that, something blazed bright blue among the carnage, a small compass-shaped something that abruptly spiraled out into the mouth of a black stone tunnel where it had no business being. Only no, it wasn't a tunnel anymore, I thought as Pritkin flung me down its maw.

It was a tomb because guess who was crowding in behind us?

I wasn't sure if the Ancient Horrors were chasing us or just trying to escape from the earthquake or the slaughter or the collapse of the world, but it didn't matter. We were engulfed by them, along with a ton of water that abhorred a vacuum and was doing its best to fill it as fast as possible. And it was doing a good job.

I suddenly couldn't see anything but crashing waves as they poured in behind us. And thousands of bubbles as we all went spilling down the stone tube at an absurd speed. Something raked claws down my armor, but I wasn't sure it knew that because there was no follow-up. Something else grabbed hold of me, but it was less an I'm-going-to-savage-you moment than a please-help-me!

But I couldn't help even myself. Like when we dropped out of the tunnel as abruptly as we'd entered it and fell at least a dozen yards into a rapidly flooding room that was supposed to be already underwater. Hadn't that been what Faerie had said, that the palace was flooded?

Tell that to my ass, I thought, as it hit stone and didn't break, but only because of the tons of water spilling out all around me. And trying to drown me as I turned over and half crawled, half dragged myself forward, trying to get out of the way of the things crashing down all around me. And then started swimming as the large space began filling up with liquid and things in the liquid that did not appear happy to be there.

That was particularly true when the ceiling cracked like a gunshot, the room shivered all around us, and the braced doors on several sides, which I guessed had kept out the flood until now, burst open.

I went under in the sudden deluge and came up spluttering because my air bubble had just collapsed. And looked up to see the tunnel spewing out dozens, if not hundreds, of the smaller Horrors before Pritkin slashed a hand through the air and sent it away again. And chopped one of the bigger specimens in two in the process, half of which left with the tunnel and the rest—

Stayed here.

A torrent of blood and the stuff the blood was attached to hit me and sent me back under, pinning me to the floor and leaving me fighting with more weight than I could manage. Until Alphonse somehow found me in all that, pulled me out from under, and dragged me back up to the pandemonium that had overtaken what had been a large room covered in plaster and mosaics. And was now—

I didn't have words for what it was now. Some Margygr had gotten through as well and were laying waste to the remaining Horrors, who they seemed to have a bigger hate-on than for than us. Maybe because those same creatures had ravaged their world and killed who knew how many of their people before they were forced to retreat and wall themselves off.

That did not appear to have been forgotten and would have been a slight relief—if I hadn't been in a drowning room filled with a churning mass of waves and foam and flailing limbs, and then of bright yellow light that spiraled up out of nowhere on the far wall, showing through an image of—

Home.

My thoughts cut out, and all the sights, sounds, and insanity instantly receded. I could hear the blood rushing in my ears insanely fast, but it didn't matter, either. My attention was wholly focused on that small, whirling yellow star and the glimpse of dark desert beyond it.

I had never realized it before, but Earth had a quality all its own. I didn't have any way of knowing where the portal was tuned to, but I didn't need it. I could smell it, taste it, sense it with every fiber of my being. I knew it as sure as I'd ever known anything, but I knew something else, too.

There was no way to reach it.

There was a war between us at the wall, which was the length of a football field away. The room was huge, I guessed to accommodate the trade that passed through the portal, some of the goods of which were still piled about the walls. And there was no way that we were getting over there, no way at all.

And that was before the room decided to fall apart. Cracks sped up the walls, causing them to crumble around us; water speared in from the two doors, threatening to drown us; and then the ceiling started following the walls, including a great chunk that would have killed us except that Alphonse caught it. And screamed in effort because something was above it, like a whole palace complex!

I crouched there, caught between a rock and a wet place, not sure whether to try to get out from under or not, as everything was coming down now. And burying people and things under the waves whenever chunks hit down. Including a battling duo who went to their graves with a trident through its stomach and its teeth buried in its opponent's throat.

And we weren't likely to be far behind because Alphonse was losing it. I looked up to see the veins in his neck standing out in full relief, the swarthy skin a red tone, and the normally impassive face anguished. We had seconds if that.

And then something hit me, but it wasn't falling masonry.

The great city, golden bright even now, with its battle scars and charred domes, began to crumble. Aeslinn, black robes flying about him, bolted out of a disintegrating corridor and stood on the farthest point of the great square, a level section of golden stone used for festivals and days of thanksgiving, as it gave the best view of the city as a whole. And stared behind him as a black, jagged line tore its way upward from the mountaintop, ripping through buildings and sending pieces of stone flying into the pale blue sky.

Until the whole grand edifice cracked and crumbled like the mountain was doing underneath it, like the world. He turned around, looking outward over the great valley below, and saw the same thing happening there. The crack that had already sundered his city scrawled down the river, the waters of which disappeared instantly.

Similar cracks shivered through the surrounding mountain range. Colossal peaks that had been there for as long as the eldest could remember were now falling, crumbling to dust, and vanishing as he watched—like his city. Like his world. Like him.

As he fell into oblivion, the rocks giving way under his feet, his last thought was, "What have I done?"

But there was no answer.

There was no anything.

"Cassie—Cassie!" Someone was shaking me again; why were they always doing that? And what was that smell? What was—

I came back to myself to see that we'd somehow gotten out from under and were hugging what remained of a wall. I couldn't see what was happening very well, as images were still crowding my mind, hazy diaphanous things obscuring my sight like sunglasses worn indoors. Everywhere I looked, people ran screaming, the sounds ringing in my ears even louder than the madness around me.

Faerie must still have her link to me, I thought dizzily. She was sending me images. Did she know it? Was it supposed to help?

Or was she too far gone to realize what she was doing and that she was threatening to take us with her? Because I could barely see, hear, or control the rest of my senses, which had been hijacked by a dying goddess. But I could smell.

What was that? It was divine, like the best meal ever, like—

Like power, I realized, managing to focus on a nearby Margygr, surrounded by a cloud of magic that sparkled in the distant portal light.

I pulled some of it to me, and as soon as it sank into my veins, I could see again. Strange shadows still fluttered across my vision, but they were annoying, not debilitating. And then I drew more in and more, and with the hits of energy came information from a dozen minds.

The Margygr had tried a collective spell to keep the room from collapsing. But it had come too late, and many of them were now dead, crushed under the weight of stone or slashed to death by the Horrors that had soon thereafter perished themselves. But their magic—

Was still here. Much of it had never been used after being released, and I drank it in, calling it to me from all parts of the room. And it came, a virtual flood of it. But this flood I welcomed, this flood I needed, as I had to find—*there.*

My vision telescoped, showing me Pritkin battling one of the Horrors by the far wall, with the crazed spider-looking thing unable to understand what was happening or refusing to care. It would die, but it would take him with it, only it wouldn't. Because I shifted him straight through the portal a second later.

I saw him fall into Bodil, who was also on the other side. I heard them screaming at each other but didn't care. I only cared about one thing and—*there.*

Æsubrand was underwater, out of view of my eyes, but not of the power surging through my veins. He had been crushed under one of the stone slabs from the ceiling, and while it hadn't killed him, he had been unable to get out. Until I shifted him, too, sending him through the raging yellow sun and into another world.

And immediately staggered under the power loss because the Pythian energy wasn't here. I was trying to run god-tier spells on Margygr power, and it might work, but it wouldn't last. So I sent Alphonse, who was yelling at me as usual and heard his voice cut off mid-shriek.

He tumbled through the portal, and I collapsed to my knees, my head going under the waves, and I didn't have the power to raise it again. Had I done too much? Where was . . . I needed more . . . I needed . . .

The room started to darken. Because there was no more power available unless you counted a few scant scraps that I could feel pinging against my skin, but that did almost nothing. They weren't even enough to let me fight off the images, which were back with a vengeance, utterly overwhelming me.

Everywhere I looked, cities were going up in flames or crumbling to dust; rivers were spewing all over the landscape, having been knocked off their courses; and avalanches were cascading down mountains, which were right on their heels, racing each other into the dirt that itself was convulsing, was splitting, was—

Dying.

I hadn't really believed it before, that an entire world could die, but I was seeing it now. And I was dying along with it because I couldn't breathe, couldn't move, couldn't see anything but carnage. And Enid's face, appearing inches away from mine.

We surfaced from the bloody waves, I guessed because she'd dragged me up, although I couldn't feel her. I was busy burning to death in a foreign city as my house collapsed around me; was chasing the family dog, who was panicked and running in a circle as multiple threads of lightning set our farm ablaze; was on a ship, going to my knees and staring with my mouth hanging open as a volcano spewed forth a cloud of fire and ash—

"Do you trust me?" Enid screamed. She was right in my face, but I couldn't answer her, couldn't speak, didn't have the strength or breath. I just nodded.

And found out why even the gods had decided to let the Margygr alone. Because Enid had wanted to fight and fight, she did. Sending a blast of something ahead of us that carved a path through Horrors and merfolk alike before grabbing me against her and all but flying through the waves.

It shouldn't have worked, but she'd caught everyone by surprise. The other Margygr had been focused on the Horrors and either hadn't noticed Enid or hadn't cared. What could a quarter fey do anyway?

That, I thought wildly, as she put on a burst of speed like a freaking torpedo, dodging or cursing anything that got in her path. And giving me a brief view through the stinging spray in my face, the blood in my eyes, and the roaring of the battle in my ears of a brilliant sun getting rapidly bigger. It reminded me of Rask and his people, who had thought they'd gotten away, only to have the world come crashing down on top of them.

I could see them now, running through a forest even as trees toppled around them. Could hear children screaming and men and women calling out for family members they'd been separated from and not finding them. Could see Rask pausing at the top of a rise, staring at the burning valley beneath him, the one his people had already started descending toward.

He didn't follow them. Young as he was, he knew the end when he saw it. Or maybe that was something else, or someone else whispering in his ear. Instead of climbing down, he turned and looked me full in the face, and his eyes said the same thing that Faerie had.

I hope I chose my champion well.

"I'll come back!" I screamed as Enid and I hit the portal's surface, and its power grabbed us, sending us spinning into the void.

I swear to you.

I'll come back.

The story continues in *Hijack the Seas: Tsunami*.

OTHER WORKS BY THIS AUTHOR

Lia de Croissets Series
Junk Magic
Weird Magic

Author's Website
KarenChance.com

Printed in Great Britain
by Amazon